The Secret Life of Lincoln Jones

Also by Wendelin Van Draanen

How I Survived Being a Girl
Flipped
Swear to Howdy
Runaway
Confessions of a Serial Kisser
The Running Dream

The Sammy Keyes Mysteries

Sammy Keyes and the Hotel Thief
Sammy Keyes and the Skeleton Man
Sammy Keyes and the Sisters of Mercy
Sammy Keyes and the Runaway Elf
Sammy Keyes and the Curse of Moustache Mary
Sammy Keyes and the Hollywood Mummy
Sammy Keyes and the Search for Snake Eyes
Sammy Keyes and the Art of Deception
Sammy Keyes and the Psycho Kitty Queen
Sammy Keyes and the Dead Giveaway
Sammy Keyes and the Wild Things
Sammy Keyes and the Cold Hard Cash
Sammy Keyes and the Wedding Crasher
Sammy Keyes and the Night of Skulls
Sammy Keyes and the Power of Justice Jack
Sammy Keyes and the Showdown in Sin City
Sammy Keyes and the Killer Cruise
Sammy Keyes and the Kiss Goodbye

Wendelin Van Draanen

Alfred A. Knopf
New York

THIS IS A BORZOI BOOK PUBLISHED BY ALFRED A. KNOPF

All rights reserved. Published in the United States by Alfred A. Knopf, an imprint of Random House Children's Books, a division of Penguin Random House LLC, New York.

Knopf, Borzoi Books, and the colophon are registered trademarks of Penguin Random House LLC.

Visit us on the Web! randomhousekids.com

Educators and librarians, for a variety of teaching tools, visit us at RHTeachersLibrarians.com

Library of Congress Cataloging-in-Publication Data is available upon request.
ISBN 978-1-101-94040-2 (trade) — ISBN 978-1-101-94041-9 (lib.bdg.) —
ISBN 978-1-101-94042-6 (ebook)

The text of this book is set in 12.5-point Chaparral Pro.

Printed in the United States of America
October 2016
10 9 8 7 6 5 4 3 2 1

First Edition

For the angels

1

An Unexpected Blow

Ruby Hobbs came out of her room, dancing and singing, buck naked, again. *"All I want is a room somewhere, far away from the cold night air,"* she warbled, her old body jigglin' and wigglin'.

Ruby being naked may sound funny, but it's a sight so disturbing even Teddy C can't take it, and that's saying something. Teddy C ogles all the oldies. Fat ones, bony ones, doesn't seem to matter to him. He's ninety, but his eye is always roving. He does the whistle, too. Or at least he tries. It's more air than sound, but there's no mistaking what he's thinking.

At first I thought the whistle was a joke, but Ma says it's for real and that his old-guy eyes see what they used to know, not what's actually there.

Except, I guess, in the case of Ruby Hobbs. "Somebody help!" Teddy C called, like he was being robbed. "She's at it again!"

"Now, now, dear," Gloria said, snatching a sheet from one of the monster-eye dryers and rushing over to wrap Ruby in it. "You can't dance at the ball without a gown on. What would the governor think?"

Gloria sure does have a way with the oldies. Maybe it's how she can jump inside whatever fantasy or memory they're in the middle of. Or maybe it's the fake flower she wears in her hair. It's the exact same one every day, but every day it seems brand-new to the folks living at Brookside. "Oh, what a beautiful bloom!" someone'll say, like it's the first time they've seen it. "As pretty as you," Gloria'll reply, which makes them blush. Like it's the first time they've been paid the compliment.

It could also be the way Gloria's voice always seems to calm things down. Her *now, nows* and *there, theres* work like she's castin' a spell.

Whatever it is about Gloria, her magic doesn't only work on the oldies. It works on me, too. Ma tells me, "Focus," but all I can think about is how dumb it is that I have to spend my afterschools here, in an old-folks' home.

Gloria, though, will give me a little smile and whisper, "Now, now, Lincoln. Remember, the more schoolwork you get done here, the less you'll have to do when you get home," and just like that, I buckle down.

But back to Ruby.

I'd been coming to Brookside every school day since September, and even though we were in the middle of November, it was still a surprise to see Ruby bust out her dance moves. Aside from her being naked, which I guess anyone can figure out how to get, the big shock is always seeing her *move.*

Normally she shuffles. *Shuff, shuff, shuff,* her slippers go. *Shuff, shuff, shuff,* slow and tired. All the oldies shuffle. Usually with walkers, or while hanging on the arm of one of the nurses. Or, I guess, "caregivers." The word seems so stiff, but Ma says I need to use it, seeing how caregivers are not actually nurses. At Brookside, nurses are the ones in white shirts, and caregivers are the ones in purple shirts. Nurses do the pills and the blood pressure and call the ambulance. Caregivers do the meals and the clothes and all the nasties. Like mopping up accidents. And changing diapers. And dressing corpses.

But back to shufflin'.

It's what all the oldies do. Going to the Clubhouse at mealtimes, to the Activities Room for entertainment hour, to the patio for a little afternoon sun . . . they shuffle and they look straight down at the floor. It's easy to get lulled into how *slow* everything goes. Which is why Ruby coming out of her room naked with her arms out and twirling is always such a shock.

This time, though, it was different.

This time, the flower and the sunny sounds from Gloria didn't help. Ruby cried when Gloria wrapped her up, and she whimpered, "Let me dance. Please. Let me dance."

This time, seeing Ruby Hobbs was more than just surprising or disturbing or funny. It was sad. And sad on top of everything else that had happened was an unexpected blow. One that knocked the wind right out of me.

2

Spinnin' Lies into Truth

The trouble at my new school began the very first day, during the very first recess. It's bad enough starting a new school when everybody else acts like they've known each other since diapers. And it's bad enough when your new teacher makes everyone read a passage aloud from a story and then fusses over your "darling Southern accent." Ms. Miller thought she was payin' me a compliment, but no boy, sixth-grade or otherwise, wants to be put in the same sentence as "darling."

But worse is recess, when you've got nowhere to go. It's time-tickin' torture. Ms. Miller had instructed us to "stay within the confines of the blacktop area for today." I had no interest in making a further fool of myself by handling a ball, so I went to go sit in the shade of a tree off the edge of the blacktop. And I was just fixin' to sit down when I noticed a stream of miniature black ants windin' around the tree's trunk. I stayed standing, studying them. They were nothing like the ants back home—those ants could haul a house away. These were small as fleas, scurryin' up and down in a thin, winding line.

"Hey!" a kid on the playground called. "We use bathrooms in these here parts!"

The voice seemed off in the distance, barely reaching my mind 'cause I was concentrating on ants.

"Hey!" he called again. "Quit whizzin' on the tree!"

What he was sayin'—and that his fake Southern accent was aimed right at me—hit like a bolt of lightning. I whipped around quick. I didn't know him, but he was standin' near the edge of the playground with a boy I recognized from my class.

"I was just lookin' at ants!" I hollered, but it was too late. They ran off, hee-hawin' like donkeys.

Back in class, Hee-Haw #2 spread it around to the guys on his side of the room. I could see them grinnin' and whisperin', spinnin' lies into truth. It was the first day of school and already the beginning, middle, and end of any hope I had for making new friends.

After that I took to hiding out. It was a whole lot safer than opening myself up to the hazards of a new school full of old friends. If they could make such a fuss over me watching ants, I didn't want to find out what they'd do if they knew where I went after school.

3

The Fling Zone

It didn't take long to settle into the new routine. I ride the school bus to Thornhill School in the mornings and the city bus home from Brookside after Ma's shift is done at night. To get from school to Brookside, I walk. It's only about twelve blocks, but it's a long twelve blocks when you're tired from school and luggin' a backpack and you're on your way to a home for oldies. It's not exactly a destination to look forward to when you're eleven.

Or even when you're ninety, now that I think about it.

If I dawdle, I hear about it from Ma. "What took you?" she whispers, giving a worried look at the wall clock. "You're not getting mixed up in anything, are you?"

"Ma-ah," I groan, 'cause I've *never* been mixed up in anything. Her asking me that came on after we moved. Maybe 'cause we're living in a "rough zone," as she calls it, but our apartment is a long ways from the route I walk from school to Brookside, so her frettin' like she does makes no sense to me.

Finally, she'll see that I'm just tired and hungry and say, "Let's get you a snack."

Snacks at Brookside are okay. Not great, but okay. They're for old folks, so they're low in fat and sugar and salt, which adds up to them being low in flavor, too. They're still better than the snacks marked *D*, which are for the diabetics and made with fake sugar, since real sugar could send them into a diabetic coma.

But the snacks are free and the juice is usually cold, which is mostly what matters. And after I'm parked at my regular table with my snack, Ma can quit worrying about me and what I might have been doing on the walk over and get back to work.

I don't tell her this, but it's not the walk she should be worrying about.

It's the bus.

I don't mean the city bus, either. She's with me on that one, so she knows what I see there. She always has advice for me when we're on it, too. "Don't stare, Lincoln," she'll whisper. "He's drunk."

Like I haven't seen drunk enough to recognize it? Like I haven't figured out it's the whole reason she dragged me halfway across the country? I know drunk, and I can usually ditch drunks. Ma . . . well, that's a different story.

But back to the bus.

On the city bus, we're allowed to sit anywhere. We can move away from trouble if it starts up, and that makes the city bus a safe zone compared to the school bus.

The rule on the school bus is little kids up front, big kids in back. And the first couple of weeks I followed that rule because it made sense to me.

Besides, what sixth grader wants to sit with first graders?

Before we moved, I used to walk to school, so I never knew how rough the back of a school bus can get. Ma doesn't want me watching R movies or playing violent video games, but the back of a school bus is as bad as both.

Usually when there's trouble brewin', I find a way to sidestep it. I hush up, duck out, and live to see another day. So that's what I tried to do on the school bus. I started bending the seating rule a little, not going all the way back when we piled on. I'm not exactly big for eleven, and I'm new, so the younger kids didn't really know any different, and they didn't seem to mind.

But the kids at the back of the bus sure did.

"Dude, ain't you in Miller's class? Why you sitting way up there?"

"Yeah, whatsa matter? You got a problem with us?" It was Hee-Haw #1. The one who wasn't in my class.

I waved at them like, no hard feelings, but I guess there were hard feelings anyway, 'cause as the bus roared along, the teasing started. First they picked on my "drawl" and how I was "a Southern boy." Then the names began flyin'. Hee-Haw #1 started off callin' me the Wiz, but one of his herd thought that was a cool name—like I was smarter'n them, or a wizard. So he moved on pretty quick from that to messin' with my name, calling me the Missing Link and the Weak Link and then just Link for short.

I knew they were trying to make me *say* something so they could make fun of the way I'd said it, but what it did instead was make me face forward and keep my mouth shut tight. But over time the names went from mean to meaner, 'til they were so bad I'd've been whupped to Sunday if I'd said them at home.

When they ran out of new names, they added shoving.

And when they got bored of the shoving, they added spitting.

By October they were up to spoon flinging. I got hit with grape bombs and tuna fish and Jell-O and whatever part of some other kid's lunch they didn't mind wasting. They were sly about it, so the bus driver never saw them, and everyone else was too afraid to do anything. Instead of trying to get rid of the flingers, the little kids tried to get rid of me. "You can't sit here," they told me, and who could blame them? I was the target, but with spoon flingin' there's lots of hits outside the bull's-eye.

I didn't know what to do about it. It's not like I could tattle. I knew where that'd get me. And it's not like I could change my mind and start sitting further back. Either way, I'd get murdered.

So I was stuck.

Stuck in the fling zone, with tuna in my hair.

4

The Great Escape

Maybe I was willin' to put up with tuna and Jell-O flying at me 'cause they were nothing compared to what I'd been hit with before the move. For Ma it was even worse.

Then on New Year's Eve almost a year ago, Ma made a resolution: we were moving.

Escaping Cliff.

Starting over.

She whispered it to me with a bloody lip and a puffy eye while I was in my hiding place, under my bed.

Ma's escape plan included stashing away cash, which meant meager eats and no extras for a good six months. It also included two small duffels and two one-ways on the Greyhound bus.

The night of the great escape I didn't sleep a wink. I had my duffel packed light, like Ma had told me—spare clothes, travelin' food, and a toothbrush, plus the only things I couldn't stand leaving behind: my secret notebooks.

When it was finally time, we walked the three miles to the station like our unders were on fire. In some ways they were, 'cause it was late July and swelterin', even at five in the morning.

Ma kept looking over her shoulder, but we made it to the station without being stopped. The only worry I had was the worry I caught from Ma, who was oozing with it. The way I saw it, Cliff was on whiskey time. He wouldn't be up 'til noon.

I'll never forget Ma's face, reflectin' in the bus window as we pulled out of the station. She didn't know I could see or she'd have hid it better, but she was one scared rabbit. "Oh, Lord," she whispered, clutchin' her bag tight. "Lord, oh, *Lord*."

She may have been scared out of her mind, but I was glad to get gone. After Cliff moved in with us, our life turned into a bad movie that got played over and over, with the fight scenes getting longer and louder.

Cliff wasn't just mean to Ma. After I called him out on a couple of lies, he took to hating me. The older I got, the meaner he got, so leaving didn't scare me near as much as staying did.

Plus, I was looking forward to meeting my aunt Ellie and my cousin Cheyenne. I figured they had to be nice, seeing how they were letting us stay with them until Ma could find a job and a place of our own.

But then we arrived.

It probably doesn't matter how nice a person is—when the apartment's small, two more bodies get in the way quick. And Aunt Ellie pushed Ma's buttons in a big way. Ma tried to explain it to me one night, keepin' her voice hushed as we camped out in the front room. "It's like we're kids again, with her bossing and criticizing and making me feel worthless!"

"Better'n gettin' beat up," I whispered back.

She muttered something but wouldn't repeat it, and it took me 'til after she was sleeping to figure out that she'd said, "Just a different kind of beat up, is all."

So Ma had problems with her sister, and it didn't take but a day or two for me to start having them with Cheyenne. She was in high school, so she got over the excitement of meeting her long-lost cousin before I was done stepping through the door. And the bathroom was definitely *hers*. Plus, she wore morning on her sleeve like a gaping wound. I swear that girl could not smile before two p.m., and by then I was too worn out from watching my step to be any kind of friendly.

"We have *got* to get out of here," Ma said after a few weeks, and I guess Aunt Ellie and Cheyenne agreed, because the instant Ma landed the job at Brookside, Aunt Ellie offered to loan her the money we needed to rent a place of our own.

The apartment we moved to is above a corner market, and it's small.

Smaller'n small.

To get to it is strange, too. First you go through a metal gate, then you go down a kind of alleyway to some metal stairs that go up to an outside hallway. Our apartment is marked *A*, and there's another door further down marked with a dangling *B*.

Our place has one bedroom and one bathroom with a toilet, a sink, and a small metal-basin shower with a wrap-around curtain. There's one plug-in burner on top of the half-sized fridge near the kitchen sink, and a two-person table off to the side of the front room, where my mattress is parked in a corner. Ma gets the bedroom, which isn't much bigger than a closet, and the only heat is from the plug-in burner.

We gave the place a Pine-Sol bath when we moved in, and when we were sitting down to jelly sandwiches that first night, Ma apologized and said, "I know it's not much, but we'll fix it up."

"I like it fine," I told her, which was the truth. I had my little corner, and we were inside our own walls. Nobody was going to be bargin' in angry or drunk or even just annoyed.

I knew it was a dump. I knew I could have hated it. But the weird thing is, even from that first night, it felt like home.

5

Kandi Kain

When Ms. Miller called Kandi Kain's name the first day of class, I thought for sure it was a joke. Maybe some kind of play on her real name that had caught on. But I learned later that Kandi Kain carries around a copy of her birth certificate just so she can set the record straight for any nonbelievers.

When I saw the certificate, all worn out from being flashed around since probably kindergarten, I became a different kind of nonbeliever.

What sort of mama gives her girl a name like that?

"My mother said it makes me unforgettable," Kandi said, the words flowin' out like warm maple syrup. "And it was better than naming me Nova, right? Or Hurra."

"Hurra's not a name," I said.

She hoisted an eyebrow at me. "And Link is?"

I frowned. "It's Lincoln," I told her, and it came out kinda proud-sounding.

Like the way Ma always says it.

Kandi was not impressed. Or convinced. "So you say," she oozed. Then she gave me a scary-sweet smile. "Can you prove it?"

"Prove what?"

"That your name's Lincoln. How do we know you're not just making that up?"

"Why would I go makin' up a name?"

"You thought I did, didn't you?"

"But your name is Kandi Kain!"

"And yours is Lincoln Jones." She gave me a cool look. "The more I think about it, the more I think you made it up. No mother names her child Lincoln. Besides, it doesn't fit with Jones." She turned her nose up a little. "Jones is ordinary. Lincoln is pretentious."

I didn't know what *pretentious* meant, but I sure didn't like the way it sounded. Like I was pretendin' to be something I wasn't. And her nose bein' up like it was didn't help, either. So I let her have it. "Ma says my names balance each other. And that Lincoln is an honorable name. One I should be proud of."

"Hmm," she said, considering me. "I guess that's true."

Darn straight! I thought, and for a second I felt good.

But then she went and said, "But 'Ma'? You really call your mom that? Where *are* you from, anyway?"

Ma always tells me that the best way to get rid of a pest is to ignore it. "If you swat at the bee, Lincoln, it'll surely sting you." And having been stung by a bee a time or two, I know she's right. But sittin' around waiting for the thing to fly off on its own is terrifying. There it is, walking on you, all fuzzy and twitchin', with its stinger fixin' to fire, while you sit holding your breath, sweating bullets.

Still, any time I've managed to not swat, I haven't been stung. I remind myself of that fact when tuna's flingin' at me on the bus. I don't swat at the pests on the bus, and I don't swat at them in the classroom.

It's hard, but that's what I do.

Now, Kandi Kain may not fling tuna, but she's still dangerous 'cause she's got that queen bee thing going on. She likes swarms of kids around her. Boys *and* girls. She holds the four-square balls hostage at recess, then directs kids around, and for some reason they do what she says. She's pretty, sure, but that's no reason for folks to act like drones.

So I kept my distance and did my own thing, but every time she'd look at me, there'd be a frown bendin' down her face. Then, one day in early October, she marched right up to me and said, "What's with you and that notebook? You writing the Declaration of Independence, or what?"

Her hands were on her hips, showin' off fingers that were painted like candy corn—yellow at the base, orange in the middle, and white at the tip. I could tell her joke about the Declaration of Independence had been brewing in her brain for some time. I could tell she thought it was smart and clever, too. Like sportin' candy-painted nails when your name is Kandi.

Too bad for her, I just thought it was dumb. "Abraham Lincoln had nothing to do with the Declaration of Independence," I told her. "He came almost a hundred years later."

That hushed her up for one whole blink of the eye.

"So what are you writing, then?"

I'd already closed the notebook when I'd seen her coming over.

I'm not stupid.

"Nothing," I told her, 'cause that's what I tell everybody when they ask. It's not rude. It's universal for *none of your business*.

But I guess when the universe revolves around you, things work a different way. "Of course you're writing something," she said. "Don't need to get all huffy about it."

"I wasn't gettin' huffy!" I said, and it came out so huffy my cheeks started to burn.

She gave me one of those scary-sweet smiles, then twitched up an eyebrow and said, "So you drawing pictures of me, or what?"

"No!" I cried, and slapped open my notebook. "It's just stories, see?"

She nosed right in, and her eyes seemed to be gulping up the words. "Annie?" she asked, pointing a candy-corn nail at the name. "Are you writing about Annie Totes?"

I gave her a blank look. Who was Annie Totes?

"In our class?" she asked.

I felt like a double fool. "No!" I slapped the notebook closed again. "It's nobody." And then, 'cause I could tell she didn't believe me, I let on a little. "The Annie in my story's a character, all right? She's an old lady."

"Like somebody's grandmother?"

"Yeah, like that," I said, even though it wasn't like that at all.

"So what's she doing?"

I stared at her a second, and for that second it felt like she wasn't just being nosy. It felt like she really wanted to know. And in that second, I was dying to tell her all about Annie and the hero of the story, Lamar, and his pet wolf, Howler, and how Annie was being haunted by chain-rattlin' ghosts.

And then that second passed and I came to my senses.

"Nothin'," I said, and put the notebook away.

6

Classmates

Not knowing who Annie Totes was was part of a problem I didn't know I had until it was too embarrassing to fix. I'd been so busy puttin' my head down and avoidin' folks that I hadn't bothered learning the names of the kids in my class. That's okay the first day or first week or even the first couple of weeks of school, but a month in, it was all-at-once embarrassing.

As in when Ms. Miller asked me to hand back papers and I couldn't. And when I slipped up on the Annie Totes question.

It's not like I knew *nobody*. There was Kandi, of course, and I'd figured out the Hee-Haws. The one in my class was named Hank, and the one who was on the bus and in the other sixth-grade class was named Ryan. Hank didn't mess with me in class and he didn't ride my bus, but when he got with Ryan at recess, it was like flippin' a switch.

I also knew Benny Tazmin. He's no bigger'n me, but he fills the room with his jokes and snickers. Remembering his name came easy 'cause Ms. Miller's on him a lot for "disruptive behavior," and the boys around him egg him on, cheering, "Ben-ny, Ben-ny!" or they tattle on him, saying, "It was Taz!"

Besides Kandi and Benny and Hank, I also knew the two girls who were always trailing after Kandi. The reason I knew their names was because Kandi acts like she's supervising them and does it using both their names like a parent: "Lexi Simmons, where have you been?" "Macy Mills, are you coming or not?" The three of them seem to be in some sort of fashion club that moves from stripes to polka dots to solids and back, and involves socks with animal designs. One of them's always messin' up in the eyes of the others, though, and half the time it seems they don't even like each other. Maybe they do and have a funny way of showin' it. Maybe they should stick to simpler socks.

And then there were my tablemates, Colby, Rayne, and Wynne. All girls. Colby's bossy, with a nose that's usually tipped up and twitchin' like she's trackin' someone's scent. Rayne's shy, with a lion's mane of dark hair, and Wynne wears wire-rimmed glasses and whispers everything, always.

So out of the twenty-eight kids in class, I knew nine.

And that included me.

That afternoon, though, it bumped up to ten when Kandi caught my eye and did a big point-point with a candy-corn finger at a girl across the classroom. She shielded her pointing hand with her other hand but didn't come anywhere near covering what she was doing. And then she mouthed a big, exaggerated "ANNIE TOTES!" that anyone could see.

I covered my face and slumped in my chair.

Kandi Kain is the worst.

7

Followed

What I thought about Kandi was proven true on my walk to Brookside that same afternoon. "Where *are* you going?" a voice right behind me said.

It made me jump, and when I whipped around, sure enough, I was face to face with Kandi.

"You take the twenty-seven bus *to* school," she panted. "But you walk this way after. And you keep on walking forever! Where are you going?"

I didn't notice I was being followed 'cause sometimes when I get to thinking about my stories, everything else sort of blanks out. In this case I was in the middle of a big fight scene in my head where Lamar and Howler corner the guy who's been faking the chain-rattlin'-ghost stuff. His name's Mr. Butte and he's meaner'n skunk spray. And now that he's trapped in the corner of a basement, he's desperate.

I like playing out scenes in my head before I write them. I'll do the same scene over and over on my way to Brookside, fine-tuning it 'til I'm itching to put it on paper. My favorite is when I get to a scene near the end of a story where the villain is trapped in a basement, or pinned in an alleyway, or tossed headfirst inside a jail cell. I live for the clank of a jail cell. Doesn't matter if the story is turning out good or bad, I finish just so I can hear the jail cell slammin' shut.

Ma doesn't get why I'm always scribblin' in a notebook. "It's not a journal?" she asked after I'd filled up the first one and was starting on a second.

"No, ma'am," I told her. "It's stories."

"Like . . . made-up stories?"

"Yes, ma'am."

She studied me for a bit. "So it's not private, then? I can read it?"

But I didn't let her. I worried that she'd say how wonderful they were because she's my ma, or that I'd be able to tell from her face they weren't any good. Either way, I didn't want her to see. I didn't want *anyone* to see.

But back to Kandi sneaking up on me.

I didn't notice it 'cause I was a long ways from school and my mind was with Lamar and Howler, down in a dark, eerie basement cornering evil Mr. Butte. That, and I don't happen to have eyes in the back of my head.

I was mad at Kandi for spooking me, and even madder

at *me* for getting spooked. And on top of getting mad and madder, I got an instant case of the worries. We were half a block from Brookside, and I sure couldn't have Kandi knowing I spent my afters at an old-folks' home!

I stopped walking. "Why you followin' me?"

"Where are you going?" she asked, like her questions mattered way more than mine. "There's nothing back this way!"

My mind was scrambling. "Well, there must be, or I wouldn't be headed this way, right?"

"So where, then?"

I was stuck. And I was mad. And my mouth kept right on being stupid. "To the intersection of Nowhere and None of Your Business," I said. "And how do you know I take the twenty-seven?"

She looked down. "Hilly's on the twenty-seven. She says Troy's pretty mean to you."

I knew which one Troy was, but Hilly? I gave Kandi a good, hard squint. "Who?"

"Hillary Howard? She's in Mr. Ulman's sixth with Troy. Short brown hair. Bracelets?"

I rolled my eyes. "Oh, her." Then I gave another good, hard squint. "Why's she sit with him if she thinks he's mean?"

Kandi looked away. "Being a girl is . . . complicated."

Like that was any kind of answer?

Then real quick she switched subjects. "But the twenty-seven picks up on the west side, and you're going due east."

"Am I?" I said, 'cause I had no idea what direction I was

headed, and hearing "due east" come out of someone with such long, shiny hair and fingernails painted like candy corn just seemed . . . strange.

"Sun's over there," she said, pointing behind us, then nodded in the direction I was headed. "So that's east."

"Well, doesn't matter which direction I'm goin'," I said. "You've got no business following me."

"Look," she said, "I've got to get home. I just wanted to make sure you're okay."

I stared at her, thinkin' that if lies were flames, she'd be one towerin' inferno.

My dark look didn't seem to affect her, though. She danced off with a little wave and called, "Tell Annie and Howler I say hi!"

"Howler's a *wolf*," I yelled after her.

"I know that!" she called back.

Which left me kinda dumbstruck.

How could she have picked that up from one little look at the page?

It didn't help my case of the worries, that's for sure. I headed on toward Brookside, wonderin' if she could read *me* just as easy.

8

The Crazies

Going inside Brookside is like pushing through a secret revolving door. On one side there's daylight and trees and cars and *movement*.

On the other there's Death.

They try to cover that up with soft music playing and a big lobby that looks like it's straight out of a magazine. I never sit there myself, and nobody else seems to use it, either. It's like a big, fancy family room missin' its family, and if you hold still in it for even just a minute, you can feel Death lurking nearby.

Even so, I was glad to step inside. Kandi might have been long gone, but her following me still had me jittery.

"Good afternoon, Lincoln! Isn't it a lovely day?" the receptionist said, shooing Death away. She's told me lots of times to call her Geri, but I was still having trouble doing that.

"Yes, ma'am. It sure is," I said as I went up to her desk.

She smiled as I signed in. "You have got to be the politest boy I've ever met."

"Ma'am?"

She stood. "We're not used to being *ma'am*'d around here, but I must say, I do enjoy it." Her heels clicked on the tile floor as she led the way across the lobby to the East Wing, which is the side where Ma works. She raised an eyebrow in my direction. "My grandson calls me dude."

Being reminded that I talk different from other folks around here had me feelin' all self-conscious. Ma says I just need to start putting the *g*'s on my words—something she's been working hard at since her sister told her, "You sound like a hick," when we were staying with her and Cheyenne. Ma fumed about it for days, but now she's correctin' *my* speech. At supper the other day she even told me that sayin' "ma'am" was "regional" and that I should maybe go easy on it. I dropped my fork. After years of drillin' it into my head, she wants me to go easy on it?

But back to being walked across the lobby.

Anyone can come into the lobby. But if you want to get to the rooms where the oldies roam, you have to sign in and someone has to let you in.

Someone also has to let you out.

Mounted on both sides of every main doorway is an entry keypad, and the folks who work at Brookside are siy about shielding the pad with one hand as they type in the secret code with the other. They're chatty while they do it, so it feels like they're playing a shell game—sly shuffling moves mixed with small talk to trick you into forgetting what's where.

I usually look away from the keypad because I know it's the polite thing to do, and I always go along with the small talk, but I never forget that once you've been shuffled in, you can't come out without the secret code.

Even Ma won't tell me the combination. "I'm not about to jeopardize my job," she said when I asked. "And you're never there without me, so you have nothing to worry about."

It still made me feel trapped. So I asked, "What if there's a fire and everyone but me's in Activities?"

"Hush, Lincoln."

"But what if—"

"Lincoln, I'm not telling you!"

So one time while Geri was letting me in, I did the sly-eye and got the combination myself. I've felt safer ever since.

But back to Geri walking me across the lobby.

She was thumbing in the code, talking about the weather, when an oldie's face popped up in the East Wing's door window.

"Oh, dear," Geri said, because it was Suzie York, looking

like a pitiful dog begging to get out. "We'd better go through Activities."

I used to think you could talk your way past Suzie York, but it's tough 'cause she's stuck in an endless loop of finding a way out. So when Geri did a U-turn back across the lobby, I was all for it, even though it was the long way around.

Activities is a really big room between the East and West Wings. Everything from exercise classes to movies to crafts happens in Activities. You can get to it from the lobby, the courtyard, or either of the wings, but from any direction you need the secret code to get inside.

So Geri keyed us in and detoured me through Activities, past the tables and chairs, which were all shoved to one side so a man with a big roll-around bucket could mop the floor. "Enjoy your afternoon," she told me as she let me into the East Wing through a side door.

"Yes, ma'am," I said, then went down a corridor, past a side hallway with a fake street sign saying DOVE LANE, and to the Clubhouse, which is what they call the big room where the East Wing oldies eat or hang out when they're not sleeping.

It's also the place I spend my afters.

Before I could make it to my usual table, though, Suzie York cornered me with sad puppy-dog eyes and said, "Where'd you come from? How'd you get in? Can you get me out?"

"Sorry, Mrs. York," I told her. "Only your family can get you out."

She gave me a puzzled look. "How do you know my name?"

"Oh, we've met before."

She glossed right over that and got back to what she really wanted to know. "Where'd you come in?"

"Down the hall," I said, keepin' it vague.

"Which hall? Where? Does it lead outside?"

Just then another lady, Debbie Rucker, shouted, "What is your name?" from across the room.

I knew she was talking to me.

She does the same thing every single solid day.

"Don't yell!" Suzie yelled, which only made Debbie yell it louder. "What is your name?!"

Debbie doesn't remember Suzie's name, either, but I still knew Debbie was talking to me. The sad thing is, Debbie's not even gray yet. And she wouldn't belong in an old-folks' home, only Brookside isn't just for oldies.

It's for crazies.

Ma gets mad when I call them that, and everyone else working there would probably hate me if they heard me say it, because Brookside's motto is "Distinguished Memory Care." But that's just a fancy way of saying Crazy Town. The fact is, everyone living there has lost their mind. Or at least part of it. They can't remember stuff. Not from one day to the next and, for some of them, not from one minute to the next. There's one oldie named Stu who seems completely gone. He just sits in a corner and drools.

At least he's quiet. Debbie? Now, that's a different

story. I used to try and ignore Debbie, but it just made things worse. She got angry and kept asking the same question louder and louder until she was throwing stuff and screaming, "WHAT IS YOUR NAME?"

"It's not her fault," Ma told me. "Her brain's damaged. Just answer her straightaway and be done with it."

So when she shouted it this time, I called over, "It's Lincoln."

"Lincoln." She said it all breathless. Like I'd just given her a beautiful gift. "Abraham Lincoln was the sixteenth president of the United States, you know. My favorite."

That right there is a good example of why crazy is something I can't figure out. How can someone not remember your name after you've told it to them every single day for over a month but *can* remember that Abraham Lincoln was the sixteenth president?

I was relieved when Ma came out of one of the bedrooms and gave me her sweet smile. "Have a good day?" she asked.

Before I could even recall, Debbie turned to her and said, "Are you his mother?"

"I am," Ma answered, like it was a brand-new question instead of the same one she answered nearly every day.

Then Suzie York pointed at me and called out, "That boy knows how to get out of here!"

The crazies who'd been watching the action perked up a little, and the ones who were half asleep in their chairs sputtered awake and turned to stare at me.

Except for Droolin' Stu, who just sat there, drooling.

"He's just here to do his homework," Ma announced, and shooed me over to my table. Then she smiled around the room and asked, "Who wants a snack?"

Which was the end of anyone's interest in me.

9

Zombie Chicken

It was only four-thirty, but Teddy C had already for-gotten about the snack and was demanding dinner. "Where's the food?" he hollered, pounding his fork and spoon on his table.

"It'll be here soon!" Gloria called as she helped another oldie to a table.

Dinnertime at Brookside is five o'clock. Two guys in hairnets roll it in on big metal carts from the kitchen. The oldies live for the carts, which hold the dinners and des-serts for all thirty folks in the East Wing, and Ma says the exact same thing goes on in the West Wing.

Once the guys from the kitchen leave, the caregivers start handing around dinner plates while the nurses make sure the oldies who get meds take them.

The oldies sit four to a table, facing each other, saying nothing, unless it's "Where's the food?" It was creepy at first to see all these old folks looking like a bunch of zombies and then *eating* like a bunch of zombies, but Ma explained that they don't talk to each other because they're concentrating. "It's everything they've got just to get the food in," she told me. "Take a minute and really watch them, Lincoln. You'll see."

So I really watched them, and really watching them is not something I ever want to do again. It's *painful* to watch them eat. Their hands shake and they *focus* on putting food in, and then it takes years for them to swallow and start on the next bite.

There are usually the same four Purple Shirts in the Clubhouse during dinner. There's Ma, Gloria, and two others named Teena and Carmen. Teena's more no-nonsense with the oldies than Ma or Gloria, and Carmen's got a voice like gravel being shoveled. Teena and Carmen don't pay much attention to me, and I return the favor.

But back to oldies eating.

Gloria's the one who spends time spooning dinners into the oldies who are really bad off. Their dinners come blended, so what might have been chicken and rice and green beans to begin with winds up being three blobs of mush on a plate.

That's painful to watch, too, so I don't, which means I get a lot of homework done during dinnertime. Or, if I'm done with homework, I take out my notebook and work on my stories, which is the best way I know to block out what's going on around me.

After dinner, there are lots of leftovers. Not after dessert, but Ma says that some things stay the same no matter how old you get.

There's no Brookside dog, but if there was, he'd be big as a blimp on leftovers. Whole enchiladas and beef patties and chicken strips and biscuits . . . it's crazy what gets left on plates. And after dinner, *slop,* it all goes into the trash.

Ma has said more'n once what a waste it is, but who wants food that's been sitting at a zombie table? Especially since lots of times there's one little bite missing. Who's gonna eat that?

But the same day Kandi followed me, I saw Ma tuck away chicken strips in a plastic bag. Right there in front of God and the Purple Shirts, she slipped chicken and biscuits into a bag and put it in her purse.

Nobody said a thing, but I knew they were all thinkin' stuff, and I was sure embarrassed. It seemed so pitiful. No kidding Ma's tight with a dollar, but this I couldn't believe. And once I got over the shock of what she'd done, my mind started screamin' in terror.

She's gonna make me eat used food?!

On the bus ride home, she didn't say a word about it, so I finally asked, "Why'd you steal that chicken?"

She looked at me like I had holes for brains. "*Steal* it?"

"Okay, *take* it."

She studied me some more, then gave me a strange little look. Like someone at school might do if they were fixin' to give you a wedgie. "Maybe I'm tired of cooking," she said.

That did me in. "Ma!" I cried. "No! I ain't eatin' zombie chicken! I'll eat cereal, day and night! You never have to cook again!"

"Zombie chicken," she said with a look that made me sure my shorts would be up to my ears if we were standing. "And what did I tell you about 'ain't'?"

"You make me eat zombie chicken and 'ain'ts' are gonna slip out!"

"Hush," she said, 'cause folks on the bus were staring now, wonderin' what sort of ma made her boy eat zombie chicken.

After a bit she leaned sideways and whispered, "And you can relax. It ain't for you."

She gave me a devilish grin, which made my mind snap like a pea pod, scatterin' thoughts all around my head.

What was that grin about?

What was she *sayin'*?

And who was it for, then? We didn't have a dog, and we didn't know any, either.

Only one thought made any kind of sense. "No, Ma!" I told her, keeping my voice low. "I won't let *you* eat zombie chicken, either!"

She gave me a stern look. "There is nothing wrong with this chicken."

"Ma, no!"

She opened her purse a bit and sniffed. "Smells delicious, if you ask me."

"Ma, no!"

She closed her purse and heaved a sigh. "The problem here is that you've never been hungry."

"I've been hungry!"

She gave me another stern look. "I've seen to it that you have not."

"But—"

"Hush."

The bus squealed to a stop, and when the doors flapped open, Ma led the way out, saying good night to the driver and nudging me to do the same when I started down the steps without sayin' it.

We walked the two blocks home without talking. It was cold out, and dark, and the streets had that scary feel they get when the only folks left on them are the ones with no place to be. I was glad to get to our corner. Glad to see light pouring out of the market.

But instead of going up to our apartment, Ma told me, "Wait right here," and headed off without me.

"Ma!" I called, 'cause she'd never done that before, and I sure didn't want to be left on my own with street folks.

"Hush!" she said over her shoulder. Then she went up to a man sitting outside the market and handed him the zombie chicken.

He looked up at her real slow. Like one of the oldies at Brookside might have. Then he raised a hand to take the food and gave Ma a nod.

He'd been there every night since we moved in, and

we've seen Mr. Noe, the man who runs the market, shoo him away from the door with a broom when he's sweeping out the place. Mr. Noe doesn't say a word to him—he just swats at him with the broom like he's a big pile of dirt.

So sometimes the man sits near the front door, and sometimes he's up the sidewalk a ways by an old pay phone that's covered in graffiti. Wherever he sits, though, he always looks the same. He wears a grimy green beanie, an old blue jacket, and gloves with the fingertips ripped out. He sits on a worn wool blanket by a cardboard box with a sign that reads:

2 TOURS
NO HOME
ANYTHING HELPS

I used to think *anything helps* meant money.
Turns out it also means zombie chicken.

10

The Demon Feather

At my old school we had desks. They were ancient, but it didn't matter 'cause yours was *yours*. The top lifted up, you could stash all sorts of stuff in it, and nobody bothered you about the mess lurkin' inside. Unless a sandwich got rotten. Or a banana went past black and into gooey. Even then, it was no big deal. The teacher'd say, "Smells like it's time for a little desk cleanin'," and everyone would throw away their spoiled food and old papers and candy wrappers.

Lookin' back on it, those desks might have been old and creaky, but they were way better'n the ones we have at my new school. What I liked most about the old desks was knowing where the borders were. Borders were simple. Nobody ever hogged up part of your desk with their stuff, or edged you out when they got carried away with a project. If they got carried away, their stuff went *smack* onto the floor.

At Thornhill School, the desks may be new, but they're really just tables. Tables for two, with a wide-open shelf for each person that barely holds a thing. There's no border on the desktop between you and your partner, not even a drawn line. So it's hard to protect your territory 'cause stuff is always creeping across the table like it's on a stealth mission.

And if that's not bad enough, we have to sit with two tables shoved together, face to face, so there are four kids at one big, square table, with no borders.

A whole continent of desktops, with no borders.

When I asked Ms. Miller if it was going to be like this all year, she explained that sixth grade is "a time of community learning" and that "this is how things are done around here."

Ms. Miller has put all sorts of reminders about being part of the community on our classroom walls and even on the ceiling. Every possible inch is covered in bright colors invitin' us to get along. There's the Global Community part, with flags and maps and art from around the world. There's the United We Stand wall, with more maps and figures from U.S. history. And there's the Our Community wall, where our projects get posted around the Golden Rule display.

Maybe I wouldn't mind community learning if my

everyday community wasn't three girls with way too much stuff. I don't understand why they have to have ten of everything and, if they do, why can't they keep it in their own territory?

Rayne's got hair accessories that stack up as the day goes by. She usually comes to school with her hair clipped down or braided with ribbons or decorated somehow, but by the end of the day it's busted loose and in full mane mode, with her headbands and clips and ribbons or what-not roamin' wild across our continent.

Straight across from me, there's Wynne, and she goes through Kleenex like air. She breathes in, she sniffles out. "Sorry! Allergies," she whispered the first time I got fed up with her tissue avalanche and pushed it back on her side. "Sorry" hasn't stopped avalanches from happening, but I feel mean just shoving them back because she looks truly miserable with her nose drippin' and her eyes waterin'.

But the worst invader was Colby's pencil feather. It's pink and fluffy and has little fake jewels that kind of clink when she writes. Why does a pencil need a feather? And why does a feather need *jewels*?

That's accessories on accessories!

I wouldn't have cared, except Colby's feather made her pencil about two feet long, and since she sat right next to me, that feather would wag around in *my* airspace with its little fake jewels all clinkin' together.

Colby gets A's on everything, which Ma told me was a good reason to put up with her feather. But during tests, that feather flaps around like a demon bird, and what that *means* is, Colby's got answers.

Right off, my stomach would tie up in knots. How could she know the answers so fast? And how come all of a sudden I couldn't think of any?

All through September and all through October I forced myself to put up with Colby's demon feather. I would scoot to the side and try everything to ignore that feather flapping through the air.

Then November rolled around and Ms. Miller gave us a math test and none of my feather-fightin' tricks worked. I just couldn't concentrate. *Flap, flap, flap, flap, flap,* that demon feather went, whippin' through the air while Colby showed all her steps. It would glide for just a second as she put a box around her answer, then take off again, flappin' its way through the next problem.

I was so distracted that instead of working on the math test, my brain went off and made up a story. In it there was a big feather that released hypnotizing eraser dust that was used as a powerful weapon by an intergalactic queen named Colby. Queen Colby had hijacked the *Inquiry*, a spaceship that, until then, had been under the command of the famous Captain Jones. The feather had hypnotized the captain and he was now a desperate prisoner on his own ship.

There's a great battle in the story, where the captain finally defeats Queen Colby by snatching the feather and tickling her nose with it, bringing her down in a fit of sneezing. It was a pretty funny scene, and I was having a great time making it better and better in my head when Ms. Miller told us that test-taking time was up.

I saw her frown when she collected my paper, but I tried to duck out to recess anyway.

"Lincoln!" she called as I was bolting for the door.

"Yes, ma'am?"

"Stay in, please."

When the room was cleared of everyone but her and me, she held out my test and said, "Can you explain this?"

So I told her about Colby's demon feather.

"Why didn't you just ask her to use a different pencil?"

"I've asked her lots of times! She says it's her lucky feather."

"Couldn't you have turned away?" She shook her head. "What *did* you do the whole time?"

I didn't want to say "Nothing," so it slipped out about the story. And since I was nervous, more slipped out than I wanted.

"Lincoln," she said with a sigh. "Don't these sound like excuses to you?" The corners of her mouth twitched like they wanted to get up but were just too tired. "Do we need to talk to your parents about getting you a tutor?"

"No, ma'am! I know how to do this stuff."

Her mouth rolled over into a frown. "Lincoln."

"I swear, ma'am! It was the feather!"

"Fine," she said after studying me for a bit. "It was the feather." Then she sat me down at the table nearest her, put my test and a pencil in front of me, and said, "You've got until recess is over."

I never worked a math test so fast in my life. And when recess was done, so was I.

Ms. Miller took the test from me with an eyebrow stretched high, then checked it over quick with a red pen in her hand.

A red pen that only touched paper once.

She looked up at me, then wrote *96%* and circled a big red A at the top. And when everyone was in from recess, she told Colby she couldn't use her demon feather pencil anymore.

"That's unconstitutional!" Colby cried, and she some-how twisted freedom of speech into freedom of feathers and got all uppity about her rights.

"Why don't I just switch seats with her?" Rayne asked, and once everyone was done being stunned by how nice it was for her to offer and what an easy fix it was, Rayne switched with Colby, putting that demon feather as far away from me as it could get on our borderless continent.

"Thanks," I told Rayne when she was all settled in.

"Sure," Rayne said, and gave me a smile that was one part twinkle and nine parts shy.

A smile that made my cheeks burn hot.

11

Talking in Circles

A strange thing happened after Rayne switched with Colby.

Kandi started stalking me.

She'd mostly left me alone after she'd followed me that day in early October. Oh, I'd see her giving me the spy-eye every now and then. My eyes hurt just seeing her do it, but maybe her eye muscles are looser than everyone else's. Maybe they're all limbered up from getting stretched around.

I don't really care that she does the spy-eye on me 'cause she seems to do it to everyone. I stuck out my tongue at her once when I caught her, but I felt stupid after, so now I just hit her with a straight-on stare, which makes her stop.

So Kandi hadn't said much to me for about a month,

but during lunch after the switch, she found me in the cafeteria and sat right across from me.

"Hi!" she said, sort of squiggling in her seat.

I kinda forgot to say hi back and just stared. I'm not used to talking to folks during lunch, especially not girls. I'm used to eating quick and getting over to the media center.

Kandi laughed. "What's the matter?"

I looked at my tray. "Uh . . . I'm almost done?"

She laughed again. "So? Just hang out and talk." She took a bite of her mac 'n' cheese. "How's your story coming?"

Her fingernails weren't painted like candy corn anymore. They were little turkeys with the tails all fanned out. "How do you do that?" I asked, 'cause the detail was crazy.

She put out a hand for me to admire. "You like?"

I was more *confused*. Or *puzzled*. Or maybe even *mystified*. Yeah, *mystified* fit the bill. "How long did that take you?" I asked.

She pulled back her hand. "You didn't answer my question."

I finished off my milk. "You didn't answer mine first."

"No, you didn't answer *mine* first."

I thought back and she was right. She'd asked me about my story. But the story about Annie and Howler was done, and I didn't want to waste time talking about my new story, I wanted to get back to *writing* it. I was at a heart-stopping spot where my main guy, Lucas, had barely escaped a killer by getting on the roof of a cabin. But the killer knew he was there and was climbing the side of the cabin by jabbing hunting knives into the wood as he went up, up, up. The wind was howling through the trees, so Lucas couldn't hear the killer coming.

That's where I'd had to stop. And since getting back to Lucas and the killer was something I wanted to do way more than talking in circles with Kandi, I stood up and told her, "Gotta go," and left.

I have a secret hideout in the media center. It's hidden by shelves of books in the far back corner, and above the shelves, clear up to the ceiling, the walls are painted with blue sky and clouds.

The librarian, Ms. Raven, goes crazy with decorations. Every inch of the walls is painted, and there are big cut-outs of characters standing around the place, and smaller ones hanging from the ceiling. There's the Reading Tree area, with a life-sized tree in the middle of a big cubby of picture books. I've seen little kids sitting around it on mats with books in their laps like they're havin' a picture-book picnic.

But back to my secret hideout.

It has a beanbag chair, soft as feathers, and that's what I sit in to write. Some lunches I wind up spending the time just staring at the painted sky and clouds, thinking about my story, but others I spend scribblin' the entire time.

My hideout's not actually *secret* as much as it is some-place no one else seems to go. Mostly, kids are at the computers. There are rows of them up front near Ms. Raven's desk, so that's where all the action is. Ms. Raven's nice, but what I like best is that she's quit askin' if she can help me. Now she just waves hello and lets me be.

And that's exactly what she did when I came in at lunch after ditching Kandi and her turkey-tail nails. Ms. Raven was over by the student stations, so I did a little double take when I passed by her desk 'cause there was a kid sitting at her computer.

There's no mistakin' whose computer it is 'cause there's an engraved brass plaque stating CARRIE C. RAVEN, LMS on it, and it has a big black bird perched on top.

I might've said something about him being back there, but Ms. Raven was lookin' right at us, so she already knew he was there. Then it clicked. "You her son?" I asked. It just came out.

"No!" he said. "She's helping me research."

The scowl on his face was tellin' me to move along—something I was more'n happy to do. I had a hero to save. A killer to stop. I needed to get Lucas off of that roof!

12

Invasion of Privacy

I didn't know I'd made Kandi mad until we were back in the classroom after lunch. Even then it took a little while to sink in because my mind was still on my story. I'd only had fifteen minutes in the beanbag chair, and the killer was now about to crest the roof while Lucas frantically looked for a way down.

"Did you hear me?" Kandi asked with a huff.

"Huh?" I asked back, 'cause I had no idea that she'd said anything.

"You were really mean to me," she said, and was she ever pouting!

"Uh . . . sorry. I didn't mean to be."

"Well, you were," she said, and stomped off.

Next to me, Rayne put a clip back in her hair and giggled.

I looked at her. "What?"

"She's not used to that."

"Used to what?"

Colby had her feather pencil out, ready for action. "Being ignored," she said without even looking at me.

Wynne leaned closer across our continent and whispered, "Can we pay you to keep doing it?" and the three of them giggled.

I didn't get it, but I also didn't care. It seemed like gossipy girl stuff to me. And then Ms. Miller started us on a timed write. *My favorite weather is . . .* , she wrote on the board, and like a switch going off, I forgot everything else and started writing.

When time was up, Kandi volunteered to collect the papers, and I could tell her eyes were slurping up words from the pages as she walked them up to Ms. Miller.

"She's reading yours," Rayne said, pulling the same hair clip back out.

"Who says it's mine?" I asked.

"Invasion of privacy," Colby called over her shoulder as she watched Kandi move toward Ms. Miller's desk.

Wynne was watching Kandi, too, and when she turned back around, she leaned forward and whispered, "You should complain."

"Who says it's mine?" I asked again, and this time they all answered me with looks that said I was dumber'n a load of bricks.

Which I guess I am, 'cause once again, I didn't hear Kandi

coming up behind me on my way to Brookside. Lucas was still on the rooftop in my mind, and I was trying to figure out how to get him down alive when she spooked me with "Don't you love this weather?"

I jumped. She laughed.

"Stop that!" I spat out.

"Why are you so skittery?"

"I'm not! I was just thinking!"

"About . . . ?"

"Look," I said, stopping dead in my tracks. "What do you want?"

"Nothing! I'm just in a great mood!" She gave me a big, sunny smile and said, "I think it's the weather. I just love the wind." She put her arms out and twirled around. "All that . . . energy!"

My jaw went for a dangle.

"What?" she asked.

"You read my paper."

"What are you talking about?" she asked, but guilt was stamped all over her face.

I gave her the stink-eye. "Don't lie!"

"Okay! So what if I read it?" she laughed. "It's not like it was personal." I was still giving her the stink-eye, so she said, "You're a good writer, Lincoln, you really are."

Then she twirled around and ran away.

13

The Vampire in Room 102

After Kandi followed me the second time, I kept a wary eye out for her and even took to going a longer way, just to throw her off my trail. I hid out from her at school, too, and after a while she started ignoring me back, which was a huge relief.

It took over two weeks, but finally one Friday it felt safe enough to take the shorter walk to Brookside, and I got there in time to see an ambulance parked by the main doors with its lights flashing and the engine running.

I hurried inside, but the East Wing and the West Wing were both closed, so I couldn't tell which side of the place the ambulance was for. I would have asked Geri when I signed in, but she was on the phone, recruitin' folks for the Alzheimer's Walk that was happening in early December.

Not that she would have told me much. She never does, unless the subject is the weather. But I would have asked anyway, especially since I've figured out that there's a vampire in Room 102.

Go ahead and laugh, but I'm not messing around. Room 102 has two beds. One of them's for Mrs. White—she's the vampire. The other's for somebody who has no idea they're about to die.

It's a sneaky situation, because Mrs. White doesn't *look* like a vampire. She actually looks like the one who's had all her blood drained. Her face is gray and bony, her hair is white and wispy, and her hands are one hundred percent knuckles.

She also *acts* dead. She just lies there, day after day, bony-faced and wispy-haired, asleep in her special motorized bed.

Ma explained to me that Mrs. White has a special bed because she's on hospice, which she also explained was a nice way of saying she's going to die. Very soon. Like, any day. Only Mrs. White hasn't died. Instead, she's outlived six roommates since Ma started working there.

Six!

Every one of those roommates was in *way* better shape than Mrs. White. They could get up and sit at a table for dinner. They could use a toilet and take a shower and go to the Activities Room, all while Mrs. White just lay there, looking dead.

One by one, though, the roommates suddenly died.

And every one of them died during the night.

And every time one died, Mrs. White bounced back to life.

"Just when you think *she's* the one who'll be gone by morning, she bounces back," Ma said after the third roommate, Cynthia, died back in early October. "I sat with her to distract her while they were clearing out Cynthia's things. Her cheeks were rosy. She smiled and talked . . . even thanked me after I changed her!"

We were on the bus ride home. And maybe it's 'cause we'd entered the month of ghouls and goblins, and spooky decorations were already up in store windows, but a funny idea about Mrs. White flashed into my brain. I kept my voice down as I broke the news to Ma. "That's because she's a vampire."

Ma gave me one of her looks. "Lincoln!"

I gave her one of *my* looks.

So she frowned at me and said, "That's the most ridiculous thing I've ever heard. She can't even get out of bed!"

"She doesn't need to," I whispered. "She's a *psychic* vampire."

"A *what*?"

"She sucks the life force out of folks," I told her.

"And how does she do *that*?"

I gave her a little grin. "You need to ask *her*."

I was just messing around, but less than two weeks later the next roommate mysteriously died during the night, and Ma kind of freaked out. "Mrs. White's cheeks were all rosy again!" she whispered on the bus ride home. "They haven't been rosy since the last time!"

"I told you," I said with a little shrug, "she's a psychic vampire." But this time I wasn't so sure I was messing around.

Then it happened *again,* and Ma really freaked out. "It's not funny!" she said. "It's the third one this month! It's like . . . it's like some sort of *hoodoo.*"

The fifth roommate dying had caused Ma to work late, so it was darker'n usual as we were walking home from the bus stop. My eyes were dartin' around, taking in the creatures of the night hangin' out in doorways. "So don't go back in her room," I said, wondering how powerful a psychic vampire could get.

Ma drew her coat in tighter. "I have to! It's my job!"

I noticed the moon, shinin' near full above us. "Well, just don't go in her room after dark, then. And maybe wear some garlic."

"Garlic? Really?" she asked.

I pointed out the moon. "Couldn't hurt, right?"

I was expecting her to accuse me of having a wild imagination, but seein' the moon did her in. "Oh, Lord!" she gasped.

She tried to dial it back, telling me we were just overreacting, but then she stopped at the corner market for some garlic. "Couldn't hurt, right?"

Ma seemed fine the next morning, but the instant I got to Brookside that afternoon, she hauled me into the

Clubhouse phone room and closed the door tight. "She noticed!" Ma gasped, and her eyes were wide as pies.

"Who noticed what?" I looked through the phone room window to see if anyone was watching, 'cause the room is small and being hauled into it felt mighty awkward.

"Mrs. White! She noticed the garlic!" Ma dropped her voice even more. "Her nose twitched! Like this," she said, then did a twitchy thing with her nose that made her look like a rabbit trying to sneeze. "And she asked, 'What *is* that foul odor?'"

I took a little step back 'cause Ma *was* smelling mighty garlicky. "Had she messed her diaper?"

"Yes! And she *still* noticed it! She acted like she was afraid of it!"

"Maybe she was talking about *her* smell?"

"She never talks about her smell, and her smell's a whole lot worse than garlic!"

"So . . . did you tell her?"

Her eyes about popped out. "That I was warding off her psychic vampire powers with garlic?!" She looked out the window to make sure no one had heard, 'cause it had come out so loud. But worse than someone hearing, the Brookside director, Mr. Freize, was entering the Clubhouse. "Oh, Lord," Ma gasped. She shoved me down in the phone chair. "Stay right here until I come get you. Look busy! Do your homework!"

"Ma, you should—"

"Hush!" she said, and hurried out of the room.

So I didn't get to tell her how garlicky she smelled.

I didn't get to tell her that she should steer clear of the director.

Too bad, too, 'cause she was all mortified on the ride home. "Did it really smell that strong?" she asked.

"Oh, yeah."

"I shouldn't have peeled them."

"You *peeled* them?"

"I didn't know! I've never had to ward off vampires before!"

"And *them*? How many did you have on you?"

"Never mind!" she snapped. Then she muttered, "They must've warmed up after I started working." She looked out the window. "It's not an easy job, you know."

We rode along for a while, quiet, until finally I asked, "You got rid of them, right?"

"Of course I got rid of them!"

She wasn't in the mood to hear it, but I felt like I needed to tell her. "It still smells, Ma."

That night she took a shower until the hot water was all gone. And the next day Mrs. White had a brand-new roommate, named Mary. "She's sweet and gentle, and her daughter seems so nice," Ma told me with tears in her eyes.

Sure enough, near the end of her second week, Sweet Mary died unexpectedly during the night. November was starting off the same way October had, and I couldn't help wondering again how powerful a psychic vampire could get. Especially with the nights getting longer. Did it give her more time to use her powers? Would she be reaching through walls soon?

"Go in there and look!" Ma said, pointing at Mrs. White's room. "Her cheeks are all rosy. She's *giggling* and wanting to go for a walk!"

"I'm not going in there!" I told her, and made a beeline for my table.

Mrs. White didn't actually get up and go for a walk that afternoon. She just lay in her special bed while they finished cleaning out Mary's half of the room.

About two weeks had passed since Mary died, so I figured the ambulance idling in front of Brookside had something to do with Mrs. White killing off her new roommate—a big, boxy woman named Pat.

The truth is, I was more worried about Ma being freaked out than I was about Pat being dead, but when the East Wing door opened, I quit worrying about either. It was Debbie Rucker who was being wheeled out, and she was as alive as ever.

Geri was still on the phone, so I hurried over to catch the door.

"What is your name?" Debbie demanded when she saw me.

"Lincoln," I told her.

"Well, Lincoln, guess what?" she said, rolling by. "I fell and I have to go to the hospital!"

"Hope you're okay," I said.

"I'll be fine!" she told me. Then in a big burst she called, "Lincoln was the sixteenth president! My favorite!"

I caught the East Wing door before it latched.

"Don't let them throw out my snack," Debbie hollered over her shoulder. "Did you hear me, Lincoln? Don't let them throw out my snack!"

I pushed the door open. All of a sudden I was ready for a snack. Maybe two!

I lost my appetite quick, though, 'cause that was the same day Ruby Hobbs begged Gloria to let her dance.

It hit me hard. I'd been spendin' my afters at Brookside for over two months and sure hadn't seen it coming, but somewhere along the line the oldies had become *people* to me. People with feelings. So as tough as it was for my eyes to take, seein' Ruby the way she was didn't seem so funny anymore.

14

Messengers

It took a lot of *there, theres* and *now, nows* from Gloria to get Ruby to stop crying and back in her room. When Ruby came out for supper a bit later, she was dressed and quiet, but in some ways her being quiet was even sadder than her crying, 'cause she just sat at the table looking down. It was like she was too tired to eat. Too tired to care.

"Why does she do that?" I asked Ma on the way home.

"Do what?" Ma whispered, looking around the bus. "And who are we talking about?"

"Ruby," I said. "Why does she come out all buck naked, singing?"

"Oh," Ma said, heaving a sigh. "I'm sorry you had to see that."

"It's the third time I've seen it!"

"I'm up to about ten."

"But why does she do it?"

Ma shook her head. "I don't know." Then she gave a little shrug and said, "Why do any of them do what they do? Like Peggy Riggs. Why does she talk to the air?"

Peggy Riggs did talk to the air. And she did it like the air was listening. Like she was sharing secrets with someone she could see. Only the secrets didn't make any sense.

"Maybe she's seeing ghosts?" I said. "There's got to be *lots* of ghosts in that place. Especially with Mrs. White on the loose at night."

"Lincoln, hush. I am just too tired to have you piling ghosts on top of vampires." She sank down in her seat a little, hugging her bag. "It was a mighty long day."

Ma turned to look out the window, so my mind wandered off. And it probably would've got totally lost if Ma hadn't snapped me back a short while later. "Huh?" I asked, 'cause she was staring at me and I knew she'd said something.

"Where do you go when your eyes get like that?" she asked.

"Get like what? What are you talking about?"

"They move around like you're watching something."

"They do?"

"Mm-hmm. So what were you thinking just now?"

I did some blinking as I remembered, then finally told her, "You don't want to know."

She gave me the same look she does when I'm about to get it for sassin'. "Yes, Lincoln. Yes, I do."

I was pretty tired, too, and sure didn't need trouble piled on top of tired. "I was just thinkin' . . . ," I said, but something told me to stop.

"Don't make me drag it out of you, boy. Just say it!"

"All right, all right!" I took a breath and started, "You know how Crazy Paula does that tapping thing?"

"Paula *Barnett*? At Brookside? You're thinking about *her*?" Then real quick she added, "And don't call her crazy."

I stared at her. "Ma, if there's such a thing as crazy, she's it."

She frowned. "You could call her Tapping Paula."

"That's worse! No one hates her for being crazy. They hate her for tapping."

Which was a fact so solid, Ma couldn't argue. Paula sits day after day, with eyes drooped to half-mast, doing nothing, then one hand starts tapping on the table, over and over and over and over, until you want to scream, *Stop it!*

"That tapping really gets to me," Ma said, twisting around to look at me. "Why does she do it? Why won't she stop?"

"*That's* what I was thinkin' about," I told her. And once that busted out, the rest started flowing. "Maybe she can't speak, but what if she can see things we can't?"

Ma sat back again and heaved another sigh. "What *are* you talking about?"

I knew she was tired. Tired and testy. I knew I should probably make up something else and not tell her what I was really thinking. But I'd had this *idea*. I could see the whole thing! "What if she can see ghosts?" I asked, lettin' more seep out. "What if they can tell her things?" Ma's eyes rolled, but I kept talking. "Paula's on the border, right? Of here and there? Of earth and after? She's got to be, right?"

Ma's whole head turned now, and she just stared at me. And I knew I should just hush up, but it was too late. I had that feeling I get when everything comes together in one picture that's big and clear and bright and . . . *amazing.*

So it gushed out. "What if all that tapping Paula does is a way of *communicating*? Like Morse code? Everyone *thinks* she's crazy, but maybe she's not! Maybe she's tryin' to tell the ghosts something! Or maybe she's tryin' to tell *us* something! Like that Mrs. White is about to strike again!"

The words hung there, hovering in the dim light inside the bus. And I had to admit—the idea had seemed way better bouncing around inside my head than it did running out my mouth.

Ma closed her eyes and took a deep breath. "Lincoln Jones, you have an imagination as wide as it is deep."

And then *that* just hung there, actin' like a compliment, when I'm pretty sure it wasn't.

At our stop, Ma gave me a little scowl as she gathered her stuff. "One thing's for sure," she said. "I'm not taking your advice about dealing with the residents. I'm done with vampires and ghosts and Morse-coding mutes."

Couldn't blame her there.

The wind blasted cold and sharp when we got off the bus, and we hunkered in against it as we walked home, me half a pace behind her. Neither of us said a word until we were almost to our corner, where Ma suddenly stopped short. "I forgot the Man's dinner," she said, then shook her head and started walking again. "It's sittin' right in the fridge."

Ever since I'd told Gloria what Ma was up to with her taking home zombie chicken, word had gotten around Brookside, and now the others helped Ma pack a dinner for "the Man."

"Sweet of you, Maribelle," they all said, but I suspect most of them thought *I* was "the Man."

As we walked along, Ma kept kicking herself for forgetting. I tried telling her to go easy on herself, but when the Man saw us coming, it was like a light went on in his eyes.

"Oh, Lord," Ma said under her breath.

And then, to make things worse, he did something he'd never done before.

He stood up.

"Lord, oh, *Lord*," Ma whimpered.

"It's okay," I told her, but it was just words, and I knew it.

"I'm sorry," she said, going up to him. "I don't have anything today."

But he wasn't looking for food. "Is your name Maribelle?" he asked.

Ma's face went a little loose.

I guess the Man knew how to read loose faces, 'cause he pointed to the pay phone and said, "You had a call. Your sister. She wants you to call her back."

"Oh, Lord," Ma said, then recovered with a polite nod. "Well, thank you very much."

"It kept ringing and ringing," the Man said, shaking his head. "At first I didn't know what it was. It never rings."

"I appreciate the message," Ma said with another nod. "Sorry if it disturbed you."

"Disturbed me?" He gave her a strange little smile. "It was no trouble."

"Well, thank you," Ma said.

When she started to leave, he said, "I'm Levi, by the way."

Then he sat back down and looked away.

15

Hide 'n' Seek

Ma handed me her key and said, "I've got to call Ellie. Go warm the stew. I'll be right up."

"But—"

"Git!"

She zapped me hard with the steely-eye, and since there's no arguing with Ma's steely-eye or her *git*, I got. But I was burning with questions! Why had Ma given Aunt Ellie the pay phone number? We didn't have a phone, but why not give Aunt Ellie the number at Brookside, like she'd done for the school when she'd filled out my forms? And why was Aunt Ellie calling, relaying messages through street folk? What was so important? It couldn't have anything to do with Ma not repaying her. Everything we did—or, more like, *didn't* do—seemed to come back to us still owing Aunt Ellie. Every time Ma got paid, she sent Aunt Ellie money, and every time I asked for something, I got told, "Not until I've got Ellie paid back." Even Snickers bars got nixed.

All this went sparking through my brain at light speed. And since Ma's steely-eye wasn't glaring at me right then, I had a full recharge of curiosity, which got me doin' an about-face back to the gate.

I opened the gate as quiet as I could, and spy-eyed the corner. I could see Ma hunkered against the phone with her back to me, so I went through the gate and edged in closer.

What I heard set my heart scampering like a rabbit. "He won't, Ellie," Ma was saying. "He can't even get himself to work. How's he ever going to get it together to track me down?" She listened for a bit, then said, "I'm sure he was! That's how he gets when he's drinking." She added the *g* at the last minute. Like she was remembering how to speak a foreign language. Then she heaved a sigh and said, "Look, if it happens again, just keep denying you've seen us. . . . Yes . . . Yes . . . I know. . . . Yes'm. And you know I appreciate it. . . . I will. And I'll put some extra in the last one. You should have it before Christmas. . . . Mm-hmm . . . I'm sorry about the trouble. Really, I am."

I should've backed away the second I knew Aunt Ellie had called about Cliff, but I got greedy, wanting to know more, and gettin' greedy always bites me in the backside.

"Lincoln!" Ma snapped when she saw me trying to steal

away. She came steaming at me like a locomotive. "Since when do you flat out disobey me?"

"Since the stairs are dark and I got scared?" I gave her my best pleading look. "You never let me go up or down by myself after dark!"

It was enough to not get me cuffed, though I'm pretty sure she knew I was playing hide 'n' seek with the truth.

She snatched the key back from me and said, "What did you hear?"

"That Cliff's after us."

"He ain't *after* us!" she said, spitting the words out hard and fast.

When Ma's not clownin' around, "ain't" means she's simmerin' in stress. And since this time the word popped out like a bubble breaking through heatin' stew, I knew it was bad.

"Sorry," she said, calming herself as she went through the gate and closed it behind us. "I don't want you to worry. He will never in a million years come out here."

As we headed up the steps, I told her, "We need to get a phone, Ma. We need to get a phone so we can call 911 if he does show up."

"It's a mighty big world, Lincoln. And he's about as enterprisin' as a barstool. Look how long it's taken him to lift his dialin' finger—we've been gone since July! Besides, no one but Ellie knows we're out here, and she doesn't know where we're livin' or where I'm workin'."

"Is that why you didn't tell her? Because you were afraid Cliff would track us down?"

"He's never gonna track us down. Not with us this far away. I'm guessin' he's finally been evicted, which is why he's callin' around now. He's at a dead end with me, so his next move'll be to sweet-talk his way into some other woman's home, Heaven help her." She locked me down with double-barreled eyeballs. "We've got nothin' to worry about, you hear?"

"Then why didn't you tell Aunt Ellie our address or where you work?"

"Maybe I didn't want her weighin' in on where we live or what I do." She shook her head. "Lord, she would have *so* much to say!"

It still didn't make sense. "But why give her the pay phone number? We can't hear it ring."

She frowned. "I didn't give her the number. She got nosy and wrote it down from caller ID when I called once before about sending her payments." She frowned even harder. "And now she's all wantin' to know who 'my man' is."

"You mean Levi?"

She flashed a look at me. "I am tryin' to *forget* his name."

"But why, Ma?"

"Because now he's not just a man." She pulled out her key and slid it in the lock. "Now he's *somebody*. Somebody's son. Or brother. Or father. Maybe all three!"

I hurried to follow her inside. "But . . . wasn't he always?"

She clicked on a lamp, then turned to face me. "Somebody named him, Lincoln. The same way I named you."

I didn't like the way that felt.

Not one bit.

So I switched back to Aunt Ellie. "Well? What did you tell her?"

"Who? Ellie? I told her the truth."

"That he's a homeless guy?"

"No! That it's a pay phone."

When she set her bag down on the kitchen table, it seemed to pull her heart down with it. "It's gonna be okay, Ma," I said, touching her arm.

The words floated around us, feeling strange.

Like I was still playing hide 'n' seek with the truth.

16

Footsteps

After the business with Aunt Ellie and the pay phone, Ma seemed to be carrying the world on her shoulders, so I got to heating what was left of the stew like she'd asked me to do before she'd caught me spying.

Ma's stew's a wonder. It starts on Sunday and usually lasts to Friday, and along the way it shrinks and grows and changes flavor. She messes with it some nights, adding spices and chopping in more stuff. I like when she goes heavy on the carrots. Something about carrots stewing in beef juices and onions makes me happy to be hungry.

It didn't take long to heat, and when I had two steaming bowls with buttered bread on the table, Ma gave me a grateful smile and we both dug in.

Most days, Ma gets me talking about school over dinner, but not this time. Two bites in, her whole face seemed to crumple and sag as she scooped up stew. Every time she slid the spoon back in, it was slow and careful, like she was looking for answers between the onions and carrots.

It wasn't until her spoon was clinking the bottom that she finally said something.

"What?" I asked, because it was more mutter than words.

She looked up like she'd forgotten I was there, then ditched the brooding and went straight to huffy. "You'd think she could have invited us to Thanksgiving."

"Aunt Ellie?" I asked, running to jump onto her train of thought.

"Of course Ellie," she snapped.

My eyebrows couldn't help creepin' up. "You told me you were working a long shift on Thanksgiving. You said there was no gettin' out of it."

"Ellie doesn't know that!"

"But . . . if she'd asked us to dinner, you'd have had to tell her no, right?"

"She didn't even bother to ask!"

I wrestled with that, trying to figure out how a person could be mad over not being asked to do something they knew they couldn't do in the first place. And after flipping it back and forth in my mind for a while, I said, "What if she was waitin' for *you* to ask?"

"We can't have Thanksgiving here! We don't even have an oven!"

"But . . . she doesn't know that, right?"

"Lincoln! Whose side are you on?"

I went back to my stew. Maybe it *was* a better place to find answers. "Didn't know there was sides," I grumbled.

She held her forehead like it was all of a sudden too heavy to hold itself up. Then she sighed and said, "I never should have asked her for help."

"But . . . if you hadn't asked her for help, we'd still be—"

"Stop, Lincoln! Just stop!" She kicked back from the table and snatched up her bowl. "I will never hear the end of Cliff 'striking terror' in her heart." She zoomed in on me and snatched up my bowl. "I can't pay that off, you understand?"

My stomach was set on having seconds, so I was about to grab for my bowl, but suddenly Ma went all pie-eyed.

"What?" I asked, 'cause she looked like some freeze-frame out of a horror movie.

And then I heard them, too.

Footsteps.

In the whole time we'd lived there, no one had gone in or out of the apartment down the hallway. There was no noise through the wall, either. I wasn't even sure it *was* an apartment next door, seeing how there was no window along the walkway like ours had. "I think it's just a storage room," I told Ma after we'd been living there a couple of weeks.

"So why's there a *B* on the door and a *B* on the mailbox next to ours?" she asked.

Which was true, only the *B* mailbox never seemed to have anything in it.

"I bet it's condemned," she said a few days later when she noticed how our floor sags by the wall we share with *B*. And after inspecting it some more, she told me, "Don't walk over here, you hear me, Lincoln? It'd kill me if you crashed to your death before I could get us in a better place."

I tested the floor myself after she'd gone to bed, and it was springy all right, but nothing that was gonna swallow me whole. Besides, the market was straight below. If I crashed through after hours, there'd be Snickers to keep my mind off the pain.

But back to the footsteps.

Since nobody ever came up the stairs and nobody ever came to our door, hearing steps outside on any other day would have been strange, but now?

Visions of Cliff popped into my head.

"Who's out there?" Ma whispered.

Like I could tell with the blinds shut?

"Switch off the light!" she told me, scurrying to put the bowls down.

"Why?"

"Just do it!" she hissed.

So I did, and after we stood around in the dark for a minute listening and hearing nothing, Ma crept over to the window, put two fingers between blind slats, and spread them apart slow and sly.

"Is it Levi?" I whispered, hoping it was the Man and not Cliff.

"Hush," she said, like she was stifling a sneeze. Then she spread the slats wider and looked down toward B.

"Is it Cliff?"

She interrupted her spying to look at me like I was dumber'n dirt. "What did we just talk about? And how on earth could it be him?"

"So who, then?"

She went back to spying through the blinds. "It would help if there was a light out there. And I don't hear anything anymore!"

I tried getting in to see, but she swatted me away. And then, like rolling thunder, those footsteps were back.

Ma jumped away from the window and sucked in a scared breath.

"Who is it?" I asked. "Did you see?"

Before she could say, our door went *bam, bam, bam*, and you'd better believe I jumped back, too.

"Hello?" a man's voice called. "I've got a delivery for next door. Can you help me out?"

"A delivery?" I whispered, exchanging pie-eyes with Ma.

"Please," the voice said. "I'm from Shop-Wise Grocers, just trying to make a delivery. My truck broke down, which is why I'm so late. I think Mrs. Graves is already asleep."

Ma did squinty-eyes at me and mouthed, *"Who?"*

She'd moved aside, which gave me a clear shot at the window. So I darted over and peeked through the blinds.

There was a man out there, but it wasn't Cliff fakin' a delivery. Or Levi the Zombie Chicken Man.

It was . . . a leprechaun.

That's what he looked like, anyway. He was short with kinda pointy ears and was wearing big boots and a green Shop-Wise ball cap. There were tufts of red hair poking out around the cap and his ears, and his stomach was like a little potbellied stove, pushing out against his Shop-Wise shirt.

"Ma!" I said, ditching the blinds and shooting her a frown. "What are you 'fraid of?" Then I switched on the light and yanked open the door.

"Oh, *thank you*," Leprechaun Man said with a mighty gust of air. "It's been a horrible day." He set two bags of groceries inside and handed Ma a clipboard. "If you could sign right here?"

Ma didn't take the clipboard. "I'm afraid you've got the wrong place."

"Don't I wish. But no, I've been here every other week for years." He smiled, and his teeth were like shiny stars flashing through deep space. "But *you're* new."

Ma just stared at him.

The stars went dark, and he heaved a sigh. "Please. If you could just give these bags to her in the morning? She's my last stop. I'd really like to get home."

"Who's your last stop?" Ma asked.

"Carol Graves? Your neighbor in *B*?"

Ma looked down the hallway. "Someone's *living* there?"

I could see a whole litter of thoughts go scampering through his mind. But all he said was, "Yes. And you'd be doing us both a big favor."

I reached for the clipboard, but Ma snatched it first. "You're signin' nothing," she growled at me, then scribbled something that was definitely not her signature and handed the clipboard back.

"Thanks," Leprechaun Man said, and he was gone before the ink was done drying.

"So now what?" I asked Ma when the door was closed.

She frowned, first at the bags, then at me. Like it was *my* fault there were strange groceries in the room.

"Check for perishables," she said, turning her frown back to the bags.

"For church food?" I asked, 'cause I didn't know what *perishable* meant and that was the first thing that popped into my head.

"*Perish*," she said, "not *parish*."

Sounded pretty much the same to me.

"Stuff that might spoil," she added, nosing through the first bag like a twitchy little mouse. "That's what the ladies at Brookside call it."

When she'd moved on to the second bag, I couldn't keep it in anymore. "Any Lucky Charms?"

She stopped nosing. "Lucky Charms?" She frowned at me. "Even if there was, I wouldn't let you at them. This food is not ours."

"No! I meant because . . ." I shook my head. "Never mind."

"There's cans of soup," she said, moving on. "And apple-sauce . . . and oatmeal . . . a bottle of cranberry juice . . . and cat food."

"There's a *cat* living next door?" I asked, caught up in the wonder of it. I'd never heard mewing or scratching or . . . anything. But right through the saggy-floor wall was a cat?

"And a person," Ma said, and she seemed to be caught up in the wonder of that, too.

17

The Silver Cat

Cats like me. I don't know why, but they do. Back in my old neighborhood they'd follow me, slinkin' along ten yards behind me like little spies. I'd coax them in with empty tuna cans and then sit and stroke them over and over and over. Something about the flick of their tails. And their fur, so soft and smooth. And the way they nuzzle in for a rub when they're done scouring tuna. Yes, sir. Me and cats get along fine.

Ma said she was beat-up tired from her long week at Brookside and went to bed early. I was so happy to not be at Brookside or school that I sure didn't want to waste free time sleeping. Besides, I needed to get back to my story. Lucas was still on the roof with a killer after him, and I couldn't just leave him there. How was he going to escape?

The killer was determined! And could fling a knife with the speed and aim of an arrow!

So I got back to writing and followed Lucas to a point where he was considerin' leaping from the roof to escape the killer. He couldn't go down the way he'd come up—that's where the killer was! But jumping would be mighty painful. It was a long way down, and if he broke bones, he'd be crumpled and crippled—a sitting duck! The killer would laugh at him—*bwa-ha-ha*—from the rooftop, then send the wicked point of a knife flying straight through his heart.

Jumping seemed the only choice, but just as Lucas was fixin' to do it, a cat appeared on the rooftop. It was a silver cat, silent as snow, with emerald eyes and abalone claws, and it ran straight for the killer, whose head had just appeared over the roofline.

The cat hissed at the villain, its mouth wide and fierce.

"Nice kitty, good kitty," the killer said as he yanked a knife from the side of the cabin. But before the villain could strike, lightning claws slashed across his face. "Aaargh!" he cried, and then down, down, down he fell.

"Well, hey there," Lucas said, crouching beside the cat. And as they both looked over the edge at the crumpled killer below, he added, "Thank you."

"Mrow," the cat said back, then nuzzled Lucas's leg, finding the pocket where a tuna sandwich had been a few hours before.

The story wrapped up great after that, and even though

it was really late when I finally wrote *The End*, I wasn't tired. I was too happy to be tired. The bad guy was defeated! And I really liked the cat. I even changed the name of the story to "The Silver Cat," and I started thinking maybe I'd write more stories about him. There was something cool and mysterious about him. Pretty soon I started imagining what it would be like if the Silver Cat had some sort of telepathy.

What if he could read Lucas's mind?

I fell asleep thinking about the Silver Cat. And when the smell and sizzle of sausages cooking woke me up, it was from a dream about the Silver Cat. I don't remember much about it except for purring. That was enough, though. The Silver Cat was happy being in my dream.

Ma seemed recharged, even hummin' a little as she fixed breakfast. And I was all for her being in a good mood. There's nothing like grits *and* eggs *and* sausage to start a day off right.

"Thanks, Ma," I told her after I was stuffed to the gills.

She smiled at me and said, "I have a hunch you're gonna need the fortification."

Sounded like trouble to me. "What are you talkin' about?"

"Carol Graves. Our neighbor."

"Why does having a neighbor take fortification? What does that even mean?"

"It means you'll be needing your strength."

"Uh . . . why?"

"Because I've been thinking," she said, clearing plates.

"Uh-oh," I said under my breath.

"We've been living here nearly three months, and the whole time we've had no idea she was in there. Who's taking out the garbage? Who's doin' the laundry? Who's cleaning the cat box?"

"Not me!" I said, twisting around in my chair.

"My guess is she's old."

"Old?" Nowhere on my wish list was getting to know another old person.

"Applesauce, oatmeal, cranberry juice, soups . . . nothing solid. I'm guessin' she's old, has trouble with her teeth, and could probably use a little help."

"Ma, no! Don't we help enough old folks every single day?"

"We?" She gave me the steely-eye. "And it's not every single day."

"But today's *Saturday*. Can't we get away from old folks on our one day off?"

"Lincoln," she warned. "I don't know what the situation next door is, but you're coming with me, and if some trash needs taking out, you're volunteerin' to do it." She frowned. "And right now, I'd like you to volunteer to do the dishes."

I didn't say what I was thinking—that volunteering was not the same as being ordered around. I just frowned right back and said, "Yes, ma'am."

But while I was doing the dishes, I started wondering

if the cat next door was silver. And if its eyes were green. And if it had claws like abalone shells.

Maybe that's why the Silver Cat had popped into my story. Maybe he *did* have telepathy!

I got so deep into picturing the cat and how it was going to purr, and feel so soft, and maybe read my mind, that by the time Ma was ready to go, I was all for taking out the neighbor's trash.

"Here," Ma said, handing me a Shop-Wise grocery bag. "You take one, I'll take the other. That way it'll seem like we're both there for a reason, not just nosing into her business."

It seemed a surprising thing for her to say. "So we're going over to nose into her business?"

Ma eyed me. "I'm pretty sure her business needs some nosing."

"But nobody wants their business nosed into. I sure don't want her nosing into ours!"

"Well, hers needs it. Ours doesn't."

"But . . . how do you know?"

"Oh, hush, Lincoln," she said, closing our door and leading me down the hallway. "Just trust me."

18

The Dangling *B*

There's no such thing as doorbells in our building, so Ma just went right up and rapped on the door with the dangling *B*.

Ma's got solid knuckles. Knuckles that mean business. Still, no one came runnin' to answer the door. She waited a minute, her ear perked near the flaky paint of the door, before using those knuckles again. "Mrs. Graves!" she shouted. "We've got your groceries!"

After another minute, I whispered, "I still say it's just storage. Or empty. Look at the knob." It was loose from the wood, and kind of sloppy. Like nothing important was stored behind it, and definitely not a person.

Which made me think that the Shop-Wise guy was actually just a wise guy who'd played some sort of trick on us. Although I couldn't really put my finger on what that trick might be.

Ma's mind wasn't on storage *or* the Shop-Wise guy. "Ha!" she huffed, giving me the sly-eye, with a grin to match. "Here she comes." She pulled her ear away from the door and whispered, "A hundred dollars says she's old."

I had all of zero dollars, so I couldn't take that bet. And that's a good thing, 'cause when the door finally creaked open, we were definitely looking at old.

Old face.

Old clothes.

Old *smell*.

"Mrs. Graves?" Ma asked, turning up the volume. "We're your new neighbors. I'm Maribelle, and this is my son, Lincoln."

She said it like she was talking to someone underwater, but the words still seemed to swim right by Mrs. Graves.

"We have your groceries!" Ma shouted.

"I can hear you, Maribelle," the old lady said, and she bared her dingy teeth a little, like a dog fixin' to bite. Then she turned to me and said, "Nice to meet you, Lincoln," and did the dog-bite thing again, which I was catching on was her way of smiling.

Ma held her bag a little higher. "Would you like us to carry these into your kitchen?"

"Not necessary," Mrs. Graves said back.

"We don't mind," Ma said. "And Lincoln would be happy to take out your trash, or whatever else needs doing."

Mrs. Graves gave me a doubtful look. "He would, would he?"

"Sure," I said after Ma nudged me. And it did seem like something I should do. Besides being old, Mrs. Graves was small. Her body was like twigs stuck together inside a heavy wool sweater.

I sneaked a peek past her, wondering how much work I might have gotten myself into. Her place was bigger than ours, but what I noticed most was sunshine. It's something that never sets foot in our place, but here, right next door, it streaked in through a window, making the air seem like it was dusted with gold.

A cat nosed in, its face poking out between the door and Mrs. Graves's leg. It was black and white and had crazy green eyes that were bright and deep and hypnotizing.

"Me-ow!" it cried, and the sound was so pitiful I had an instant wish for a can of tuna.

I knelt down to pet it and could see another cat padding over that looked like the twin of the first cat, but wasn't. It was the mirror image. All the markings were in the exact opposite place, except the white tip of the tail, which was in the exact *same* place.

I was so busy figuring out the Mirror Cats that at first I didn't see a third cat coming from the other side of the room. It was dusty gray and small, with one eye insistin' on sleeping while the other one was wide open, scouting things out. I thought, *Pretty neat trick,* but as the cat moved closer, I figured out that the one eye wasn't sleeping after all. It was missing.

My mind started flashing around. Whatever had happened must've been epic. Maybe dogs had cornered him in a dark alley! Maybe he'd been viciously attacked! Left for dead with a geyser of blood spurting from his eye!

I was just picturing him staggering home in a tattered war uniform, with a crutch and a lame leg to go along with his bloody eye, when Mrs. Graves pushed One Eye aside with her foot.

It was a quick move, and she did the same thing to the other two without even looking down. "Just leave the bags there," she told Ma, pointing to the ground at our feet.

"They're heavy," Ma said. "Why don't you let us—" But the door was already closing in Ma's face.

After staring at flaky paint for a solid minute, Ma finally set her bag down next to where mine was already resting. "Did you see the cats?" I whispered on our way home, and I was all pumped up.

"I didn't have to see them to *smell* them," she said, letting us into our apartment. "How can she even breathe in there?" Her head quivered like the tail of a snake, and what rattled out of her mouth was, "Where are her kids? Where is her family? What is *wrong* with folks?"

"What do you mean?"

"Didn't you notice? There were dishes everywhere! And piles of garbage!"

I almost let out, "There were?" but I pulled back the reins in time and said, "Maybe she doesn't have kids?"

"I saw pictures. In frames. By her couch."

"You *did*?"

"I've got a good eye for these things," she said, giving me a stealthy look.

I couldn't believe how we'd been looking through the exact same doorway and had seen such different things. "Were they pictures of *people*?" I asked.

"What else would they be of?"

"I don't know . . . cats?"

She grinned at me like she thought I was joking, but when she saw I wasn't, she got all serious. "Her kids need to know."

"Need to know what?"

"That she's living in unsanitary conditions with seventeen cats!"

"*Seventeen?* I only saw three!"

"Where there's three, there's seventeen," she said with a huff.

That made no kind of sense to me, but she sure seemed serious.

And I liked the happy feeling that it might be true.

19

The Laundromat

Saturday is Ma's one full day off, but she treats it like a workday, which means it's a workday for me, too. Groceries. Laundry. Cooking. Cleaning. It's a full day of gearing up for the next week, and the only part of it that feels like any kind of time off is being at the Laundromat.

I like the Laundromat. I like the way it smells, the way it sounds, the way it's noisy and quiet and busy and still all at the same time.

The folks who use it are interesting, too. They're fun to watch because you can tell they've got *stories,* which I try to piece together from the way they act and the things they say and do.

What kind of ruins the Laundromat for me, though, is Ma. She'll fidget and frown and flip through one abandoned magazine after another without reading much of anything. Once in a while she'll get up to check the machines to see how much longer it's gonna be.

"Wish *I* had a good book," she'll grumble when she goes past me. Or, worse, she'll nose in and say, "What *are* you writing?" when I'm scribbling fast on a story.

One time I sat a bit away from her and tried to pretend she was a stranger, just to see what story I might put together from watching her. I couldn't get past *knowing* her, though, and then she went and slapped down her magazine and said, "What *are* you doing?"

I guess my spy-eye wasn't being too sly.

I've also tried a bunch of times to get her to go do the other errands and let me watch the clothes, but she always does a leery-eye around the place and whispers, "I'm not leaving you with derelicts and drifters, Lincoln."

I tell her, "They're just doin' their laundry," but what I always get back is a highfalutin "Mm-hmm" and a look that says my mind's turned to mud.

The day we got shut out by Mrs. Graves and her cats, though, Ma seemed different at the Laundromat. She wasn't flipping through magazines or pacing around. She was just sitting there, staring off into space.

"What, Ma?" I finally asked, 'cause her being so still was making it hard to concentrate on my new story, which was about a hunched old lady who magically transformed into a fierce and awesome ninja cat at night. Or maybe she was fierce and *evil;* it was too soon to tell.

But back to Ma.

I had to ask her, "Ma?" again and give her a little shake before she turned to me and said, "What? Oh." And then her face started doing this witchy-twitchy thing like she was either about to cry or trying to cast some sort of spell on me.

"Ma!"

The witchy-twitchy thing stopped. "How old are you?"

You better believe that sent worry shooting straight through me. Was working with old folks all day making her lose her mind?

Was crazy *contagious*?

"Ma!"

She swiped a hand in front of her face like she was erasing one thought and starting over with another. "What I mean is, are you going to remember all this?" She looked around the Laundromat. "How's it going to settle in your mind?"

Her eyes were going all glassy, but I couldn't figure out why. "What are you *talking* about?"

She turned her glassy eyes on me. "Are you going to look back and hate me?"

"Hate you? Why would I hate you?"

She shook her head. "I'm trying, Lincoln. Really, I'm trying."

"I know that!"

She looked down at her hands. And after a long, quiet spell she said, "My life started going bad at eleven. It was almost surely goin' bad before then, but I remember eleven being when I really started feelin' it. Eleven's when I started to *see* things."

"Like what?"

"Like about my ma and the way she . . . the way she wasn't there for us." She shook her head. "And Lord, did I resent Ellie for steppin' in."

"I thought your ma was dead."

"She is. But she was gone long before she died."

Ma always steered clear of the subject of her ma, but now she was diving right in.

In public.

Comin' clean in a Laundromat.

"Why you thinkin' about all this?" I whispered. "Did something happen?"

"It's just everything." She wiped her eyes, and after another quiet spell she said, "I guess sometimes it's the parents doing the abandoning, and sometimes it's the kids."

I chewed on that a minute, but it didn't explain a thing. "What kids?"

Ma was digging through her bag. "I need to call Ellie," she said, standing up with a fistful of coins.

Which made no kind of sense to me, either.

She started to hurry off but stopped long enough to shoot me a pair of arrow-eyes. "Don't you ever leave me alone in a place with seventeen cats, you hear me, Lincoln Jones? Don't you dare."

Then she swept out the door.

· · ·

A sly-eyed drifter came up to me while Ma was off phoning Aunt Ellie. "Spare some change?" he asked. He looked like he'd been shovelin' dirt for about twenty years, so using money for a wash and dry would have been putting it to good use. But I could tell from his eyes that's not where it'd be going. They were watery. And red. And when he blinked, it seemed slow and painful. Like his eyelids were lined with bits of sharp glass.

"Can *you*?" I asked back. "'Cause I got nothin'."

I worked at making myself look bigger than eleven. Like, maybe, thirteen. And he did back off, but then he stood skulking around, checking me over with his painful eyes.

I tried to ignore him and get back to my story, but I couldn't concentrate with him there. He was scary. Not in a big-bear way. More in a sneaky-snake way. Like any minute he might pull out a knife and strike.

"Git!" I finally told him. "I got nothin'!" It just sort of popped out and made me feel like I'd bit my own tail. To my surprise, though, he took one last painful look around, then left.

I played what had happened over and over in my mind, and it kept getting better. Soon I had teeth that were flashing like diamonds when I said, "Git!" and there were actual energy beams shooting from my eyes to his. Beams that could lift him off the ground!

By the time Ma came back, I had been made Supreme Leader of Laundrovania and was using my magic energy-eyes to excavate secret tunnels behind dryer portals—escape routes that the frightened citizens of Laundrovania could use if the Drifter returned with an army of derelicts.

"Sorry that took so long," Ma said, getting busy folding clothes.

I hadn't noticed the dryer'd stopped tumbling, but Ma didn't scold me for slacking. She just set about folding like a machine, getting my T-shirts stacked while I got busy pairing up socks, wondering why she'd run off to call her sister. Her eyes looked a little puffy, but she was acting . . . solid. Like there might have been a leak, but now things were dammed up tight.

"You talk to her?" I asked.

"Mm-hmm," she said. She smoothed out a T-shirt. Snapped out another. Folded it, too, then smoothed it flat.

"So?" I finally asked.

"So . . . we're in a good place. Better'n we've been in years." She snapped out another shirt. "Maybe ever."

"So . . . she invite us for Thanksgiving?"

Ma laughed. "No, but that's a good thing." She slid a look my way. "Besides, I'm working, remember?"

I stared at her, then got back to sorting socks.

It was a whole lot simpler than sorting out Ma.

20

Magically Delicious

Early the next morning, Ma left for her half day of work like she does every Sunday. And I would have rolled over and gone back to sleep like *I* do every Sunday, only then I remembered.

There were Lucky Charms in the kitchen!

It was a mighty miracle that I'd talked Ma into buying them, but they'd been in the specials aisle with a big cutout leprechaun's talkie bubble saying, "Magically Delicious!" and a sign boasting $2.50 for the giant size.

"Please, Ma?" I begged, and after a pause that included a sigh, a frown, and one stretched eyebrow, she said, "Just this once," and put a box in the cart.

She wouldn't let me touch them when we got home, though. "A treat for Sunday," she'd said.

But now it *was* Sunday!

It was dark out, with everyone but Ma still snoozing off Saturday, but that didn't change the day. It was Sunday! And there was a giant box of magic deliciousness and a whole gallon of milk right over there! How could *anyone* sleep through that?

I ate the first bowl, feeling nothing but happy. The second bowl, I slowed down a little, giving the marshmallow stars and moons a little time to soften while I thought about my story. I'd already written six pages, but I still wasn't sure if the Ninja Cat Woman was good or evil.

It was weird not knowing. And after a while it crossed my mind that maybe she was both. Or somewhere in between. But thinking that made me feel like I was wearing a scratchy shirt that needed switchin' out of. And quick!

So I poured myself another bowl of Charms, got my notebook, and got back to the Ninja Cat Woman, hoping she would show her true colors if I kept going. But after writing two more pages, I was feeling itchier than ever, and my stomach was killing me. I'd gobbled up half the Milky Way, and now a whole constellation of moons and stars was expanding at light speed inside of me. I was dying to get up and *do* something.

Ma has only one rule for me on Sundays, and every Sunday she repeats it: "Don't you leave the apartment, Lincoln Jones." She'll usually tack on something cheerful, like, "There's folks out there who'd kill you for your empty pockets." And when I ask her, "Who'd do that?" she'll say,

"Lord, child, think! Folks who don't know your pockets are empty! And that's about everybody out there!"

One time it was, "Don't you leave this apartment, Lincoln Jones. I don't want to have to peel your splattered body off the street." So I told her, "I know how to cross a street, Ma!" and she hit me back with, "But not everybody behind a wheel knows how to drive!"

So that's how she makes sure I don't get antsy to go anywhere. And usually, staying inside is not a problem. Usually, I sleep in and laze around and then read something or write a story. Usually, I love Sunday mornings and being alone and safe in my own place with new groceries.

It's my favorite part of the week.

This Sunday, though, was different. It wasn't even ten o'clock and I was sick of everything. I didn't want to read, the Ninja Cat Woman story was going nowhere, and I sure didn't want to eat.

And then a little voice started pointing out that Ma hadn't done her usual don't-leave-the-apartment scolding on her way out the door. Maybe she'd still been caught up in thinking about her sister and just forgot. Or maybe she'd figured the rule had already sunk deep enough inside my skull. Or maybe she couldn't think of any new terrible thing that might happen to me if I left the apartment.

The little voice got a little bigger, reminding me how Ma had left me alone at the Laundromat and nothing bad had happened. Ma was probably starting to see that she didn't need to fret so much. That I was fine on my own. *Responsible.*

'Course, if I actually went off and got splatted on the street, my poor mangled body would get whupped to Sunday.

Next Sunday, which, believe me, would be a whole lot of whuppin'.

My brain was doing double shifts, though, and what it worked out was that next door was the place to go. I could offer to lend a hand to an old lady . . . who had cats! And since I wouldn't be leaving the apartment *building* . . . how could Ma be mad?

So I got up and walked out of the apartment without looking back.

Or locking the door.

Or checking to see if there were chunks of Charms stuck in my teeth.

21

The Admiral in Undies

When my knuckles hit on Mrs. Graves's door, my heart also started knocking.

And it got to knocking *hard*.

It was stupider'n spit, I know, 'cause I wasn't doing anything *wrong*. And I wasn't going to get *hurt*. Mrs. Graves was an old lady. And right next door! What could happen?

But in my brain Mrs. Graves had suddenly transformed into the Ninja Cat Woman. She had secret moves. *Stealthy* moves. Moves that could kill you.

The door didn't open with the first knock, but that didn't surprise me after the way she'd taken forever to answer it the morning before.

Maybe she was switching out of her ninja costume.

So I knocked again, louder, and my heart knocked louder, too. "Mrs. Graves!" I called. "I'm here to help!"

I stood there staring at the door, waiting for something to happen, and when nothing did, I put my ear up to the flaky paint.

Right away I heard a sound.

It was like sandpaper on wood.

Scratching.

I stooped down low and called, "Hey, kitty, kitty!" through the door, then put my ear against it again.

I heard more scratching, but now there was a voice, too. It sounded a long ways off and I could make out only one word.

Help.

"Yes, I'm here to help!" I shouted, stretching out the words like old folks need you to do. "But you have to open up."

I put my ear back on the door.

"Meowwwww, meowwwww," scratch, scratch, scratch, "Help!"

"Ma'am?" I called. It just slipped out. Like I didn't know what else to say because I didn't quite believe what I was hearing.

"Help!" she called back.

It was a jittery sound. Weak and wailing.

Like a trapped little lamb.

"Do you need help?" I called back, still not sure what to do.

I listened again, and the cats were going crazy meowing and scratching, but through all that I heard, "Help!"

The doorknob wobbled in my hand like it might fall

apart, but it didn't turn. So I rattled it and twisted harder, but it still didn't give.

"I'm coming!" I hollered, then stepped back as far as I could and charged the door, ramming it with my shoulder.

All that did was put a mighty dent in my arm and make my shirt flaky with paint. "Ow!" I yelped, my arm already throbbing.

Now I was mad at the door for hurting me, so I stepped back and kicked it, *bam*, right next to the knob, just like they do in the movies.

Swoosh, the door swung open!

Reeeeeeeeerrr, the cats went flying!

And before the cats could even think about escaping, I was inside, closing the door. "Mrs. Graves?" I called, not seeing her anywhere.

"Here!" she cried. "The door's stuck!"

It was the bathroom door, and I only had to lean into it a little before it squeaked open.

"That does it," she said, marching out in nothing but a shirt and saggy undies, acting like she was ready for battle. "That door is coming off!"

"Ma'am?" I asked, looking away from her and her saggy undies.

"I was trapped in there all night!" she snarled. "That door needs fixing, and since that's never going to happen, I'm taking it off!"

"Ma'am?" I asked again, 'cause now I was testing the door, and it seemed just fine. Maybe a little sticky, but nothing a mouse couldn't nudge open.

"Don't you tell me it's fine," she said, rattling through a drawer. "Maybe it's fine for you, but you don't live here!" She held up a screwdriver. "Ha!" she cried, then went back to searching the drawer. "Why do I need a door, hmm? There's nobody here but me!"

She turned to me, gripping a hammer in one hand and the screwdriver in the other. And with her feet planted apart like they were, she looked like an action figure. Well, an old-lady action figure. In saggy undies. But she did have light-up eyes—kaleidoscope eyes, with beams of power shooting straight at me!

Then her mouth started moving. "Lincoln," she said. "Take. Down. That. Door."

Her words hit me like a stun gun. First off, she remembered my name. How could *that* be? She had to be at least ninety! Next off, she was commanding me around like an admiral squadron leader. And last off, she was doing all of that in saggy undies like it was an everyday thing that didn't matter a hoot.

The combination had me dumbstruck.

Well, except for one word that managed to sneak out. "Ma'am?"

"Here," she said, shoving the tools at me. "Take down the door."

I'd never taken down a door before. But since there were screws going into the frame at the hinges, I figured undoing them was a good place to start.

"Stop!" the Admiral in Undies commanded when I started twisting a screw. "Just pop up the pins!"

I looked at her, back to thinking she was crazy. A door didn't have pins!

"Here," she said, then led me inside the bathroom, where she flicked a bony finger at a little groove that ran around one of the hinges. "Just tap that up and pull the pin out. Do all three and the door will come right off."

I stared at the hinge in wonder. I had opened and closed doors my whole life, just lettin' them swing back and forth for me. I'd never even considered *how* they swung, but now the hidden secrets of hinges had been revealed.

By an old lady in saggy undies.

"Go on," she said. "Put the end of the screwdriver right there and smack it upward. Once it starts, it'll go easy."

I did what she told me, and sure enough, a thing like a big brass nail came up, up, up, until it popped right out and clanked onto the floor.

"Do the other two," the Admiral commanded, "while I get dressed. I'm cold as ice!"

I did what she said, and when the third pin clanked to the ground, I jumped back, expecting the whole door to fall right off. It didn't, though. It just stayed put.

The Admiral was already back, wearing faded orange pants that looked like they were as old as she was. "That's it," she said, spying the pins on the ground. "Now pull the door straight off and set it out here against the wall."

So I gave the door a bear hug and yanked, and the hinges came apart like separating gears, half still screwed to the frame, and half still screwed to the door.

I put the door down, feeling like I'd just figured out another magic trick. "Wow."

The Admiral was frowning at the bathroom, muttering, "It could have been worse, I suppose. At least I had water and a toilet." She turned to me and showed me her yellow teeth. "And a competent new neighbor."

The Mirror Cats were nosing up to me. I didn't want to scare them off, so I let myself down to the floor real slow, 'til I was sitting cross-legged.

"That's Cleo, and that's Patrick," the Admiral said.

"What about that one?" I asked, pointing under a chair where One Eye was watching us.

"That's Jack."

"What happened to him?"

"Only he really knows." She moved into the kitchen, calling, "Don't have much in the way of boy food here, but if you want soup, I'm having some. My blood sugar's down and I'm cold to the bone."

I was still up to the gills with Lucky Charms, but I wanted to buy some more time with the cats. They were so soft. And Cleo was purring, a hum low and smooth, hypnotizing me. So I told her, "I'll have a little."

"Hmm," she said, studying me.

"Ma'am?"

"Not the answer I was expecting."

Then she turned away and got busy with a can of soup.

22

One-Eyed Jack

The Admiral ate her soup by hunchin' over it with her face practically inside the bowl. She didn't look up once as she shoveled, and that was fine by me. If she had, she'd have caught me sneaking little soupy chicken chunks to the cats.

When she'd drained the last drops into her mouth, I told her I needed to get going and asked if she wanted me to take a load of trash with me on my way out.

She wiped her cheek with the back of her hand and frowned. "I don't have much."

I couldn't help giving her counter a look. It was covered with trash. Empty cans, empty paper-towel tubes, plastic bread bags . . .

"Don't touch it," she said in a kind of growl.

"But . . ."

"They come in handy," she said. "Or could."

"If . . . ?"

"You never know." She frowned at me and stood up. "You just never know."

I stood up, too, and took the bowls over to the sink, which was crazy full of dishes. And since Ma's made me a pro at dishes, I got busy without even asking.

"Hmm," she said with a frown, but instead of stopping me, she left the kitchen.

I didn't see any dish soap around the sink, so I looked in the cabinet underneath, which was damp and musty and crammed full of junk. There were a lot of old scrub brushes and ugly toothbrushes. Plus miles of crusty cleaning stuff with labels so old you couldn't even read them. But I did find a bottle of yellow dish soap, and when I stood up, One-Eyed Jack was watching me from up on the counter.

I sneaked a peek around the kitchen wall. The Admiral was sitting in a sunny chair looking out the window, so I leaned in closer to Jack and studied his permanent wink. "How'd you lose it, huh?" I whispered.

He just sat on the counter, his tail doing a lazy little twitch from side to side.

"Keepin' it a secret?" I whispered, then got after the dishes. And soon my mind was changing Jack's story. He wasn't a war soldier—he was a pirate cat. *Argh!*

"Were you in with pirates?" I asked. "Did they smack you around?"

He seemed to give me a little smile. It was only on one side, but I swear his mouth stretched up a bit.

"Or maybe one of the ship's rats fought back?"

Then I had an even better idea!

"Did an evil seagull swoop down from the crow's nest and *peck* it out?"

The half smile was long gone, and Jack was now just doin' the lazy twitch, giving me a bored one-eyed stare.

So I dived into the dishes and got lost in picturing Jack on board a pirate ship on the pitching sea, battling rats and birds and sea monsters. I ran through five fierce eye-gouging battles, the most thrilling one involving a sea serpent with scales sharp as knives.

In all the battles, Jack lost the same eye. I just kept re-setting it and starting over until the sea serpent showed up in my mind. I could just see it, scales all green and blue and shiny, slitherin' through the waves, rearin' its head, flashing its deadly black eyes. . . .

Jack was lucky he hadn't lost his life!

When I was done with the dishes, Jack was still just sitting on the counter, watching me. Winking at me. Which made me think that maybe he *did* have telepathy. Maybe he could see everything that was going on in my head! Why else would he sit still for so long?

"We need to get you an eye patch," I told him as I hung up the raggy towel I'd used for drying. "You'd look sharp in a patch."

"Mrow!" he said, and nudged right up to me.

As much as I liked hanging out with One-Eyed Jack, I knew I'd best get home before Ma did. The Admiral was snoring in her chair, so I was planning to just sneak out, but as I was tiptoeing to the door, she sputtered to life, then saw me tiptoein' and screamed.

It was a short scream, though, choked off by something in her throat. Spit? Cat hair? Beats me, but it started her up coughing and wheezing and gasping like she was bound to die.

I fetched her a cup of water quick. And after she'd got things mostly under control, she wheezed, "You're still here."

She seemed mad about it, so I said, "Yes, ma'am. I did your dishes."

"Right, right," she said, still catching her breath. Then she nodded and warbled, "You can't go. The door needs repair."

"Ma'am?"

"You broke it."

I stared at her and finally said, "You told me to."

Her top lip lifted a quarter inch. It was the most sarcastic look I think I've ever seen. But I asked, "You want me to put it back together?" even though it was tough to keep being polite with that lip curled back like it was.

"Some toothpicks should probably do the trick."

Toothpicks?

"And a bit of glue wouldn't hurt."

Glue?

I wanted to holler, "Ma! Help!" 'cause she deals with crazy all day long. But then the Admiral creaked to her feet and said, "I do appreciate you breaking it down, Lincoln. Really, I do. But I can no longer turn a screwdriver with any force, so if you wouldn't mind helping fix it?"

I almost slapped myself silly. It was the front door she was talking about, not the bathroom door!

I followed her back to the kitchen. She said nothing about the shiny-clean sink, but she seemed very pleased when she found a smashed box of toothpicks buried in the back of a drawer. "This way," she said, like she was riding a winning streak, and led me to a little room that might've once been for a washer/dryer but was now serving as the cat yard.

My nose tried closing down as my eyes stretched wide at seeing and *smelling* the four litter boxes. I looked around, but no cats were standing by to take credit for their sand-swept sculptures.

Ma would have been going, "Oh my *Lord*," but Mrs. Graves acted like she was reaching over roses instead of turds as she fetched a bottle of glue from a cupboard. "Eureka!" she said, holding it out to me.

I took it and said, "Uh, ma'am?" 'cause she was turning to go like there was nothing wrong.

She looked at me lookin' down at the sculptures, then bent a little lower to see what I was staring at. "Oh," she said. She stooped even lower. "Oh, yes. That does need attention."

It needed a whole lot more than attention.

It needed a bulldozer!

She spread open the top of a big black garbage sack that was on the floor near a food-and-water tower. The sack already had something in the bottom, but I didn't get what it was until she said, "You mind dumping them in?" And since I was just standing like a cow-eyed rock, she nudged me with, "Just pick up the boxes one at a time and empty them in here. Then we'll fill them up fresh."

So I put down the glue, held my breath, and made like a bulldozer. And when I was done, there was a whole acre of stinky desert stuffed in the sack.

"You want me to take it down to the trash?" I asked after I'd filled the boxes with clean kitty litter, 'cause who wants a big sack of cat turds hanging around?

She shook her head. "There's still plenty of room in it."

"But, ma'am, it's already mighty heavy."

"Leave it," she commanded, then nodded at the glue and said, "Let's get that door fixed."

When I'd kicked down the door, I'd busted out some screws, and the wood where they'd been was now too spread out for the screws to bite into. But Mrs. Graves showed me that shoving toothpicks into the holes and breaking them off so they were about level and then squirting in a little glue to help things hold together would close in the holes so the screws had something to grip.

After I'd repaired the first hole, the Admiral quit barking orders while I worked and started getting nosy instead. She asked me about school and where I was from, and then she asked about Ma.

"Where is your mother today? I trust she knows you're here?"

"She's at work," I said, doing a little answer dodge as I put some muscle into flushing down a screw.

"Oh? And where's that?"

"She works at"—I caught myself from saying Crazy Town—"an old-folks' home."

The Admiral was quiet for a long time. So quiet that I found myself looking to see if she was still there. Which she was.

"What are you going to tell her?" she asked, and she didn't seem like the Admiral anymore. She seemed like a cornered mouse.

"Ma'am?" I asked.

"I'm fine," she said, finding her voice. "You tell her I manage just fine."

She left while I was cranking in the last screw, and when she came back, she had a little fold of money. "Thank you for your help, Lincoln," she said, putting it in my hand. "And I trust you won't make trouble for me."

"Trouble?" I tried to give the money back 'cause I knew Ma would not be happy about me taking it. Plus, it felt like hush money. "You don't have to—"

But the next thing I knew, I was shoved outside, standing face to face with her flaky front door, the hush money still in my hand.

23

Hush-Money Trouble

The hush money turned out to be three dollars. Three measly dollars. How much hush was she expectin' to buy with three measly dollars? It was worth a pause. Maybe an extra breath. Nobody would actually *hush* for three bucks.

I should've crammed the money under the Admiral's door, but I wasn't thinking straight. What I was thinking was Snickers.

The trouble with hush money is, it comes with voices. Whisperin' voices that started whooshin' through my head.

Go! No one will know!
Yeah! You'll be back in a flash!
You deserve a Snickers!

Think of all the work you did!

Yeah! Breakin' down doors!

Takin' down doors!

Fixin' up doors!

Yeah! And think of all those dishes!

And those nasty cat boxes!

The voices went quiet for a bit, giving me time to think, like they'd told me to. I also started thinking how, according to what had happened each and every Sunday before, I still had thirty minutes before Ma walked through the door. And that the market was right downstairs! Only two minutes away!

The voices were back.

You really think she's gonna let you keep it?

You need to spend it!

Yeah! 'Cause if you don't spend it, where you gonna hide it?

And if you do hide it, what happens if she finds it?

I had to admit, those were some mighty good points.

Time's tickin'.

What're you waiting for?

Go!

I hit the stairs running and didn't stop 'til I got to the gate. Then I double-pie-eyed the street. To the left, to the right, across it, and to the left again.

No muggers in sight.

No Ma, either!

So I slipped through the gate and hurried past Levi and his ANYTHING HELPS sign like he wasn't even there.

Inside the market it was dark. Like the belly of a big bear. One that had been roaming campsites, raiding food bins, having a snack party.

It was also quiet. Like a big-bellied *hibernating* bear. Which made me feel like I should be stealthy. Smooth. Tiptoe, even.

It's dangerous to wake a hibernating bear!

I ninja'd past the liquor wall and made a quiet beeline for the candy rack. Mr. Noe was at a computer behind the counter, looking through glasses that were straddlin' the end of his nose. He rolled an eye up and over my way, then went back to looking at his computer while I studied the candy rack.

According to the prices, I could get two large Snickers. Or a Snickers and a Kit Kat. Or a Snickers and a pack of Sour Patch! Or a Snickers and Red Vines!

I love Red Vines.

It's funny how you can set out knowing exactly what you're gonna do and end up confused. And I guess I was taking forever deciding, 'cause Mr. Noe was now aiming double-barreled eyeballs at me. "How much you got?" he asked.

I showed him my money, then glanced over my shoulder.

He looked toward the door, too. "Why are you so nervous?"

"N-nervous?"

He frowned. "You steal, I prosecute."

I tried to say, "I just showed you my money!" but my

mouth was all dry and my words just shriveled up. And the longer Mr. Noe's aim was on me, the more *I* shriveled up.

What was I doing? I'd come in for Snickers. I should get Snickers! So I plopped two king-sized on the counter, shoved my bills over, and walked away with two big candy bars and some change.

Change that was now jingling in my pocket like a little tattletale alarm.

If I'd've had more time, I'd've spent the change. Or, if it'd been found money, I wouldn't have worried. But it was hush money. What was left of it, anyway. It held a story that I wasn't allowed to tell, but it jingled and jangled like *nah-ner-nah-ner* in my pocket, giving away that I had something to hide.

I tried walking smoother, but I could still hear it, deep in my pocket, metal on metal, laughing.

How do you hush up hush money?

How do you stop it from tattling on you?

Outside the belly of the bear, sharp daylight blinded me. And I was so busy squinting and thinking about hush-money change and looking over my shoulder for Ma instead of looking where I was going that I nearly tripped over Levi.

"Oh, sorry!" I said, scampering clear of his setup.

He didn't say a word, but from his half-cocked grin and the way he was eyeballing the Snickers bars in my hand, I pieced together quick that he'd been watching me.

Watching me watch for Ma.

I stood still as a statue, calculating the situation at light speed. Then I reached in my pocket for the tattler coins and locked eyes with him as I slid them into his box, giving him a silent message: *Here's some hush money. You know what I'm sayin'?*

He gave me back a caterpillar eyebrow and a twitch of a grin, speaking without saying a thing. *You call that hush money?*

His eyes swept back down to the chocolate-colored wrappers in my hand and tossed up a twinkle when they looked at me again. I heard what he was saying without him saying a thing. *A Snickers—now* that's *hush money.*

I gave him a candy bar and skedaddled.

24

Trapped

Aside from voices, the other trouble with hush money is, it comes with a price.

A big price.

I didn't know that at the time. I just knew that Ma would be home any minute, and the only place I could think to hide a king-sized Snickers was my stomach. Maybe because it was the place I *wanted* to hide it. But I was short on time, so I sat in my corner, chewing and stuffing like a skittery squirrel.

I'd been wanting a Snickers forever. And the parts were all there—the chocolate and caramel and crunchy peanuts—but it didn't taste the same. It didn't even taste good.

It tasted like gulping down fear.

When it was gone, I felt sick. Sick, and jumpier than ever. Like I was back to hiding from Cliff.

Then I started worrying about the wrapper. First I stuffed it in my pocket. But then I started thinking . . . what if it worked its way up? What if I forgot and pulled it out? What if Ma checked my pockets while I was sleeping?

So I took it out of my jeans and buried it at the bottom of the kitchen trash.

But there wasn't much in the trash bin, and I could just see the wrapper flashing to life somehow. Unfurling like a flag, surrendering to Ma as she threw something else away!

So I dug it out quick, found some scissors, and made for the bathroom like a cat escaping a hose. Two heartbeats later, "Lincoln!" came cryin' through the door. "Lincoln, where are you?"

Lightning hit my scissors and cut up that candy wrapper. "Here, Ma! Be right out!" I hollered.

"Oh, thank the Lord," Ma cried.

I pressed the toilet lever, calling, "What's wrong?" 'cause I could tell something was and I was praying it had nothing to do with me.

"It's the Man."

"Levi?" The cyclone of water was sweepin' candy wrapper evidence round and round and down the drain as dread went washing over me. "What happened to him?" I stashed the scissors quick and found Ma rag-dollin' in a kitchen chair.

She sat up some, and her hands covered her mouth as she shook her head. "They tased him."

"*Tased* him? Who did? And why?"

"The police." She looked square at me. "He was shouting and cussing and . . . and wouldn't do what the police told him to."

"What were they telling him to do?"

"To calm down and put his hands up."

"But . . . why? What did he do?"

"I have no idea. Maybe it was being surrounded by uniforms that set him off. I tried to get him to calm down, but he didn't even seem to know who I was. And the things he was saying . . . it's like he was someone else. Some*place* else."

"Things like what, Ma?"

"I don't remember! None of it made sense! He was acting crazy! He lunged at one of the cops and they tased him." She sat panting, her eyes brimming like she was going down in choppy waters. "They tased him and hauled him off."

I wanted to say, "But he was fine! I saw him! He was twinklin' and negotiating hush-money candy! There was nothing crazy about him!"

But I didn't.

I just stood there, watching Ma drown in the things she'd seen.

"It's okay, Lincoln," she said, tossing *me* a life preserver. "We don't know what's going on in that man's mind. What voices he hears. What battles he's still fighting."

I wanted to tell her everything, but I was afraid she'd freak out. Afraid she'd be mad. Afraid everything would be . . . different. So what finally came squeakin' out of me was, "You think he'll be back?"

She was quiet plenty long enough to make me squirm. Then she sighed and said, "There's got to be someplace better for him than a dirty sidewalk. Let's hope he lands there instead."

She stretched out her arms, and when she wrapped them around me, it was like she was holding on for dear life.

I just stood there with my mouth locked down tight.

Trapped.

25

Tattletale Toilet

The next morning, Ma sprang my cage. "Lincoln!" she called from the bathroom. "Why are there bits of Snickers wrappers swimmin' around the toilet?"

I was in the middle of a dream, trapped inside the corner market by a decrepit old man who was trying to tase me for sneaking Snickers to homeless folks. His Taser was slick and could shoot from a distance, but his aim was all shaky and he was shufflin' along like a zombie in short red socks, wearing a hospital gown that was gaping wide open in back. "Don't you know it'll kill 'em?" he was shouting as I dodged him. "Send 'em straight into a diabetic coma!"

"Lincoln!" Ma hollered again. "What's a Snickers wrapper doing in the toilet?"

I was glad to shake off the zombie in red socks, but now

my mind was dodging around for another escape route. How could there be wrapper left in the toilet? I'd seen it go down! And I'd used the toilet since! Had some pieces stuck to the sides? Had they made their way back upstream? How could this be?

"You sure it's not somethin' else brown?" I called back.

"Lincoln Jones, I know the difference between somethin' else brown and a candy wrapper." Her head popped out of the bathroom. "And I'm guessin' no 'No' means you got some explainin' to do?"

It was early, the clock said we were running late, and she was dropping *g*'s left and right, which all spelled trouble. "Let me see," I said, buying time.

"Mm-*hmm*." She stepped aside with hips fisted and a look that said hot water was coming to a boil and she was fixin' to dunk me.

"Maybe it's like the alligators in Florida," I said, sweating over two scraps of Snickers wrapper floating in the bowl. "You know the ones that fight their way upstream 'til they pop up someone's toilet?"

"And maybe you best quit the bobbin' and weavin' and answer me."

In class, Ms. Miller taught us about the Great Divide. It's the crest of the Rocky Mountains, where rain either rolls down west to the Pacific or east to the Atlantic. An inch one way or the other and a raindrop ends up in a completely different ocean.

During the lesson Ms. Miller was already moving on to something else when I raised my hand and asked, "What if you were a raindrop and you landed smack-dab in the middle?"

I could see her mind doing a slow step back. "Well . . . eventually you would roll one way or the other."

"But what if you balanced right there *on* the Divide? Then what?"

"Then other raindrops would join you and pull you one way or the other."

"Well . . . what if they didn't?" The rest of the class was starting to whisper, but something about being a single raindrop on the very center of the crest of the Great Divide was messing with my head.

Ms. Miller nodded and said, "Then the sun would evaporate you, and you'd condense and join a cloud, and the cloud would drop you again. Eventually you would have to go one way or the other."

So maybe what I said next to Ma was on account of knowing I couldn't stay on the Great Divide forever. Or maybe it was wanting to take down the Zombie in Red Socks, who was still staggering around in the corners of my mind. But probably it was because I couldn't take another second of feeling like *I* was the bad guy who needed lockin' up.

"Do you think Levi's dead?" I asked, cringing.

"What?"

"I think I might've killed him," I confessed, gazing into the tattletale toilet.

"Child, what are you talking about?"

"I'm not a child, Ma. I'm a murderer." I turned to face her. "I gave him a candy bar. A big one."

I could see Ma's brain shifting gears, pressing the gas, then lettin' up, trying to figure out what to say. "A candy bar can't kill a man," she finally said.

"What if he's diabetic? Ms. Miller told us that—"

"Lincoln!" She was full throttle now, like the city bus gunning it into traffic, dark exhaust puffing out all around. "What were you doing with a candy bar in the first place? And more important, why were you down on the street?"

Before I could stop it, a confession came spurting out of me. It felt like I was heaving up my guts, spraying all over Ma. And just when it seemed like I was done, more would come blurting out until finally my gut was empty. Empty, and glad to be rid of the secret.

Ma just stood there, pie-eyed, like anyone would if they'd just been hurled on. And when she was sure I was done spraying the ugly truth all over her, she gave one good, hard blink and took a mighty breath.

I hunkered down, expecting the worst, but I guess what I'd spewed was too big a mess to clean up right then, 'cause she swallowed that mighty breath, squared her shoulders, and said, "I appreciate you tellin' me the truth, Lincoln. We'll sort through this tonight. Right now we best get movin' or we'll miss our buses."

"Yes, ma'am," I said, grateful to be escaping for now.

"Eat something," she hollered over her shoulder as she scurried to get ready for work.

"Yes, ma'am!" I hollered back, 'cause all of a sudden I was starving.

26

From Bad to Worse

Seems like when a day starts off bad, it only gets worse. Could be that you're so distracted by one bad move that you wind up making others. Or maybe some days are mixed into your life to prove you can survive them. Maybe it's like leveling up.

I got to the bus stop in the nick of time and shuffled on last. Everyone else found seats quick, but I was shut out cold, with kids expanding their territory when they saw me coming down the aisle, making like there was no room on their bench in case I was thinking of squeezing in.

Nothing new there.

And then I heard my name. "Lincoln! Lincoln! Back here!"

I recognized her voice right off, and a sly-eye proved that, sure enough, it was Kandi.

My day was racing along the fast track from bad to worse. Why was she even on my bus? I checked around quick for a place to sit, pretending I hadn't heard her.

"Lincoln!" she hollered again. "Back here!"

Now everyone was staring at me, and the back of the bus started treating me like I'd been drinkin' stupid water. "Dude, what's wrong with you?" "Wake up, man!" "Helllllloooo, moron . . ."

No grapes or tuna were flingin' around yet, but I was imagining spoons getting unholstered and Troy commanding the troops.

Ready. . . .

I could feel it—spoons were being loaded.

Aim. . . .

They were cocked back and quivering!

Fire!

No food came zinging through the air, but Kandi's voice sure did. "Lincoln!"

I finally looked at her square-on. She had a hand slapped down on a seat beside her. Holding it for me. There wasn't a spoon in sight.

"Lincoln!" the bus driver hollered into her big bus mirror. "Sit down!"

"Why were you ignoring me?" Kandi hissed when I took the seat she'd saved.

"What are you doing on this bus?" I asked back.

She full-on frowned at me. "Why'd I even bother to save you a seat?"

About then is when it sank in: I was in the fling zone

and no one was hurling food *or* insults. "Where's Troy?" I asked, sly-eyeing around to be sure I wasn't about to be ambushed.

Hilly Howard was sitting across the aisle from Kandi and me, messin' with her bracelets. "I see what you mean about him not answering questions," she said over me like I wasn't even there. "It *is* annoying."

Kandi gave me the stink-eye and called, "And I'm definitely annoyed!"

So yeah. Girls are confusing. First they save you a seat, then they act mad when you're sitting in it.

Kandi crossed her arms. Her little turkey-tail nails were chipped here and there, like they were tired of looking so festive. "Aren't you going to apologize?" she asked with a huff. "Or at least thank me?"

"For what?"

"Another question," Hilly said, causing trouble. She wasn't even looking at me. She was pulling at her bracelets, moving them around and around her wrist, and it made me notice that her fingernails were painted just like Kandi's, only the turkeys looked brand-new.

"See?" Kandi cried.

"Which is another question from you," I pointed out. "You're the one who never answers questions!"

Hilly quit messing with her bracelets and squared off with me. "You could start by thanking her for saving you a seat."

I nearly broke it to her that I'd rather pick tuna out of

my hair, but she leaned across the aisle and whispered, "Or how about for getting Troy kicked off the bus?" She gave me laser-beam eyes. "Not that the world needs to know that, but you should."

My head whipped back to Kandi. "How'd you do *that*?"

She got busy chipping at a turkey tail. "I told Ms. Miller."

"But . . . *why'd* you do that?"

"Because Hilly told me how bad it was. And someone needed to do something. And I'm not afraid of Troy Pilkers."

"But . . . he's gonna think it was *me*."

It came out sounding like no one I wanted to be. I didn't sound like Lamar or Lucas or any of the heroes in my stories. I sounded like a scaredy-cat.

A coward.

Hilly leaned over the aisle again. "I'm not seein' a famous journalist in him, Kandi."

"Me?" I asked, pointing to myself like the word alone wouldn't do.

Kandi smiled at her. "You'll see."

"What are you *talking* about?" I asked, whippin' my head from side to side.

Hilly gave me a look that said I was way smaller than my britches. "Kandi was up all night predicting your future."

"What?" I was gettin' whiplash from looking back and forth.

"Hilly!" Kandi cried.

"Well, you were," Hilly grumbled. Then she frowned at me and said, "You need to thank her, stupid." She went back to her bracelets again, her little turkey tails reeling them around her wrist. "Nobody liked what Troy was doing. Even if you are a dork."

"He's *not* a dork," Kandi said.

I don't know if I was sticking up for myself or Kandi, but something made me look right at Hilly and say, "That's right. I'm not."

The bus was pulling into the drop-off zone, and Hilly stood up while it was still moving. "You are until you thank her. After that, we'll see."

They both focused double-barreled stares on me, Hilly from above, Kandi from the side.

So I broke down. "Thank you."

Kandi's nose tilted back and a little air came puffing out of it. "No problem," she said, but the look she gave me said she was lyin'.

27

Girls

At my old school, recess was indoors as much as it was outdoors. What kept us in was sometimes rain, but mostly heat or it being too humid to do much but sweat. Chasing or bouncing or dodging a ball on a swelterin' day was not my idea of fun.

Besides, I wasn't any good at sports. Ma didn't like them, and Cliff—when he came into the picture—might have been good with a bat, but he wasn't interested in swinging it at baseballs.

So sports and I never really got acquainted, and that was okay. Nobody made a fuss over it 'cause lots of other kids were spending recess indoors, too. And as long as you didn't mess with stuff or start trouble, nobody cared what you were doing in a corner by yourself, which, for me, was usually reading comics.

I love comics. The superhero kind. Which aren't funny, but for some reason they're still called comics. Ma bought them for me once in a while, but my old school's media center had a secret stash of them in a back room, and Mr. Willard, the librarian, slipped them to kids who asked. "Here you go, Mr. Jones," he'd say with a wink, and I'd be glued to the thing any chance I got.

On the back cover of every comic Mr. Willard had taped a list of vocabulary words. Words that were used in the comic. That was good for when you were reading and didn't know what a word meant, but the payback was you had to know all the words when you checked the comic back in.

"Ready, Mr. Jones?" Mr. Willard would say in a voice all hushed and secretive. Then he'd run through the list, sweepin' the room with a sly-eye as he went down it, like any minute the two of us might be hauled off to the principal's office.

"Why're there such hard words in comics?" I asked him once, 'cause after a while my brain was loaded up with vo-cab-u-lar-y.

"Because they're really for adults," he whispered. "Ready for another?"

At Thornhill there are no comics. On the second day of school I asked Ms. Raven, hoping she might have a secret stash like Mr. Willard had, but the answer was no. And when I asked Ms. Miller where indoor recess was held, she gave me a strange look and said, "We do recess outside."

I walked away feeling funny inside. Like I was alone in the middle of a school full of kids, with no place to go.

So I found a secret spot off to the side of the blacktop between a building and a fence, and that's where I'd go to work on my stories at recess. No one bothered me or even knew I holed up there.

That is, until Kandi went and messed things up.

"Why are you always hiding back here?" she asked during morning recess on the day she'd invaded the bus. She was holding on to a four-square ball and had Macy Mills and Lexi Simmons with her. They were havin' a polka-dot day. Just lookin' at them made me dizzy.

I'd jerked when Kandi had asked, 'cause I was already jumpy, worried that Troy might pop up out of nowhere and let me have it. But her asking like she did also shocked me. How long had she known about my spot?

"You want to play four square with us?" she asked.

"No thanks," I said, shaking my head.

She frowned. "If you don't watch out, you'll wind up like Isaac Monroe."

"Who?"

But they were already running off.

I grumbled, "Great. Now I'm gonna have to find a new spot." But I couldn't figure that out right then, so I got back to my story. The Ninja Cat Woman was moving through the shadows of the city's night streets, tailing a sneak thief who had stolen Old Yeller—a yellow diamond worth over a million dollars. I was putting in double agents and heart-pounding twists, so it didn't take long to forget about Kandi and four square and where Troy Pilkers might be lurking.

When recess was over and we were lined up outside the classroom, I noticed a lot of whispering behind me, but I didn't know it was *about* me until we were sitting in our seats and Colby clued me in.

"You shouldn't be writing about us," she hissed across territories. "It's not nice!"

"What?" I said, 'cause it was like a snake had struck out of nowhere.

"You heard me," she hissed.

Rayne was next to me, fiddlin' with a hair ribbon, and Wynne was across from me, wringin' the life out of a Kleenex, looking every which way but at me.

"I'm not writing about you!" I said. "Not any of you!"

"Prove it!" Colby said. She had whipped out her feather pencil and was now leaning across territories, shaking it at me like she was about to cast some deadly feather spell.

"Colby!" Ms. Miller called from the front of the class. "Put that away this instant!"

Colby put it away with a huff, but her attitude didn't go away with it. She was shootin' eye darts at me the whole rest of the morning. Then at lunch she and Rayne and Wynne surrounded me at my table. "Prove it," Colby demanded.

Rayne and Wynne still weren't looking at me, but they were there, which meant they were in the same camp as

Colby. And looking around, I saw they had backup, including Macy and Lexi and their zillion polka dots. Lots of other kids were staring at me, too. It was like a mob out there, armed with plastic pitchforks, itchin' to do me in.

I couldn't believe it. Was this what I got for minding my own business?

Was this what I got for writing in a notebook?

The whole school hated me?

It felt like I was in an oven, roasting. And since I could see only one way to bust the door open and escape, I pushed my notebook forward. "Here," I said.

Colby snatched it like she had every right to have it, and for a split second I panicked, remembering my story about Queen Colby and the spaceship. But that one had just been in my head—I hadn't actually written it down.

They huddled over my notebook like a three-headed monster, gobbling up pages while I sat there feeling mad and embarrassed.

"Who's Agent Leroy?" Rayne asked.

"What's a Ninja Cat Woman?" Wynne whispered.

They flipped through the notebook fast, until Colby finally said, "These are just . . . stories."

I yanked my notebook back. "See? Nothing in there about anybody!"

They stared at me, *sorry* written all over their faces.

And then, like someone had waved a magic wand, *poof*, Kandi appeared, rosy-cheeked and out of breath. "Guess what?" she said, sitting beside me.

Colby got right in her face. "You can't sit here! That's what!"

"Why?" Kandi said, looking all hurt.

"Leave!" Colby said, and now Rayne and Wynne were leaning in, too, like a flock of crows swooping down on roadkill.

Kandi gave me a look that was crying out for help, but I wanted nothing to do with her or the trouble she'd caused. And since I could tell I was on the verge of saying something either stupid or mean, I grabbed my stuff, gave the whole bunch of them a scorching look, and took off.

28

Catfight

It was probably stupid to think that my disappearin' into a beanbag chair for fifteen minutes meant my problems would disappear for good.

The fifteen minutes was nice, though. Agent Leroy had ducked through a maze of corridors and was now tailing the Ninja Cat Woman, who thought she was tailin' a double agent! I even laughed out loud once 'cause the picture in my head was so funny.

Then lunch was over and I went back to class in time to see Colby shove Kandi. They were over by the Golden Rule board, but I guess it's hard to read about doin' unto others when you're coming to blows, 'cause Kandi cried, "Hey!" and shoved her back, hard.

Benny Tazmin—who sits by the United We Stand wall

and had just before lunch been scolded for "disruptive behavior"—jumped up and called, "Catfight!" and seemed super excited that someone besides him might be getting in trouble.

"Girls! Girls!" Ms. Miller cried. "Stop that!" She broke them up like a referee sending boxers back to their corners. "Now, what is the problem?"

The rest of the class was moving in for a better look. "I'm sick of her spreading rumors!" Colby said, shooting eye darts at Kandi.

"I wasn't spreading rumors!" Kandi cried. "I was trying to help!"

"Help?" Ms. Miller asked. "Help who?"

A turkey-tail nail shot out in my direction. "Lincoln!"

I tried to stop my eyes from gettin' big and my face from screwin' sideways, but they just wouldn't stay put.

Benny pointed at my face and laughed, "Dude, that's priceless!" which made everyone else laugh, too.

I tried to do a face erase, but Colby kept the horror going. "He doesn't need help," she shouted at Kandi. "You just can't stand that he ignores you!"

How had this happened? All I'd done was mind my own business.

"Girls!" Ms. Miller cried. "Calm down!"

Her words had the opposite effect on Kandi, who burst into tears and went flying out of the room.

Ms. Miller sighed and said, "All right, everyone take your seat." Then she went over to the classroom phone and called the office.

The rest of the day was awkward. Kandi didn't come back, and although Ms. Miller tried acting like nothing had happened, she was the only one. Notes were slippin' around like they'd been buttered, and anytime I looked, I caught someone staring at me.

Not at Colby, at *me*.

They weren't mean looks. Not like I was trapped in enemy territory. It was more like I was some weird animal in a cage at the zoo.

When the end-of-school bell rang, I bolted out of there. I checked over my shoulder every two minutes on my way over to Brookside, making sure nobody was tailing me, and I was finally starting to breathe a little easier when Kandi stepped out from behind a tree and planted herself in front of me.

"Aaaah!" I cried, jumping back. "Noooooo!"

"Do you hate me?" she sniffed.

"Yes" and "Leave me alone" would have ended things right then, but she was still crying, and her eyes were all puffy, and most of her turkey tails were completely chipped off. Which added up to me saying, "No!" like I actually meant it.

Sometimes I really am dumber'n dirt.

"Stop walking," she whimpered. "*Please* stop walking."

She sat down on a concrete step near the tree and patted the space next to her. "I'm really sorry. I was just trying to help!"

I wasn't about to sit down, but I also couldn't stop from asking, "Help with *what*? Troy? It doesn't help that now he has an actual *reason* to be mad at me! And tellin' folks I was writin' about them . . . I told you that wasn't so!"

"I told them you were a journalist," she whimpered. "I was trying to make it sound important! I didn't know the difference."

"What difference?"

"Between a journalist and someone who makes up stories!" She grabbed a stick off the ground and started jabbing at the dirt. "Colby told me."

"But why'd you tell anyone *anything*?"

She shrugged. "I was trying to help."

"Help with *what*?"

"Friends."

"Friends?"

"Lincoln," she said, looking at me like I was a poor, dying puppy, "you have no friends."

My cheeks got hot and my eyes pied out, and for the second time that day I could not do a face erase.

And then with a sniff, she gave me a look that was all parts sad. Like she felt just awful about breaking the news to me. "The people in your stories are not real, Lincoln."

I could feel my whole face go hot. "What do you know?" I shouted, then started running away from her as fast as I could.

29

Walker Wars

I used to have friends. That was back before Cliff. After Cliff I was too busy hiding what he was like from my friends to notice I was losing them. I didn't want them knowing the trouble I'd been in. I didn't want them seeing the marks on me, which sometimes took weeks to clear up.

So I hid the cryin' and started lyin'.

Back then, I believed the things Cliff yelled at me—that him being mad was all my fault. I thought *I* was the reason he was hurtin' Ma.

Back then, I didn't understand about whiskey time.

By the time Ma figured out what Cliff was up to while she was at work, I was used to doing the hush-and-hide. And her trying to fix things only made it worse for me when she wasn't looking.

One of the places I'd go to hide was inside my stories. I could be there for hours, quiet as a mouse. And when I was in the middle of an exciting part, or when the jail cell was about to clang loud with the sound of justice, I didn't miss having friends. The friends I made up were enough.

So Kandi saying what she did felt like a sucker punch. What did she know? About any of it?

I was madder'n a hairy hornet, but once I was at Brookside, I got distracted by what was going on in the East Wing.

Two oldies named Linda and June were facing off, fighting over a walker. Linda was on the inside of the walker, scooting forward, shouting "Move!" at June, who was on the outside, grabbing the crossbar, shouting, "Give it back! It's mine!"

Linda wasn't about to. She shoved forward. "Move, you old coot!"

Two oldies fighting over a walker wasn't anything new or shocking. What was new *and* shocking was these two doing it. Linda and June were best friends and usually quiet, zoning out in front of the TV holding hands. But now they were shooting killer eye darts at each other, actin' like they'd wrestle to the death over a walker.

I looked around for a Purple Shirt—any Purple Shirt—but Ma and Gloria weren't in the Clubhouse, and neither was Teena or Carmen.

Then Debbie Rucker shouted, "What is your name?" at

me, and Suzie York came up asking, "Do you know how to get out of here?" and Crazy Paula started tapping on the table like she was sending out a frantic message. And through all that, the Walker War was escalating.

"It's mine!" June shouted, shaking the bar.

"Let go, or I'll flatten you!" Linda yelled, shoving forward.

"Catfight!" Teddy C called, sounding mighty gleeful from the comfort of an easy chair.

Across the room, Debbie Rucker turned up the volume. "WHAT IS YOUR NAME?"

So I shouted back, "LINCOLN!" And since no Purple Shirts were showing up, I put myself in the middle of the Walker War, telling the battling oldies, "Now, now," just like Gloria would have.

"Tell her to let go!" Linda shouted.

"Tell her to give it back!" June shouted louder, shaking the crossbar.

Across the battlefield, Debbie hollered, "Lincoln was my favorite president!" while Suzie York tugged on my sleeve and begged, "Get me out of here!" and Teddy C cheered, "Catfight!"—this time from up on his feet.

In the nick of time, Gloria came running out of Mrs. White's room and saved the day. "June Bug, dear! There, there! What's wrong?"

"This thief stole my walker!" June snarled, keeping her eyes locked on Linda. "And now she's saying it's hers!"

Gloria put her arm around June, and in a real soothing

voice, she said, "Have you seen your zucchini? I think one might be ready to harvest."

"Is it?" June asked, turning to face her.

"Mm-hmm," Gloria said, gently pulling one of her hands off the walker. "Lincoln can show you."

I gave Gloria a look like, I can? But she gave me a pleading one back and whispered, "Mrs. White's roommate just passed. . . . It would help me so much if you could—"

"Sure," I said, calculating that Ma was probably inside the Psychic Vampire's room and, with another roommate down, there wasn't enough garlic on the planet to risk leaving her alone in there.

So the next thing I knew, the Walker War was over and I was headed outdoors with Looney June to find a zucchini. *Shuff, shuff, shuff,* we walked, with her holding on to my arm and me thinking that walking old folks was not something that should be left to the young. It hurts to walk that slow. You can feel yourself growing old, walking that slow.

Right outside the patio door, there's a sunny table where the same small group of oldies hangs out on any nice day. There's Sir Robert, who Ma says is not really a sir or named Robert. There's Alice, who calls everyone sweet pea and claims she feels naked without her pearl necklace. And there's Pam, who has little pom-poms strapped to her walker and wears a cheerleader top of some kind or another every single solid day. The school it's from doesn't matter—if there's a megaphone on it, it'll do.

Alice may dress all proper, but she's trouble. She's worse than Teddy C, 'cause instead of a whoop or a whistle, Alice grabs your backside.

I'm not fooling.

The first time she grabbed mine, I whipped around, not believing what had happened, and she said, "Hello, sweet pea," and gave me a wicked grin.

The next time, I told her, "Don't do that!" and she just laughed and said, "Do what, sweet pea?" which made her and Pam laugh like a couple of wrinkly-faced hyenas.

Now I just swing wide when I have to walk by her. And that's exactly what I was doing when Sir Robert called out, "Good evening, m'lady!" to Looney June.

"She's no lady!" Alice snapped at him.

"Certainly not," Pom-Pom Pam said, sizing June up with a frown.

But June had her eyes on Sir Robert, who was all decked out in his usual button-down shirt, with a silky scarf tucked in around the collar. "Good evening!" she said with a little bow.

"Where are you off to on such a glorious evening?" Sir Robert asked.

June's smile wilted as she tried to remember. Then it boinged back to life and she said, "Why, right here!" and headed for the only empty chair at the table.

"No!" Pam said. "You can't sit here!"

Alice grabbed the arm of the empty chair and pulled it away from June. "Go away!"

And I was in the middle of thinking that Brookside was just like school but with wrinkles when a voice behind me said, "Lincoln?"

I could feel my blood do an instant curdle, and when I turned around, sure enough, it was Kandi.

30

Jailbreak

I stared at Kandi like I was seeing ghosts, my mind holding its cheeks, screeching in terror at the sight of her. How could this be? What was I gonna do? There was no escaping the way this was going to haunt me at school.

"How'd you get in?" I choked out.

"I told them I was your friend," she said, looking around. "And I met your mom. She was, um, disposing of diapers?"

"You are not my friend!" I said through my teeth. "You're a stalker!"

"Lincoln," she said, like a pouty little puppy. "I'm just trying to *help*."

"Go away!"

But now Sir Robert and the ladies were all tuned in.

"Hello, sweet pea," Alice said, twiddlin' her pearls as she checked Kandi over.

"Beautiful hair," Pom-Pom Pam said.

Alice nodded. "I could rule the world with hair like that."

"I once did!" Pam said. "I could grow it for miles. Best hair on the cheer team, hands down."

Alice let go of her pearls and scowled at June. "Good thing your granddaughter didn't inherit *your* lousy hair."

June looked confused. Like she wasn't really sure who these people were or why they were being mean to her.

Kandi was keepin' quiet, which was a relief until I saw that she was soaking it all up like a giant sponge.

The same way she'd soaked up my story.

That put me skidding into a double worry. How could I stop her from spreadin' this all over school?

"Guess you won't be needing this," Alice said, yanking the chair free from June.

"Yes, have a nice walk," Pam added.

They were telling us to move along clear as a ringin' bell, and with the chair yanked back, June was now hanging on to me for dear life.

"Where are we going?" June asked as I pulled her along.

"To look at your zucchinis, remember?"

"Oh, that's right," she said.

We shuffled down the walkway a few steps, and I guess latching on to one arm wasn't enough for her, 'cause she grabbed Kandi's, too, turning us into a human walker. "I'm glad you're here," she said, smiling at Kandi. "Do you want to see my zucchinis?"

"Sure," Kandi said, smiling back.

Then June asked her, "How's your mother?"

"My *mother*?" Kandi looked like she'd been goosed, then turned to me with question marks flashing.

I faked like I didn't see.

June frowned. "Why doesn't she ever visit me?"

"Visit you?" Kandi asked, sneaking pie-eyes my way.

I gave her a dark look, which was all she deserved after nosing her way into Crazy Town.

"It'd be nice to get a visit from her every now and then," June said with a huff. "Is that too much to ask?"

Kandi, for once, was speechless.

"Well," June said, shuff-shuff-shuffing along. "It's nice that *you're* here, dear, even if your mother can't be bothered."

"Who *is* this?" Kandi mouthed at me.

Which earned her another dark look.

The "courtyard" at Brookside is a maze of walkways that go winding around the Activities Room and the two wings. It's where the oldies get their sunshine and go for walks. There are nice plants and garden decorations, but if you look past the flowers and trees and fake squirrels, you start to see that you're trapped inside the walls of a fort.

As we shuffled to a T in the walkway, where the choice was to go left toward the garden and the West Wing or right to a dead end, we saw about six oldies congregating at the dead-end fence.

I didn't recognize any in the group, and for a minute I thought the guy in the middle might work at Brookside. He had a head of thick brown hair and didn't look *that* old, but then I saw he was wearing pajama pants. And he was barefoot.

The rest of the group were all women, and even though they were trying to whisper, they were fighting about something.

"No! I get to go first!"

"No, *I* do!"

"He said *I* could!"

Pajama Man was trying to look over the dead-end fence but couldn't reach high enough. So he gave up and said, "Line up!" in a gruff voice.

Two of the women had walkers and they jockeyed to get up front, but a tall lady in pink pants elbowed her way in.

Pajama Man was stooped over now with his hands laced together.

"What are they doing?" Kandi whispered.

"Escaping," I whispered back, forgetting that I was givin' her the silent treatment.

Pajama Man tried to give Pink Pants a boost, but she couldn't seem to push herself up. And then there was a rush of feet from the left and a man's voice shouting, "Stop!"

"Quick!" the oldies all cried. "They're coming!"

"Sergeant Baker!" the man who was running shouted. "Sergeant Baker, stand down!"

Pajama Man straightened up, then drooped, his whole body a flag of surrender.

The others grumbled, and a couple of them cussed, but

they all turned away from the dead end and started shuffling back toward the West Wing like a litter of naughty puppies.

Gloria hurried up behind us, and when she saw that the group was heading back to the West Wing, she let out a big breath and asked me, "Maybe you can take June inside?" Then she smiled at Kandi and said hi, and eyed us back and forth like she was trying to figure out the situation.

"I'm Lincoln's friend," Kandi said, lying through her teeth. "It's nice that he comes here every day, isn't it?"

"It sure is," Gloria said, giving me one of her sweet smiles.

Then Kandi asked, "Is everyone here . . . ?" and she wiggled a finger around by her head.

"Oh, yes," Gloria said with a laugh.

And that was it.

I was doomed.

31

A Day Full of Learnin'

As soon as Kandi got what she wanted, she was gone. I was left feeling like a skunked dog, knowing that kids at school were gonna start holding their noses around me and whispering behind my back. *Did you hear? Lincoln spends his afters in a looney bin! His mom works there changing crazy geezers' diapers!*

Ma wanted to know who my friend was, and she asked like it was something exciting.

I went at her like a snapping turtle. "She's *not* my friend! I hate her!"

Ma tried finding out more, but I shut her down. And since she was still on the clock, she left me alone at my table, where I pictured everything that would happen at school the next day over and over in my mind until it felt like *I* belonged in Crazy Town.

With all that had happened at school and after, I'd forgotten about what had happened before—about the Snickers and Levi and the tattletale wrapper.

Ma hadn't.

My first reminder was when I saw Ma pack up leftovers. That made everything else flood back and made me want to stay put at my table in Crazy Town, even though Paula was tapping, and Debbie was shouting, and Ruby was trying to pull off her clothes.

Anything was better than facing Ma about the Snickers.

But instead of lighting into me like I'd been dreading, Ma was quiet on the walk to the bus stop. And then *on* the bus, she was still not acting mad when she said, "There's something I need to explain to you."

I waited, not sure where this was going.

"You're eleven," she said.

It didn't sound like she was asking this time, but she did have a worried look on her face. Like my being eleven might be a deadly condition. "So?"

"So if something happens to you while I've left you home alone, they could take you from me."

"What? Why?"

"Because here you need to be twelve to be left alone."

"Why?"

"It's the law. Ellie told me. I didn't believe her at first, but I checked, and it's true. And if social workers found out you were on your own and saw where we're living . . ."

"What's wrong with where we're livin'?"

Her look threw me back into the zoo. Only instead of

making me feel like some freak creature in a cage, this look said I was something cute and cuddly. "Ma! Why you lookin' at me like that?"

She kissed me on the forehead and sighed. "Oh, Lincoln."

This was definitely not going the way I'd expected. And something about that made me blurt out, "Ma, I'm sorry for sneaking out, okay? It was just downstairs. That's all."

"I'm more worried about the lying."

"I didn't lie!"

"You did some pretty fancy dodging, which has the same intention."

I looked down.

"I'm also worried about where you got the money."

I frowned and thought hard about how to answer.

"Lincoln. Tell me."

"You have to promise not to . . . not to *do* anything."

"Do anything like what?"

"Like anything!"

"Child, if you're gettin' mixed up in—"

"I'm *not*. I'm not mixed up in *anything*. I got three dollars for helping an old lady, okay?"

The rest came busting out like a sack of marbles scattering across the floor. I told her about breaking down a door, taking off a door, and fixing up a door. And I tried to hold back about the kitty litter and garbage and the three dollars being hush money, but that all clattered out, too. By the time I quit talking, my sack of secrets was empty.

I held my breath, watching Ma collect all the things I'd said. She seemed to be picking them up one at a time.

Carefully.

Putting them inside a sack of her own.

"Ma," I said. "Mrs. Graves doesn't want folks knowin'. Or interferin'."

Ma nodded. "Like I don't want folks knowin'. Or interferin'."

What she was saying took a second to sink in. "You mean with us?"

"Mm-hmm." She shook her head. "But with us, you're getting bigger and stronger. With her . . . it's just downhill. And if she can't even open her bathroom door . . . ?"

"That's not a problem anymore." I frowned. "She doesn't want to wind up at Brookside."

Ma frowned back. "She'd be lucky to wind up at Brookside. Most places aren't near as nice as Brookside."

"So why's Suzie York always lookin' for a way out?"

Ma kept quiet.

"Besides, Mrs. Graves remembered my name. And it's not like she can't throw out her garbage. She just doesn't want to."

"And why's that?"

"She . . . she's waitin' for the stuff to come in handy."

Ma leveled a look at me, then shook her head again and sighed. "Lincoln, she needs help."

"*She* doesn't think so!" I leaned back and crossed my arms. "And after today, I'm done with folks meddlin' in my business, and I sure don't want to meddle in theirs." I shot her an arrow-eye. "Or have a ma who does."

She checked me over. "Does this have to do with that girl?"

I gave a snort, and on the subject of Kandi Kain, that's all I was spillin'.

When we got to the corner market, Levi was not in his spot.

Another guy was.

The new guy was younger but had long stringy hair and watery eyes. His sign said:

WHY LIE? I NEED A BEER!

Ma offered him the wrapped-up leftovers, and he took them but didn't thank her. And after we'd set off toward the gate, the food came flying at us, hitting Ma in the back. "I ain't no *dog*," he yelled.

Ma grabbed me when I made like I was gonna clock him, and she pulled me along quick, without even looking back.

After we'd ducked through the gate, she held still a minute, then took a deep breath and said, "It's been a day full of learnin'."

It seemed crazy to me that she'd say that after being smacked in the back with leftovers.

Then again, it seemed like the only sane way to sum up the day.

32

The *Bulletin*

It wasn't until we were eating supper that I thought to ask. "The Psychic Vampire struck again, huh?"

Ma's head wiggled. "It's unbelievable." She lowered her voice like she was afraid Mrs. White might hear. "You know what she said to me?"

"What?"

"'No one's taking *my* window seat!'"

"She said that?" My voice was whisperin' now, too. It all seemed so creepy.

"Mm-hmm." She leaned in a little. "She claims folks come in at night and beat her up so they can get her spot."

"Beat her up?"

"But she fights them off."

"She can't even sit up!"

Ma sat back. "Well, she's holding on to her window, I can tell you that."

I gave that a minute, then asked, "So who's next?"

"There's talk of leaving the bed empty."

"Really?"

"Mm-hmm." She scooped up some stew. "Despite the waiting list."

"Seems to me there's a big waitin' list to get *out* of that place," I said. "You should have seen the crazies trying to climb the fence today!"

She frowned. "I heard. Gloria spotted them on the monitor."

"The monitor?"

"The whole outside's covered by cameras. You never noticed?"

I shook my head. "So there's no hope of them escapin'?"

"Hope? What do you mean, hope?"

"They're never gonna bust free?"

She was quiet, picking around her stew for a minute. "They're not prisoners, Lincoln."

I about sprayed my food. "Tell that to Suzie York. Or to that Sergeant Baker guy."

"Who?"

"The guy giving crazies boosts over the fence!"

She frowned. And when she spoke again, it was quiet, but in a way that was tellin' me to hear her loud and clear. "You need to stop calling them crazies. They have dementia."

"That's just a nice way of saying they're crazy."

She went on like I hadn't said a word. "And if they did get out, they'd be lost or dead in no time. They're like children, Lincoln. Someone needs to care for them."

Questions went flyin' through my head. Like, *Well, who put 'em in there? Why don't they take care of them?*

But those questions also sent *pictures* flying through my head. Pictures of crazies, living with us. Paula at our supper table, tapping. Debbie off in a corner, hollerin', "WHAT IS YOUR NAME?" Any one of them leaving puddles on the furniture or screamin' bloody murder in the shower or flingin' food around the place—all stuff I'd seen at Brookside.

Instead of asking my questions, I said nothing. But Ma was quiet, too, which usually means a talk is brewing.

Sure enough, right before bed Ma came and sat on my mattress. She had some folded papers in her hands and said, "The folks living at Brookside weren't always crazy."

I just nodded, wondering which way this was going.

"I know it's hard to picture, but they were once eleven, just like you. And I promise you, they never thought they'd be living at Brookside."

A vision of kids from school all shriveled up and hunched over walkers popped into my head. Colby's walker was decorated with feathers, and she looked like an old bird, hobbling along. Troy Pilkers was yellin' stuff and hurling food, Hilly Howard was in a corner, staring at her bracelets, and Kandi was bossing everyone around, teeth clacking and diaper showing.

"I've been reading these," Ma said, pulling me out of my

nightmare. "They've helped give me understanding and patience when I'm about out."

"What are they?" I asked.

She handed them over. "Every one of these has a 'Resident Spotlight.' That's the part to read."

"What's a Resident Spotlight?"

"You'll see. Just read." Then she stood up and went to bed.

When I unfolded the stack, I found myself face to face with the *Brookside Bulletin*. On top was the November issue, behind it was October, behind that, September and clear back to June—back to before Ma was even working there.

The front page of the November issue had a boxed-in part about Veterans Day, inviting folks to come to a celebration honoring the veterans who were living at Brookside. The date was already past, and I sure hadn't heard anything about it, but according to the newsletter, the celebration included refreshments and a movie called *Flags of Our Fathers*.

It sounded like a party.

Outside the box there were three announcements about November activities, with headlines reading Follies to Perform at Brookside and Experience the Junior Jazz Trio and Lori's Casuals Fashion Show.

I stared at the page, wondering if this was the same Brookside I'd been going to every day.

Then I turned the page and saw big bold letters announcing RESIDENT SPOTLIGHT—the part Ma had told me to read—and saw that the article was about Paula.

Crazy, tapping Paula.

There was a picture of her looking just like I knew her. But none of that matched a whole page of small print about her. It was written by her two daughters and started with where Paula was born and about her family, where she grew up and went to school—regular stuff. But then it told how she'd worked for thirty years as a civil rights attorney and loved to go rock-climbing.

By the end of the article, my jaw was dangling. I could not picture Crazy Paula rock-climbing. Or working as a lawyer! All I could see was a shriveled-up woman with drooping eyes, tapping.

So . . . maybe all that tapping came from hearing the judge slam a gavel for thirty years. Maybe that sound was stuck so deep in her brain that it was the last thing to go.

But . . . an *attorney*?

What had happened to her? Had she fallen off a rock and hit her head?

I went back to the article and found out that, no, she hadn't hit her head. She'd just slowly lost her mind.

When I was done with that Resident Spotlight I read the others, and they were all just as flabbergasting. I learned that Peggy Riggs used to teach calculus, Mrs. White had done missions in Africa, Droolin' Stu used to be a mechanical engineer, and Suzie York had six kids and seventeen grandkids.

"Ma?" I called, and when she didn't answer, I went to her room. "Ma?"

"What is it?" She was in bed, sounding mighty drowsy.

"Why do some old folks lose their minds and others don't?"

She propped up a little. "They don't really know. But they're trying to figure it out."

"Who is?"

"Scientists. Doctors. Folks like that."

"So it's not from drinking too much booze or hitting your head or eating aluminum?"

"Eating aluminum?"

"Well, drinking soda out of a can. Someone told me once it can give you Alzheimer's."

She laughed a little. "Well, I don't know about that. And liquor and hitting your head won't *help,* that's for sure, but Debbie Rucker's the only one at Brookside I know of who had something like that happen. A blood vessel broke in her brain."

"But . . . why'd that make her want to know folks' names?"

Ma yawned. "The brain is complicated, Lincoln. I'm not sure anyone can really answer that question." Her eyes were drooping, but she patted the bed, and when I sat on it, she held my hand and said, "I only want two things from you regardin' this, okay?"

I nodded, waiting.

"Appreciate being young. I know that can be hard, but you'll be old soon enough, and there's no goin' back."

I nodded. "And?"

"And quit callin' them crazies. They can't help the state they're in."

I looked down.

"Is that a 'Yes, ma'am'?" she asked, and one eyebrow was cocked way up.

I nodded.

"So let's hear it."

"Yes, ma'am."

She gave me a pat. "Now go to bed."

Something I was more'n happy to do.

33

Facing the Truth

I woke up knowing I had to survive only one day of Troy Pilkers tracking me down and Kandi Kain spreading stories about me at school before having five days off for Thanksgiving break.

Just one day of duckin' and dodgin' and five days of *ahhhh*.

Then Ma went and monkey-wrenched me.

"You're going to have to come with me tomorrow and Thursday. And Friday," she said, bustling around the kitchen.

"What?"

She tased me with a look. "Got wax in your ears, child?"

"Ma! You can't be serious!"

"Where else you gonna go?"

"I'll just stay here!"

"No, you won't."

"But, Ma!"

"Get movin'. I can't have you missin' the bus."

The bus was about to leave when I got to my stop, but the driver saw me coming and flapped the doors back open. And when I ran up the steps, she gave me a wink and a grin. "Good morning, Lincoln," she said. "We should be smooth sailing for the rest of the year."

"Ma'am?"

She leaned over a little and lowered her voice. "Our problem is definitely not returning." She gave me another wink and wagged her head to the back of the bus. "Go on."

I moved along but my mind was a jumble. Had the bus driver known all year that food was flingin' in the back of her bus? And if she had, why hadn't she kicked Troy off the bus a long time ago?

Or maybe she knew something was going on but couldn't peg what. Maybe she found food splats all over at the end of the day and cursed whoever was doing it. Maybe Kandi tattling was the break she'd been waiting for all year.

As I walked along looking for a seat, I got a sick feeling in my stomach. Not like the one I got every day, knowing I was moving toward the fling zone. This one was from feeling like a coward. I hadn't stuck up for myself—I'd just taken it. Instead of swattin' at the bee, I'd let it sting me, over and over and over. Things hadn't gotten any better with me ignoring Troy—they'd gotten worse.

Until Kandi had come along and stuck her nose in things.

I was smashed between the gears of wanting to throttle Kandi and knowing I should thank her for real. Like I meant it.

It was a terrible place to be caught.

Hilly was waving from the back of the bus. "Hey!" she called. "Back here!"

I moved along, acting like a snake might jump out and bite me, but I did end up sitting next to her.

"So?" she said, twiddlin' her bracelets.

"So?" I said back.

"How are things with you and Kandi?"

I slid her a look. "Painful."

"Ooooh," she said, reading way too much into one word. Then she slid me a look back and said, "Well, you should be nicer to her."

Her telling me that sent me in the opposite direction. "I'm plenty nice to her!"

She crossed her arms and full-on looked at me. And after she got done sizing me up with a frown, she said, "If that's your idea of nice, then no wonder you don't have any friends."

"What? How would you know about my friends? How would you know anything?"

She just shrugged and went back to messin' with her

bracelets, and I turned away from her, feeling hot and mighty angry.

And then Ma's voice started running through my head.

On our long bus ride escaping Cliff, Ma told me that in fights, nothing makes a person madder than the truth. "Anger won't change the truth. It just works like a drug that makes you feel better for a while. But no matter how much you yell or blame or how many fists you throw, the truth'll be there waiting for you when you sober up. The only way out is to face the truth and try and fix things."

It had started off with her talking about Cliff but had turned into something that felt bigger than him. Her eyes were drilling into me as she spoke, and her voice was powerful in how quiet it was. Even as tired as I was, I could tell she wasn't just explaining things.

She was *warning* me.

I didn't really understand why on that bus, but as I got off this one, it hit home.

I was mad.

I was plenty mad!

But the sick feeling in my stomach was coming from the truth.

A truth that had nothin' to do with anyone but me.

34

Steamed

It was a complicated feeling. One that I sure wasn't going to be able to sort out before class started. On the one hand, Kandi had gotten Troy Pilkers kicked off the bus. On the other, she had spied on me, followed me, and nosed her way into stuff that was none of her business. And worst of all, she *talked*. What a mess she'd made, tellin' folks about my writing. And now that she knew where I went after school, everybody would know!

I headed for the media center to hide out, picturing how the day would go. I could just see it—kids whispering, their eyes scooting around, watching me. That grew into me imagining kids whispering and pointing, with nobody even bothering to do the sly-eye. Soon my mind was in a house of terrors, with kids ballooning in size, pointing and laughing. *HHHA-HA-HA! HHHA-HA-HA!*

Then a voice broke into my house of terrors. "She's kidding, right?"

Poof. The laughing kids disappeared, and I was outside the media center with a real boy standing right next to me. The one I'd seen working at Ms. Raven's computer.

His hair was wild, and his backpack looked like it weighed more than he did. He was grabbing the shoulder straps tight. "It's going to be closed all day?" he said, pointing to a sign taped to the door.

I would have been upset, too, but I got distracted by the strap where his hand had been.

It had a name written on it.

Isaac Monroe.

A bell went clanging inside my head. And then Kandi's voice started clanging beside it. *If you don't watch out, you'll wind up like Isaac Monroe.*

I stared at him, trying to figure out what Kandi had meant. He looked pretty normal to me. Well, except for the backpack making him look like a pack mule. And his hair making him look like a wild sea anemone.

"Why are you staring at me?" he said.

"I . . ." But before I could think of something to say, he clomped away.

I could feel my cheeks burn. I hadn't just been looking, I'd been fool-faced *staring*. And even though I was kicking myself for doing it, I was mostly mad at Kandi.

Why'd she have to say anything about Isaac Monroe?

Why'd she go around talking about folks?

Thinking that made *all* of me hot. Like steam was

building up inside of me. The feeling I'd had on the bus was long gone. This was *Kandi's* fault. If she had just left me alone with my stories, nobody would've thought I was writing about them! But she nosed and nosed and then went and said stuff like, *If you don't watch out, you'll wind up like Isaac Monroe.* Even before I knew who he was, I thought there was something off about Isaac Monroe, all because of Kandi.

Well, Isaac Monroe might look like a wild anemone pack mule, but at least he didn't paint his fingernails like candy corn or turkey tails!

I steamed along looking for Kandi 'cause I'd had enough. And I knew what she was doing! Right that instant she was tellin' someone that Lincoln Jones's ma worked in Crazy Town.

Like it was anyone's business?

It wasn't hard to find her. She was on the playground talking to a group of kids—boys and girls—waving her hands through the air and laughing.

The other kids were laughing, too.

I ran at them, full speed ahead. "Stop it!" I shouted, plowing into the group like a runaway train. I looked right at Kandi. "Stop nosing in other folks' lives, stop following them around, and stop talking about stuff that has nothing to do with you!"

Kandi did stop.

Everybody else stopped, too.

And they all stared at me.

"You think it's something to make fun of," I shouted, "but it's not!"

Kandi blinked at me, not saying a word. But the other kids started asking, "What's he talking about?" "Make fun of what?" "Why's he so mad?" "Kandi, what's going on?"

Kandi just shook her head, then turned and gave me those stupid puppy-dog eyes. Like, *Oh, you poor, sad boy.*

"Stop that!" I shouted at her. And because it felt like the world wasn't quite spinning the way it's supposed to and I needed to get my footing back, I said, "And what's so weird about Isaac Monroe?"

Everybody turned back to Kandi.

"I never said he was weird," she said softly. "He's just . . . a loner."

"So what?" I shouted.

"Calm down, Lincoln," she said. "Really, it's okay." Then she leaned in and whispered, "I didn't tell anyone anything."

When it sank in that she was telling the truth, an *oops* flattened out my face. And when I stepped back, I saw that the group was about twice as big as it had been when I'd come crashing in. Colby was there. So was Benny. And Hank and Troy. And Rayne.

"What's wrong?" Rayne asked.

"Nothing," I said, backpedaling, then running away.

What I meant, though, was *everything.*

35

Half Sweat, Half Shower

I was mighty relieved when school let out. Not that anything happened during it, but I kept expecting it to, which was maybe worse than if it actually had.

I kept my radar up for Kandi on the walk to Brookside, but she didn't pop up anywhere, and neither did Troy. I almost jumped for joy when I made it to Brookside without being ambushed.

The minute I was inside, though, I came skiddin' to a stop. Thanksgiving decorations were all over the place. There were full-on hay bales and cornstalks, but it wasn't like being on a farm. It was all *fancy*. Like a scarecrow dressed in a tux and wearin' shades.

Geri said, "Nice transformation, isn't it?" And after I'd signed in, she hurried around from behind her desk. She was wearing little white sneakers and blue jeans and moving faster than usual. "Wait until you see the Activities Room! It's almost ready for tomorrow."

"Tomorrow?" I asked.

"For our Thanksgiving celebration?"

"But . . . tomorrow's Wednesday."

"That's right. We do it on Wednesday so families can celebrate here with their loved one and have their own celebration on Thursday." She keyed in the pass code. "It works out better that way."

"Wow!" I said, taking in the Activities Room, which had been made into a dining hall, with white tablecloths and Thanksgiving decorations everywhere. "Who did all this?"

"The activity director's in charge, but everybody helped out. It's fun and festive, don't you think?"

I nodded. "It looks great."

"You're joining us tomorrow, right?" She gave me a sweet smile. "You're family now, too, you know."

"Uh, yes, ma'am." And I should have left it right there, but the "family" part was messin' with my head a little, so I let slip, "Ma says I have to."

Geri laughed.

"I didn't mean it like that!"

She chuckled. "Believe me, I understand." Then she keyed me into the back door of the East Wing and said, "But we'll have a great time, I promise."

The back hallway of the East Wing looked the same as usual—not a stick of Thanksgiving decoration. I could

173

hear snifflin' comin' from down Dove Lane, but that wasn't anything shocking. Tears spring up quick at Brookside, but if Gloria's nearby, a few *there, there*s and they disappear just as fast.

But when I glanced down Dove Lane, it wasn't one of the oldies doing the snifflin'. It was Gloria. And Ma was the one standing by, making soothing sounds.

"What's goin' on?" I asked, and right away Gloria flicked back her tears and said, "Oh, nothing, dear."

Ma was a little more truthful. She scowled down the hallway and said, "Wilhelmina's son says we're doing a slipshod job of taking care of his mother."

I knew who Wilhelmina was. She stayed in her room most days, but according to Ma, she was a terror. She hit and bit and screamed bloody murder over everything. Ma would come out soaked after bathing her. "Half sweat, half shower," she told me on a bus ride home. "Lord save me from having to bathe that woman ever again!"

I spy-eyed the hallway toward Wilhelmina's door. "Doesn't her son know how much trouble she is?"

Gloria put on a brave smile. "She's been here a year, but this is his first visit. He can't know what we go through."

"But he should," Ma growled. "And him threatening to have us fired? That's . . ." Ma's head wobbled and steamed and looked mighty close to exploding.

"Can he do that?" I asked.

Gloria shook her head. "It just hurts to hear. Especially when you try so hard."

Ma finally spouted off. "Who does he think he is anyway, comin' in and bossin' us around like that?"

"Uh . . . Wilhelmina's son?" Gloria said with a shaky little grin. Then she took a mighty breath and grabbed Ma by the arm. "Come on. We should get back to it."

It didn't take long for Gloria to make like she was over what had happened, but I could tell something was still knotting her up. She kept checking the main East Wing door like she was expecting something bad to come bustin' through it. And then she came up to me all fidgety and asked, "Dear, would you mind playing with them?" She was pointing out a table where Pom-Pom Pam and June were sitting with an oldie named Marla, putting together Scrabble letters on the bare table. "They lose their way. And I can't handle a squabble right now. Not with"—she gave the door a worried look—"all I need to do before tomorrow."

"Sure," I told her, and went right over, filling the fourth seat at the table.

"Oh, good," June said to me, then pointed at a word that would have put me in hot water if I'd've said it at home. "Make her take it off."

"If it's in the dictionary, it's fair play!" Marla said, giving me a twinkle. "And that baby's in the dictionary!"

"It's crude," June said, reaching for the word. "And I'm taking it off!"

Marla slapped her away. "Hands off!"

"Now, now," I said, putting them back in their corners, like I pictured Gloria doing. "It's Pam's turn, right?"

They all gave me the wary-eye, but finally nodded.

At Brookside, players don't bother to hide their Scrabble letters. They keep them faceup in front of them, but it doesn't seem to affect the play. I guess it's hard enough for them to make words without worrying about anything else. So since I could see Pam's spread of letters, I pointed to her *L* and said, "You don't have to take off Marla's word, just change it with that."

"Ha!" June chortled. "Do it! Do it!"

So Pam turned the word to "LASS" like she was making a royal move, and then Marla went and shocked everyone by saying, "Now *that's* how you play. Good move."

I was feeling mighty proud for snuffing the fuse of that situation when a man walked into the Clubhouse. He was wearing slacks, polished shoes, and a tucked-in polo shirt, and he was talking on his phone.

I'd never seen him before, but I knew right off that he was Wilhelmina's son. I could just tell. He was keeping his voice down, but it filled the room with a low growl, and he was moving like a dog fixin' to bite.

Which I guess is why nobody stopped him when he started going inside bedrooms. Most of the doors were wide open, but even the ones that weren't he opened anyway, doing a quick tour before moving on to the next one.

Ma and Gloria stayed back, twitching as they watched him. Teena and Carmen were steerin' clear, too, delivering laundry to rooms he wasn't anywhere near.

After seeing him go in and out of so many rooms, I

started getting a dangerous case of the snoops. What was he doing?

When he went into Mrs. White's room and didn't come out, I could see Ma and Gloria whispering, wondering if they should go find out what he was up to.

Or maybe they were hoping Mrs. White was using her vampire powers!

A few minutes later he was *still* in there, so I got gutsy and went over and spied through the door. My heart was jumping like a jackrabbit, but his back was turned, so I held still and listened while he talked on the phone.

"They better not have a problem with it," he was saying. "Why would they? The second space is empty! . . . No, it's not by the window, but the woman in here is on hospice and doesn't look like she'll make it through tomorrow. . . . Why wait? We pay a lot of money to have her here! . . . Well, I think it *is* reasonable to demand that they move Mom now. She doesn't like her room, and her roommate *moans*. Have you heard it? It would drive me crazy! And this one's just lying here like she's already dead! . . . Well, I don't care. This is a much better room, and when this roommate goes, we'll make sure Mom gets the window. . . . Well, isn't that typical of you? . . . No, *you* listen. You're not roadblocking me on this! I don't care if you are the legal authority, I'm not leaving here until I get her moved!"

He jabbed at his phone, and I ducked to the side quick, but he never even noticed me. He stormed out of Mrs.

White's room and snapped his fingers at Ma, commandin' her to let him out of the Clubhouse.

When he was gone, Ma and Gloria both swooped down on me. "What did you hear?" they whispered.

So I told them, and they listened with their eyes stretched high and their mouths stretched low.

When I was done, Ma whispered, "He said all that? Right there by Mrs. White?"

"Yes, ma'am."

"Lord!"

Gloria looked toward the main door. "I'll bet he's gone to talk to Mr. Freize. And I'm sure he'll get his way." But when she turned back, I could see she was trying to fight off a tickling at the corners of her mouth.

Ma noticed it, too. "Gloria?"

Gloria shook her head a little, but the tickle wasn't letting up. And finally she said, "Poor Wilhelmina."

Slowly, Ma's mouth took up the tickle.

Mine did, too.

Poor Wilhelmina.

36

Good Shirt Math

Ma got off work really late. Partly that was because of moving Wilhelmina into Room 102—something her bossy son watched over the whole time. And partly that was because of everything that needed doing before the next day—giving oldies showers, mostly. And tidying up. And readying clothes for any oldie whose family was coming to the Brookside Thanksgiving.

"Why's everything got to be so perfect?" I asked on the bus ride home.

"Some folks only visit on holidays. It's important the residents look their best."

"But . . . isn't that like faking it?"

"It's the same as cleaning yourself up before family comes to supper." She looked out the window. "Just a whole lot more work when a body has trouble moving on its own."

I was going to leave it right there, but she turned back and stared at me.

"What?" I asked.

Behind her stare, I could see tired wheels turning toward trouble. And before long she took up blinkin'—something I knew to be a dangerous sign.

"No, Ma. Whatever you're thinkin', no. There's only so much one day can take."

But she yanked on the stop cord, and before I knew it, we were off the bus miles from home, marching along the sidewalk.

"Where we goin', Ma?"

"To fetch you some clothes. I'm wearin' my work uniform tomorrow, but you can't be showin' up in that."

I was tripping all over myself to keep up. "I've got clean stuff at home!"

"Did you see Brookside today?" She tossed me a look that was half angry, half helpless. "I had no idea all this would be such a fuss or I'd have planned better." She started walking even faster. "Lord, I hope they're still open."

"Who, Ma?"

But then we turned the corner and I knew.

Goodwill.

The lights were on, and we made it with seven minutes to spare. And in seven minutes, Ma tracked down some slacks, a button-down shirt, and a pair of shoes. The shoes were at least two sizes too big, but it was the only pair that came anywhere near fitting me. "Better too big than too small," Ma said, and headed for the register.

The clothes came to six dollars and fifty-two cents. That left Ma with a little change from the seven dollars she handed over, and left me with an eye on the stack of comic books by the register. They were tattered and torn, but I heard them crying out, *Lincoln* . . .

"They're only a quarter, Ma, please?" I begged.

Ma looked at me, at the change in her hand, at the comics, and back at me.

I could feel my face start to crumble.

That was not her cavin' look.

That was her stand-firm look.

But . . . why? She had a quarter right there in her hand! And couldn't she hear the comics calling my name?

And then the girl behind the counter said, "One free comic book with the purchase of a traditional Thanksgiving outfit."

I stared at her, not believing my ears. She had eyes that looked like they'd lost a battle with a fat-tipped Sharpie and had pins sticking through an eyebrow, but her voice was like angels singing.

"Go on," she said. "Take one."

She didn't have to say it again.

Back on the bus Ma leaned against the window and closed her eyes. "Four of those comics equals one good shirt," she said, sounding worn to the bone.

I knew she was explaining why she hadn't jumped at

the chance to buy me a comic, but it gave me an instant case of guilt over the hush money I'd wasted.

I tried to smooth it all over by kiddin' around. "So . . . can I take the shirt back?"

Her head turned toward me. Slowly. Like it was in need of oilin'.

"You're a funny boy, Lincoln Jones."

"Yes, ma'am," I said, grinning at her.

She raised a disapprovin' eyebrow, then turned back to the window, but I could see her in the glass, smiling.

The next morning we were up early, same as every Wednesday, but instead of getting on the school bus, I got on the city bus with Ma. My Goodwill clothes and comic book were in my backpack, along with a notebook for stories.

"So," Ma said once we were settled in, "I've been thinking."

"Not already . . . !" I moaned.

"What am I gonna say?" she asked, her proper tone instantly slippin' away.

"Somethin' havin' to do with me doin' somethin' besides readin' my comic book?"

"Hmm," she said, sizing me up. "How'd you know?"

"Ma!"

"And didn't you read the whole thing last night?"

"It was a speed-read! To see how it ended! I need to go back and read it right."

She sighed. "Look, Lincoln, I didn't ask if it was okay for you to spend the whole day with me. I figured it'd be fine, but after all the fuss yesterday, I don't want to jeopardize my job."

"But Gloria said—"

"Gloria's been workin' there five years and everybody loves her. No one's firin' Gloria." She took a deep breath. "Me, I'm new, and not as . . . sunny as Gloria."

"So . . . why was she the one so shook up yesterday and not you?"

Ma gave me a long, hard stare, then nodded and said, "I guess we can thank Cliff for that."

"What's Cliff got to do with this?"

"I'm done takin' the blame for stuff I haven't done. I'm done with Cliff and anyone like him, which means I ain't cowerin' to the likes of Wilhelmina's son."

My jaw went for a tumble. "You think he's as bad as Cliff?"

She gave a little snort. "Same animal, different claws. I don't know what he said to the director, but he got Wilhelmina moved like *that,* so I think he's got a way of gettin' what he wants. And last night he wanted me and Gloria fired."

"But—"

"I cannot lose this job, Lincoln. So I'm gonna stand my ground, but I'm also gonna make sure I don't give Mr. Freize some other excuse to fire me." She turned double-barrels on me. "So if you don't mind, I've been thinkin'."

I swallowed hard. "Yes, ma'am."

"I need you to be helpful today. Helpful and cheerful. No broodin' about bein' at Brookside on your day off, no callin' folks crazies. I want you to help with the snacks, help clear the dishes, do table activities with the residents, or just sit and talk with them. Make like you're happy to be there, and be *thankful*." Her lips pinched together hard, and I could see tears springin' up in her eyes. And finally what she was thinking came slippin' out around the rock choking off her throat. "Remember last year, and be thankful."

Funny how you can move away from a place, but the memories of it move right along with you. Suddenly my mind was at last year's Thanksgiving, with me hiding from Cliff under the table as he went after Ma, yelling at the top of his lungs, "Orange glaze don't belong on a Thanksgiving bird! You know I hate sweet with my meat! How am I suppose'ta eat that?" He had her up against the wall, spraying whiskey breath in her face. "Answer me, woman! How?"

I would have tried to make him let go of her, but the times I'd done that before, he'd sent me flying across the room and then doubled down on Ma. So I held my breath and waited while Ma choked out, "Sorry," over and over until Cliff finally shoved her aside.

"I'm glad you got us out of there, Ma," I said.

She gave me a little smile, but I could see she was still battling the rock in her throat. So when she started turning back to the window, I touched her arm and said, "I am thankful, Ma. Mighty thankful. And I'm happy to help."

She raised an eyebrow. "Remember that when Paula starts tappin'."

I raised one back. "And Debbie asks what my name is?"

"And Peggy starts talkin' to the air."

"And Alice grabs my backside?"

Both Ma's eyebrows went flyin'. "She does that?"

I laughed, "Don't worry. I've learned to steer clear."

She laughed, too, and something about seeing her head thrown back with laughter made me feel lucky.

Lucky to be spending the day with her.

Even if it was in Crazy Town.

37

The Demon Gasp

Ma's shift started with the news that Wilhelmina was definitely still alive.

So was Mrs. White.

"Oh, Lord," Ma said when she heard squalling coming from Room 102.

"Can you get that?" Gloria called. She was dealing with Teddy C, who was spittin' out his dentures and cussin' up a storm.

"Sure," Ma called back, and for some reason I followed her inside the Vampire's suite.

"She's not getting my window!" Mrs. White wheezed. She was looking straight up like she was talking to the ceiling. "Tell her! She can't have my window!"

Wilhelmina was standing by the window. The hair on

the back of her head was mashed flat like someone had lifted a boulder off a field of dry grass. "What is she doing in my room?" Wilhelmina demanded, turning to glare at Mrs. White.

"*Your* room?" Mrs. White hacked out. "This is *my* room!"

Wilhelmina gave Ma a look that oozed like a cut onion. She pointed at Mrs. White and said, "Get. Her. Out!"

"*You* get out," Mrs. White wheezed. Her head creaked toward Ma. "Arrest her!"

"Arrest *me*?" Wilhelmina cried. "They should arrest you for making me feel like I'm in a death ward!" She glared at Ma. "Why is she here?"

I could see Ma box away all the mean things Wilhelmina had said and done to her. I could see her reminding herself that Wilhelmina was ornery because she was confused and frustrated. Frustrated over losing her mind.

Ma grabbed a framed photo from Mrs. White's side table and shoved it at me. "Distract Mrs. White while I take Wilhelmina out of here."

I almost blurted, "No! Not me!" but a fierce look from Ma set me moving to Mrs. White's bedside with the photo.

The Vampire was even scarier close up. Her teeth were brown and her hands were bony bird claws. I could see blue veins crossing her almost-bald skull like a road map, and there were little patches of raw skin spotting her face.

She was back to looking straight up and hadn't seen me yet, and I had an urge as big as Texas to run. But I'd promised to help, so I looked at the picture in my hand, tryin' to figure out what to say.

Most of the oldies have pictures of their family surrounding them. I've seen Gloria and the others pick up a picture and hold it in front of an oldie and say, "Is this your daughter?" or "Tell me about him," or "My what a beautiful bride you were!" and get them talking about something happy.

In her whole half of the room, Mrs. White had one picture, and I was holding it. It was a group shot of a bunch of boys on a patch of bone-dry dirt in front of a hut. The boys had on no shoes and barely any clothes, but they were laughing and smiling. In the middle of the boys was a woman dressed in safari clothes, and her smile was even bigger than the boys' smiles.

And I was just wondering if the Safari Lady might be Mrs. White's daughter when I flashed back to what I'd read in the *Brookside Bulletin* about Mrs. White being a missionary in Africa.

I looked at the Safari Lady closer. And closer. She looked nothing like the Psychic Vampire. But . . . why else would this picture be here?

"Is this *you*?" I asked, showing her the picture.

I must have startled her because she jerked a little. Then her claws reached out for the picture, and for the first time, her eyes turned on me. They were blue and so faded. Like a sky burnt to white by summer heat.

And then suddenly the sky started rainin'.

188

"You're here," she said, her eyes spillin' over. "I thought you'd never come."

She rested the picture in her lap and reached a shaky hand over, grabbing mine.

It was like a corpse coming to life, and my mind was screamin', *Zombies! Run!* but the Icy Bird Claw of Death was *clamped* on. "Please stay," she begged.

My mind was reeling in terror. Was this how she pulled the life force out of folks? Was I the Psychic Vampire's next victim? But much as I wanted to run, there was something about her watery eyes that kept me in place.

"How are the others?" she asked, looking back at the picture and then at me. "Are they here, too?"

I've seen Ma and Gloria do the smile-and-play-along with the oldies enough to know it's the best way to keep things from breakin' down. So I tried, "The others are fine. But no, it's just me."

The Weepy Vampire held on tighter. "Sit with me."

I looked over my shoulder for help, but Ma was long gone, and since the Vampire's grip was deadly and her eyes were on me like laser beams, I sat in the chair by the bed.

"Thank you," she said through her cracking lips.

Her head creaked back to center, so at least she was looking straight up again instead of at me. But even though her eyes had released me and were closing, her hand was still clamped on tight.

Holding the hand of an almost-corpse is plenty creepy, but when the hand may be pulling out your life force, it's also *scary*. And piled on top of creepy and scary was painful, since my hand was stretched and twisted over the bedrail.

I sat there watching her breathe, waiting for the chance to slip free. I could see the ribs in her chest go up and down, up and down, like they were trying to poke through her tissue-paper skin.

I read once that birds have tendons in their feet that keep them clamped on to a wire or perch when they sleep. They don't have to think about it or make it happen—it's a reflex. Even though Mrs. White was still clamped on tight to my hand, she seemed to be asleep, so I pulled my hand free.

"No!" she cried, sputtering to life.

Her head creaked my way, and she looked so relieved to see I was still there that when she reached through the bars for my hand, I gave in and let her hold it. "Don't go," she croaked out. "Please stay."

When Gloria breezed in a few minutes later and saw me holding the Psychic Vampire's hand, her eyebrows went flying. "My," she whispered, like I was some sort of superhero.

It left me feeling like I couldn't ask her to help me escape, even though that's exactly what I wanted to do.

Gloria checked Mrs. White over, then tucked an extra blanket around her and told her, "Sweet dreams."

Mrs. White held on to me tighter.

After Gloria left, I rested my head against the bed rail

and waited for Mrs. White to really go to sleep. I don't know how long I sat there with her hand clamped on mine, 'cause I got lost in thinking about flying through the city like superheroes do. First I had a cape, then I had a bodysuit with an *L* for Lincoln on my chest, but folks on the street were crying, "Loserman!" so my mind erased the *L* and went for a symbol of wings instead.

Once I had the picture of wings on my chest, I sprouted them on my back. I didn't need a cape to fly—I had wings!

The wings changed everything. I became powerful and mobile. I was Angelman, and villains didn't have a chance! I swooped around the city, ridding it of evil.

But even being a superhero angel doesn't erase the creepiness of holding hands with a psychic vampire, so after a while I veeeery sloooowly pulled my hand away.

This time, she didn't budge. So I veeeery sloooowly pushed myself out of the chair. And I was veeeery sloooowly turning to go when Mrs. White's eyes flew open and a screeching sound came out of her mouth.

Or *into* her mouth.

Her jaw dropped open, her bony chest went up, and her eyes stayed cranked wide while the horrible sound happened.

It was like a demon was being sucked inside her.

"Help!" I cried, and bolted for the Clubhouse. "She's possessed!"

The oldies at the tables didn't budge or even look over, but Ma sure did. She came racing toward me, and since I couldn't *explain* what I'd just seen, I made like Mrs. White, cranking my eyes open and making a sound like a demon was entering my body.

She seemed to understand that evil forces were at work in the Vampire's room. "Stay here," she commanded, holding a stern finger in front of my face.

"You can't go in there!" I cried when I realized she was going in for battle.

"Stay!" she said, doing the finger thing again.

Then Gloria appeared, asking, "What happened?"

So I cranked my eyes and did the demon gasp again, and Gloria went in to back up Ma.

Angelman must still have been operating inside me, because I couldn't just stand by and let them battle the demon alone. I took a deep breath, puffed out my chest, and went inside.

Ma and Gloria were both standing over Mrs. White, and Gloria had just clicked off a walkie-talkie.

Good! They were calling for more backup!

Only . . . Mrs. White wasn't looking possessed. Her eyes were closed and she was back to looking like skin over bones.

Bones that weren't moving.

At all.

I said, "She was . . . she was . . ."

Gloria gave me a soothing smile. Like *I* was crazy!

"No!" I cried. "Her eyes were all cranked back and she was gasping like, ghaaaaaaagh, and—"

"There, there," Gloria cooed. "That was just her agonal gasp."

"Her what?"

Ma put her arm around me. "Her last breath, Lincoln." A nurse walked in as Ma walked me out, and that's when I finally got the picture.

The Psychic Vampire was dead.

She wouldn't be sucking up any more life forces. Or saying mean things to Ma. Or screeching at folks about her window.

She was dead.

Finally dead.

And the confusing thing was, I couldn't stop crying.

38

Phantom Flavor

A chill was swirlin' through me like an ice storm. I couldn't get the sight of Mrs. White or the sound of her demon gasp out of my mind, and her icy bird-claw seemed to still be clinging to my hand.

Ma parked me in the phone room and apologized all over the place for asking me to help. I told her it wasn't her fault that Mrs. White held on for nine hundred years and decided to let go while she was holdin' on to me. I tried acting like I was all recovered, but I was pretty wigged out and Ma knew it.

"Just stay in here," she said, twitching with nerves. "Just stay in here and read your comic book."

I warmed right up to that idea. And since we could hear clankin' and bangin' and Teddy C hollerin' about needin' his teeth, I told Ma, "Go on! I'm fine."

After she left, I holed up with my comic book, and it did help. A lot. But out of the corner of my eye I could see Ma and Gloria working away, and after a while guilt started pangin' through me. They were doin' a nonstop hustle in and out of rooms, changin' diapers, wiping up spills, delivering snacks, and fetching Teddy C's teeth, which he kept hurlin' across the room.

They also performed a magic trick when the medical folks were taking Mrs. White away. All they really did was talk to any oldie the stretcher needed to roll by, but it was like a hocus-pocus of smiles and words and gentle touches. I swear the oldies had no idea one of their own was dead and going, going, gone.

After that, Ma and the others started setting up for lunch, and that's when the guilt pangs took over. Ma hadn't sat down once the whole time, and here I was, lazin' around reading comics?

So I went out and helped with lunch and then was busy the whole rest of the afternoon. I did some cleaning up, but mostly what Ma and Gloria wanted was for me to hang out with the oldies, starting with Ruby Hobbs. "If you could just sit and visit with her? She's about to go tearful on us."

Tearful I could take, as long as she didn't go naked!

When I sat by her and said, "Hi, Ruby," her weepy face dried right up and she started babbling about things that made no sense whatsoever. I tried to follow what she was saying, but she seemed to be stringing random words together and I didn't have the decoder.

It must've made sense to her, though, 'cause she was smiling like she was telling a happy tale, and all I had to do was nod and say, "Wow," or "Really?" to keep her going. When she was all tuckered out from talking, she closed her eyes right there in her chair and nodded off.

After Ruby, I asked Ma what else I could do, and she said, "Just make the rounds," which meant going from one table to the next, playing cards or helping with a puzzle or just visiting. It was easy 'cause things seemed pretty much under control. At the moment, Tapping Paula was Napping Paula, Sir Robert was outside with Sweet-Pea Alice and Pom-Pom Pam, June and Linda were by the TV holding hands, and except for Teddy C—who was still fussin' about his teeth—everyone else seemed to be doing okay.

All that changed when Teena cleared away Debbie Rucker's snack dish.

"Bring it back!" Debbie shouted. "I said, bring it back! There's a lot of flavor left in that bowl!"

She was talking about a plastic pudding bowl that looked pretty scraped out to me.

Teena said, "You're done, Debbie," and kept clearing dishes while Debbie got madder and madder.

"Did you hear me? Give it back!"

"You're done, Debbie."

"GIVE IT BACK!"

Teena ignored her, piled up the dishes, and left. But even though the dish was long gone, Debbie kept shouting, "GIVE IT BACK! GIVE IT BACK RIGHT NOW!"

Ma finally came out of one of the rooms with her blue sani-gloves on. "Is there any way you can get her to quit squalling?" she begged me.

So I went over to Debbie and said, "Hi."

She was all red in the face, but she did change subjects. "What is your name?"

"Lincoln."

"What is your last name?"

"Jones."

"Lincoln Jones," she said, taking a deep, choppy breath. "Can you please bring me a pudding? They took mine away before I was done."

"They're all gone. But we're having Thanksgiving dinner really soon."

"We *are*?"

"Yes, ma'am. I heard there's turkey and mashed potatoes and stuffing. . . . It's going to be a feast."

"Really?" Her red edges were fading fast. "What about pie?"

"I'm guessin' pumpkin? Maybe apple?"

She let out a happy sigh, and her eyes got glassy. "Lincoln Jones?"

"Yes, ma'am?"

"Will you go for a walk with me?"

My eyes went shiftin' around, but my mouth went, "Sure."

She smiled and latched on to me as we headed for fresh air. "Lincoln Jones?"

"Yes, ma'am?"

"I like pumpkin pie."

"Yes, ma'am. Me too."

We walked a little further. "Lincoln Jones?"

"Yes, ma'am?"

"I love Thanksgiving."

"Me too."

Outside now, she looked up at the sky and took a deep breath. "Lincoln Jones?"

"Yes, ma'am?"

She smiled at me. She seemed so calm now. Like a different person. "I'm glad you're here."

I smiled back, and it was truly a wonder to feel the same.

39

Ruby's Family

Since families had to sign up to come to the Brookside Thanksgiving, the staff knew how many places to set. The tables in the Activities Room were put up banquet-style, which really meant picnic-style, with folding tables hiding under white tablecloths. Only about half the oldies had folks coming. I guess there's no sense signing up for a feast if your oldie's stuck in bed or would rather sleep than eat.

When families from both wings started arriving, Ma had me change into my new clothes, which she'd starched to practically standin' during one of her breaks. I was not looking forward to being boxed in by buttons and starch, but when Gloria saw me, I changed my mind.

"My, how handsome you look, dear!"

I could feel my cheeks get hot. "Thank you, ma'am."

The caregivers had to wear their work shirts so folks would know who to ask if they needed help, and since Ma's shift was extended to overlap with the night crew, there were Purple Shirts all over the place. Some were taking care of the oldies who were not coming to Thanksgiving, and the rest were working the feast.

"Where should I sit, Ma?" I whispered when I found her in the Activities Room. The place was buzzin' with folks, and it felt like my first day at Thornhill, where everybody but me seemed to know somebody.

Ma looked around, sizing up the place. It was fillin' in fast, and I could tell she hadn't thought about where I'd be sitting until just now.

Then, coming up behind us from the East Wing, we heard singin'.

Loud, warbly singin'.

"The hills are alive with the sound of muuuusic . . ."

We turned around, and sure enough, it was Ruby Hobbs.

"Mother," a lady beside her was saying, "we'll sing after dinner, okay?"

"With songs they have sung for a thousand yeeeeears . . ."

"Mother, shh. We'll sing after dinner."

There was a man with them, and trailing behind the three grown-ups were a sour-faced girl and a boy.

A boy I knew from school.

My forehead went poppin' with sweat, but before I

could dive for cover, Isaac Monroe recognized me. His eyes went shifty—like he wanted to duck for cover, too.

Somehow Isaac's ma picked up on the situation. "Do you two know each other?" she asked.

I was waiting for Isaac to say something, and I guess he was waiting on me, 'cause we were both standin' there, dumbstruck, when Ruby went and shocked everybody. Not by strippin', but by smiling right at me and saying, "This is Lincoln."

The whole Monroe family was staring at me now, and I could see new questions springin' up in their minds. So I dodged the new ones by answering the old one. "We go to the same school."

I could see Mrs. Monroe's mind clicking with connections. "This is your son, Maribelle?" she asked, smiling at Ma.

"He sure is," Ma said, putting a hand on my shoulder.

"It is such a pleasure to meet you," Mrs. Monroe said, sizing me up from head to oversized shoes. "I see your mother every Tuesday and Friday morning when I visit." She turned to Ma and smiled. "We're like old friends by now, aren't we, Maribelle?"

Ma gave her a smile back, but there was a twitchiness to it. Like her *face* had been starched to standing but could crumble any minute.

Mrs. Monroe had already turned to herd her kids forward. "This is Isaac," she said, directin' the introduction at Ma. "And this is Liza."

"A pleasure to meet you both," Ma said, soundin' mighty proper. Then she saw that Ruby had started to droop, and she waved the family along, saying, "You should probably go find seats. We're glad you all could make it!"

Mrs. Monroe had only gone a few steps when she turned back and said, "Are you here with other family?"

She was lookin' straight at me, so I shook my head.

"Why don't you come sit with us?" She smiled at Ma. "If that's okay with your mother?"

"That'd be very nice," Ma said, not even botherin' to wonder what I thought of it. Not that I *knew* what I thought of it, but havin' supper with a bunch of strangers was not my idea of a good time. Even if one of them went to my school.

"Come join us, Lincoln," Mrs. Monroe said, and Ma pushed me along, whisperin', "Mind your manners!"

Once we got settled at a table, Isaac's ma was friendly, but Isaac was just quiet, and Liza was in a dark mood. Then their folks started talking to the folks taking chairs next to them, and the rest of us were left sittin' around all awkward while Ruby spaced out.

"I can sit someplace else," I finally said.

"No!" Isaac said, like his voice was tryin' to stop something from falling.

"How does she know you?" Liza asked, sliding a look my way.

"Ruby?" It came blurting out before I had the good sense to stop it.

Liza looked at me like I'd stung her. "You call her by her first name?"

I started scooting back from the table. "I think I should probably go sit someplace else."

"Sorry. Not your fault," she said, stopping my chair. "Being here's just painful. First I hated Saturdays. Now Thanksgiving, too."

Isaac leaned across the table, whispering, "It's not Thanksgiving, and she can't help it."

"Like I don't know that?" Liza said, her words like spit on a skillet. She leaned forward at him now, saying, "How's your research coming? Still think you're going to find a cure?"

"Shut up!"

"You shut up!"

"Kids!" their ma hissed across her ma. "Not now! Spend a little time talking to your grandmother."

"Why? She doesn't even know who I am!" Liza hissed back, right across Ruby. Then, louder, she said, "Do you, Grandma?"

Mrs. Monroe turned up the volume, too. "Of course you remember Liza and Isaac, right, Mother?"

Ruby gave Mrs. Monroe a quivery smile. "What was that?"

"Your grandchildren! You remember Liza and Isaac, don't you?"

"I have grandchildren?"

Liza pushed back from the table. "I'm going for a walk."

"What? No!" her ma cried.

"They're not even close to serving," Liza said, and took off toward the East Wing.

Mrs. Monroe gave Isaac a pleading look, so he said, "I'll find her," like it was something he was used to being asked to do. He pushed back and looked at me, saying, "Come on."

Come on? I barely knew him. And I sure didn't want to chase down a girl who was shooting off attitude.

Best to stay away!

But . . . if I didn't follow Isaac, I'd be stuck sittin' by myself next to Ruby Hobbs, which was bad enough right there, but who knew what she'd do?

I hopped up quick and hurried after Isaac.

40

Cool Air

We found Liza outside in the dark, mopin' at the table where Sweet-Pea Alice and Pom-Pom Pam usually hung out with Sir Robert.

"Go away," Liza growled at us, her breath puffing white in the cold air. But before either of us could say a word, she leaned forward at me and said, "How can she possibly know you and not me?"

"I don't know," I said, tiptoeing through a minefield of words. "Maybe because Debbie makes me say my name every afternoon?"

"Debbie?" Her head started quivering. "Who's Debbie?"

"The one who's always shoutin', 'WHAT IS YOUR NAME?'"

Her eyes were squinting now. "Every afternoon? Are

you saying you're here *every afternoon*? Why haven't I seen you before?" She turned to her brother. "Have you seen him here before?"

Isaac shook his head.

I looked down and toed a crack in the concrete. "I'm not here weekends," I said, going with what she'd said earlier about hating Saturdays. "Just during the week." I peeked up and they were both staring at me now. "I come after school."

"*Why?*" Liza said, squinting harder.

Isaac stepped in. "Look, it's not his fault Grandma knows him. If she sees him every day, he's become part of her new memory map. Which makes sense since—"

"Stop!" Liza cried. "I don't care about any 'memory map'!"

"But it probably explains why she knows him and not us! She sees him over and over—he's part of her new memory map!"

Liza rolled her eyes. "Genius here's looking for a cure. You know that, right?" she said in my direction.

"Knock it off, Liza," Isaac growled.

"Is that what you research in the media center?" I asked.

He nodded, but he and Liza were still glarin' at each other.

So I tried smoothin' things over. "Well, someone's got to find a cure, right? Why not him?"

Isaac gave me a look that was all parts grateful, but Liza

frowned at me like I had beans for brains. "Well, let's see. For starters . . . he's eleven years old!"

"So?" Isaac said.

"So?! It's a disease, Isaac! It shuts your body down! It *kills* you!"

"I know that! Stop treating me like I'm a stupid kid. I know a lot more about this than you do! And at least I'm trying to do something about it instead of saying she'd be better off dead, like you do!"

"Well, she would be," Liza grumbled. "And she's going to be! I heard the director tell Mom that most people last here about two years. Grandma's been here a year and a half. She'll be dead before you're out of elementary school!"

Isaac's face freeze-framed, and his eyes kinda glazed over. Not like he was gonna bust out in tears, more like he was doin' some complex calculations in his mind. Finally he blinked and said, "Maybe if we took some of her DNA and—"

"STOP IT!" Liza yelled. "There's nothing *you* can do about it! And I'm sorry, but I don't want to hear any more of your crazy ideas or your technical explanations for why she knows *him* and not me!"

"Not *us*," Isaac said with a frown.

"I know, but I'm older. I've known her longer. She saw me every day after school since I was in kindergarten! And before that she saw me the whole day while Mom and Dad were at work! I should be mapped into her brain so deep she could never forget me!" She turned a glassy look on me. "But no. She knows *him* and not me!"

"She doesn't *know* me," I said. "She's never said my name before. I was as shocked as you. And I bet if I went in there now, she'd look at me like she'd never seen me before."

Liza stared at me for a solid minute, then sighed and leaned back in her chair. "How do you take being here every day?"

"It is pretty crazy," I said.

Liza snorted. "Talk about an understatement."

"But none of 'em's my kin, y'know?"

"Your *kin*?"

I looked away, not wanting to get grilled about what hole I'd crawled out of. "Family. None of 'em's family."

A cloud of quiet moved in and hung overhead until Isaac asked, "So your mother's a caregiver?"

I shrugged. "Every day but Saturdays."

"I can't believe you come here every day," Liza said. "Do your friends know?"

The question felt like a bee sting, and she must've seen how uncomfortable it made me, 'cause she snorted and said, "Yeah, people judge. Even when you try to explain, they just don't get it."

I thought about the truth in that. How if someone had told me even a little of what I'd seen while spending my afters at Brookside, I'd have laughed or hurled or called them a liar.

But seeing it day after day?

Watching what the Purple Shirts go through?

Having Mrs. White die holdin' my hand?

I got it, all right.

And I was pretty sure I wouldn't be forgetting it any-time soon.

41

Zombie in a Wheelchair

Isaac checked his watch and said, "We should get back," but it was probably more the cold than the time that got Liza up and moving. Her teeth were actually chattering when she said, "Good idea."

Problem was, we were locked out. The door we'd come through had been propped open before but was now closed up tight, and knocking brought nobody to our rescue. Even after pounding, nobody came.

Liza took up worrying between banging on the door. "What if they started serving? Mom's going to be so mad! Why isn't anyone in there?"

Through the door window, I could see Droolin' Stu sittin' in his corner and Peggy Riggs on a couch talking to air, but other than that, the place looked deserted.

I was itching to punch in the code and let us inside,

but I stopped short of doing it. I reminded myself that the only good secret is a kept secret, and this sure didn't seem like anything worth jeopardizing Ma's job over.

So after Liza banged again, I said, "Let's try another door."

"Fine," she huffed, and started running away from the East Wing and around the corner toward the back side of the Activities Room.

Isaac and I chased after her and were closing in when all at once she turned around, screaming, "Aaaaaahhhh," and came flying our way.

"What's wrong?" Isaac cried, reeling backward.

"Over there!" she screamed, pointing behind her as she tore by. "A zombie! In a wheelchair!"

Our jaws went danglin'.

A zombie in a wheelchair?

Isaac and I watched her go, then cocked eyebrows at each other. Neither of us had to say it, 'cause there are just some things you have to see for yourself.

We weren't takin' chances, though. No, sir! We moved like sneak thieves up the walkway, our eyes peeled. "You believe in zombies?" I whispered.

"Nah. You?"

"Nah."

Then we saw it.

"Aaaah!" we both cried, coming together like magnets.

We watched it sitting there, in a wheelchair between shrubs, white as moonlight, twitching.

"What is it?" Isaac breathed.

It still wasn't jumping up to get us, so I stepped in closer. "It's only a mannequin," I whispered over my shoulder. "They use 'em for training."

"Why's it in the bushes? And why's it *moving*?"

"Maybe they wanted to hide it from folks 'cause they couldn't get it to stop twitchin'?"

"Maybe they should just disconnect the circuitry?"

"Maybe they didn't know how? Or ran out of time?" I shrugged. "They've been workin' hard all day to make everything perfect."

That seemed to snap loose circuits together in Isaac's mind. "We have *got* to get inside." He looked back the way we'd come and shouted, "Liza!" then took off, saying, "We're going to be in so much trouble!"

"Come back this way when you find her!" I called after him. "I'll get someone to let us in!"

"Right!"

Racing to the back door of the Activities Room, I passed by a big window and looked inside. Mr. Freize was talking, and Purple Shirts were lined up on either side of him. Ma was on the very end, looking around.

Looking for me.

I keyed in the code quick, opened the door, and slipped in a rock to keep it from closing again. Then I raced back to find Isaac and Liza. "Over here!" I called when I saw them coming. "They let me in!"

I flicked the rock out of the way without them noticing, and we made our way back to our seats, trying to be as smooth as possible—which wasn't that smooth, seein' how the director was making a speech and everyone else was quiet and listening.

Mrs. Monroe rolled her eyes as we settled in, but she seemed more relieved than mad, since the dark look Liza had been wearing before was gone.

After a minute had passed and Isaac knew he was off the hook, he nudged me under the table and mouthed, "Zombie in a wheelchair!"

I did my best to keep from laughing, but it was hard.

42

Yellow as Jell-O

I was still grinnin' like a fool about the zombie in a wheelchair when I heard Mr. Freize say Ma's name. And right after, the whole room broke out in applause. Big applause. Like my ma was the winner of some important award.

Was I missing something?

A few folks stood up, still clapping, and then more folks stood up. Pretty soon all the families were standing up, clapping. I looked around in wonder, then gave Isaac a little shrug and stood up, too.

When folks started sitting again, the director laughed and said, "I was going to suggest you give our team a round of applause, but I can see that you already understand what an incredible job they do. So this seems like a good time to remind you that our caregiver Christmas donation box is in the foyer. In the spirit of giving and thanks, remember to give generously!" He picked up a glass and lifted it. "Thank you for coming tonight. Thank you for trusting us with your loved ones. Now please enjoy our Brookside Thanksgiving."

So all the clapping and cheering wasn't just for Ma. But it was *partly* for Ma, which still left me feeling partly stunned. And then Isaac's ma leaned over and caught my eye. "You have no idea how much I appreciate your mother. She's an angel, she really is."

Ma? An *angel*?

Guess she'd never seen Ma draggin' home after work. Or been hollered at by her for running late. Or been cuffed for sassing.

I was still wrapping my head around all the standing and clapping and folks thinking Ma was an angel when food started appearing in front of me. First a little plate of salad slid in. Then metal tongs came over my shoulder and left a roll on another little plate. Then a big plate with a turkey slice and mashed potatoes and marshmallow yams and green beans got delivered. It all happened so fast that I was still busy with one thing when the next showed up.

"They *are* efficient," Mrs. Monroe said with a smile.

I guess most folks were busy trying to keep up with the deliveries, 'cause there was more clinking of dishes than talking going on. You could even hear the background music. It was the fancy kind, with violins and horns and cellos and stuff.

And I was just thinking how the horns sounded like someone was playing them into a pillow when a voice broke through like reveille, shouting, "Stop that!"

I looked over in time to see Sir Robert fling the water from his glass at Teddy C. Teddy got hit, but not as bad as Pom-Pom Pam, who got a big, wet splat on the side of her hair.

Teddy C looked stunned, but Pam was up like a shot.

Like she was back on the field, cheering again.

Only she wasn't cheering.

She was flinging mashed potatoes, shouting, "You ruined my hair!"

I'm pretty sure she was aiming at Sir Robert, but her throwing arm was probably not in practice, 'cause she missed by a mile and hit Alice instead.

Alice didn't waste time calling her sweet pea. She broke into language so nasty she'd have been suspended from school for life. And with her words came food, flingin' through the air. Potatoes. Rolls. Green beans. Yams. She threw everything she could scoop up but still couldn't seem to hit Pam. She hit everyone around *but* Pam.

Then the volcano erupted. The oldies who'd been hit started hurling food and insults.

"Take that, you wrinkled prune!"

"Who you callin' wrinkled?"

"You, you ugly, shriveled pile of wrinkles!"

"If I'm a prune, you're a . . . a big, fat *cauliflower*!"

"Prunes?" Debbie Rucker called. "I love prunes! Can I have some?"

But while Debbie was asking for prunes, the rest of the room was going nuts.

"Stop stealin' my food!"

"It's my food!"

"I need seconds! Someone bring me seconds!"

"He means ammo! Don't bring him anything!"

And all the while, food was flying.

"Who did that?" someone screamed. "Who hit me? You?"

"No! It was her!"

"Liar! I'll sue!"

"I'll sue you for calling me a liar!"

"Prunes!" Debbie shouted. "I want prunes!"

Mashed potatoes thumped against my head. Isaac saw and said, "This is crazy!"

I peeled the mush out of my hair. "Reminds me of ridin' the school bus."

"Yeah, right?" Isaac laughed.

"You ride the bus?" I asked, still peelin' out mush.

"The thirty-three. Hate it."

"I'm on the twenty-seven. Hate it worse!"

Ruby had been quiet until then, but she perked up now and started ripping at her blouse, singing at the top of her lungs, *"Just a spoonful of sugar helps the medicine go down!"*

"Mother!" Mrs. Monroe cried. "What are you doing?"

Buttons were poppin' all over the place. *"Medicine go down . . ."*

"Mother!"

"Medicine go down!"

"Mother, stop that!"

"Just a spoonful of sugar—"

"MOTHER!"

While Mrs. Monroe tried putting Ruby's clothes back together, Sir Robert—who was wiping food off his face with his neck scarf—shouted, "You're as yellow as Jell-O!" at Teddy C.

"Jell-O?" Debbie hollered. "*I* want Jell-O!"

Food stopped flying.

There was a murmur of "Is there Jell-O?" and then the place went quiet.

All the oldies looked around.

"Can we have Jell-O?" Debbie asked.

All eyes turned to the director. His suit was spotted with potatoes. His face was twisted in terror.

"Sure," Gloria said, taking charge. "I think we have some in the kitchen." She gave a stern look around the tables. "But you have to behave. If you can't behave, you can't have Jell-O. Do we have a deal?"

All the oldies nodded.

The families let out huge sighs of relief.

And just like that, the food fight was over.

43

Leftovers

Ma got off work even later than expected. *"Lord,"* she said, collapsin' into a window seat on the bus ride home. "I am worn clear down to the bone."

She settled in, with her bag on her lap and a care package of leftovers at her feet. The director had forced monster-sized helpings of food on any of the day-shifters who'd stayed late to clean up. They were packed in plastic containers and put inside big cloth bags.

I wasn't sure what-all was in ours.

I was praying there was no zombie turkey.

Ma might have been worn clear down to the bone, but her mouth sure wasn't actin' like it. The minute she sat down, it started flappin' away, forgettin' all about her fancy *g*'s.

"All that work we did makin' sure everything was perfect?" she moaned. "Why'd we bother? It was like bein' in a room with two-year-olds." She gave a little snort. "That's what everyone says, right? They become children again. They squall and cry and demand and fight. And I've seen 'em swipe food, or spit it back out, but *Lord,* an actual food fight? And the families just *sat* there."

"It was pretty crazy," I offered.

"Yes," she said, turning to face me square-on. "Yes, it was. There is no other word to describe it. You can say it again."

"Ma'am?"

"It's okay. Say it again."

"Crazy?"

"Yes. That is the one and only word for tonight. Crazy."

I laughed. "And here I was tryin' to quit sayin' it."

She laughed, too, then heaved a big sigh and went quiet. I just sat watching the wheels turn in her head, until finally what she was thinking began slipping out. "Today was hard the whole way around." She slid a look my way. "Except for one thing."

I thought back, trying to figure what that might be. It had been a long one, that's for sure, from Mrs. White dying to cleaning up after a food fight.

"You and Isaac," she said, saving me from recalling the details.

"Me and Isaac?"

"Mm-hmm. It was so nice to see you *playin'* with someone."

"We weren't *playin'*."

"Maybe I was readin' those happy cheeks wrong?"

"What happy cheeks?"

"The ones you were wearing when you came sneakin' in from whatever mischief you two were up to outside."

I tried to wipe the *uh-oh* from my face.

She laughed, and for all the weight of tired I knew she was carrying right then, that laugh lifted her like an invisible balloon. "Doesn't matter, and I don't care. I just liked seein' the two of you havin' a good time."

"I thought you might be mad about us comin' in when the director was talking."

She gave me a sweet smile. "He was just doin' the introductions. It was a good part to miss."

"It got you a standing ovation, though. That was nice, right?"

"Yes, it was," she said. And after a minute, she added, "It's nice to be appreciated."

I could see her driftin' off in her mind again, and when she came back, she said, "I wish there was a way folks could know what it's like without actually livin' through it."

"You mean bein' . . . havin' . . ."

"Alzheimer's. Dementia. It's hard. It's hard any way you look at it. For them, for the families, for us." She let out a heavy sigh. "You try to give folks dignity to the end, but you lose your own along the way."

"What do you mean?"

She gave me a never-mind shake of the head.

"Ma?"

She tested me with a good, long stare, then said, "I change diapers, Lincoln. Big, messy diapers. It's not in a world anywhere near glamorous."

"You do a lot more than change diapers!" It came out a whisper.

This time her smile was small and sad. "I know, but none of it erases the diaper changin', now does it?"

I kept on whisperin'. "Isaac's ma said she thinks you're an angel."

"That's nice. . . ." Her voice trailed off, and I could see her mind leapfroggin' from one tired place to another.

"Ma?"

"Hmm?"

"What are you thinkin'?"

"Oh, just that Isaac's ma's an interior designer."

"A what?"

"She styles folks' homes."

"How do you style a home? What does that mean? And why you thinkin' about that?"

She shook her head. "Never mind."

"But . . . what does it have to do with her callin' you an angel?"

She turned to me, and her face seemed so . . . pained.

"Ma? What's wrong?"

She stayed quiet, and her eyes were holding mine like she was waiting for *me* to say something.

"Ma?" I said again. "Tell me."

Her head wobbled again as her eyes broke away.

Then she leaned against the window and stayed that way for the rest of the ride home.

44

Shot of Knowledge

The second time I woke up the next day, it was from knowing what I should have said to Ma on the bus.

It rang through my head like a shot in the woods.

I wanted to race downstairs and call her from the pay phone, but she'd made me promise something when she'd woken me up earlier. "You can stay here today," she'd whispered, "if you swear you won't go downstairs."

"Huh?" It was dark and cold in the apartment. It felt like the middle of the night.

"I have to catch the bus. Now swear it, unless you want me draggin' you along."

She was leavin' for work? How could it be time to leave already? My whole body felt sore from the day before. Sore and tired. Like I needed to sleep for days.

"Swear," she whispered louder. "Swear or get your shoes on this instant."

"I swear," I said, and I meant it.

All two words of it.

Then I went back to sleep and stayed that way for another four hours, which is when I woke up with the shot of knowledge ringing through my head.

I stumbled to the kitchen sink for a drink of water, and after slurpin' upside down at the faucet, I found a note on the table. A note outlining things I was to do and not do.

Nowhere on the *Don't* list was *sleep all day,* so I fell back into bed, thinking that at least I wasn't breaking any rules. And then I just lay there, wishing I could go downstairs and call Ma.

I needed to tell her what I should have said on the bus.

After frettin' about it for a while, I decided I'd write her a note. I'd get the words just right and hand them to her when she got home. But try as I might, I couldn't get the words even close to right. I went through page after page trying, but it kept coming out wrong. How could I write whole stories but not a little note?

Finally I gave it a rest and tended to the list Ma had made. I wiped down the counter, swept the floors, scrubbed the toilet, cleaned the mirror, and picked up around the place.

Then I ate a peanut butter sandwich and got caught up in thinkin' about Ma.

Why was I so bad at *saying* this?

Maybe I was using too many words.

Maybe I should make her a list instead.

Yeah, a list!

So I got busy with that, only to discover it made what I was trying to say doubly dorky.

So I ripped it up, too, and went back to Ma's list.

Fix Carol Graves a plate and take it to her popped out at me. I figured chances were slim to none that Carol Graves would answer the door, so I didn't get fancy fixin' the plate. I just shoveled some Brookside Thanksgiving left-overs on and took it over.

I knocked on the door, *bang, bang, bang,* holding the plate away so no flakes of paint landed in the food.

I waited, then put my ear up to the door, wondering if I'd get a peek at One-Eyed Jack. Just the thought made my heart speed up. Made me remember—One-Eyed Jack might be telepathic!

So I tried again, *bang, bang, bang,* and this time when I listened, I could hear coughing. A slow, grinding kind of cough. Like someone tryin' to turn over a motor when the battery's about dead.

I knocked again and was fixin' to call out, "Just deliverin' Thanksgiving supper!" but changed my mind as the words were set to launch. "Delivery from Shop-Wise Grocers!" I called. "Need you to sign!"

It came out sounding all leprechaun-y, too.

My ear told me the coughing was getting closer. Very slowly closer. I also heard, "Coming," but it was feeble as could be. Nothing admiral-y about it.

When the door finally opened, Mrs. Graves was panting hard and didn't even seem to care that she'd been tricked. I was expecting to have to do some fancy talking, or even stick my foot in to keep the door from slamming in my face, but she took one look at me and started shuf-flin' back the way she'd come, still coughing.

"I brought you a Thanksgiving meal," I said, following her to her sunny spot by the window. The Mirror Cats were coming out to see me, mewing like they wanted the food themselves. I looked around for Jack but didn't see him. "You want me to heat it up?" I asked.

She was in her seat now, coughing away. I waited for an answer, but I think it was too hard for her to cough and nod.

There were lots of cups and mugs on the coffee table near her, and thinking that one might have something she could drink to help with the coughing, I checked them over and saw mold floating inside them.

I raced to the kitchen and fetched some fresh water from the tap. When I delivered it to her, she was too shaky to hold the cup herself, so I held it up for her and let her sip until she pushed it away.

"Are you okay?" I asked, though it was pretty easy to see she wasn't.

She nodded. "Take Jack home with you."

Her voice was so little I could barely hear her, and I was sure I'd heard her wrong. "Ma'am?"

"Jack. Take him home. The others will kill him."

Kill him?

The Mirror Cats were right there beside us, meowing and flicking their tails, but I still didn't see Jack.

"Where is he?"

"Hiding. Promise me you'll take him."

I nodded. "Are they hungry?" I asked, watching the Mirror Cats.

"They have food."

"How about you?" I took in all the dishes beside her. Most were scary gross with mold. "I'll heat up the food I brought."

She nodded like she barely cared and closed her eyes.

I went to the kitchen, keeping my eyes peeled for Jack. "Here, kitty," I called, but that just brought the Mirror Cats closer, mewing at my feet.

I took the plate I'd brought, put it inside the microwave that was buried in the corner of her counter, and set the timer at only one minute. I'd learned from Gloria that oldies like their food warm, but barely. If you heat it so *you* think it's just right, they'll scream that their mouth is on fire.

Or spit it back at you.

While the microwave was going, I checked the cat zone and found that the food-and-water tower was knocked over. The Mirror Cats were right there, crying, so I set the tower up and got it working again. "There you go," I told them, and when they pounced in to eat, I took up calling for Jack. "Here, kitty, kitty."

I couldn't find him anywhere, so I went back to the microwave, and as I was pulling out the plate, I felt him standing alongside me.

He wasn't touching me, I just knew he was there.

"Hey, fella," I said, stooping down with a piece of turkey in my hand. He had claw marks scabbed across his muzzle and some newer blood on his side. "Here you go, boy," I said, tearing off little pieces of turkey and placing them on the floor.

When he'd finished, I took him and the plate over to Mrs. Graves, along with a cup of juice. She was sound asleep, and every breath she took gurgled. Her lips were cracked and her eyes looked crusted. It was like she was drowning and drying out, all at the same time.

"Ma'am?" I said, sitting in a chair beside her. "You need to eat something." When she didn't answer, I nudged her. "Ma'am? Please. At least have some juice."

"Just leave it," she whispered. "I'll be fine."

I watched her falling back to sleep and nudged her again. "Ma'am? I think I should get you to the hospital."

"No," she gurgled. "Just leave me here in the sun. It's what I want." She opened her eyes to see Jack sitting on my lap. "But take him with you. He deserves someone like you. Take anything you need. There's food."

"Can *you* try to eat?" I begged. "Just a bite or two?"

She shook her head. "Maybe in a little while." She closed her eyes, and the wrinkles on her face smoothed away. "Come back then."

She was falling asleep again, so I stood and said, "I will."

Then I tucked a blanket over her and leaned in, whispering, "Sweet dreams."

45

Not Alone

By the time Ma came home from work, I had a lot of explaining to do. There was a litter box in the bathroom, kibble in the kitchen, and a one-eyed cat roaming around.

Ma took it all in as she unloaded from work. "Lincoln Jones, you have a lot of explaining to do."

"Yes, ma'am. I know."

"So . . . ?"

There was one thing I wanted to clear up right off the bat. "I did not go downstairs. Everything's from next door."

"And . . . ?"

"And I only went next door 'cause it was on your list."

"And . . . ?"

"And before I tell you about that, there's something else I want to tell you."

She was sitting now, at the table that I'd set for dinner, with the chair turned out to face me. Her arms were movin' into the crisscross position that meant she was holdin' back from sayin' what she was thinking. "Well . . . ?" she demanded.

"I'm sorry I didn't say it on the bus last night. And I'm sorry I couldn't figure out how to say it on paper. I tried, and I tried hard, but it just sounded stupid."

"Lincoln, what *are* you getting at?"

And that's when the jumble of words came tumbling out. "You get up in the dark and don't come home 'til after dark. You work all day at makin' other folks comfortable and dignified, which leaves you tired to the bone and feelin' undignified. And I know the reason you work so hard isn't just to give oldies dignity. It's 'cause of me. 'Cause you want me to have a life where I'm safe and don't have to hide under the bed. And if that means changin' big ol' messy diapers, that's what you're willing to do."

Ma's eyes were startin' to run, so I took in a deep breath and got to what I was really wanting to say. "What I should have said last night was that I'm *proud* of you. I think you're a wonder. I wouldn't trade you for anyone's ma. Not anyone's!" Her eyes were spillin' over now, so while she was reaching for a napkin to dry her face, I finished up quick. "And I don't want to live someplace that's been styled. I like it here. It's styled just fine the way it is."

Ma wiped her face and blew her nose and sniffed. Then

she gave me a look that was one hundred percent suspicious. "Is this your way of buttering me up about the cat?"

"No!"

She laughed and sniffed some more and put her arms out. And when I came in for a hug, she whispered, "I would have said yes anyway."

"Ma!"

She laughed again. "Now tell me what happened. How'd we get a cat?"

So I told her about Mrs. Graves and the Mirror Cats attacking Jack and how I'd been going back every hour all afternoon to check on things next door. "She doesn't want me to call anyone, and she doesn't want to go to the hospital. I think she just wants to die, Ma, right there in her sunny window."

"What if a doctor could help her?"

"She told me a hundred times to let her go in peace."

Ma was quiet for a long time, staring at the floor, her head shaking back and forth from time to time. Finally, she heaved a sigh and said, "Take me there?"

So I did, and after Ma checked Mrs. Graves over, she pulled a chair right alongside her and held her hand. "You can go home, Lincoln, but I need to stay here," she said. "So she knows she's not alone."

"I think she wants to be alone, Ma."

Ma looked at me with a smile that was three parts sad and seven parts wise. "No one wants to be alone, especially now."

"But she's sleepin'," I whispered. "She's been sleepin' all afternoon. She doesn't even know we're here."

"Oh, she knows, Lincoln." Her face was now all parts wise. "She knows."

So I pulled up a chair alongside, too. I didn't know how long I could take just sitting there, but I did know one thing.

I didn't want Ma to be alone, either.

46

Freedom

Mrs. Graves passed during the night. I was asleep in the chair when Ma shook me awake and whispered, "She's gone, Lincoln. Let's get home."

I was still half in a dream where I was trying to leave a strange room but the door going out took me right back inside the very same room. I kept going round and round and round, not knowing how to get out.

And now I was wakin' up in a strange room with a dead body in it.

I was feeling mighty bamboozled.

"What are we supposed to do now?" I asked.

"Shh."

Didn't seem like much of an answer to me. And I wasn't sure why we were bein' quiet, or why tiptoein' was in order.

It wasn't like we were going to wake her up. But I was too tired to put up a fuss and more'n happy to go. I followed Ma out the door, glad it didn't take me back inside the very same room.

When we were in our own apartment, I went straight for my mattress. And I was half asleep and half wishing for an extra blanket when Ma came over and whispered, "I'll be back. I need to make a few calls."

I don't know how long she was gone, but when she slipped back in, I thought I was dreaming, 'cause there was a cat curled up at my chest, purring.

And then I remembered—I had a cat!

"Ma?"

"Shh. Everything's fine."

The purring at my chest made me believe it was so.

Ma did not take pity on me in the morning. "You're coming with me," she said soon after her alarm went off.

"But, Ma!"

"Don't fuss. You're comin'."

"What about Mrs. Graves?"

"They came and got her last night."

"Who did?"

"The coroner's office. You didn't hear?"

"No!"

"Well, they did. Now get movin'."

"But, Ma!"

"Get movin'!"

On the bus ride to Brookside, I noticed the dark bags under Ma's eyes, but she wasn't lettin' on how little sleep she'd had, if she'd had any at all. She told me that the Mirror Cats would be fine and that everything else would be taken care of without us. "Families have responsibilities, whether they like it or not."

"She had family?"

"I told you she did."

"But . . . who are they?"

"Two feuding sons. One's in Florida, the other's in Los Angeles."

"How do you know?"

"I found a letter and instructions in a drawer."

"You went nosin' through her stuff?"

"Mm-hmm," she said.

It was a highfalutin *mm-hmm*, too. One that said loud and clear that I'd best not be passing judgment.

Still, I couldn't help thinking about it. How could someone have two kids and wind up dyin' with strangers? What were her sons like? Why were they feuding? Did they know where she was living? Did they know *how* she was living? Did they know their ma had lost track of what was garbage and what wasn't?

Did they know she needed help?

At Brookside, I tried escapin' into my notebook. Into a story. I had to be at Brookside all day, and I just wanted to block it out. Before, I could always do that with writing stories, but now I couldn't seem to get into one. I couldn't tune out bein' there. And bein' there felt like it was sucking the life right out of me.

"You doing okay today, dear?" Gloria asked me after lunch. "Your mother told me about what happened. You've had quite a couple of days, haven't you?"

I just nodded and told her I was fine. But I felt strange. Like something inside me had changed.

Ma seemed to have changed, too, but in a different way. "I got a raise!" she whispered on the bus ride home.

"Really?"

"A good one! It came with a glowing review from the director, too. He said he likes my work ethic and my patience with the residents. He told me he always hears good things about me and that he's grateful for the way I stepped up during Thanksgiving. He also noticed the way you pitched in and told me I'm raising a fine young man."

"He said that?"

She gave me a look that was all parts mischief. "Well, he doesn't know about you callin' folks crazies or forcing garlic on me to fight off psychic vampires."

"I didn't force garlic on you! And I sure didn't tell you to *peel* it!"

She laughed. A big, smiley, cheek-poppin' laugh. I hadn't seen her this happy in . . . ever.

"You know what this is?" she asked, wagging a Brookside envelope with her paycheck in it.

"A Brookside envelope with your paycheck in it?" I ventured.

"It's more than that. It's freedom. Tomorrow I'll send

Ellie what I owe her, plus some thank-you money, and then I can start savin' for *us*."

"Uh . . . can the thank-you money and the savin' maybe wait 'til after Christmas?"

She turned a cool look on me. "What? Getting a cat's not enough?"

My face flashed wide, but it came back in quick. The truth is, if she'd have asked me what my wildest dreams would bring me for Christmas, I'd have said a cat. Jack had just arrived early, is all.

She laughed at my face flashing around and said, "We'll have a fine Christmas, Lincoln. I promise. And next year? What do you say we start looking for an apartment with heat in it?"

"That would be nice," I agreed.

"Mighty nice," she said, and she smiled the whole way home.

47

Brave

The best thing about what was left of Thanksgiving break was Jack. He was like my new shadow, followin' me everywhere I went. And when I sat down or rested on my bed, he'd curl up right there with me. I spent a whole lot of the weekend talking to Jack.

I also spent a whole lot of the weekend wishing Jack could talk to me. I had questions! Had Mrs. Graves taken him in after he'd become One-Eyed Jack? Or had the Mirror Cats slashed his eye? I wished he could tell me.

The worst thing about the weekend was not the shopping or the chores. It was Sunday morning, when it was just Jack and me in the apartment and Ma was at work. I almost wished she'd made me go to Brookside with her.

It wasn't just being trapped by my promise to stay

inside the apartment. It was everything that was going on outside the apartment. I guess they wanted to clear Mrs. Graves's place out quick, 'cause even though it was Sunday, workers were walking back and forth, back and forth, emptying out the apartment. I spied on them through the window blinds, careful not to let on that I was home. Someone figuring out I was home was the first step in them knowing I was home alone.

The workers did carry out some boxes of stuff, but mostly what they hauled away were black trash bags, stuffed full and round. One after the other after the other. It was like an army of big black ants marching past, working in a line.

I wondered about Mrs. Graves's feuding sons. Where were they? The men cleaning out the apartment were hired workers. I could tell by their boots and shirts and the way they marched along and worked together. This was a job. They didn't care about anything else.

So why weren't the sons here? Didn't *they* care?

I also wondered about all the stuff Mrs. Graves had saved, thinking she might need it someday. Toothbrushes, toilet-paper rolls, butter tubs, bread bags . . . it was all being hauled off to the dump. She treated it like treasure, but to everyone else it was just trash.

It all felt sad. And it lingered in my mind long after the army had stopped marching. I couldn't figure out answers for any of it, and after Ma was finally home, she was no help at all. "Hoarding's a common problem with seniors, and folks have fallings-out, Lincoln. You can't solve all the world's problems. You gotta start by fixin' your own."

Seemed kinda funny coming from someone who'd delivered zombie chicken to a homeless guy and sat up all night with a dying stranger. And what had Ma meant about "fixin' your own"?

I was almost asleep when I remembered how Ma had called her sister to patch things up. She could have just left things as they were, but she'd called Ellie and tried to make them better. I lay there in the dark, figuring out, finally, how important that was.

Then my mind started rewinding. Working backward in time, thinking about all the things that had happened since Ma had made her resolution on New Year's almost a year ago.

I always knew Ma worked hard. And I knew she'd made a plan and was sticking to it. As tough as everything was, she was sticking to it.

But there was something else. Something I hadn't known before. And right there, in the dark, it clicked. More than any of the heroes in my stories, more than any other person I'd ever known, Ma was brave.

Truly brave.

And seein' that clear as day right through the dark made me know something else. It had come and gone in little waves before, but it was settling now, way down inside.

I could be brave, too.

48

Surprises

Isaac was waiting for me when I got off the bus Monday morning. "Hey!" he called.

His hair was combed back and still a little wet. I went over to him, thinking that instead of a wild anemone mule, he looked like a turtle walking on two legs. "What's in there?" I asked, slapping his backpack.

"Oh, everything!"

He sounded mighty excited, and it made me laugh. I slipped him a wily look. "Like . . . a zombie in a wheelchair?"

He laughed, too. "Wish I'd known you were going to be at Brookside on Friday," he said. "I'd have come."

"To Brookside?" My face went a little screwy. "*Why?* And how'd you know I was there?"

"My mom. She said she saw you looking all miserable in a corner."

"She did?" I thought back to Friday. It *had* been a long and miserable day. One that would have been a whole lot better with Isaac there. "It was the slowest day ever. . . ."

"No food fights?"

I laughed again. "Dentures went flyin', but that's about it."

"Hey, are you doing the Alzheimer's Walk on Saturday?"

"Uh . . . I don't think so. It's Ma's only real day off."

"Well, my mom said if you wanted, you could come home with me Friday after school and we could camp out in the tree fort and then do the walk on Saturday."

My mind went twirlin'. "You have a tree fort?"

"Yeah! It's got a trapdoor, a pulley-system dumbwaiter, and a telescope for stars."

I was in. I was all in. "I need to ask Ma, but . . . sure!"

The warning bell rang. "Hey," he said, "you want to meet up at lunch?"

I laughed. "For a food fight?"

He smiled, big and bright. "I'm up for that!"

"Maybe they're servin' Jell-O!"

He laughed, too, then said, "What do you do at recess?"

I shrugged, not wantin' to say I hid out somewhere with my notebook.

"I could meet you right here if you want. We could hang out?"

For the first time since school started, I was bubblin'

inside. Bubblin' with the excitement of findin' a friend. "Sure!"

Then Kandi came running up. Her cheeks were all rosy, and her fingernails were painted white with red stripes. Like candy canes. She probably thought she was being clever, but I thought it was annoying. December was still a day away, and she was already claimin' it as *her* month.

She looked back and forth between Isaac and me with nosy written all over her face. "So . . . did you have a nice Thanksgiving?"

I slid a look at Isaac.

He slid a look at me.

"It was fine," I said, and Isaac nodded his agreement.

"I didn't know you two were friends," she said, and she was twitchin' a little. Like she was feeling guilty for what she'd said about Isaac.

"Uh-huh," I said, giving her a cool look.

"I'm glad," she said, still twitching. And since we weren't saying anything more, she ran off, calling, "We need to get to class!"

"Her mother died last year," Isaac said, watching her go.

"What?" I wasn't even sure he'd actually said it. It was so out of the blue.

"Brain cancer. It happened quick."

"What?" I still wasn't sure this was a real conversation.

"My sister says she's a mess."

"Your sister does?"

"Yeah. She knows her sister."

"Whose sister?"

"Kandi's sister."

"Kandi has a sister?" I said it like it was the world's biggest revelation. I have no idea why.

Isaac laughed. "A lot of people do."

The blacktop was almost cleared, and we were going to be late, so we took off running. "I'll meet you at recess!" I called.

"Righty-o!" he called back.

In class, Kandi was being chatty with everyone around her. She sure didn't seem messed up to me. She seemed nosy. And annoying. And seeing her flit around, smiling all the time . . . seeing her boss folks like a camp director . . . seeing her throw little tantrums when things didn't go her way . . . none of it added up to her being messed up. It added up to her being kinda *spoiled*.

But maybe I'd added things up wrong.

It felt like when I'd read the Resident Spotlights in the *Brookside Bulletin*. I'd thought I had folks all figured out, then it turned out I didn't know much about them at all. But it was more than that. All this time I'd been writing stories about made-up people that I could see clear as day, but the real folks around me had stories I'd been completely blind to.

The thought put me in a wobbly mood. Ms. Miller, though, was in a great mood, and very excited about our new writing assignment. "You're going to detail your

Thanksgiving experience," she said, pacing around like a caged tiger. "I want you to use all the senses. What you saw, what you heard, what you smelled, what you tasted. . . . Make me feel like I was there."

Colby's hand shot up, and when Ms. Miller called on her, Colby asked, "So you want us to describe Thanksgiving dinner?"

"You don't have to limit yourself to dinner. The buildup to dinner, the cleanup after dinner, the family traditions, the games you played or movies you watched. Did you travel? What was that like? How about Black Friday? Did you go shopping?" She laughed, like she was going back in her mind, remembering. "Lots of sights and sounds there!"

Benny called out, "How long does it have to be?"

"This is a volume piece. The longer the better," she said. "Grab me with your opening line and go! I will not be grading on syntax. I want you just to write, write, write. I want you to *enjoy* the process and not worry about anything but getting your experience down on paper."

"So how many pages for an A?" Colby asked.

"Hmm," she said, studying her. "How about ten? Yes, ten!"

She was winging it like no teacher I'd ever known.

"Ten?!" Benny cried. "I can't write ten pages!"

"Then maybe you'll only write seven and get a C." She leveled a look at the class. "You had five days off. Tell me about them."

Back before Thanksgiving break, I could have written ten pages about any made-up story, easy. Which means that before Thanksgiving break, I could have *made up* a story of what happened on my Thanksgiving break, easy. Like, I could have made up a story about Aunt Ellie and Cheyenne coming over to our big house for a feast. Wild turkeys could have been flappin' and gobble-gobblin' in the backyard tree, tryin' to escape their doom. Our dog— a big, happy hound—could have been barking and bounding around all over the place, trying to reach the turkeys. I could have planted our own garden in the story, where corn and yams and carrots were just waitin' to be harvested.

I could have, and who would've known it wasn't true? Nobody.

And nobody would've cared.

But now I felt strange inside. Like I was done with making stuff up. Done running from things. Done hiding.

But I couldn't write about what *had* happened. If I told the truth, Ms. Miller might call the cops. Besides, how could I explain how I'd spent most of my vacation with folks who had lost their minds? How I'd seen two old ladies die? How I'd eaten leftovers from a food-fight Thanksgiving meal for four days running and had hidden out from an army of ants in an apartment with my new, one-eyed cat?

There was no explaining it. Not in ten pages, not in a hundred.

So while Colby's feather pencil flapped around and Rayne and Wynne had their noses low over their pages and scribbled away, I sat on the edge of our continent with a blank page, feeling stuck.

Stuck and alone.

49

I Do Declare

After that first half hour of writing, we had a math lesson, and then we were back to writing again 'cause Colby raised her feather and begged, "Can we have more time on our essay? Please?"

I'm guessin' she'd had a Thanksgiving worth writing about.

I watched her feather do the mad flap for a while, and then I guess I was staring at Rayne's paper, 'cause she asked, "Why aren't you writing?"

I hunkered down, shielding my blank page after that. And I *tried* to come up with something, but I was tangled up inside. All I had for my essay when the recess bell rang was a title: "My Thanksgiving."

When Ms. Miller released us, I busted out of the room

and cut across the blacktop toward where Isaac said he'd meet me. I was hoping his class had to write a Thanksgiving essay. I thought maybe he could help me figure out what to do.

I was almost at the spot when Troy Pilkers stepped in my way. "I do declare!" he said. "If it ain't the Missing Link."

He was making fun of me being from the South.

He was also baiting me.

I didn't bite, but my heart was beating fast as I tried sidestepping him.

He sidestepped, too. "Whassamatter, sugar? Cat got your tongue?"

I tried sidestepping again, but when he blocked me again, I squared up and said, "It's not my fault you got thrown off the bus."

"Well, shut my mouth! If that don't put pepper in the gumbo!"

"*What?*" I gave him a good, hard squint. "That makes no sense."

He dropped the Southern thing. "Yeah? So who was it?" He shoved me. "Who got me thrown off?"

The shove wasn't that hard, but it set something off in me. I wanted to run. Find a corner somewhere and wait for it to be over.

But my feet stayed planted, and I drilled him with a look that said he was dumber'n dirt. "*You* did. Driver's got a mirror, you know."

Before Troy could answer, Isaac stepped in. "Hey! Why'd you shove him?"

Troy zeroed in on him. "You really taking me on, Dweebly?"

Out of nowhere, Kandi was there, too, with a four-square ball tucked under her arm. "Oh, grow up, Troy."

Troy took in the three of us, then stared at her. "These two? Seriously?"

"You don't know anything about them, okay? Maybe if you did, you wouldn't be so mean."

"I was just goofing around," he said with a shrug. "He could have asked me to stop, you know."

I stretched up an extra inch. "Like you need to be asked to quit flingin' tuna in someone's hair?"

"Yeah," Kandi said. "Only an idiot would need to be told that's not cool." And then she did the most surprising thing I'd ever seen at school. She softened her voice like Gloria always does to calm down the oldies and said, "I don't think you're an idiot, Troy. So just be nice, would you? It's not hard."

He stared at her some more, then grumbled, "Whatever," and walked away.

"Wow," I said, watching him go.

Isaac nodded. "That was unexpected."

Kandi smiled at us, then looked out at the four-square court, where kids were waiting for her to return with the ball. "You guys want to play?"

"I'm terrible," Isaac said, shaking his head.

"Me too."

Kandi punched her free hand to her side. "Oh, just come, would you? Everyone's terrible. It doesn't matter. It's just fun."

I looked at Isaac and shrugged.

He shrugged back.

And we followed Kandi to the four-square court.

50

Opening Up

Trouble was waiting for me inside the classroom. During recess, Ms. Miller had gone around to each desk and looked over our essays. "Lincoln," she said, and wagged a finger for me to follow her outside.

As quiet as she'd said it, the whole class knew I was in trouble. And as hard as they tried, their sly-eye watching me go was nowhere near sly.

"I thought you loved to write," Ms. Miller said when the door was closed.

I stared at my shoes.

"Lincoln? Look at me."

I looked up, then went back to my shoes.

"Lincoln, you can write about anything. Anything that happened over Thanksgiving break. It doesn't have to be about the dinner."

I nodded.

"Lincoln?"

"Yes, ma'am."

"Do you celebrate Thanksgiving?"

I nodded, which seemed to send relief streakin' through her.

"Well, then, what's the problem? I thought you would love this assignment! You are my very best writer, did you know that?"

I shook my head.

"You have a wonderful way with words. I always look forward to reading your essays."

"Thank you, ma'am."

She stood lookin' at me for an endless minute. Finally she said, "Is everything all right at home?"

I nodded.

"Lincoln?"

She had a look on her face that was all parts doubt, and it set a wave of panic crashing through me. "No!" I said, lookin' straight at her. "Things at home are *fine*. They're great. Actually, they've never been better!"

"So . . . ?"

I shrugged and went back to looking down. "So there's no explainin' the Thanksgiving I had."

She shook her head. "I don't understand this. You love to write, everything at home is fine, you celebrate Thanksgiving—"

"Well, I don't know if you'd call it *celebratin'*."

She gave me a curious look. "So what *would* you call it?"

I thought about that. "Surviving? I survived it?" Then, under my breath, I added, "Which is more'n I can say about some folks."

She crossed her arms. "Okay. Now I am completely confused."

"I know, ma'am, see?"

"No! I don't see!"

"Exactly! There's no explainin' it."

"Well." She studied me hard while I did the same to my shoes. Finally she said, "How can anyone understand if you don't at least try to explain?" Then she softened up and said, "I know you're new here, and I know that's not easy. I have no idea what you're going through or why your vacation was . . . difficult. But I can see that you have a story to tell, and your story *matters*."

I peeked up at her.

"I promise you, Lincoln, it matters." She gave me a little smile. "Can you please just try?"

"I have tried, ma'am. I don't know how to start."

My not knowing how to start seemed to make her very happy. Her eyes popped wide and her finger popped up. "Ah!"

"Ma'am?"

"Start anywhere! In the middle. At the end. It doesn't matter. Just start. And once you start, weave your way back. Or forward. Don't worry about where—just start."

Ms. Miller made it sound so easy, but it was Kandi who made me think I should actually figure out a way to do it.

"Lincoln! Lincoln, wait!" she called, catching up to me on my way to Brookside.

It was a little strange to be happy to see her. Might've had something to do with the way she'd brought Isaac and me into playing four square again at lunch and made sure no one cheated us. I'd made it to first square for three whole serves, something that qualified as a miracle.

And a happy one at that.

She got straight to the point. "I wasn't going to tell you, but I think you should know—Colby showed around your essay while you were out with Ms. Miller today."

"What?"

"She said you must be too embarrassed to write about your Thanksgiving."

"What?"

"I told her to shut up and mind her own business."

I felt like I'd been put in an alternate universe, what with Kandi tellin' someone else to mind their own business and all. But before I could get my bearings, she said, "Are you blocked?"

"Blocked?"

"You know—when a writer can't figure out what to write, they call that being blocked." I didn't say anything, so she went on. "I'd be blocked, too, because I had the worst Thanksgiving ever. But you know what? I'm not writing about that. I'm writing about a made-up Thanksgiving. The decorations are great, the food is delicious, everyone's happy and having a good time. . . . Fiction is fun, and I totally see why you do it."

"You been readin' up about bein' a writer?"

"How'd you know?"

"Well, you know way more about it than I do."

We walked along until what I was thinking finally popped out. "Isaac told me about your ma. I'm sorry." I slid a look her way. "I'm guessin' that's why you had a bad Thanksgiving?"

She nodded, and her eyes got all glassy. "I'm just trying to do what she said: keep my chin up, remember that life is precious, and be a force for good in the world." She burst into tears. "But it's so hard! Sometimes it's just so hard."

Talk about unexpected. I stopped walking and stared.

Kandi wiped her eyes on her sleeve and sat down on a walkway step, her arms propped against her legs, her head sagging like she was just too tired to carry on. "People don't know what it's like," she choked out. "They just don't."

I sat beside her. I couldn't claim to know what it was really like, but just the thought of losing my ma put a rock in my throat. And it was coming to me clearer now that all this time I'd figured Kandi was one thing when it was turning out that she was another.

Finally I ventured, "Maybe you've been workin' so hard

at hiding what you're going through that folks have no idea, and no way of understandin' it."

She turned her weepy eyes on me. "Isn't that what you do?"

The truth in that was undeniable, but I denied it just the same. "No!"

She stared at me, then shook her head and wiped away her tears. "Never mind. Sorry." She stood up. "I've got to go."

She was already hurrying off. "Wait!" I called, chasing after her.

"It's okay, Lincoln. I had a little breakdown. Sorry. I'm fine."

"But—"

"Look, you don't want to talk about yours, I don't want to talk about mine. And even if I did, the truth is, nobody really cares."

My mouth shot open. "I do!"

The words stunned me, but there they were, stopping Kandi in her tracks while they shot a bolt of fear through my heart.

"What did you say?" she asked.

I wanted to run.

Hide!

My heart was galloping in my chest. My mouth was dry. But I could see now that being brave—truly brave— was about more than facing off with Troy, or derelicts at the Laundromat, or even Cliff.

It was about facing off with the truth.

So I stood by my words. "I do," I said, then looked at her square-on. "Writing about some phony Thanksgiving isn't gonna make anyone know what you're goin' through. And you're right—I've been doin' the same thing as you." I took a deep breath. "I love writin' stories, and I'm gonna keep writin' stories. But I'm starting to see that there's a time for stories and there's a time for truth, and I'm thinkin' this is a time for truth. So how about we make a deal: you write about your real Thanksgiving, and I write about mine."

She looked at me for an endless minute. "You're serious?"

I was sweatin' bullets, but I held my ground with a nod.

"Deal," she said. Then she stuck out her hand.

And I shook it.

(51)

Full Circle

After Kandi went her way and I went mine, I started losing my nerve. I wanted to hold up my end of the deal, but . . . how could I ever explain my Thanksgiving?

How could I write about my secret life?

I thought about it the whole rest of the way to Brookside.

I thought about it when Geri said, "Good afternoon, Lincoln! Isn't it a lovely day?" as I signed in.

I thought about it when Suzie York asked me, "Do you know how to get out of here?" and Debbie Rucker called, "What is your name?" and Alice said, "Why, hello, sweet pea," and grabbed for my backside.

I thought about it when Teddy C wolf-whistled at Gloria, and when Ma gave me one of her sweet smiles and asked if I was wantin' a snack. I thought about it when I saw that there was a new oldie in Room 102 who had the window-side bed, instead of Wilhelmina.

I thought about it as I passed by Droolin' Stu, and when June and Linda shouted for somebody to make Paula quit tapping.

But how could folks understand if I *didn't* find a way to explain? How could they understand why living in a place with no heat and a sagging floor or sitting up all night with a dying stranger were things to be thankful for, if I didn't explain?

I sat at my table and pulled out my notebook and thought about it for a long time. There was so much stewin' around in my brain. So many *ingredients* in the story. Some sour, some sweet, some salty, some spicy . . . I wasn't sure what to put in.

Or, especially, what to leave out.

And where in the world should I start? I couldn't explain Thanksgiving without explaining stuff that happened be-fore. It wouldn't make any sense! But how far back did I have to go? A week? Two? Back to zombie chicken? Back to the first time the Psychic Vampire struck? Back to when we moved? Back to *why* we moved? It all tied together, and none of it made sense standin' alone.

So . . . where to start?

I was deep into stirring my mental stew when a sound came out of one of the oldies' rooms.

A warbly sound.

Singing.

I snapped to attention and turned away quick, knowin' what was comin' next.

Everyone knew what was comin' next.

Even the oldies who couldn't seem to remember anything else knew what was comin' next.

"Stop her!" Teddy C cried.

"Not again!" Pom-Pom Pam wailed.

But there she was.

Ms. Miller's voice popped into my head—*Start anywhere! In the middle. At the end. It doesn't matter*—and just like that, my pencil took off writing.

Ruby Hobbs came out of her room, dancing and singing, buck naked, again. . . .

About the Author

Wendelin Van Draanen is the author of many award-winning and beloved books, including *Flipped*, *Swear to Howdy*, *The Running Dream*, the Sammy Keyes mystery series, the Shredderman quartet, and the Gecko & Sticky books. Read more about her books at WendelinVanDraanen.com or follow her on Twitter at @WendelinVanD.

Wendelin lives in central California with her husband and two sons. Her hobbies include the "three R's": reading, running, and rock 'n' roll.

SCRIBES AND SCHOLARS

SCRIBES
AND SCHOLARS

A Guide to the Transmission
of Greek and Latin Literature

BY

L. D. REYNOLDS

Fellow and Tutor of Brasenose College, Oxford

AND

N. G. WILSON

Fellow and Tutor of Lincoln College, Oxford

SECOND EDITION
REVISED AND ENLARGED

CLARENDON PRESS · OXFORD
1974

Oxford University Press, Ely House, London W.1

GLASGOW NEW YORK TORONTO MELBOURNE WELLINGTON
CAPE TOWN IBADAN NAIROBI DAR ES SALAAM LUSAKA ADDIS ABABA
DELHI BOMBAY CALCUTTA MADRAS KARACHI LAHORE DACCA
KUALA LUMPUR SINGAPORE HONG KONG TOKYO

CASEBOUND ISBN 0 19 814371 0

PAPERBACK ISBN 0 19 814372 9

© *Oxford University Press 1968, 1974*

FIRST EDITION 1968
SECOND EDITION 1974

*Printed in Great Britain by
Butler & Tanner Ltd, Frome and London*

PREFACE

This book is designed as a simple introduction for beginners to a field of classical studies which generally remains little known or understood despite its importance and intrinsic interest. In schools and universities students read Greek and Latin authors in editions equipped with an apparatus criticus, but they are too often un-acquainted with the historical facts which make such an apparatus necessary, and are at a loss to evaluate the information that it gives. There are few works in English to which they can be referred, and a short guide is needed, especially one which can be read by those whose linguistic and historical knowledge is limited.

We have attempted to outline the processes by which Greek and Latin literature have been preserved, describing the dangers to which texts were exposed in the age of the manuscript book, and showing to what extent ancient and medieval readers or scholars were concerned to preserve or transmit classical texts. The history of texts cannot be separated from the history of education and scholarship, which also bulk large in these pages. On the other hand, matters of pure palaeography receive attention only if they are of direct importance for transmission.

The book is intended in the first place for students of Greek and Latin, but the theme handled is so inextricably connected with the cultural history of the Middle Ages and Renaissance that we think our account may be useful to anyone concerned with these periods. We also hope that students of biblical scholarship may find something of interest.

Reasons of space have compelled us to compress the material to the utmost and to omit some topics which we should have liked to treat, such as the general history of scholarship since the Renaissance. In addition it has sometimes been necessary to make a simplified statement of points that the expert reader will regard as complicated and controversial. Detailed footnotes, apart from increasing the price of the book, seemed out of keeping with the character of such an introductory work, but in general we have tried to indicate the primary sources in brackets in the main body of the text. The shelf-marks of manuscripts, often abbreviated and perhaps unfamiliar to the reader, are expanded and to some extent explained in the *index codicum*. Our major debts to the work of others are indicated in the Bibliography. Technical terms are explained where necessary, not in a separate glossary, and the reader who wishes to refer back to the explanation may find it through the index.

We should like to record here our gratitude to Professor R. G. Austin, Dr. R. W. Hunt, Mr. E. J. Kenney, Professor H. Lloyd-Jones, Professor Sir Roger Mynors and Mr. D. C. C. Young for much valuable advice and assistance. We should also like to thank the British and foreign libraries indicated in the notes to the plates for their permission to reproduce photographs of manuscripts in their possession.

June 1967   L.D.R.
                                                                N.G.W.

PREFACE TO THE SECOND EDITION

In preparing this new edition we have attempted to retain the principal feature of the original, a readable text unencumbered by a heavy apparatus of learning, and at the same time to meet the criticism that the absence of notes might make it difficult for readers to pursue any topic of special interest to them. We did not wish to go to the length of documenting all our statements with footnotes and hope that the addition of short notes to each chapter, largely bibliographical in character, will achieve a satisfactory compromise.

A new chapter, necessarily very selective, has been added in order to carry our survey down to the modern period. We have also made a number of additions and corrections to the original text and brought details up to date. We have profited a great deal from the kindness of friends and reviewers, and from the particular circumstance that the book has been subjected to the expert and critical eye of those responsible for the Italian and French editions. Much of the new material was prepared in the first instance for a French translation about to be published by Les Éditions du Seuil and we owe a special debt to M. Pierre Petitmengin of the École Normale Supérieure, whose acute suggestions have enabled us to make many improvements in both detail and substance.

December 1973   L.D.R.
                                                         N.G.W.

CONTENTS

  A*

1. ANTIQUITY

I. ANCIENT BOOKS

A description of the processes by which classical literature has been transmitted from the ancient world to the present day may conveniently begin with a brief outline of the origin and growth of trade in books. In Greece of the pre-classical age literature preceded literacy. The nucleus of the Homeric poems was handed down through several centuries during which the use of writing appears to have been completely lost; and in the latter part of the eighth century, when the Phoenician alphabet was adapted for the writing of Greek, the tradition of oral literary composition was still strong, with the result that it was not immediately thought necessary to commit the Homeric poems to writing. According to a tradition frequently repeated in antiquity the first written text of the epics was prepared at Athens in the middle of the sixth century by order of Pisistratus. This account, though not above suspicion, is plausible; but it does not follow that copies of the text of Homer began to circulate in any considerable numbers, for Pisistratus' object was in all probability to ensure the existence of an official copy of the poems to be recited at the festival of the Panathenaea. The habit of reading epic poetry instead of hearing it recited will not have been created overnight, and books remained something of a rarity until well into the fifth century. On the other hand the growth of forms of literature which do not depend on oral composition ensured that from the seventh century onwards there was a need for authors to put their works in writing, even if only one copy was made for the purpose of reference; thus Heraclitus is said to have deposited his famous treatise in a temple, and perhaps for this reason it survived to be read by Aristotle in the middle of the fourth century (Diog. Laert. 9.6). The multiplication and circulation of copies was probably extremely limited, and it may be conjectured that the first works to reach even a modest public were either the writings of the Ionian philosophers and historians or those of the sophists. There must also have been a certain demand for copies of the poetic texts that formed the basis of school education. It is not until the middle of the fifth century or a little later that a book trade can be said to have existed in Greece: we find references to a part of the Athenian market where books can be bought (Eupolis fr. 304K), and Socrates is represented by Plato as saying in his *Apology* (26) that anyone can buy Anaxagoras' works for a drachma in the orchestra. All details of the trade, however, remain unknown.

Of the appearance of the books that were produced in classical Greece not much can be said with certainty. The number of books or fragments surviving from the fourth century is so tiny that it would not be reasonable to regard them as a representative sample. The general statements that follow are therefore based primarily on Hellenistic material, but it may be inferred with some plausibility that they are true also for the classical period. An attempt will be made to show how the physical differences between ancient and modern books affected the ancient reader in his relation to literary texts.

The form of the book was a roll, on one side of which the text was written in a series of columns. The reader would unroll it gradually, using one hand to hold the part that he had already seen, which was rolled up; but the result of this process was to reverse the coil, so that the whole book had to be unrolled again before the next reader could use it. The inconvenience of this book-form is obvious, especially when it is remembered that some rolls were of considerable length; one of the longest surviving (P. Oxy. 843) contained when complete the whole of Plato's *Symposium* and must have been about twenty-two feet long. Another disadvantage was that the material of which it was composed was by no means strong, and damage easily ensued. It is not difficult to imagine that an ancient reader faced with the need to verify a quotation or check a reference would rely if possible on his memory of the passage rather than go to the trouble of unwinding the roll and perhaps thereby accelerating the process of wear and tear. This would certainly account for the fact that when one ancient author quotes another there is so often a substantial difference between the two versions.

The standard writing material was papyrus (Plate I), prepared by cutting thin strips from the fibrous pith of a reed that grew freely in the Nile delta; in the first century A.D. there were also minor centres of production in Syria and near Babylon. Two layers of these strips, one laid at right angles over the other, were pressed together to form sheets (Pliny, *N.H.* 13.68ff.). The sheets could then be glued together in a long row to make a roll. Many sizes of sheet were made, but the average book allowed a column of text between eight and ten inches high, containing between twenty-five and forty-five lines. As there was only one large source of supply the book trade was presumably exposed to fluctuations arising from war or a desire by the producers to exploit their virtual monopoly. Some such difficulty is implied by Herodotus' remark (5.58) that when writing material was in short supply the Ionians had used sheep and goats' skins as a substitute. In resorting to this expedient they seem to have followed the practice of their Oriental neighbours. But leather as a writing material compared unfavourably with papyrus, and was no doubt used only in emergency. In the Hellenistic period, if Varro can be trusted (cf. Pliny, *N.H.* 13.70), the Egyptian government placed an embargo on the export of papyrus, which seems to have stimulated the search for an acceptable alternative. At Pergamum a process was devised for treating animal skins to give a better writing surface than leather, the result being what is now called parchment (otherwise known as vellum); the word owes part of its etymology to the name Pergamum, and the derivation can be seen more clearly from the Italian form *pergamena*. But if this tradition is true the experiment was at first short-lived; one must assume that the Egyptian embargo was soon removed, for it is not until the early centuries of the Christian era that parchment comes into common use for books; early examples are fragments of Euripides' *Cretans* (P. Berol. 13217) and Demosthenes *On the false embassy* (Brit. Mus. Add. 34473 = P. Lit. Lond. 127).

To what extent the supply and price of papyrus hindered or encouraged its use in Greece is impossible to say. But when employed for the production of a book it was almost invariably covered with writing on one side only. The form of the book made this necessary, since a text written on the back of a roll would have been very easily rubbed away, and perhaps the surface of the papyrus contributed to the formation of this convention, since scribes always preferred to use first the side on which the fibres ran horizontally. On rare occasions we hear of rolls written on both sides (Juvenal 1.6, Pliny, *Epp.* 3.5.17), but such books were exceptional. A shortage of writing material did, however, sometimes cause a literary text to be written on the reverse across the fibres: a famous example is the manuscript of Euripides' *Hypsipyle* (P. Oxy. 852). It is important to note in this connection that the quantity of text carried by an ancient book was very small: the copy of Plato's *Symposium* mentioned above, though very large by ancient standards, contained a text which does not occupy more than about seventy printed pages.

Finally it should be emphasized that the text as arranged on the papyrus was much harder for the reader to interpret than in any modern book. Punctuation was never more than rudimentary. Texts were written without word-division, and it was not until the middle ages that a real effort was made to alter this convention in Greek or Latin texts. The system of accentuation, which might have compensated for this difficulty in Greek, was not invented until the Hellenistic period, and for a long time after its invention it was not universally used; here again it is not until the early middle ages that the writing of accents becomes normal practice. In dramatic texts throughout antiquity changes of speaker were not indicated with the precision now thought necessary; it was enough to write a horizontal stroke at the beginning of a line, or two points one above the other, like the modern English colon, for changes elsewhere; the names of the characters were frequently omitted. The inaccuracy of this method, and the state of confusion to which texts were soon reduced by it, may be seen from the condition of the papyri containing Menanders' *Dyscolus* and *Sicyonius*. Another and perhaps even stranger feature of books in the pre-Hellenistic period is that lyric verse was written as if it were prose; the fourth-century papyrus of Timotheus (P. Berol. 9875) is an instance, and even without this valuable document the fact could have been inferred from the statement that Aristophanes of Byzantium (c. 257–180 B.C.) devised the traditional colometry which makes clear the metrical units of the poetry (Dion. Hal., *de comp. verb.* 156, 221). It is to be noted that the difficulties facing the reader of an ancient book were equally troublesome to the man who wished to transcribe his own copy. The risk of misinterpretation and consequent corruption of the text in this period is not to be underestimated. It is certain that a high proportion of serious corruptions in classical texts go back to this period and were already widely current in the books that eventually entered the library of the Museum at Alexandria.

II. THE LIBRARY OF THE MUSEUM AND HELLENISTIC SCHOLARSHIP

The increase of the book trade made it possible for private individuals to form libraries. Even if the tradition that sixth-century tyrants such as Pisistratus and Polycrates of Samos possessed large collections of books is discounted (Athenaeus 1.3a), it is clear that by the end of the fifth century private libraries existed; Aristophanes pokes fun at Euripides for drawing heavily on literary sources in composing his tragedies (*Frogs* 943), and his own work, being full of parody and allusion, must have depended to some extent on a personal book collection.

There is no trace of any general library maintained at the public expense at Athens, but it is likely that official copies of plays performed at the leading festivals such as the Dionysia were kept in the public record office. Pseudo-Plutarch (*Lives of the ten orators* 841f) ascribes to the orator Lycurgus (c. 390–324 B.C.) a proposal to keep official copies in this way, but the need would probably have arisen earlier. We know that after the original performance plays were revived from time to time. New copies of the text must have been needed for the actors, and if they had been obliged to obtain these by a process of transcription from private copies it would be surprising that such a complete range of plays survived into the Hellenistic age.

The advance of education and science in the fourth century made it only a matter of time before academic institutions with their own libraries were founded. It is not surprising to find Strabo reporting (13.1.54) that Aristotle built up a large collection of books, no doubt representing the wide diversity of interests in the Lyceum. This collection and that of the Academy were the models emulated shortly afterwards by the king of Egypt when establishing the famous library at Alexandria (Diog. Laert. 4.1, 5.51).

The main interests of the Lyceum were scientific and philosophical, but literary studies were not neglected. Aristotle himself
wrote on problems of interpretation in Homer besides his well-
known *Poetics* and *Rhetoric*; and in connection with the latter
there is some evidence that he and his successors were interested in
the study of Demosthenes' speeches.

Of much greater significance were the literary studies undertaken at the Museum in Alexandria. This was formally, as the
name implies, a temple in honour of the Muses presided over by a
priest. It was in fact the centre of a literary and scientific community, and it is essential not to underestimate this last aspect of
it; the librarian Eratosthenes (c. 295–c. 214 B.C.), though a literary
man, was also a scientist who achieved fame for his attempts to
measure the circumference of the earth, and it is probable that
other distinguished Alexandrian scientists were members. The
Museum was maintained at the expense of the king, and the members of it had study rooms and a hall in which they dined together.
They also received a stipend from the royal purse. It has been
observed that there is a superficial resemblance between this
institution and an Oxford or Cambridge college, but the analogy
breaks down in one important respect: there is no evidence that the
scholars of the Museum gave regular instruction to students. The
community was probably set up by Ptolemy Philadelphus c. 280
B.C., and it soon won a reputation, perhaps arousing jealousy
through the lavishness of its arrangements, for we find the satirist
Timon of Phlius writing of it c. 230 B.C. 'in populous Egypt they
fatten up many bookish pedants who quarrel unceasingly in the
Muses' bird-cage' (Athenaeus 1.22d).

An essential part of this foundation, housed in the same complex
of buildings or in the near neighbourhood, was the famous library.
It seems that some steps had been taken already in the previous
reign by the first Ptolemy to set up a library, by inviting Demetrius of Phalerum, the eminent pupil of Theophrastus, to come to
Alexandria for the purpose c. 295 B.C. The library grew rapidly.
The number of volumes is variously estimated by the ancient
sources, but owing to the inaccuracy with which all large figures
given by classical authors are transmitted it is difficult to calculate
the true figure. If we accept as true the tradition that in the third

century the library contained 200,000 or 490,000 volumes (Eusebius, *Praep. Evang.* 350b, Tzetzes, *prolegomena de comoedia*), allowance must be made for the fact that a single roll would contain no more than a Platonic dialogue of moderate length or an Attic play. There is also no means of knowing to what extent the libraries made it their policy to stock duplicate copies. But despite this uncertainty it is beyond doubt that great efforts were made to form a complete collection of Greek literature, and there are anecdotes which throw light on the spirit in which the business of the library was conducted. The king is said to have been determined to obtain an accurate text of Attic tragedy, and persuaded the Athenians to lend him the official copy from the public record office. The Athenians asked for a deposit of fifteen talents as security for the return of the texts, but having once obtained these the Egyptian authorities decided to keep them and forfeit their deposit (Galen 17(1).607). We also learn from Galen that in their anxiety to complete their collection the librarians were frequently deceived into purchasing forgeries of rare texts (15.105).

The task of the librarians in reducing to order the mass of books flowing into the Museum was enormous. The principle of arrangement in the library is not known, but one indication of the vast labours involved is that Callimachus, who was not himself chief librarian, compiled a kind of bibliographical guide to all branches of Greek literature, which occupied one hundred and twenty books (the *Pinakes*, frr. 429–53). Owing to the conditions of ancient book production the librarians faced certain problems that do not trouble their modern counterparts. Texts copied by hand are quickly liable to corruption; to make an accurate copy of even a short text is a harder task than is generally realized by those who have not had to do it. In addition to this pre-Hellenistic books gave no help to the reader in any difficulty. Consequently there must have been numerous passages where the author's meaning could no longer be discerned, and many others in which various copies of texts reaching the Museum showed serious discrepancies. The incentive that this gave to the librarians to put the text in order led to a great advance in learning and scholarly methods. It is no coincidence that five of the first six librarians (Zenodotus, Apollonius Rhodius, Eratosthenes, Aristophanes, and Aristarchus) were among the most famous literary men of their day, and it is in no small measure due to the success of their methods that classical Greek texts have come down to us in a state that is reasonably free from corruption.

In one case we can see clearly the influence which the scholars of the Museum exercised on the state of texts in common circulation. Of the many fragments of ancient copies of Homer a modest proportion are as early as the third century B.C. The text in these papyri is rather different from that now generally printed, and there are numerous lines added or omitted. But within a short time this type of text disappeared from circulation. This suggests that the scholars had not merely determined what the text of Homer should be, but succeeded in imposing this text as standard, either allowing it to be transcribed from a master copy placed at the disposal of the public, or alternatively employing a number of professional scribes to prepare copies for the book market. Discrepancies in the text of authors other than Homer were probably less serious, but not enough early papyri are preserved for us to form a judgement; it is a reasonable assumption that the Alexandrians did what was necessary to prepare a standard text of all authors commonly read by the educated public.

After the standardization of texts the next feature of Alexandrian scholarship that merits attention is the development of a number of aids to the reader. The first step was to ensure that fifth-century books coming from Attica, some of which must have been written in the old alphabet, were all transliterated into the normal Greek spelling of the Ionic alphabet. Until 403 B.C. Athens had officially used the older alphabet in which the letter epsilon represented the vowels epsilon, epsilon-iota and eta; similarly omicron was used for omicron, omicron-upsilon and omega. The drawbacks of this script need no comment, and already before the end of the fifth century the more accurate Ionic alphabet was being used for some Athenian inscriptions on stone: probably the same was true of Athenian books. Nevertheless it is certain that some texts reaching the Alexandrian library were in the old script, for we find Aristarchus explaining a difficulty in Pindar as due to misinterpretation of the old alphabet; he tells us that at *Nemeans* 1.24 an adjective which appears to be in the nominative singular (ἐcλός) is incorrect for metrical reasons and must be understood as the accusative plural (ἐcλούς) (cf. schol. ad loc.). Another point at which the critics showed their awareness of the old alphabet was Aristophanes, *Birds* 66. It is important to note that the adoption of the Ionic alphabet for early Attic texts has been recognized as the norm since the Alexandrian period. In contrast to the procedure used for editing texts in all other literatures there has never been an attempt to restore the original orthography of the authors in its entirety.

A second aid for readers was an improvement in the method of punctuation and the invention of the system of accentuation, both commonly ascribed to Aristophanes of Byzantium. In a text lacking word-division the addition of a few accents gave the reader a substantial help, and it is rather strange that they did not immediately come to be regarded as indispensable to a written text. But though they were sometimes written over words that would otherwise have been difficult or ambiguous, in general it is hard to see what principle determines their addition in ancient books, and they were not regularly added until the beginning of the tenth century.

Although these improvements in the outward appearance of literary texts had significant and lasting results, they were of far less importance than the advances in scholarly method made by members of the Museum. The need to establish the text of Homer and the other classical authors inspired scholars to define and apply the principles of literary scholarship more systematically than had been attempted before. Discussion of difficult passages led not merely to the production of a reliable text of the authors in question, but to commentaries in which the problems were discussed and interpretations offered. There had previously been some isolated works devoted to Homer; Aristotle had written on problems in the text, and much earlier Theagenes of Rhegium (c. 525 B.C.), perhaps spurred by Xenophanes' attacks on the immorality of the Homeric gods, had attempted to remove this embarrassing weakness of the poems by resorting to allegorical interpretation. But now a mass of critical literature was produced for the first time. Some of it was highly specialized; for instance Zenodotus apparently wrote a life of Homer and a treatise on the length of time required for the action of the *Iliad*. Aristophanes wrote on grammatical regularity (περὶ ἀναλογίας) and compiled corrections and supplements to the bibliographical guide to Greek literature that Callimachus had composed. Work of this character was not confined to Homer; we hear of monographs on the characters of comedy by Hypsicrates and on the myths of tragedy by Thersagoras (P. Oxy. 2192). These explanatory works were in all cases written as separate texts independent of the work that they illustrated; apart from brief and rudimentary notes commentary on an author was not at this date added to the margin of a text, but occupied another book. In the case of Homer especially, and less frequently in lyric poetry, drama, Demosthenes, and Plato, a number of conventional signs were put into the margin of the text to indicate that the passage was interesting in some way, for instance corrupt or spurious, and that the reader would find comment on the point in the explanatory monograph. Although very little survives from this class of literature in its original form, there is one famous example in the papyrus of part of a work by the later scholar Didymus (1st cent. B.C.) on Demosthenes (P. Berol. 9780). But in general our knowledge of these works comes from fragments of them that have been incorporated into the later form of commentary known as scholia; these are regularly transmitted in the margins of medieval manuscripts, and more will be said of their history below.

We come now to a brief discussion of the critical signs and the commentaries. The first and most important sign was the *obelos*, a horizontal stroke placed in the margin just to the left of a verse. It was used already by Zenodotus, and indicated that the verse was spurious. Some other signs of less importance and frequency seem to have been devised by Aristophanes. The final development of the system as applied to Homer was made by Aristarchus, who produced complete editions of both *Iliad* and *Odyssey*. He used six signs: apart from the *obelos* we find the *diplē* >, which indicated any noteworthy point of language or content; the dotted *diplē* (περιεcτιγμένη) >̣ referred to a verse where Aristarchus differed in his text from Zenodotus; the *asteriskos* ✳ marked a verse incorrectly repeated in another passage; the *asteriskos* in conjunction with the *obelos* marked the interpolation of verses from another passage; and finally the *antisigma* Ɔ marked passages in which the order of the lines had been disturbed (Plates I and II).

It is natural that a complicated system of this kind, which had the drawback that the reader wishing to discover a scholar's reasons for placing a sign at any given point had to consult another book, commended itself to scholarly readers only. No more than a tiny proportion of the surviving papyri, about fifteen of more than six hundred, display them. In the medieval manuscripts of the tenth century and later they are usually omitted; but there is one famous and important exception to this rule, the tenth-century Venetian manuscript of the *Iliad* (Marc. gr. 454), which preserves a vast collection of marginal scholia. As the commentary on an author was written in the margins by this date, and not in a separate book, there was perhaps less incentive to transcribe the signs; but fortunately the scribe of the Venice manuscript was determined to copy what he found in his exemplar without omission. Consequently the book shows a great number of the conventional signs, and it is by far the most complete and reliable source of our knowledge of this feature of the work carried out by the Alexandrians. It does not, however, always agree exactly in the use of the signs at the points where it can be compared with a papyrus, and there are signs which are not linked with a corresponding note in the scholia.

Though the Homer commentaries of Aristarchus and his colleagues are lost, enough of them can be reconstructed from the extant scholia, which are more copious than those on any other Greek author, to allow us to form a good judgement of the scholarly methods of the time. It is clear that many copies of the Homeric text reached the Museum from widely different sources; the scholia refer to texts coming from such places as Massilia, Sinope, and Argos. These were sifted and evaluated by the scholars, but it is not clear which text, if any, was taken to be the most authoritative. The procedure which made the Alexandrians notorious was their readiness to condemn lines as spurious (ἀθετεῖν, ἀθέτηϲιϲ). Their reasons for doing so, though possessing a certain specious logic, generally fail to convince the modern reader. One ground frequently alleged was undignified language or conduct (ἀπρέπεια). The first passage of the *Iliad* which was condemned in this way will serve as an example. At the opening of book I (29–31) Agamemnon, when refusing to release Chryseis, says to her father the priest: 'I will not set her free; no, sooner shall old age overtake her in my palace at Argos, far from her home, where she shall work the loom and serve my bed'. The lines are obelized in the Venice manuscript, and the ancient commentary on them reads as follows: 'the lines are athetized because they weaken the force of the meaning and the threatening tone . . . it is also improper for Agamemnon to make such remarks'. Another typical instance occurs at *Iliad* 3.423–6, where Zenodotus rejected the lines on the ground that it is unbecoming for the goddess Aphrodite to carry a seat for Helen. And naturally all passages that tended to show the gods in an unflattering light were an easy target for critics of this frame of mind; hence there were some who athetized the affair between Ares and Aphrodite in *Odyssey* VIII.

Scholars capable of treating a text so drastically, especially in their willingness to condemn lines as spurious for inadequate reasons, might have done great damage to the text. But fortunately for subsequent generations of readers the Alexandrians avoided the temptation to incorporate all their proposed alterations into the text itself and were content to note proposals in their commentaries; but for this restraint our text of Homer would have been seriously disfigured. It is interesting to note that most of their proposals did not commend themselves sufficiently to the ancient reader to become part of the ordinary text in circulation; this of course is not necessarily to be taken as evidence of the superior judgement of the reading public in antiquity, which may scarcely have given any thought to such matters. A count of the emendations made by the Alexandrians has shown that of the 413 alterations proposed by Zenodotus only 6 are found as readings in all our papyri and manuscripts, and only a further 34 in a majority of them, whereas 240 are never so found. Of the 83 emendations that can be ascribed to Aristophanes only one found universal approval, and 6 others appear in a majority of witnesses to the text, while 42 are never found in the text. Aristarchus was more influential, but even his suggestions were not readily accepted; out of 874 readings 80 are universally found, 160 occur in the majority of texts, and 132 in the scholia only.

It would be wrong to end this account of the Alexandrians without mentioning some more favourable specimens of their criticism. Certain parts of their work were of a high enough standard to be of permanent value. Their attempts to identify verses or passages of dubious authenticity were not always based on weak reasoning. They were suspicious of *Iliad* X, the story of Dolon, and had doubtless recognized that it was different in style from the rest of the *Iliad* and loosely attached to the narrative. In Odysseus' descent to the underworld in *Odyssey* XI Aristarchus noticed that lines 568–626 did not belong to the main thread of the story. Perhaps most interesting was the observation by Aristarchus and Aristophanes that the *Odyssey* ought to end at 23.296. Modern scholars might prefer to avoid condemning these passages as spurious and to regard them instead as products of a later stage of composition than the main body of the text; but this does not detract from the merit of the critics' observations.

Another matter for which the ancients, especially Aristarchus, deserve praise is the development of the critical principle that the best guide to an author's usage is the corpus of his own writings, and therefore difficulties ought to be explained wherever possible by reference to other passages in the same author (Ὅμηρον ἐξ Ὁμήρου σαφηνίζειν). This notion underlies many notes in the scholia which state that a given word or expression is more typically Homeric than the alternative possible reading. The principle was naturally liable to abuse if employed by a critic of mediocre intelligence, as happened all too often; for it might be taken to imply that if a literary text contains an expression that is both unique and difficult it must be modified in order to agree with the author's general practice. Such an extreme interpretation of the rule could have led to disastrous results, and it is greatly to the credit of Aristarchus that he appears to have devised a complementary principle, that there are many words or expressions in Homer which occur only once but should be accepted as genuine and left standing in the text (cf. schol. A on *Iliad* 3. 54). Problems which require the correct application of these principles still cause great difficulty to critics of the present day.

Finally it should be made clear that though the critics concerned themselves mainly with notes of a linguistic or antiquarian character, they were not blind to the literary merits of the poetry, and occasionally offer an apt comment on a fine passage. An example may be taken from the famous episode in *Iliad* VI, where Hector takes his leave of Andromache and Astyanax, and the poet describes how the child is frightened at the sight of the plume on his father's helmet. The critics commented: 'these verses are so full of descriptive power that the reader does not simply hear the sound of them but sees the scene before him; the poet took this scene from everyday life and copied it with supreme success'. Shortly afterwards comes the comment: 'while representing everyday life with such success the poet does not in the least destroy the stately tone appropriate to epic' (cf. schol. T on *Iliad* 6.467, 474, from MS. Burney 86 in the British Museum).

Most of this account of Alexandrian scholarship has been concerned with the text of Homer because of the copious evidence available. But it is certain that Alexandrian work on other authors was of great importance, and a few facts may be briefly enumerated. The text of tragedy was established, probably by reference to the Athenian official copy, as was mentioned above. The colometry of the lyric passages was devised by Aristophanes of Byzantium, so that they were no longer written out as if they were prose. A number of treatises on various aspects of the plays were written, and Aristophanes is credited with the authorship of the arguments outlining the plot prefixed to the plays; it is generally held, however, that the arguments now surviving are either not his work or have been considerably altered in the course of time. Marginal signs to guide the reader were much more sparingly used than in editions of Homer. The commonest was probably the letter chi, which indicated a point of interest in much the same way as the *diplē* in the Homeric text; this sign is mentioned in the scholia and occasionally is found in a medieval manuscript. A specially interesting feature of Alexandrian work on tragedy is the detection of lines altered or added by actors, generally in the plays of Euripides, who was more popular than the other dramatists. These interpolations are probably quite numerous, but it is not easy in every case to be absolutely certain that the line or lines in question are not original; and if they are clearly late, it may be obscure whether they should be attributed to Hellenistic actors (or more strictly producers) or to later interpolators. The scholia, however, which depend ultimately on Hellenistic work, do designate some lines as actors' interpolations. At *Medea* 85–8 the scholiast accuses the actors of misunderstanding the proper punctuation of 85 and altering the text in consequence; he adds rightly that 87 is superfluous, and its origin is not far to seek. At *Orestes* 1366–8 the chorus announce that one of the Phrygians is about to come out onto the stage through the front door of the palace, whereas in 1369–71 the Phrygian says that he jumped down off the roof. According to the scholia the original stage direction required the actor to make the jump, but this was regarded as dangerous, and so the actor descended by the back of the scenery and came out through the front door. In an effort to disguise this change 1366–8 were composed. Though these lines are needed in order to give a proper introduction to the new character and are linguistically blameless, they can be used to put us on the track of a more extensive interpolation.

Other Alexandrian works that should not go without mention are the editions of comedy, Pindar and the lyric poets. Here too the colometry had to be determined, and at one point we can see how Aristophanes rightly used it to show that a phrase which did not correspond metrically with the antistrophe should be deleted from the text (schol. on Pindar, *Olympians* 2.48). The task of editing comedy was undertaken in the same way as that of tragedy. We do not know what copies of the text were taken as the basis of the edition, but the rich collection of material contained in the surviving scholia to Aristophanes shows that his plays were studied with energy and enthusiasm.

III. OTHER HELLENISTIC WORK

The great age of Alexandrian work occurred in the third and second centuries; in the early part of the period the Museum was unrivalled. After a time, however, the rulers of Pergamum decided to challenge this position by founding a library of their own. The scheme is primarily associated with the name of king Eumenes II (197–159 B.C.): vast buildings were erected, and excavation by German archaeologists in the last century brought to light some sections of the library. Much less is known of the Pergamene library than of the Alexandrian. The librarians clearly undertook bibliographical studies on a large scale, and literary men found it useful to consult their work along with that of the Alexandrians (Athenaeus 8.336d, Dion. Hal., *de Dinarcho* 1). But the Pergamene scholars are not credited with editions of the classical authors and appear to have confined themselves to short monographs on specific points, sometimes directly in controversy with the Alexandrians. Their interests were not exclusively literary; Polemon (c. 220–160 B.C.), though he collected examples of parody, was first and foremost a student of topography and inscriptions; these important topics of historical scholarship had both remained outside the usual range of studies undertaken in the Museum. The most famous name linked with Pergamum is that of Crates (c. 200–c. 140 B.C.). He is known to have worked on Homer; some of his proposals for emending the text are preserved in the scholia, and he paid special attention to geography in Homer, attempting to reconcile it with Stoic views on the subject. He was also the first Greek to give lectures on literary subjects in Rome (see p. 19).

The Stoics gave a good deal of attention to literature. To them an important part of interpreting Homer was the application of allegorical explanations, and one of their treatises on this by a certain Heraclitus has survived. Apart from Homeric studies they dealt with grammar and linguistics, elaborating a fuller terminology than had previously existed. But the first formal Greek grammar was by Dionysius Thrax (c. 170–c. 90 B.C.); he appears to have been just old enough to have been a pupil of Aristarchus, but is not to be counted as an Alexandrian in the full sense, since his teaching was done largely in Rhodes. His grammar begins with a definition of the parts of the subject, the last of which, described by the author as the noblest of all, is the criticism of poetry. He then goes on to deal with parts of speech, declensions and conjugations, but matters of syntax and style are not discussed. This brief guide enjoyed a lasting vogue, as is attested by the volume of commentary upon it written by later grammarians. It was the basis of Greek grammars until comparatively modern times, and had the distinction of being translated into Syriac and Armenian in late antiquity.

The best Alexandrian work had now been completed; the decline of the school was brought about by the action of Ptolemy Euergetes II, who instituted a persecution of Greek literary men (c. 145–4 B.C.); among others Dionysius Thrax, who had begun his career in Alexandria, went into exile. The only eminent figure in the remaining part of the Hellenistic age is Didymus (1st cent. B.C.). He achieved notoriety in the ancient world through the bulk of his writings (but the story that 4,000 books came from his pen must be an exaggeration, even if it is assumed that many of these may not have been any longer than modern pamphlets). His name is mentioned frequently in scholia, and it is clear that his work extended over the whole range of classical poetry. As far as can be judged from the fragmentary nature of the evidence his activity was not so much composition of original commentaries as compilation from the already huge mass of critical work, and he is important because his compilations were evidently one of the main sources of material used by the later scholars who drew up the scholia in their present form. One book of his whose influence can be traced in extant works is his collection of rare or difficult words from tragedy (τραγικαὶ λέξεις); from this source derive a number of entries in the later dictionaries such as Hesychius. Didymus is also important for his work on prose authors; he commented on Thucydides and the orators, and the only substantial passage from his writings that is still preserved is part of a monograph on Demosthenes (P. Berol. 9780). This book when complete contained notes on speeches IX–XI and XIII. It confirms the usual view of Didymus as a compiler without any great originality or independence of mind; there are many quotations from sources otherwise lost, such as Philochorus and Theopompus, whereas Didymus' own contribution is very small. He goes so far as to record without comment a report that speech XI is a compilation of Demosthenic topics put together by Anaximenes of Lampsacus; yet this view, whether correct or not, demands discussion from any commentator. Not all interesting passages are discussed, but this kind of monograph was often less comprehensive in scope than its modern counterpart would be. On the other hand it is a welcome surprise to find that the commentary, instead of being confined to matters of linguistic interest or of value only to teachers of rhetoric, deals with chronological problems and historical interpretation.

IV. BOOKS AND SCHOLARSHIP IN THE ROMAN REPUBLIC

Although written records may have existed from very early times, Latin literature did not begin until the third century B.C. Inspired by Greek example, it was probably committed from its first beginnings to the form of book which had long been standard in the Greek world, the papyrus roll. By the middle of the second century Rome had a considerable body of literature of her own, poetry and plays and prose, and the growth of such a sophisticated literary and philosophical society as the Scipionic circle implies that books circulated freely within a limited class of Roman society. A century later, when Cicero and Varro were at their peak, the world of books had become very much a part of the world of the educated Roman.

Little is known about the ways in which Latin literature was handed down during the first two hundred years of its life. In the days when there was no organized machinery for the multiplication and circulation of books, no established libraries to preserve them, and before scholarship had begun to take a critical interest in their contents, the channels of transmission must have been casual and hazardous. Some works fared better than others. The national epics of Naevius and Ennius enjoyed a special status and received some scholarly attention at a comparatively early date. Prose was probably less fortunate. The one work of Cato which has been transmitted to us directly, his *De agri cultura*, appears to have been mangled and modernized through frequent and uncontrolled copying. There seems to have been no corpus of his speeches available in Cicero's day; Cicero protests against the neglect into which they have fallen (*Brutus* 65f.) and says that he had managed to gather together more than 150 of them. Dramatic texts had their own particular hazards, as we can see clearly in the case of Plautus. His plays were written for performance, bought by the magistrate or his agent, and transmitted initially as stage copies. We know from the prologue to the *Casina* that the plays were revived from time to time, and a subsequent restaging would mean that the script was cut, padded out, recast, or modernized to suit the taste of the producer or the audience. There are still traces of this early tampering with the text in our manuscripts; the different versions of the last scene of the *Poenulus* are an obvious example. Plautus' popularity was so great that he readily attracted spurious accretions and we are told (Gellius 3.3.11) that at one time no less than 130 plays were circulating under his name. Terence's plays enjoyed a more sheltered transmission, but some manuscripts preserve an alternative ending of the *Andria* which may go back to an early date.

This period of fluid transmission may account for many of the corruptions in these texts. In one place Varro has preserved for us (*L.L.*7.81) the authentic description of the shifty Ballio sidling through the door (*Pseud.* 955):

> ut transvorsus, non provorsus cedit, quasi cancer solet.

An attempt to get rid of the archaic *provorsus* produced the flat version of the line presented by both the surviving recensions of the text, the Ambrosian palimpsest (A) and the remaining manuscripts (P):

> non prorsus, verum ex transverso cedit, quasi cancer solet.

But in the *Miles Gloriosus* (24) A preserves the Plautine *epityra estur insanum bene* ('his cheese and olive spread is madly good eating') while both P and Varro (*L.L.* 7.86) read *insane*. In general the text of Plautus seems to have suffered surprisingly little since the days of Varro. The survival of what we have of early Latin literature is largely due, in the first instance, to the renewed interest which was taken in these writers during the last century of the Republic, and the comparative soundness of their texts we owe in part to the work of the early Roman grammarians.

According to Suetonius, the study of grammar was first introduced into Rome by the Homeric scholar Crates of Mallos. Crates came to Rome on a diplomatic mission, probably in 168 B.C., broke his leg in a sewer and turned his enforced convalescence to good use by giving lectures on poetry. The gradual infiltration of Hellenistic culture was doubtless governed by more complex factors than the breaking of a bone, but we must be thankful to Suetonius for turning his colourful spotlight onto a point in time when the Romans, who by the death of Ennius had a

well-established literary tradition of their own, were ready to take
an academic interest in their literature and language. He names
two grammarians of this early period, C. Octavius Lampadio and
Q. Vargunteius. Lampadio worked on the *Punic War* of Naevius
and may have been interested in Ennius too, but the evidence is
suspect: a copy of the *Annals* thought to have been corrected by
Lampadio himself was still extant in the second century A.D.
(Gellius 18.5.11). Vargunteius is reported to have given well-
attended lectures on the *Annals*. Outside professional circles, a
strong preoccupation with literary and linguistic matters is
apparent in the poetry of Accius and Lucilius.

But the first of the great Roman grammarians was L. Aelius
Stilo, of whom our ancient authorities speak with the highest
respect. A firm and perhaps significant date in his life is the year
100 B.C., when he followed Metellus Numidicus into exile at
Rhodes. It has been plausibly conjectured that he may have
acquired his knowledge of Alexandrian scholarship there, from
Aristarchus' own pupil Dionysius Thrax. At all events, Aelius is
the first scholar who is recorded as having employed at Rome the
conventional critical signs of the Alexandrians. The evidence for
this is found in a remarkable document known as the *Anecdoton
Parisinum*. This tract, preserved in a manuscript written at Monte
Cassino towards the end of the eighth century (Paris lat. 7530),
describes the critical signs used by Aristarchus and his successors.
It almost certainly derives, with similar accounts, from the lost
De notis of Suetonius. An important sentence reads (when some of
the names have been conjecturally restored):

His solis [*sc.* notis] in adnotationibus Ennii Lucilii et historicorum
[= writers of comedy?] usi sunt Varro Servius Aelius aeque et pos-
tremo Probus, qui illas in Vergilio et Horatio et Lucretio apposuit, ut
Homero Aristarchus.

The name Aelius is not in doubt, and his interest in Plautus and
the elucidation of archaic texts would naturally involve him in
scholarship of the Alexandrian type. Although Plautus is no substitute for Homer, the nature of his text and the circumstances
of its transmission presented problems similar to those which had
exercised Hellenistic scholars and for which their critical methods

had an obvious relevance. Plautus' text needed to be standardized: there were a mass of spurious plays, and the genuine ones contained later accretions and interpolations and varied considerably from copy to copy. The production of a list of the genuine plays had already exercised Accius; Stilo occupied himself with the problem, as did others, and pronounced twenty-five to be genuine. His son-in-law Servius Claudius was certainly interested in detecting interpolations, for Cicero speaks of his skill in saying 'hic versus Plauti non est, hic est' (*Fam.* 9.16.4). Aelius had a great influence on his pupil Varro (116–27 B.C.). Varro was a polymath, with a special interest in literary history, drama, and linguistics. He seems to have played a decisive part in selecting which plays of Plautus should be passed on to posterity as the genuine article. Although he accepted others as authentic, Varro singled out twenty-one plays as being unquestionably Plautine and this canon, known as the *fabulae Varronianae*, must coincide with the twenty-one plays which have come down to us. The establishment of the text of these early writers involved other questions of textual criticism besides authenticity, and Varro's awareness of routine problems is clear from his definition of *emendatio* as *recorrectio errorum qui per scripturam dictionemve fiunt* (fr. 236F).

Another activity for which there was ample scope was the interpretation of obsolete or difficult words. Evidence for this activity abounds in Varro and in what poor remains we have of the first Latin lexicon, the important and influential *De significatu verborum* of the Augustan grammarian Verrius Flaccus. This survives, partly in the abbreviated version made by Pompeius Festus, partly in the still more jejune epitome of Festus made by Paul the Deacon in the eighth century, with scattered references elsewhere. For instance, the *Nervolaria* of Plautus contained a trenchant description of decrepit prostitutes:

scrattae, scruppedae (?), strittabillae, sordidae.

These ladies were already encrusted with learning by Varro's time: he quotes (*L.L.* 7.65) the views of three different writers on the second word. Since the interpretations of these difficult words were often written between the lines of one's copy (as Varro himself testifies, *L.L.* 7.107), they could easily win a place in the text or give rise to doublets. For instance, at *Epidicus* 620 the P recension offers the reading *gravastellus* ('little old man'), while A has *ravistellus* ('little man with grey hair'); both variants were known to Festus and so go back at least to Augustan times. At *Miles Gloriosus* 1180 we have three variants, all ancient: the authentic reading is *exfafillato bracchio* ('uncovered'), preserved by P and attested by ancient authorities; but *expapillato* ('bared to the breast') can be traced back to antiquity; and A appears to offer a third variant (*expalliolato*), which must be at least as old as A itself (5th cent.).

The expansion of literature and scholarship in the late Republic was accompanied by important developments of a practical nature, and it is not surprising that during this period we first hear of plans for a public library at Rome and of the existence of more organized facilities for publishing books. There were already large private libraries. Greek books in particular had flowed in as part of the *praeda belli* and Lucullus' library, open to those who wished to use it, was famed. Cicero took enormous trouble to build up a fine collection of books; he received much help and advice from his friend Atticus and was fortunate to inherit the library of the scholar Servius Claudius. But it was Caesar who first planned a large public library. He commissioned Varro (among whose many works was a *De bibliothecis*) to collect books for it, but the plan was not realized: the first public library at Rome was founded in the Atrium Libertatis by C. Asinius Pollio in 39 B.C.

We hear nothing of a book trade at Rome before the time of Cicero. Then the booksellers and copyists (both initially called *librarii*) carried on an active trade, but do not seem to have met the high standards of a discriminating author, for Cicero complains of the poor quality of their work (*Q.f.* 3.4.5, 5.6). It was perhaps to fill this gap that Atticus, who had lived for a long time in Greece and had experience of a well-established book trade, put his staff of trained *librarii* at the service of his friends. It is not easy to see whether Atticus is at any given moment obliging Cicero as a friend or in a more professional capacity, but it is clear that Cicero could depend on him to provide all the services of a high-class publisher. Atticus would carefully revise a work for him, criticize points of style or content, discuss the advisability of publication or the suitability of a title, hold private readings of the new book, send out complimentary copies, organize its distribution. His standards of execution were of the highest and his name a guarantee of quality.

From the exchange of letters between Cicero and Atticus we can get a good idea of the casual and fluid nature of publication in the ancient world. There was no copyright or royalty (hence the importance of literary patronage) and private circulation could easily pass by degrees into full-scale publication; an author could incorporate changes into a published text by asking his friends to alter their copies, but other copies would remain unaltered. Cicero drastically reshaped his *Academica* when Atticus was in the process of having copies made and consoled him for the effort wasted with the promise of a superior version. But copies of the first draft were in existence; both 'editions' survived, and we have a more substantial part of the first than of the second. Cicero also protests that his *Oratio in Clodium et Curionem*, of which fragments have survived in some scholia, was published without his consent. In the *Orator* (29) he had incorrectly attributed some lines of Aristophanes to Eupolis and asked Atticus to rectify the mistake quickly in all copies. In this case he succeeded in correcting the tradition which has come down to us, but he was not so lucky when in the *Republic* (2.8) he wished to alter *Phliuntii* (as he had wrongly called the inhabitants of Phlius) to *Phliasii*; the sole manuscript of the work which has survived still has *Phliuntii*, and it is the modern editor who makes the change which Cicero requested.

V. DEVELOPMENTS UNDER THE EARLY EMPIRE

By the end of the Roman Republic the institutions and processes which govern and guard the transmission of the written word were already in existence, and under Augustus and his successors they were refined and consolidated. The book trade flourished and we soon hear of the names of established booksellers: Horace speaks of the Sosii, later Quintilian and Martial tell of Tryphon, Atrectus, and others. By the time of the Younger Seneca book collecting had become a form of extravagant ostentation. Augustus founded two public libraries, one in 28 B.C. in the Temple of Apollo on the Palatine, the other, not long afterwards, in the Campus Martius.

Thereafter libraries were a common form of both private and imperial munificence, in Rome and the provinces; one of the most famed and lasting was the Bibliotheca Ulpia founded by Trajan, which long survived the disasters of fire and strife and was still standing in the fifth century. Given an enlightened emperor, patronage could foster scholarship as well as literature: under Augustus Hyginus was appointed Palatine librarian and Verrius Flaccus was made tutor to the imperial children. It was during this period that school education too took the form which it was to keep for centuries and, with the state taking an increasing interest in education, it became standardized throughout the Roman world.

Secondary education at Rome was provided by the *grammaticus* and this largely consisted of the careful reading and detailed interpretation of poetry. Prose was more the concern of the *rhetor*, but their provinces to a certain extent overlapped. An important development was begun sometime after 26 B.C. by Q. Caecilius Epirota, a freedman of Atticus, who instituted in the school which he had opened the practice of studying Vergil and other modern writers. Vergil's entry into the normal school curriculum may have been at the expense of Ennius. From now on a successful poet, a Horace or an Ovid, saw his works passing into the school syllabus before he was decently dead and this continued until the archaizing reaction at the end of the first century interrupted the process and froze the canon of classical authors. Although poets like Horace and Lucan continued to be read in the schools, two poets were studied above all others, Vergil and, more surprisingly, Terence; in prose Cicero and Sallust occupied a similarly pre-eminent position.

The intense and minute study which was devoted to commonly read authors by expert and inexpert alike could affect their text for both good and ill. The large demand for popular works and those in the school curriculum might be expected to have flooded the market with poor copies and, while the close attention of scholars and grammarians would tend to safeguard the purity of the text, it is unfortunately only too apparent that scholars at all periods and with the best intentions have the power to deprave as well as to emend a text which passes through their hands. On the whole, neither the ill effects of popularization nor the interference of pedants appear to have muddied the main stream of our textual traditions nearly as much as might have been feared, but there is interesting evidence of some early corruption in standard authors. As early as the sixties Seneca (*Epist.* 94.28) quotes one of the unfinished lines of the *Aeneid, audentis fortuna iuvat* (10.284), with the supplement *piger ipse sibi obstat.* The gnomic quality of the half-line and the inviting vacuum which it left to be filled might so easily have generated a proverb that it is going too far to assume that Seneca actually used an interpolated copy of Vergil, but there is no doubt that those who wished to improve the national epic were already at work. Livy offers a clearer case. Quintilian, writing about thirty years after Seneca, tells us (9.4.74) that the preface to Livy's history began with the dactylic opening *facturusne operae pretium sim*, and that this should be preferred to the corrupt version current in his day. We owe the stylistic nicety of Livy's opening words, with their epic ring, to Quintilian, for all the manuscripts of the Nicomachean family, on which we depend at this point, read *facturusne sim operae pretium.* In the next century Gellius complains (20.6.14) that Sallust's *maiores vestrum* (*Cat.* 33.2) had been corrupted to *maiores vestri*, and the surviving manuscripts show that his complaint was justified. In the case of such authors it was never too soon for the textual critic to ply his trade.

The great Augustan scholar Verrius Flaccus still devoted his attention to the early writers, but his contemporary Julius Hyginus, a man of wide learning, wrote a work on Vergil which included observations on his text. He would read *sensus . . . amaror* for *sensu . . amaro* at *Georgics* 2.247 on the alleged authority of a manuscript *ex domo atque ex familia Vergilii* (Gellius 1.21); in *Aeneid* 12.120 he would emend *velati lino* to *velati limo* (*limus* being a sacrificial apron), more plausibly perhaps, but it is difficult not to conclude that Hyginus was more interested in improving Vergil than Vergil's text. Remmius Palaemon, an influential grammarian, continued to put the emphasis on modern authors, and Asconius, who stands out amongst ancient commentators for his good sense and integrity, wrote on Cicero, Vergil and Sallust. But of the scholars of the first century the most famous in his own day and in later ages was M. Valerius Probus of Beirut. His dates fall somewhere between A.D. 20–105 and his period of scholarly activity probably belongs to the closing decades of the century. He is a controversial figure, for our information about him is scanty and easily exaggerated. Such facts as we have about his life come from Suetonius (*De gramm.* 24). He tells us that Probus, disappointed in his hopes of military promotion, turned to the study of the old authors whom he had learned to admire at school in the provinces and who were now out of fashion at Rome. He gathered together a large number of texts and went through them in accordance with Alexandrian methods, providing aids to the reader and adding critical signs in the margin: *multaque exemplaria contracta emendare ac distinguere et adnotare curavit.* He did not set himself up as a teacher, but had a few followers with whom he would very occasionally read texts; he published only a few short pieces, but left behind a fair-sized *silva observationum sermonis antiqui.* His use of the tools of Alexandrian criticism is attested by the *Anecdoton Parisinum* (see p. 20): he is credited with the use of certain *notae* (the *asteriscus, asteriscus cum obelo, diplē*) and his employment of others is stated or implied in later commentaries; he is said to have worked specifically on Vergil, Horace, and Lucretius. Traces of his activity, some perhaps apocryphal, are found in later commentators, Servius and Donatus, and in Gellius. For instance, at *Aen* 1.44 he wished to emend *pectore* to *tempore*; at 8.406 he found the expression *coniugis infusus gremio* unbecoming and read *infusum*; at 10.173 he put a comma after *trecentos*; at 10.539 he would replace *armis* by *albis*; in Terence's *Adelphi* he assigned the words *quid festinas, mi Geta* (323) to Sostrata; in Sallust's *Catiline* (5.4: *satis eloquentiae, sapientiae parum*) he wished to foist upon Sallust the word *loquentia.* Little of this inspires confidence. It is not certain that he collated manuscripts, but he may have had access to at least one authoritative text: he claimed that his knowledge of Vergil's use of *i* and *e* in such accusatives as *urbes/urbis* and *turrem/turrim* was based on a manuscript corrected by Vergil's own hand (Gellius 13.21.1–8). It is difficult to assess his influence on our textual traditions. Probus has been such a convenient peg upon which to hang flimsy reconstructions of the early history of a number of texts that he has been credited with authoritative editions of Vergil, Terence, Horace, Lucretius, Plautus, Persius, and Sallust. Evidence of his work on Vergil and Terence is found in Servius and Donatus and others, and we have a couple of isolated references to an interest in Plautus and Sallust. A life of Persius exists which claims to have been taken *de commentario Probi Valeri*. Of his alleged editions of Horace, Lucretius, and Plautus we have nothing but conjecture. Copies which he had corrected doubtless circulated in antiquity, some of his written work was available, and the views which he had expressed in his informal seminars, handed down by word of mouth, were accessible to a later generation, as Gellius demonstrates. Such a legacy would account for the evidence; much more is needed to demonstrate a series of authoritative editions shaping the main streams of transmission. At all events, there is little trace of Probus' known corrections and emendations in our extant manuscripts. This is reassuring evidence of the strong respect which the Romans had for the authentic text. Our tradition of Vergil shows how little the scholarly work which grew around an author need affect his text.

VI. ARCHAISM IN THE SECOND CENTURY

The marked decline in creative literature which set in during the second century was accompanied by a widespread academic interest in the writers of the past. In particular, there was a resurgence of enthusiasm for the early writers of Rome. The beginnings of this archaistic revival can be seen in Probus; it was encouraged by Hadrian, and its influence can be traced in the works of Fronto, Gellius, and Apuleius. This cult of the archaic, besides producing the most baroque effects in the prose of the period, ensured that the writers of the early Republic— Ennius, Plautus, Cato, and lesser figures as well—were taken down from the shelves and studied with passionate interest. To this revival we owe much of our knowledge of these early writers. Their chances of ultimate survival were slim; their language was too archaic and obscure for them to survive the narrowing interests and declining literacy of the ages to come, and, with some notable exceptions, they lived on only in the fragments and gossip preserved by Gellius or one of the later collectors of words and facts.

We can glean from the pages of the *Attic Nights* of Aulus Gellius a remarkable picture of the antiquarian book trade in the second century A.D. He tells us that he saw on sale in a bookshop at Rome an ancient Latin version of the *Annals* of Fabius Pictor (5.4.1), and relates how one of his teachers, in order to look up a word, procured at immense pains and expense an old manuscript of Ennius' *Annals* 'almost certainly corrected by Lampadio himself' (18.5.11). Valuable finds could still be made in the libraries of Rome and the provinces: at Rome he found a rare work by Aelius Stilo (16.8.2), at Patras a venerable copy of Livius Andronicus (18.9.5), at Tibur a manuscript of the Sullan historian Claudius Quadrigarius (9.14.3). One of his friends had a Vergil *mirandae vetustatis, emptum in Sigillariis xx aureis* (2.3.5), quite a find to make, if the story be true, at a Christmas fair. Fronto corroborates this antiquarian's paradise when he speaks of the high price and prestige attached in his day to manuscripts of Cato, Ennius, Cicero, and other Republican writers, when they had been written by such men as Lampadio and Aelius Stilo, edited by Tiro, or copied by Atticus or Nepos (*Ad M. Caes.* 1.7.4). It is tempting to think that the venerability of the books still to be found at this period has been exaggerated by commercial guile or the enthusiasm of the collector, and there seems little doubt that some of the more recherché items were expensive and egregious fakes; but the important features of the situation remain even if some of the details are suspect, the continued availability of Republican writings, the value attached to old authors and old manuscripts, and the keenness of scholars to hunt these out, sometimes merely in the hope of recovering an authentic reading. The practice of consulting other manuscripts in order to improve one's own copy must have happened at all times, but is only sporadically documented. The earliest evidence for anything on the scale of a recension goes back to this period and concerns the activity of Statilius Maximus, a known Ciceronian scholar of the late second or early third century. In a manuscript of Cicero's speeches discovered in 1417 (see p. 122) the second speech *De lege agraria* begins with a note which has travelled down with the text and takes us back so many centuries: *Statilius Maximus rursum emendavi ad Tyronem et Laecanianum et Domitium et alios veteres III. oratio XXIIII.* The general sense is clear: Statilius corrected the text with reference to a number of manuscripts, including one which claimed to go back to Tiro.

VII. THE COMPENDIUM AND THE COMMENTARY

The intellectual decline which had begun in the second century
was accelerated by the economic breakdown and political chaos
of the third, and no major literary figures emerged until the age of
Claudian. Many of the works produced during this period, though
they may be dreary in themselves, are important for the history of
classical texts. Some are important because they ensured the con-
tinuance of the classical tradition through the Middle Ages, when
the great works of literature were either not available or unsuited
to the needs and capacities of the time; some are still of value,
because their sources have been lost or mutilated. Among these
was the compendium. Florus had written an abridgement of
Roman history in the reign of Hadrian and an epitomized Livy
was known before that. These were followed in the third century
by Justinus' epitome of the Augustan writer Pompeius Trogus,
and in the fourth by the abbreviated histories of Eutropius, Aurelius Victor, and others unnamed. Some of these were widely read
in ages which could not assimilate the rich fare of Livy and had
lost the works of Tacitus. Already in the late third century the
emperor Tacitus (275–6) is alleged to have ordered that the works
of his namesake be copied ten times a year, *ne lectorum incuria
deperiret* (*Hist. Aug.* 27.10.3). This story is almost certainly a
fabrication of the late fourth century, but it is *ben trovato*. Apart
from the political disasters of the third century, which must have
taken their toll, the prominent absence of any real literature strongly
suggests that the preservation and transmission of the literary
heritage may likewise have suffered from neglect and misunderstanding. In other fields we have Festus' epitome of Verrius
Flaccus and Solinus' plundering of Pliny and Mela. The period
which produced so many potted handbooks was also the great
age of the commentator and scholiast, of whom the best known are
Acro and Porphyrio on Horace and the two great scholars of the
fourth century, Aelius Donatus and Servius; Donatus wrote on
Terence and Vergil, Servius contributed to the great Vergilian
commentary which bears his name. Donatus was also the author
of two grammars, the *Ars Minor* and *Maior*, which, together with

the *Institutiones grammaticae* of Priscian (6th cent.), provided the Middle Ages with their textbooks on grammar.

Two other compilations should be mentioned here in view of their significance for a later age, the *De compendiosa doctrina* of Nonius Marcellus, of uncertain date, and the *De nuptiis Philologiae* of Martianus Capella, written in the first part of the fifth century. The first is a dictionary, still valuable in that it contains many quotations from works now lost; the author appears to have excerpted two tragedies of Ennius himself. The *De nuptiis* is an allegorical treatise on the seven liberal arts, which appear as bridesmaids at the wedding of Mercury and Philology. By the late fourth century the liberal arts had been standardized as grammar, rhetoric, dialectic, arithmetic, music, geometry, and astronomy. The canonical seven were handed on to the Middle Ages and became, in theory, the basis of medieval education. In time they split into two groups, the *trivium* (grammar, rhetoric, dialectic) and the *quadrivium* (arithmetic, music, geometry, astronomy), an elementary and a more advanced course.

The grammars and compilations of late antiquity served a double purpose, for the quotations which they used to illustrate a word or fact provided the men of the Middle Ages with what was at times the sum of their knowledge of ancient literature, and allowed them to give their writings a veneer of learning which was pathetically at variance with the narrowness of their classical reading.

VIII. FROM ROLL TO CODEX

Between the second and fourth centuries a development took place which is of the utmost significance for the history of the book and therefore for the transmission of classical texts in general. This was the gradual disappearance of the roll in favour of the codex, that is to say the adoption of a book with essentially the same appearance as the one we use today.

Down to the second century A.D. the standard vehicle for all literary texts had been the papyrus roll, but from the earliest times an alternative medium had existed in the writing tablet, which consisted of a number of wax-coated boards fastened together with a thong or clasp. These were used throughout antiquity for letters, school-exercises, rough notes, and other casual purposes.

The Romans extended their scope by using them for legal documents and took the important step of replacing the wooden tablets with parchment leaves. These parchment notebooks (*membranae*) were in use by the end of the Republic, but it took a long time for them to achieve the status of books.

The first mention of literary works being published in parchment codices is found in Martial, in a number of poems written during the years 84–6. He emphasizes their compactness, their handiness for the traveller, and tells the reader the name of the shop where such novelties can be bought (1.2.7–8). Although there is one surviving fragment of a parchment codex in Latin written about A.D. 100 (the anonymous *De Bellis Macedonicis*, P. Lit. Lond. 121), the pocket editions which Martial was at pains to advertise were not a success. The codex did not come into use for pagan literature until the second century; but it rapidly gained ground in the third, and triumphed in the fourth. It could be made of either papyrus or parchment, but it was the parchment codex which eventually won the day. Although a papyrus roll might last as long as 300 years (Galen 18(2).630), the average life would be shorter, and parchment was a much more durable material; in time its toughness was to prove a vital factor in the survival of classical literature. The impulse to change the format of the book must have come from the early Christians; for while the pagan codex was a rarity in the second century, the codex form was already universal for biblical texts.

The advantages of the codex over the roll were many: it was handier, more capacious, easier to consult. Reference was made still easier by numbering the pages, and the addition of a list of contents guarded against forged interpolations and other interference with the text. These were important considerations in the days when much of life revolved around the authoritative texts of the Scriptures and the Code. The importance of the codex for religion and law is obvious. It had a relevance for literary texts too: a book which could hold the contents of several rolls meant that a corpus of related texts or what was considered the best of an author's work could be put under one cover, and this was attractive to an age which was inclined to trim its intellectual heritage to a manageable form.

The change from roll to codex involved the gradual but whole-sale transference of ancient literature from one form to another. This was the first major bottle-neck through which classical litera-ture had to pass. It must have been somewhat reduced in the process, but the losses are not easily specified or assessed. There was the danger that little-read works would not be transferred to codex form, and in time their rolls would perish. A voluminous author, if some of his rolls were not available at a critical moment, might never recover his missing books.

Since some of the earliest surviving books of antiquity are parch-ment codices of the fourth century, it may be appropriate to mention at this point the separate question of the main scripts used in Roman times for the production of books. These were Square Capitals, Rustic Capitals, Uncial, and Half-uncial. Square Capitals survive in only a few imposing manuscripts of Vergil and seem to have been reserved for *de luxe* editions. The main book-hand of the classical period was the Rustic Capital (Plate IX), more fluid than the square variety and written with the superficial negligence which has given it its name. The earliest specimen which we can date is a fragment of a poem on the battle of Actium (Naples, P. Herc. 817), written between the event it describes (31 B.C.) and the destruction of Herculaneum (A.D. 79), where it was found. This hand continued in much the same form down to the early sixth century; famous manuscripts in this script are the codex Bembinus of Terence (Vat. lat. 3226) and the great codices of Vergil, the Mediceus, Palatinus, and Romanus. A handsome rounded script, Uncial, emerged as a fully developed hand in the fourth century and lasted until the ninth. An early example is the Vatican palimpsest of the *De republica* (Vat. lat. 5757 of the late 4th or early 5th cent., Plate X); one of the finest is the fifth-century Puteanus of Livy's third decade (Paris lat. 5730, Plate XI). The admixture of minuscule forms led to mixed forms of Uncial, in particular Half-uncial. There are a number of classical texts written in this script, mainly papyri, but it was predominantly used for Christian writings.

IX. PAGANISM AND CHRISTIANITY IN THE FOURTH
CENTURY

The fourth century witnessed the final clash between Christianity and paganism. In 312 the first Christian emperor Constantine dramatically reversed the policy of his predecessor Diocletian by allowing the Christians freedom of worship, and within the space of a few decades they had taken the war into the pagan camp. The climax of the struggle found expression in the dignified debate which took place in 384 between Ambrose, then bishop of Milan and coming to the height of his power, and Q. Aurelius Symmachus, the pagan writer and administrator, who made a moving plea for the restitution of the Altar of Victory which had been removed from the Curia. In 394 the leader of the last pagan resistance, Virius Nicomachus Flavianus, was defeated by Theodosius and committed suicide in the old tradition. At the centre of the pagan opposition in the West were the Roman senators, who recaptured for a time the spirit of their ancestors and rallied to the defence of their traditions and heritage.

A vivid and sympathetic memorial to this movement is still extant in Macrobius' *Saturnalia*. The relevance of this learned symposium lies in the setting and *dramatis personae*. In the year 384, on the occasion of the Saturnalia, a number of cultivated upper-class Romans meet on successive days in the houses of Vettius Agorius Praetextatus, Virius Nicomachus Flavianus, and Symmachus, and have much learned talk about religion, history, philology, and in particular their great pagan poet Vergil. Among those present are other known opponents of Christianity. Servius is there as a representative of professional scholarship, a little over-awed by the company. We know Praetextatus had died in 384, Flavianus in 394; Macrobius has nostalgically recreated the great pagan society of the past as a framework for his learned compilation and we see its members, before their world had crumbled around them, discussing the minutiae of Roman life and literature with the sophisticated learning of the great Romans of the Republic.

But these men have left their own memorial, modest but effective, in the notes, generally called subscriptions, which are attached to a number of Latin texts. The production of correct texts of the Latin authors, if only with the modest aim of having a readable text on one's shelf, happened all the time. But the subscriptions suggest that there was a sudden increase in this activity towards the end of the fourth century and the intensification of the process was in origin a facet of the pagan revival. Fortunately it outlived paganism: the great Roman families of late antiquity carried on the tradition, and the descendants of the Symmachi and Nicomachi and others, pagan and Christian alike, continued to guard their national heritage as wave after wave of barbarians poured into the Empire.

Fortunately the triumph of Christianity did not remove the need for readable texts of the pagan authors. Christians who were hostile to pagan literature found themselves in an acute dilemma. It was clearly ill suited to be the basic stuff of Christian education. The poets were polytheistic and the tales they told about their gods, and particularly about the father of them all, were usually devoid of edification or downright immoral; Roman rhetoric, though it could be useful if employed in the right cause, encouraged glibness in speech and argument out of keeping with simple piety; even the philosophers, who had so much to offer to the Christian thinker, also contained much that was inimical to religious faith and the Christian way of life; the magnitude of the pagan achievement in all spheres of human activity, of which its written as well as its material remains were a constant reminder, might tend to sap confidence in new values and institutions. On the other hand, the enormous debt which Christians owed to the classical heritage and the extent to which they could still benefit from it was obvious even at times when the tension between the two cultures was at its highest. Just as Ambrose in his *De officiis ministrorum* was able to produce an influential manual of Christian ethic by reworking the basically Stoic content of Cicero's *De officiis*, so Augustine, writing at a time when he was least sympathetic to secular letters, in his *De doctrina Christiana* successfully adapted classical Roman rhetoric and in particular the theory of the three styles as elaborated by Cicero in the *Orator* to the needs of the Christian preacher. The agony of the dilemma which faced the orthodox Christian nurtured in the pagan schools is in human terms most dramatically reflected in Jerome as he runs through the gamut of conscience and renunciation, temptation and compromise. The last was inevitable. In general it was recognized that pagan literature could be plundered with profit provided that due caution was observed and the end justified the means. Jerome uses the analogy of the captive woman in Deuteronomy (21: 10–13) who may be taken to wife and made a true Israelite when she has had her head shaved and her nails pared (*Epist.* 70.2). Augustine sanctions the use of secular learning by likening it to the despoiling of the Egyptians (*De doctrina* 2.60). Although the Christian attitude to pagan learning remained complex and fluid and generalization is dangerous, these two simple parables did echo through the ages and provided a handy justification for those who wished to have the best of both worlds. For the moment practical necessity had the last word: the old Roman system of education continued, for the simple reason that there was no alternative. Christian writings were not suitable for the school syllabus, the basic textbooks were all pagan, and in any case the ordinary cultivated Roman had few qualms about the traditional education; the obligations of polite society and his own highly developed sense of style made it difficult for him to turn over to the less sophisticated diet of Christian literature. The Roman educational system, authors and gods and all, continued until the monastic and episcopal schools were able to replace it with an education which, however much it owed to the traditional system, was essentially Christian in direction and purpose.

X. THE SUBSCRIPTIONS

The subscriptions provide a series of fascinating testimonies to the interest evinced in late antiquity in classical literature and its preservation. These notes, originally appended at the end of a work or the books of a work, have sometimes been copied from manuscript to manuscript along with the text. But the scribe might easily omit them, and the survival of so many is an indication of the extent of the activity. The work which Praetextatus did on the correction of texts is recorded in his epitaph (Dessau, *ILS* 1259, 8–12), but there is no trace of it in any surviving manuscripts, though the family tradition continued into the sixth

century: the Vettius Agorius Basilius Mavortius who worked on
the text of Horace sometime after 527 must have been a member
of the same family. One of the few subscriptions with a claim to be
original is that found in the codex Mediceus of Vergil (Laur. 39.1,
Plate IX), where Asterius, consul in 494, records that he had
corrected and punctuated the text.

The subscriptions begin towards the end of the fourth century
and continue into the sixth. They vary from the simple *Iulius
Celsus Constantinus v.c. legi* (Caesar's *Gallic War*) to a more detailed
statement giving the date, place, and circumstances of the revision.
As often as not the writer turns out to be an administrator, or
even an army officer, rather than a professional scholar. In some
cases the amateur corrector sought expert help or had access to
another manuscript, in others he confesses, with a *cri de cœur*,
that he has worked *sine exemplario* or *prout potui sine magistro*.

Among the earliest is the subscription attached to Apuleius'
Golden Ass:

Ego Sallustius legi et emendavi Romae felix, Olibrio et Probino v.c.
conss., in foro Martis controversiam declamans oratori Endelechio.
Rursus Constantinopoli recognovi Caesario et Attico conss.

This is an interesting document which goes back to the pagan
revival. The years in question are 395 and 397 and the Sallustius
who carried out the revision would be a member of the family
closely connected with Symmachus. The work was carried out
under the eye of Endelechius in the forum of Augustus, which,
with the neighbouring forum of Trajan, accommodated schools of
rhetoric and grammar. One of the three families of Martial manuscripts goes back to an ancient recension which was corrected by
Torquatus Gennadius in 401, also in the forum of Augustus, and
the imperial fora remained as intellectual centres down to the end
of the ancient world.

The most celebrated series of subscriptions are those found in
various books of the first decade of Livy:

Nicomachus Flavianus v.c. III praef. urbi emendavi apud Hennam.
Nicomachus Dexter v.c. emendavi ad exemplum parentis mei Clemen-
tiani.
Victorianus v.c. emendabam domnis Symmachis.

The Nicomachean recension of Livy's first decade was a collaborative effort on the part of the related families of the Nicomachi and Symmachi, who had the ambitious project of editing the whole of Livy. Nicomachus Flavianus is the son of the pagan leader, Nicomachus Dexter is his grandson; Victorianus, who is here helping the Symmachi, edited one of the works of the elder Flavianus. Part of the work of revision was done at the villa of the Nicomachi at Enna in Sicily.

The continuation of this tradition can be seen in the subscription to Macrobius' commentary on Cicero's *Somnium Scipionis*:

Aurelius Memmius Symmachus v.c. emendabam vel distinguebam meum [*sc.* exemplar] Ravennae cum Macrobio Plotino Eudoxio v.c.

Here the great-grandson of the Symmachus who appears in the *Saturnalia* is seen correcting another work by Macrobius, and helping him is a grandson of the author himself. The chain extends to the very threshold of the Middle Ages, for this Symmachus, consul in 485, was the father-in-law of Boethius.

2. THE GREEK EAST

In the early centuries of the Roman empire intellectual life in the
Greek provinces was in a state of decline. Despite the existence of
institutions of higher education such as the schools of philosophy
and oratory at Athens, Rhodes, and elsewhere, there were few
outstanding achievements in literature or scholarship. The
Museum at Alexandria still existed; although the end of independent government in Egypt brought to a close the royal
patronage of scholarship, the situation was soon restored, for we
find Strabo reporting (17.1.8) that the Roman emperor now supported the Museum, and there are explicit references to scholars
entitled to its privileges. But notable works of scholarship do not
seem to have been produced. Only the library continued to render
service as a leading collection of material for the scholarly public;
the tradition that Caesar was accidentally responsible for its
destruction during his visit to Egypt (48–47 B.C.) has been widely
accepted, but the sources are not entirely in agreement as to the
extent of the damage, and it seems likely that no more than a
section of the library was burnt, or that the deficiencies were made
good by Antony, who was said to have transferred the Pergamene
library to Alexandria (Plutarch, *Antony* 58); total destruction is
also difficult to reconcile with the fact that Strabo apparently did
his geographical research in Alexandria. Literary work is harder to
trace. In the Augustan age Aristonicus did further selection of the
Homeric commentaries, and Tryphon studied and classified figures
of speech (the treatise which now passes under his name has been
revised by later redactors). During the reign of Tiberius there
are again signs of some activity; Theon commented on various
poetic texts, especially Hellenistic, such as Theocritus, Apollonius
Rhodius, and Callimachus; a scrap of his notes on Pindar's
Pythians has recently come to light (P. Oxy. 2536). Apion prepared
a glossary to Homer that is quoted by Hesychius and Eustathius
(a little of it survives in P. Rylands 26). Heliodorus wrote a com-

mentary on the metres of Aristophanes, parts of which are found in the extant scholia. But as far as we can see none of these works was outstanding as an advance in scholarly method or critical principles. Much the same is true of the second and third centuries, except that the grammarians Apollonius Dyscolus and his son Herodian were important in their own field, and some of their works survive independently of the scholia. Apollonius was the first grammarian to write on syntax in something approaching the modern sense of the term; the name Dyscolus is said to have been given to him owing to the difficulty of his subject-matter. Among other things he characterized the Greek perfect tense as a description of a present state; also he showed clearly for the first time the difference implied by the use of present and aorist in moods other than the indicative. In both these matters he made an advance on the Stoic theorists, who had already managed to develop a useful terminology for the tenses.

The decline of scholarship and criticism does not need to be explained purely as part of the general decline of the time. There was another more tangible influence at work. Though school education included the reading of Homer and the other poets, especially tragedy and comedy, there was increasing emphasis on the study of rhetoric. As a result a large number of handbooks on oratory were written, and the Attic orators, in particular Demosthenes, received more attention than before. Interest was to some extent diverted from the poets. A more fundamental change in education may have been connected with the fact that the poverty of Greece and her evident inferiority to Rome in all spheres easily bred a nostalgic admiration for the achievements of the classical period; if men could no longer perform acts worthy of the great days of old, they might at least attempt to rival them in literary style. The growth of this feeling can be traced as early as the reign of Augustus, and it became especially prominent in the second century A.D. By this time the Greek language had undergone considerable changes, as can be seen from a comparison of the classical language with that of the New Testament or the letters and documents among the papyri. A desire to write in classical style at once created a need for manuals of instruction, and the energy of men with literary tastes was turned to the writing of these textbooks. Dictionaries composed by Aelius Dionysius and Pausanias under Hadrian (117–38) have survived in fragments; we have also complete works by Pollux and Phrynichus dating from the reigns of Marcus Aurelius (161–80) and Commodus (180–92). These books all gave guidance to the would-be writer of classical Attic prose; in general they listed words or constructions current in everyday use which a writer might be tempted to employ, and then added the correct classical idiom. Any cultured person who interlarded his prose with modern expressions not found in the great Athenian writers was considered to have spoiled his style seriously and to have made a shameful display of ignorance and bad taste; this emerges quite clearly from the dedicatory letter which Phrynichus prefixed to his *Ecloge* and in the heading to the work. These experts in classical Attic did not always agree in their recommendations, nor were they equally strict in the construction of the rules they propounded. Some, such as Phrynichus, failed to appreciate the distinction between poetic and prose diction, and recommended usages which are found only in Greek tragedy; this made them unreliable guides for the school or university student. A certain degree of controversy arose among them. One issue was whether a single occurrence of a word in a classical author justified its usage, and three times in the *Ecloge* (206, 258, 400) we find Phrynichus stating that he is not satisfied to recommend words in this category, since he wishes to follow the well-established and common usage of Attic authors. Controversy also arose when incorrect instructions were given by a purist; there is a work by the so-called 'Anti-Atticist' showing that a number of prohibited expressions could be traced in Athenian texts earlier than c. 200 B.C.

Although the fashion was artificial in the extreme and had undesirable effects on literary compositions of every kind, the practice of Atticism lasted a very long time; it was the governing principle for all literary men not merely under the Roman empire but right to the end of the Byzantine period. The Byzantines may as a rule have been less successful in their imitation of ancient models than the writers of the Second Sophistic age such as Lucian and Aristides, but there is no doubt that their aims were identical, since lexica of Attic diction were composed by later scholars, for example Photius in the ninth century and Thomas Magister in the fourteenth; and as late as the fifteenth century we find the historian Critobulus writing an account of the fall of Constantinople to the Turks in 1453 in a style which is clearly intended as an imitation of Thucydides. Stylistic archaism on this scale has no parallel except perhaps in China, where it is still possible for Mao Tse Tung to think it worth writing lyrics in the style of eighth-century poets like Li Po.

Atticism had another important and less unfortunate consequence. The requirement to use only Attic diction of the best period ensured that in schools the classics of Athenian literature continued to be read as part of the regular curriculum, and this in turn meant that new copies of the text of major works were being steadily produced in sufficient numbers to guarantee the survival of most of them; only Menander was an exception. Even when the Eastern empire was at its lowest ebb the tradition of reading classical literature in the schools was never quite obliterated.

Close linguistic study of Attic texts led to other results. The occurrence of non-Attic words in a text supposed to come from the classical period might rouse suspicions as to its authenticity; and in fact we find Phrynichus remarking that the speech *Against Neaera* in the Demosthenic corpus is to be regarded as spurious partly on account of its impure language (*Ecloge* 203). But the minute linguistic observations of the schools were not entirely beneficial. They had the effect of instilling the forms and inflections of the Attic dialect so deeply that, when an educated man was transcribing a text, he tended to replace forms drawn from other dialects by the Attic forms which he knew so well. This is clear in works which contain Doric dialect, such as the lyrics of tragedy or Theocritus' *Idylls*; in many parts of the text original Doric forms have been eliminated by successive generations of copyists. The text of Xenophon has suffered in the same way. Phrynichus tells us (*Ecloge* 71) that Xenophon departed from his native Attic dialect by writing the word for 'smell' as *odmē* instead of *osmē*; similarly Photius in his *Lexicon* says that Xenophon used the poetic form of the word for 'dawn', *ēōs*, instead of the Attic *hĕōs*; but in both these cases the surviving manuscripts of

Xenophon regularly show the normal Attic forms. Here too the influence of the scribes is clear.

II. THE CHRISTIAN CHURCH AND CLASSICAL STUDIES

The effects of the growth of the Christian Church upon education and literary studies must now be considered. In earlier antiquity religious toleration had been the rule rather than the exception, and adherents of many different faiths had lived peacefully side by side, but the animosity with which Christians and pagans regarded each other brought about a substantial and permanent change. Many influential clergy disliked equally the unbelievers and the classical Greek literature which they studied with enthusiasm, and so the members of Christian communities were advised not to read such books. If this attitude had been adopted by all the clergy it would in due course, as the new religion became universal by the fifth century, have imposed an effective censorship on classical literature; as it is there can be little doubt that one of the major reasons for the loss of classical texts is that most Christians were not interested in reading them, and hence not enough new copies of the texts were made to ensure their survival in an age of war and destruction. But the literary merit of the classical authors was sufficient to tempt some Christians to read them, particularly as there were, at least in the early period, comparatively few Christian literary classics which could be recommended as an acceptable substitute for the traditional texts studied at school. Allegorical interpretation might be used to make certain passages inoffensive to Christian taste. Another important consideration was the need to make Christianity appeal to the well-educated pagan, and one means to this end was the demonstration that some of the important concepts of the new faith could be discussed in terms borrowed from the classical philosophers, especially the Stoics and Plato. The fusion of Greek and Christian thought in Justin and Clement exemplifies this attitude.

Early church fathers of the highest authority were content that Christians should read some pagan texts during their education. When Saint Gregory Thaumaturgus attended Origen's school at Caesarea in 233–8 he found his master encouraging pupils to read classical literature, and especially the philosophers; only those authors who denied the existence of a deity or a divine providence were to be avoided (Migne, *PG* 10.1088A, 1093A). It should be noted that Origen's willingness to learn from pagan culture extended to the realm of textual criticism. The interpretation of the Old Testament had become a matter of controversy, since the Septuagint was at variance with some other early Greek versions, and difficulty arose if precise interpretation of a passage was required. Origen adapted the system of marginal signs used by the Alexandrian critics to the Old Testament; an obelus marked a passage found in the Greek but not in the Hebrew, and an asterisk passages in which the Hebrew agreed with translations other than the Septuagint. In his *Hexapla* Origen went further and devised a method of presenting the Hebrew text and the translations in parallel columns. The successive columns were the original Hebrew, the Hebrew in Greek letters, the Greek translations of Aquila, Symmachus, the Septuagint, and Theodotion. The resulting book, a cumbrous anticipation of a modern apparatus criticus, must have been enormous, and no doubt partly for that reason it has not come down to us in its original form, except that fragments of a five-column version omitting the text in Hebrew characters survive as the lower script in a Milan palimpsest (Ambros. S.P. 11.251, *olim* O. 39 sup.).

The outlook of the fathers of the fourth century was no less liberal. Saint Basil wrote a short treatise advising the young on the best method of profiting from Greek literature (Homily 22), and Saint Gregory of Nazianzus criticized the majority of Christians for their complete rejection of pagan works, some of which he believed to be useful (*PG* 36.508B). There was in general no attempt to alter the school curriculum by banishing the classical authors. For a brief period Julian's persecution of the Christians in 362 tempted Apollinaris (c. 310–90) to construct a totally Christian curriculum, for which he and his father composed a long poem in Homeric style on the antiquities of the Jews and a paraphrase of the Psalms, also in hexameters. But the persecution soon ended, and pagan and Christian continued to use the same educational system without serious polemic or controversy. Some professors of rhetoric were Christians, but they did not exclude pagans from their classes: in the fourth century at Athens the Christian

Prohaeresius won the admiration of his staunchly pagan student Eunapius. Similarly at Gaza in the early sixth century the leading figures Procopius and Choricius pursued classical and Christian studies together.

The major classical texts, which had a firm position in the curriculum, were read by believer and unbeliever alike; but the survival of other texts was immediately put in danger when the new religion became universal, since the mass of the public, after the completion of their education, had no further interest in reading pagan books. It is sometimes asserted that the Church formally imposed a censorship and burnt pagan books as a matter of policy. The policy, if it ever existed as such, took a long time to have its intended effect; in the seventh century the poems of Sappho were still being read in Egypt (P. Berol. 5006). Occasionally there is a report of the burning of pagan books; Jovian in 363–4 is said to have burnt a library assembled at Antioch by his predecessor Julian (*Suda*, s.v. Iobianos). But this was an isolated case of vindictiveness: such destructive fervour was usually reserved for the works of fellow Christians who had deviated into heresy, and several ceremonial bonfires of unorthodox books are recorded in the fourth and fifth centuries.

The attitude of the church remained substantially unaltered throughout the Byzantine age. Classical authors maintained their place in the schools. Eminent members of the higher clergy figure among the most competent students of classical Greek at all times. There is no reliable evidence for censorship. A famous statement by the humanist Petrus Alcyonius (1486–1527), to the effect that the ecclesiastical authorities caused the texts of pagan poets to be burnt, is not supported by any other evidence. The numerous authors he mentions in this connection had probably been lost through other causes by the end of the Dark Ages. The Byzantine church was only concerned to destroy books by heretics; for instance in 1117, when the metropolitan Eustratius of Nicaea was examining arguments against the views of the Armenian church, he discovered works by Saint Cyril that appeared to contain heretical tendencies, and when copies of these works by Cyril began to circulate he brought the matter before the authorities, who ordered that all copies should be sent within forty days to

Santa Sophia to be destroyed. Again in 1140 it came to the ear of the patriarch that a monk's heretical works were being circulated; after a search three copies were found and burnt. On the other hand no case has yet come to light in which the Church took similar measures against a classical text; even the works of the detested apostate Julian survived.

III. THE EARLY BYZANTINE PERIOD

While the general condition of the ancient world declined rapidly higher education in the Eastern part of the empire was more flourishing than ever before. Schools can be traced at Alexandria, Antioch, Athens, Beirut, Constantinople, and Gaza; they were in effect the universities of the ancient world. They varied in character and importance: at Alexandria Aristotle was one of the main topics of study; the chief subject at Beirut was law. The need for such institutions was created by a vast increase in the Roman civil service in the fourth century. The government required administrators of liberal education and good prose style, as the emperor Constantius stated explicitly in 357 in an edict preserved in the Theodosian code (14.1.1). The study of classical poetry and oratory continued in the schools as before; special attention was given to cultivating Attic prose style, and for this purpose a number of rhetorical tricks of style had to be mastered. The works of the early Atticist writers of the second century A.D. such as Lucian and Aristides were regarded as models no less deserving of imitation than the classics of ancient Athens; this equal valuation of Attic and Atticist lasted right through the Byzantine period. Literary education seems to have held its own for some time against the claims of more practical disciplines; but at the end of the fourth century we find Libanius, the head of a famous literary school, complaining that students are being attracted to the study of law and Latin, which were also of obvious benefit to potential civil servants (*Autobiography* 214 and 234). One by one the schools declined or closed, until by the middle of the sixth century only Constantinople and Alexandria remained: Justinian himself had closed the philosophical school at Athens in 529, and the other cities had been much reduced by war or natural disasters.

The emphasis on rhetoric and Atticism did not encourage much scholarship in the modern sense of the term. One achievement, however, which may belong to this period, is the redaction of ancient commentaries into the form of scholia now placed in the margins of a text instead of occupying a separate book (Plates II and III). In particular there is reason to believe that work on Demosthenes and the other orators was carried out in the school at Gaza. The task was essentially one of compilation and selection, requiring intelligence in the choice of material selected from previous exegetical works; but in practice the scholia to all authors are marred by stupid or irrelevant notes. The date of this activity is usually placed in the fourth or fifth centuries, but it remains uncertain, since the identity of the compilers cannot be established. The idea of entering copious scholia in the margins of a text may have arisen at any time after the codex became the normal form of book; yet copious marginal scholia are not commonly found until the ninth century.

In this connection it should perhaps be mentioned that Procopius of Gaza (c. 460–c. 530) is supposed to have invented a form of literature that bears some resemblance to scholia, namely the catena, a running commentary on a book of the Bible which puts together the opinions of several previous interpreters, frequently with verbatim quotations of their arguments. This invention marked a new stage of biblical studies; but whether the catena is to be regarded as a forerunner of classical scholia or as an imitation of them is a question that has not yet been answered.

The last feature of this period which merits discussion is the progressive narrowing of the range of literature normally read. After the third century it becomes more and more uncommon to find any educated man showing knowledge of the texts that have not come down to the modern world. To explain this fact Wilamowitz formulated the theory that in the second or third century a school syllabus was selected by a prominent schoolmaster, and this became so influential that all schools adopted it. With the general decline of culture and impoverishment of the empire no texts outside this range were read and copied often enough to be guaranteed survival. To take an example: seven plays by Aeschylus and seven by Sophocles were selected, and because of this no others have come down to us; nine or ten plays of Euripides were chosen for reading in school, but in this case a lucky chance led to the survival of a single manuscript containing a number of other plays. Though the theory has much attraction there is reason to think that it presents too schematic a view of the history of texts. An initial objection is that there is no positive evidence as to the identity of the schoolmaster in question. One possible candidate would be Eugenius, who in the fifth century wrote on the colometry of fifteen plays. If this figure is correct it hints already at a selection of nine plays from Euripides and three from each of the other dramatists; but the reduction of the set books to the number of three is more probably a feature of the revised curriculum of late Byzantine schools. However, when so much remains unknown, it would be wrong to lay emphasis on our ignorance of the origin of the selection. More important is the reading of texts outside the syllabus in late antiquity; there are fifth-century fragments of Euripides' *Phaethon* and *Melanippe Desmotis*, and seventh-century fragments of Sappho and Callimachus, and three of the four documents in question come from the country districts of Egypt, where a taste for reading the less common pagan texts might have been expected to die out at a rather earlier date. By contrast Menander was still being read in the school at Gaza in the sixth century, but did not survive into the middle ages. Last and most important, it is clear that not all the losses of ancient literature took place so early. In the ninth century Photius was able to read a large number of books that have subsequently disappeared and are known to us from no source except his own account of them. For these reasons it is perhaps best to abandon the idea that a conscious act of selection by an individual was a primary factor in determining the survival of texts.

By the latter part of the sixth century the decline of learning and culture was serious. The imperial university at Constantinople, refounded by Theodosius II c. 425, and a new clerical academy under the direction of the patriarchate, were the only major educational institutions in the main part of the empire; the school at Alexandria continued, but rather in isolation. The exhausted condition of the empire did nothing to encourage learning, and before any recovery could take place matters were made worse by the religious controversy over icon-worship. For some three centuries there is little record of education and the study of the classics. The iconoclasts were not finally defeated until 843, when a Church council formally restored the traditional practices of image worship. Very few manuscripts of any kind remain from this period, and there is little external evidence about classical studies. The only works of the epoch which deserve mention are those of Choeroboscus, a lecturer in grammar at the seminary in Constantinople, and the *Canons* of Theognostus, a lengthy work on orthography from the early ninth century; owing to the change in the pronunciation of Greek, spelling was as much an obstacle to schoolchildren as it is in England today.

IV. GREEK TEXTS IN THE ORIENT

Here a brief digression is needed in order to mention a rather neglected chapter in the history of transmission, the significance of translations of Greek texts into Oriental languages. At some point during late antiquity Greek texts began to be translated into Syriac, activity being centred in the towns of Nisibis and Edessa. The lands of the eastern Mediterranean are commonly believed to have been bilingual under the Roman empire. But this view is exaggerated, and the mass of the population probably spoke little or no Greek. When the authoress of the *Peregrinatio Aetheriae*, a very early account of pilgrimage, visited the Holy Land about 400, she noted that at church services the officiating priest conducted the liturgy in Greek, and an assistant immediately gave the Syriac version of what he had just said (ch. 47). The Church could only achieve its purposes by use of the vernacular.

Probably the first text to be translated was the New Testament, followed shortly by a range of patristic works. The earliest manuscripts of these versions go back to the fourth and fifth centuries, and it is well known that they are of value to theologians. It comes as a surprise, however, to find that other forms of Greek literature were translated. The schools of Nisibis and Edessa are known to have prepared versions of Aristotle, and a section of Theophrastus' *Meteorology* survives in Syriac alone. Philosophy and science were not the only concerns of the Syrians. They translated some Lucian and the grammar of Dionysius Thrax, as if attempting to give their pupils the benefits of a Greek literary education in translation.

These latter translations are not of any great value to the modern scholar interested in establishing the correct form of the Greek text; it sometimes happens that the Syriac, instead of helping to correct the Greek, has to be corrected from it.

Arabic versions of classical texts are perhaps more numerous than their Syriac counterparts and certainly better known; this may be due to the accident of survival. The stimulus to make these translations seems to have come purely from a desire to use the best handbooks of science and philosophy available, and it is unlikely that a translation of the Bible preceded that of classical texts. As a rule the translations were made from an existing Syriac version, and so allowance must be made for two stages at which the inaccuracy of a translator could mar the expression of the original. When an Arabic version exists side by side with the Greek tradition one cannot assume as a matter of course that it will substantially help in determining the Greek text. Yet a famous example will show that utter pessimism is unjustified. In Aristotle's *Poetics* the Arabic text, though exceptionally difficult to understand, offers a few readings which the editor must accept and several more which he must consider seriously, a reasonable harvest if the brevity of the treatise is borne in mind. That the *Poetics* should have been translated is a cause of some surprise at first sight; but the explanation of both the Syriac and Arabic renderings may be simply that all the writings of 'the master of those who know' were held to be important enough to justify translation. For the most part, however, it was science and philosophy that interested the Arabs. Plato, Aristotle, and Theophrastus were much studied. The mathematicians received special attention; the version of Apollonius of Perga *On conic sections* is important because several books of it have been lost in the Greek; the same is true of Philo of Byzantium's *Mechanics* and works by Archimedes and Hero of Alexandria. The medical writings of Hippocrates, Galen, and Dioscorides were closely investigated. By no means all the versions that are attested have yet been found in Arabic manuscripts; we know of many of them only from references to them in medieval Arabic encyclopedias. But since the study of Arabic manuscripts still has much progress to make there is hope that more versions will be recovered.

What has been said above about the general quality of the translations needs to be qualified in one respect. It is clear that in the ninth century there was one translator whose scholarly attainments were at least equal to those of his contemporaries in Byzantium. Hunain ibn Ishaq (809–73) was competent in Arabic, Persian, Greek, and Syriac, the last apparently being his mother tongue. He began his work as a translator at the age of seventeen, and if his command of languages was already good at that age it seems that he must have grown up in a multilingual community. He appears to have lived in Baghdad, where he founded a school of translators, and he refers to meetings in that city at which Christians gathered to read their ancient literature. Though he does not make it clear whether this reading was of originals or Syriac versions, he does say that Greek communities, perhaps using monasteries as focal points, preserved the use of the language, and that it was possible to find Greek manuscripts all over the Islamic world. He himself searched for them in Mesopotamia, Syria, Palestine, and Egypt. In a letter to a friend who had asked for a detailed list with indications of content of all Greek medical works known to him Hunain gives a long account of his method of work. He writes at length about Galen, and considers particularly which texts have been translated into Syriac only and which into Arabic also, who the translator was, to whom the work was dedicated, and where Greek manuscripts might be found of works not yet translated. His comments on his predecessors are revealing. He frequently claims that they were incompetent in linguistic knowledge, or were certainly working from damaged or illegible manuscripts, a hindrance which Hunain himself had to face from time to time. In such cases he collates the faulty existing version against as many Greek manuscripts as he can find and produces a revised rendering. The quantity of Greek books that he had access to and their damaged condition are emphasized more than once. It is possible that the scrupulous consideration and comparison of divergent texts was a technique that he learnt at least in part from Galen, who employs much the same methods in handling the difficult text of the Hippocratic corpus. Such merit as Arabic versions possess may well be due to the scholarship of Hunain and his associates.

One other language should be mentioned. Translation into Armenian probably began for the purposes of the Church as it did in Syria. The Armenian version of the Bible is one of the most celebrated. In the field of patristic literature some works by Philo have come down to us in the Armenian alone, and the same is true of part of Eusebius' *Chronicon*. As to classical texts, the translations of Plato and Dionysius Thrax are mentioned in another context (see pp. 16, 53). An intriguing and tantalizing report suggests that other Greek books of purely literary and secular character were translated; apart from a number of historians there is mention of unnamed works by Callimachus. An account of the plot of Euripides' *Peliades* comes from an Armenian source.

V. THE RENAISSANCE OF THE NINTH CENTURY

The first real achievements of Byzantine scholarship belong to the middle of the ninth century. There were men of outstanding ability who were able to exercise their powers to the best advantage in the more peaceful condition of the empire. In 863 the assistant emperor Bardas revived the imperial university, which had disappeared in the turmoil of the preceding centuries, by founding a school in the capital under the direction of Leo, a philosopher and mathematician of distinction; other professors appointed at the same time were Theodore the geometrician, Theodegius the astronomer, and Cometas the literary scholar; the last of these may have specialized in rhetoric and Atticism, but he also prepared a recension of Homer. Leo's scholarly temperament can be seen from an episode during his residence on the island of Andros. He met a learned man who gave him some tuition in rhetoric, philosophy, and arithmetic; this made him wish to pursue the subjects further and he crossed over to the mainland in order to search for books in monastic libraries. His motive is characteristic of the changed atmosphere in Byzantium; during the Iconoclastic era emperors like Leo the Armenian had hunted for books merely in order to find texts which could lend them support in theological controversy.

The revival of learning coincided with, and was perhaps assisted by, certain changes in the appearance and production of manuscripts. Hitherto the standard script of books had been the uncial character, which had reached its fully developed form as early as the fourth century, and had changed surprisingly little in the course of centuries. Despite its impressive appearance it had the serious disadvantage that it was slow to write and so large that the quantity of text on each page was strictly limited. When the cheaper writing material of the ancient world ceased to be readily available, as the papyrus plantations were either exhausted or used mainly by the Arabs after their conquest of Egypt in 641, the demand for parchment must have increased sharply; even in an age which was not much interested in literature, theological and liturgical texts were required and the needs of the civil service had to be satisfied. To meet this difficulty it appears that the expedient was devised of adapting for use in books the script that had been current for some time in official circles for letters, documents, accounts, and the like; the modern technical term for the revised script is minuscule. It occupied far less space on the page and could be written at high speed by a practised scribe. The first dated example belongs to the year 835, and is known as the Uspensky Gospels (Leningrad gr. 219). As the script of this book is by no means immature or primitive, the adoption of this style should probably be dated at least half a century earlier. The place of its origin is not known for certain, but there are some grounds for thinking that it was popularized by members of the important Stoudios monastery in the capital, which was a well-known centre of book production at a later date. Gradually the uncial hand was abandoned, and by the end of the tenth century it was no longer used except for a few special liturgical books. The new script facilitated the copying of texts by making more economical use of parchment, and not long afterwards the situation was improved by another invention. In 751 the Arabs had taken some Chinese prisoners of war at Samarkand and learnt from them the process of paper-making. Soon Arab production in the East and in Spain reached substantial proportions, and in due course it was exported to Byzantium. Hostilities between the two empires may have had an unfavourable effect on the trade, but there is no doubt that paper came to be widely used in Byzantium, and it seems to have been used in the imperial archives from the middle of the eleventh century.

The transliteration of old uncial books into the new script was energetically undertaken by the scholars of the ninth century. It is largely owing to their activity that Greek literature can still be read, for the text of almost all authors depends ultimately on one or more books written in minuscule script at this date or shortly after, from which all later copies are derived; the quantity of literature that is available to us from the papyri and the uncial manuscripts is only a small proportion of the whole. In the process of transliteration mistakes were sometimes made, especially by misreading letters that were similar in the uncial script and therefore easily confused. At many points in Greek texts there are errors common to all the extant manuscripts which appear to derive from the same source, and this source is usually taken to be a ninth-century copy. A further assumption generally made is that one minuscule copy was made from one uncial copy. The uncial book was then discarded, and the minuscule book became the source of all further copies. The theory has a certain a priori justification on two grounds, since the task of transliteration from a script that was becoming less and less familiar would not be willingly undertaken more often than was absolutely necessary, and there is at least some likelihood that after the destruction of the previous centuries many texts survived in one copy only. But these arguments do not amount to proof, and there are cases which can only be explained by more complicated hypotheses. In the tradition of Plato one manuscript (Vienna, supp. gr. 39) differs greatly from all others in its errors, and it is difficult to believe it derived from the same ninth-century exemplar; it may derive from the transliteration of a different uncial book, so that at least two old books would seem to have survived the Dark Ages. A confirmation of this is that when a Greek text has been translated into an Oriental language at an early date, perhaps the fifth century, the readings which are characteristic of the Oriental translation may occur also in a small group of the Greek manuscripts. This is true of the Armenian version of some of Plato's dialogues, the Arabic version of Aristotle's *Poetics*, and, if the example of a patristic text may be admitted here, of the Syriac translation of Saint Gregory of Nyssa's *De virginitate*. Another argument pointing in the same direction can be drawn from the difficulty which arises in the study of the manuscripts of some texts that were very frequently read during the Middle Ages, such as the Euripidean plays included in the school curriculum. Here the relation of the manuscripts cannot be established precisely by the usual method, since they do not fall into groups that coincide regularly in error. This situation presupposes that medieval scholars and schoolmasters frequently compared their own copy of the text with others and made alterations or added variant readings above the line; this process is known as contamination. In such cases it may be that more than one copy survived the Dark Ages to be transcribed, so that two or more transliterations took place; alternatively, only one transliteration was made but this copy was deposited in some central place where it was consulted by interested readers and received as marginal additions the variant readings that had been found in other copies. It is easy to imagine, though there is no external evidence for the assumption, that such deposits of semi-official copies took place in the library of the academy set up by Bardas. It is also possible that similar copies existed in the patriarchal academy, for there is a manuscript of Plato's *Laws* (Vat. gr. 1) written in the early tenth century with marginal variants added in the next century by a scholar who refers to these additional readings as coming from 'the patriarch's book'; unfortunately we cannot be sure whether this was a private copy or part of the library in the seminary.

The Bardas university was founded under favourable conditions, and was probably the centre of a lively group of scholars concerned to recover and disseminate classical texts of many different kinds. Yet it does not seem to have had the influence that might have been expected, for there is very little reference to it at later dates. Its professors are completely overshadowed by their contemporary Photius (c. 810–91), a man of remarkable attainments who is perhaps as important for his position in the Church and the affairs of the government as for his devoted encouragement of learning. Twice he held the patriarchal throne of Constantinople (858–67, 877–86), and in these years some of the negotiations which led to schism between the Eastern and Roman churches took place; it is only one of the consequences of this schism that efforts to obtain assistance for the weakened empire of the fourteenth and fifteenth centuries were seriously impeded by the estrangement of the two churches. For our purpose, however, the most interesting phase of Photius' life is the time before his sudden and rapid elevation to the patriarchate (he was still a layman until a week before the appointment). As a young man he had always been a keen student of a wide range of subjects, and from an early age succeeded in leading two different careers simultaneously. Jealousy and spite gave rise to a tradition that, rather like Faust, he achieved his knowledge by making a bargain with a Jewish magician, giving up his Christian faith in return for success, learning, and riches. He was much in favour at the court, and occupied positions of trust in the circle of the emperor; but apart from this he conducted a kind of private literary club. In 855 he was appointed to an embassy with the task of negotiating an exchange of prisoners of war with the Arab government. Before going on the long and dangerous journey Photius wrote, as an offering and consolation to his brother Tarasius, a summary of books that may have been read or discussed at the gatherings of his circle, especially those which Tarasius himself had not been able to attend. The resulting work, known as the *Bibliotheca* (alternatively *Muriobiblos*), is a fascinating production, in which Photius shows himself the inventor of the book-review. In 280 sections which vary in length from a single sentence to several pages Photius summarizes and comments on a wide selection of pagan and Christian texts (the proportions are nearly equal, and 122 sections deal with secular texts). He claims to have compiled it from memory, but it is generally regarded as a revised version of the notes he had made in the course of his reading in the last twenty years. It is not arranged according to any plan. Photius claims that the order of the authors reviewed is that in which they occurred to him, and he had not the time to be more systematic. Its value to the modern scholar is that Photius summarizes many books that are now lost: that applies for example to some twenty of the thirty-three historians he discusses. Much can be learnt of the interests of a prominent Byzantine figure of the time: in the secular texts historians are most numerous, but among others there are orators, novelists, and compilers of Atticist dictionaries. The latter are significant, for they show the author's concern with stylistic considerations, which is also shown by his frequent brief characterizations of the style of an author; the desire

c

to write and appreciate a good Attic style was never far from the thoughts of Byzantine literati. The breadth of Photius' interests is enormous. That a pious man and future patriarch should bother to read the Greek novelists is surprising; he enjoyed them linguistically, but could not bring himself to be favourable to their contents. It is also notable that he read anti-Christian tracts; this is incidentally a strong argument against the notion that the ecclesiastical authorities attempted to impose a censorship. Philosophy is not well represented in the *Bibliotheca*, but there is evidence of his knowledge in this field elsewhere in his works. The most serious limitation of taste shown in the book is the absence of poetry. One wonders whether in this respect it is a true record of Photius' own reading. It is a possible but not certain inference that classical poetry was not yet a subject of interest in intellectual circles; the fact that surviving manuscripts of the poets are not datable earlier than c. 925 may be relevant here. Cometas' interest in Homer mentioned above is not a serious objection to this view, since the epics enjoyed an inviolable position in the school curriculum which put them in a class apart from all other poetry.

Photius' only other work deserving mention here is his *Lexicon*, the first complete copy of which was discovered in 1959 in a remote monastery in Macedonia. It is a typical work of its class, valuable for its brief quotations of classical texts not now available. The purpose was to amalgamate and revise various existing books of the same kind; in the *Bibliotheca* Photius remarks how useful such a book would be. In his Atticism he was moderate and willingly admitted words from poetic sources if they seemed the most expressive means of conveying a notion. These quotations from the poets do not imply a reading of the full text, but were probably drawn as such from his sources. Besides this lexicon he was partly responsible for the compilation of at least one other, and he further shows his stylistic pedantry by correcting the usage of friends' letters.

The sudden appearance of so distinguished a person after the obscurity that had previously reigned is remarkable; it is all the more strange that nothing is known of the identity of his tutors, nor of the sources from which he was able to acquire knowledge of so many rare texts. From this time onwards, as a result of the activity in Photius' salon and in the new university, there is a practically continuous tradition of classical studies in Byzantium. Literary texts were copied regularly and more technical works, especially mathematical and medical, were much studied, not least because they were still in general the best textbooks available. The first major result of these new stimuli to scholarship can be seen in Arethas (c. 860–c. 935), who became archbishop of Caesarea in Cappadocia; again it is a churchman who shows great interest in learning.

Whereas Photius' own books do not survive, or at least have not been identified, several volumes from the library of Arethas still exist, and copies derived from other lost volumes are known, so that a good picture of his collection can be obtained. The preserved volumes are masterpieces of calligraphy on fine quality parchment, and it happens that the prices of some of them were recorded by the original owner. For his Euclid (D'Orville 301, A.D. 888) he paid 14 gold pieces; the cost of his Plato, a thicker volume of larger format (E. D. Clarke 39, A.D. 895, Plate III), was 21 pieces. In relation to contemporary incomes such prices are an indication of the high cost of a book; civil service salaries started at 72 gold pieces per annum, and might rise in exceptional circumstances to 3,500. Book collecting was not a hobby for men of modest means.

Arethas commissioned books from professional scribes, in the main monks of monasteries which accepted regular orders on a commercial basis, and he then wrote a large amount of commentary in the margins in his own hand (Plate III). Though he was not a critic of great power or originality these marginal commentaries are valuable because they were drawn from good sources; the notes in his copies of Plato and Lucian are examples of this. Surviving volumes of his library include Plato, Euclid, Aristotle's *Organon*, Aristides, Lucian, and some Christian writers. Others that can be inferred from various evidence are Pausanias, Dio Chrysostom, and Marcus Aurelius; the last of these was probably the exemplar which ensured the further survival of this text. Once again there is an absence of interest in poetry, while Atticist writers are well represented; but Arethas evidently differs from Photius by showing no taste for historical writing.

The sources of Arethas' collection are unknown. The copies of

Plato and Euclid were acquired while he was a deacon. At this date he was probably living in the capital, where copies of most authors must have been readily available for some time. For rarer texts it may have been necessary to look further afield, but we do not possess any information about the book trade that throws light on Arethas' acquisitions. However, since a historian of c. 800, George Syncellus, refers to old and valuable books coming from Caesarea in Cappadocia, one may speculate that when Arethas arrived in his archbishopric he made some discoveries there.

VI. THE LATER BYZANTINE PERIOD

With the death of Arethas some time in the thirties of the tenth century a new period begins, in which eminent scholars and bibliophiles are much more difficult to identify. Some stimulus to learning was given by the activity of the erudite emperor Constantine VII Porphyrogenitus (913–59). During a long period of enforced semi-retirement he compiled various manuals of state-craft which survive partially. These took the form of encyclopedic compilations based on a very wide range of historical sources, and as such are of some importance to classical scholars, since many of the texts do not survive elsewhere. This great activity of Constantine was doubtless not carried out by him single-handed, but nothing is known of the collaborators. Shortly afterwards, perhaps in the reign of John Tzimisces (969–76), the collaboration of scholars resulted in a work which is of value for much the same reason as the works of Constantine; this is the *Suda*, less correctly known as Suidas (as if it were a proper name), which might be best described as a combination of dictionary and elementary encyclo-pedia. It has articles on a great number of classical personages and topics, and despite a certain amount of dubious or erroneous material transmits much useful information. Some of its sources can be traced; among those most frequently used are the text and scholia to Aristophanes, for which the *Suda* is in effect a fairly im-portant witness. However, it is the lost sources, some not now easily identifiable, which give it its value. Though the intelligence of the authors cannot be rated very high, their work does mark some advance, in so far as it is considerably more than a lexicon of Attic diction and is one of the earliest books with a claim to the title of encyclopedia, and perhaps the earliest encyclopedia to have alphabetical arrangement.

It should not be assumed that because individual scholars of this date remain unknown, the impetus given to literary studies by Photius had entirely ceased to have effect. Extant manuscripts of classical texts make it clear that even in the early tenth century the reading of classical poetry other than Homer had begun; the earliest copies of Theognis (Paris supp. gr. 388) and Musaeus (Barocci 50) almost certainly belong to this date. Several other poetic texts were being read by the middle of the century or a little later, and in fact some of the most valuable of all surviving manuscripts are the result of this activity; one may give as instances the text of the Greek Anthology, sometimes known as the *Palatine Anthology*, which serves to distinguish it from the anthology later composed by Planudes (Heidelberg gr. 23 + Paris supp. gr. 384); the Venice *Iliad* (Marc. gr. 454, Plate II), the importance of which is even greater for the scholia than for the text; the Ravenna Aristophanes, which is the only medieval manuscript to contain all eleven plays (Ravenna gr. 429); Laur. 32.9, which besides being the only medieval copy of all seven plays of Aeschylus is also of fundamental importance for the texts of Sophocles and Apollonius Rhodius. Prose authors were not neglected, and we can instance the leading manuscript of Polybius, written by the monk Ephraem, probably in 947 (Vat. gr. 124), and two copies of Demosthenes (Paris gr. 2935 and Laur. 59.9). These three codices were written by scribes whose hands can be identified elsewhere, and thus we can form some impression of the range of books written by a single scribe, even if they were often commissioned works and hence not representative of the scribes' own interests. Ephraem can be identified as the scribe of three other books: Venice, Marc. gr. 201, Aristotle's *Organon*, A.D. 954; Athos, Lavra 184, *Acts* and *Epistles*, undated; Athos, Vatopedi 747, Gospels, A.D. 948. The Paris Demosthenes was mainly written by the scribe of the Plato mentioned earlier (Vat. gr. 1), while the other Demosthenes is probably in the same hand as the Ravenna MS. of Aristophanes. Many manuscripts of classical authors written at various dates in the Byzantine period can be connected in this way by identification of the scribe's hand. Though the surviving books may not be more than a small proportion of those copied, the number of possible identifications does suggest that the copying of ancient texts was in the hands of quite a small group of scholars, schoolmasters, and professional scribes.

Classical learning and education continued in the eleventh century much as before. The major change of this epoch consisted of a reorganization of the imperial university; whether this was provoked by a decline in the institution in the form that Bardas had given it is unknown, but the new arrangement included the setting up of a faculty of law and another of philosophy. The changes were made under the aegis of the emperor Constantine IX Monomachus in 1045. The law school does not concern us here, except to note that its foundation antedates by some years that of the famous faculty at Bologna, from which modern law faculties ultimately derive their origin. The philosophical school, which also gave instruction in grammar, rhetoric and literary subjects, was under the direction of Michael Psellus (1018–78), much the most versatile man of his generation, who distinguished himself as civil servant, senior adviser to several emperors, historian, and academic philosopher. His literary output attests his wide reading of the classics, but his intellectual interests were rather more in philosophy, and his eminence as a lecturer and teacher led to a renewed interest in Plato and to a lesser extent Aristotle. The fortunes of the school were not entirely favourable. For reasons which seem to have been political rather than intellectual, the school's teachers fell into disfavour at the court, and Psellus himself had to retire to a monastery for a time; but he returned to important positions in due course, and it is likely that the school continued its work.

A further revival of philosophy, this time with Aristotle as the main author for study, can perhaps be traced to the early twelfth century. Anna Comnena, the princess who was forced to live in the seclusion of a monastery and composed a famous *History*, was connected with two scholars who wrote commentaries on Aristotle, Eustratius of Nicaea and Michael of Ephesus. The most interesting fact about this activity is that their treatises are devoted largely to the *Politics* and the zoological works; these texts had not yet been supplied with commentaries, despite the enormous amount of study of Aristotle that had taken place in the ancient world and early Byzantine period. It rather looks as if Anna may have noticed this gap and decided to commission the necessary commentaries.

From the twelfth century onwards the story can be carried forward once more by reference to outstanding individuals. Undoubtedly the most eminent figure in the scholarship of this age was Eustathius (fl. c. 1160–92), who after being a teacher of rhetoric in one of the leading institutions of the capital was appointed to the archbishopric of Thessalonica in 1175. During his teaching career in the capital he must be assumed to have accomplished most of his scholarly work. The libraries of Constantinople no doubt held treasures not yet exploited by men of learning, and one may suspect that Eustathius did not entirely relish the promotion which removed him to another city; though important, Thessalonica does not seem to have been at that date a centre of intellectual life. His interest in classics did not prevent him from taking his clerical duties seriously, and we still possess a treatise by him on the reform of the monastic life; among other things it shows that most monks had no interest in books or learning and were unworthy of their vows, and the bibliophile in Eustathius comes out in an anecdote he tells of an abbot who sold a beautiful calligraphic copy of Saint Gregory Nazianzen because his monastery had no use for it. This section of the tract serves to remind us that the tradition of learning was alien to the spirit of many members of the Church, however much high prelates set an example by their display of deep learning. Eustathius himself knew a number of texts that have since been lost and would be useful to us if still preserved. This is apparent partly from his use of otherwise unknown sources in his commentaries and partly from a quotation he gives of a few lines of Sophocles' *Antigone*; here he refers to 'good copies' (ἀκριβῆ ἀντίγραφα) which give the full text of lines 1165–8, whereas all the manuscripts of Sophocles now reduce the passage to incoherence by omitting one of the lines. Eustathius had evidently noted the unsatisfactory state of the text and compared other copies until he found one with the right text. It seems quite likely, to judge from a remark in his introduction to Pindar, that he read more of his *Epinicia* than we possess today.

His major works were his commentaries on classical authors. What he wrote on Pindar does not survive except for the introduction, and of his notes to Aristophanes no more is known than minute fragments preserved in late manuscripts. But we have his notes to Dionysius Periegetes, a late poet of little merit who wrote an account of geography in about 1,000 hexameters; these verses have come down to us in so many manuscripts that they must be presumed to have served as the textbook of geography in Byzantine schools. More important and much more voluminous are his commentaries on Homer; that on the *Iliad* fills about 1,400 large pages of print in the Leipzig edition of 1827–30. Both these commentaries are essentially compilations, with very little that has been contributed by Eustathius himself. The scale of the commentary, especially that on Homer, is enormous; the discussion of the first line of the *Iliad* runs to 10 pages, and if even a modest proportion of this was ever used by a teacher in the Byzantine classroom, the result must have been to confuse the pupil by a mass of learning of dubious relevance and at the same time to prevent him reading through the text at a pace sufficient to yield some enjoyment. Eustathius is fond of allegorical interpretations, and criticizes Aristarchus for not adopting them. The work is useful to the modern scholar occasionally, but only because of those qualities which made it unduly cumbersome for the author's contemporaries; as far as relevance is concerned it is no advance on the average standard of commentary produced in the ancient world.

Two of Eustathius' lesser contemporaries deserve mention. John Tzetzes (c. 1110–80) was not in holy orders but appears to have run a school in Constantinople. Apart from some letters which reveal a good deal about his personality and day-to-day life his writings include commentaries on three plays of Aristophanes, Hesiod, and part of Homer. He is inferior to Eustathius in knowledge and intelligence, and is quite unjustifiably conceited about his own attainments: it is not easy to respect the man who in the middle of a note on Aristophanes (*Plutus* 677) states that he would not lengthen his explanation but for the fact that there is a good deal of space left on the present page of his book. Nevertheless the allusions in his letters show his wide reading, and we know that he attended meetings at which interpretations of classical texts were discussed; more information about this philological club would be very welcome. Like Eustathius he too had read some books that we no longer have, including some Callimachus and Hipponax. The same is true of Michael Choniates (otherwise known as Acominatus), a somewhat younger man who corresponded with Eustathius and like him was elevated to a bishopric at some distance from the capital, in this case Athens. In his letters he bemoans his fate; to have the use of the undamaged Parthenon as his cathedral was no compensation for the loss of educated society, and his congregations of ignorant peasants were incapable of appreciating the beauties of his high-flown Atticist sermons. But he was the proud owner of one very rare book no longer extant, the *Hecale* of Callimachus, and delighted in quoting from it in his letters. He and Tzetzes are the latest Byzantines of whom we can say with certainty that they could read more classical poetry than we can.

The reason for this lies in an event of the utmost importance which Michael Choniates lived to see, the capture and sack of Constantinople by the Fourth Crusade in 1204. Great damage was done, and there is little doubt that libraries suffered severely. For the historian of literature this sack of the city was a greater disaster than the more famous one of 1453. In 1204 the rare texts mentioned in the previous paragraph were destroyed; at any rate there is no trace of them when the seat of government was restored to Constantinople in 1261 after the fall of the Latin kingdom. If the events of 1204 had not taken place these texts might well have found their way to the West through the agency of the numerous Italian visitors and book collectors who went to Greece and brought back manuscripts. By the time that the city fell into the hands of the Turks little remained to be discovered by the collectors; the only substantial and well-attested loss is recorded in the statement of Constantine Lascaris that a complete copy of the *Universal History* by Diodorus Siculus was destroyed by the Turks.

While the capital was occupied by the Franks and most of Greece was parcelled out among Western barons, the Byzantine administration dragged out a precarious existence at Nicaea, preserving the empire's possessions in Asia Minor. Despite the drastic reduction in the wealth and power of the empire this period of exile in Nicaea was by no means one of the worst for literary studies. The emperors John Vatatzes and Theodore Ducas Lascaris were concerned to promote schools and libraries and eventually built up quite a tradition of secondary education. Little is known in detail, since very few manuscripts can be identified as having been written in the Nicaean empire, but it seems clear that poets and orators were studied, and some of Theodore's own letters display cultivated and scholarly attitudes. Other scholarly work was done by the monk Nicephorus Blemmydes (c. 1197–c. 1272), who wrote on many topics, including logic, physics, and geography, and made a journey to parts of the old empire now under Latin control in search of books that could not be found in Asia Minor. This is one of the few short periods in which literary studies flourished outside the capital. It is also possible that the thirteenth century was an age of considerable culture in the outlying Byzantine province in the heel of Italy; Sicily and the extreme south of Italy were largely Greek in speech during the Middle Ages, and a good deal is known of the numerous Greek monasteries there. The part of this territory most closely in contact with Constantinople was the district of Otranto, where there was a famous monastery of Saint Nicholas that maintained a school and a large library. A number of books written there and in the neighbouring towns of Nardò and Gallipoli do suggest a reasonably flourishing state of school education; there are copies of Homer, Hesiod, and Aristotle safely attributable to these centres, and a number of other books, including some lexica, may have been written there. But there is no trace of any advanced scholarship or any attempt to write commentaries on classical authors.

The Latin kingdoms in Constantinople and Greece were brought to an end in 1261, and the Greek emperors reigned once again from their traditional capital; but their empire was reduced in size and power, being gradually whittled away by the invasions of the Turks on the eastern side and the encroachment of Italian trading states such as Genoa and Venice in Greece and the islands; mercenaries hired to assist the empire often did more harm than good, as for instance a band of Catalans who did an immense amount of damage before setting up a small independent state in

Athens. Nevertheless the late thirteenth and early fourteenth centuries saw some of the best Byzantine work on classical texts. Though little is known of the leading institutions of the capital, there appear to have been several schools in Constantinople and Thessalonica, presided over by men of learning. In an account of this brevity there is not room to describe more than two of them. The first is the monk Maximus Planudes (c. 1255–1305), who worked in the capital and achieved much in a rather short life. Besides running a school for a time he was sent on a diplomatic mission to Venice, and either before or during this acquired a good working knowledge of Latin, an exceptionally rare attainment in Byzantium (otherwise it appears to have been confined to a few lawyers and interpreters). He read widely in Latin, evidently with considerable interest, for he prepared a large number of translations, among which figure Augustine, Boethius, Macrobius and very remarkably Ovid's *Heroides, Metamorphoses,* and amatory works. Not all these translations have yet been printed, but it has been plausibly suggested that those of the theological works might yet prove useful as an introduction for Greek theologians to the Latin fathers; the conservatism of the Greek literary language is such that Planudes' versions could be printed with little change, but the more serious obstacle, the Greek refusal to be reconciled to the Western Church, has remained essentially unaltered until the present day. The first contact between Byzantium and the West for purposes other than trade agreements or religious disputation had no immediate result; but in the next century the monk Demetrius Cydones continued the task of translation with some works of Aquinas, and a traffic of ideas moving in the opposite direction was begun by the Italians who came to Constantinople to learn Greek. Of more practical and immediate importance was Planudes' study of Greek texts. He is generally thought to have been responsible for the production of a large volume (preserved in Florence as Laur. 32.16) containing a collection of classical poetry, which includes school authors and others such as Nonnus. But his interests were far from being confined to the usual range of school texts; we find him searching for Plutarch's works, of which he compiled a catalogue, and he drew up a revised version of the Greek Anthology which includes quite a number of epigrams that do not occur in the Palatine manuscript; of this latter work his autograph is now in Venice (Marc. gr. 481). His method of dealing with Greek texts was not always such as to commend him to modern editors; in one case, the didactic poem on astronomy by Aratus (c. 315–c. 240 B.C.), which was probably used as a textbook on astronomy if the subject was taught in school, Planudes could not resist the temptation to revise some parts of the text which were factually inaccurate. Instead of simply recording in a commentary the advances in knowledge, he replaced lines 481–96, 501–6, and 515–24 by passages of his own composition (Plate VI). Further information about his interests can be gleaned from his letters. He mentions manuscripts of the abstruse mathematical writer Diophantus, and we know that he was interested in other scientific authors such as Ptolemy and Euclid; he also wrote a pamphlet about the introduction of Arabic numerals (in general the Greeks still used the cumbrous alphabetic system of numerals). Another feature of his letters worthy of mention is that he frequently requests one of his correspondents who lives in Asia Minor to obtain for him some parchment, and is irritated when his friend can do no better than find him some asses' skins. The shortage of writing material experienced by one working in or near the capital is very surprising. It may be worth noting in passing that though he had been employed by the emperor on an embassy and was clearly a scholar of distinction, there is no sign that he ever obtained imperial patronage or support for his scholarly work, and this is generally true of Byzantine scholars with the partial exception of those working under the kingdom of Nicaea.

Rather less catholic in his tastes but no less important as a scholar than Planudes was Demetrius Triclinius, a schoolmaster who is known to have lived in Thessalonica c. 1305–20. His work on the standard poetic texts of the curriculum can be traced partly through autographs that survive and partly in the numerous later books which contain commentaries headed by his name (Plate VII). His chief claim to a place of honour in the history of scholarship is that he was the first Byzantine to have a grasp of the metres of classical poetry and to exploit his knowledge. All his predecessors had either virtually ignored metrical questions or had failed to appreciate the potential utility of the subject for a student

of classical poetry. But Triclinius came across a copy of the
ancient metrical treatise by Hephaestion and grasped the essentials
of it with a view to correcting the many passages in classical
texts which were suspect or undoubtedly corrupt. It seems
likely that he or his elder contemporaries were the first to emend
texts systematically, and in the case of Triclinius enough documents survive to allow us a view of him at work. Though his knowledge of metre was by no means perfect he could correct iambics;
sometimes he achieved a result that has won the general approval
of modern critics, but often he resorted to facile measures such as
the insertion of stopgap words to heal a metrical fault, and it is
evident that he was not sensitive to questions of linguistic style in
classical poetry. In more complicated metres than iambics he was
less sure of his ground, but had one vital weapon: he knew that the
lyrics of the chorus in tragedy and comedy were intended to have
exact metrical responsion, and the text of Euripides which contains
his autograph corrections (Laur. 32.2) shows him willing to use
Procrustean violence in order to achieve the desired result (see
p. 211). Despite his many mistakes in the use of his knowledge it
remains the most important step forward in the treatment of
poetic texts at this date. Textual criticism was thus raised again to
the level which it had reached in the ancient world, but the task
awaiting the critic had increased, since the practice of copying by
hand for a millennium and more had necessarily introduced many
new errors into the texts.

Triclinius' other main work was a redrafting of the scholia on
various authors. He sifted the material of the old scholia and
selected what he believed to be most useful for school instruction.
The resulting new commentary contained a certain number of
additional glosses or other elementary notes added by himself, and
it tended to omit or reduce parts of the scholia which are most
valuable for modern scholars; ancient learning was not always
directly relevant to the text and Triclinius did not have the modern
scholar's reasons for wishing to preserve it. Being conscious of the
importance of his metrical knowledge he composed a separate
metrical commentary on many plays; in the case of Aristophanes
he had some guidance from the ancient metrical commentary by
Heliodorus which survived in the old scholia. In his autograph

copies he arranged in separate columns the metrical commentary of his own composition and the old scholia which he had revised.

By his work on text and scholia, which was on the whole more thorough and competent than that of his colleagues, Triclinius deserves to be counted as the forerunner of modern editors. Like other scholars he hunted for fresh manuscripts in the hope of improving the texts. In some of his notes he refers to the different readings of the various copies that he had been able to consult. On one occasion his searches appear to have been rewarded by a dramatic discovery: he came across a text of nine plays of Euripides that were otherwise almost unknown in Byzantium; the copies of this book that he had prepared by his pupils or in a local scriptorium, to which he added a good many alterations in his own hand, are our only source for the text of these plays. We therefore owe largely to Triclinius our knowledge of about half the surviving work of Euripides.

Planudes and Triclinius may be selected as the most important representatives of their age, and the latest Byzantines whose activities had any lasting effect on classical texts. Though they were not followed by men of comparable ability, they were not without colleagues and rivals in their own day, and the work of the latter can be seen in much the same way from surviving manuscripts. Some manuscripts of this comparatively late date are important for the constitution of texts. They contain good readings which are due to the acumen of contemporary scholars or represent branches of tradition that cannot be traced earlier. Classical studies enjoyed great popularity; not only the literature was being read, but technical and scientific works written in antiquity were still sufficiently up to date to demand and reward attention. With some justification the period is referred to as the Palaeologan Renaissance, the name being drawn from that of the ruling house of the time. Secondary education seems to have increased substantially although the general condition of the empire was anything but satisfactory. Schoolmasters devoted themselves to the elucidation or correction of texts that can scarcely have formed part of the regular school curriculum; we have seen for instance how Planudes worked on Nonnus and scientific texts, while Triclinius' study of the newly found Euripidean plays apparently had no bearing on the school programme, for there is no evidence that any of them was added to the normal syllabus. This consisted of Attic or Atticist prose writers, textbooks of the art of rhetoric, especially Hermogenes and Aphthonius, and the poets, primarily Homer (Plate IV) and the selected plays of tragedy and comedy. By the late thirteenth century it had become the custom to read three plays of each tragedian and Aristophanes, sometimes known as the 'triad'; the habit may go back to the twelfth century or earlier, for Tzetzes composed a full commentary on only the three Aristophanic comedies that later were standard reading. Most manuscripts of these four authors contain only the triad; some of the later manuscripts have only one or two plays, which may well be an indication that the curriculum had been still further reduced. The plays outside the triad might easily have been lost through neglect, but fortunately they were preserved just long enough to be rescued by the Italian visitors and collectors of the Renaissance; all the most important manuscripts of these texts reached Italy during the Renaissance and many are still to be found there. The dramatic texts are only one instance of a general process. The chief merit of the Byzantines was that they took an interest in a wide range of classical texts and thus preserved them until scholars of another nation were in a position to use and appreciate them. The tradition of scholarship was taken up by the Italian humanists, who resembled their Byzantine colleagues in many ways. A vast number of manuscripts were brought back from the Byzantine empire in the last century of its history, and the collectors were active long after, so that today the libraries of the Greek East are virtually denuded of classical texts. This process was undoubtedly necessary in order to ensure the survival of Greek literature.

3. THE LATIN WEST

I. THE DARK AGES

The sixth century saw the final collapse of what remained of the Roman empire in the West. In Italy the relatively enlightened rule of Theodoric (493–526) was given distinction by the two most notable figures of the transition period from the ancient to the medieval world, Boethius and Cassiodorus; but it was followed by the destruction of the Ostrogothic kingdom by the Byzantines and a spectacular cultural decline. The provinces were to fare little better. North Africa, now in Vandal hands, was soon to pass beyond the pale of Western culture; some of its literary achievement, such as the *Latin Anthology*, was transmitted in time to Europe and so to posterity. Spain, prey to external attack and internal strife, was to see a revival of Visigothic culture in the later sixth and early seventh centuries, reaching a modest peak in Isidore of Seville, but it too was to succumb in the early eighth century to the Moslem invaders. Though traces of the older Roman culture lingered on among the upper classes in Gaul, the Frankish Merovingian dynasty founded by Clovis (481–511) was grotesquely ill-suited to foster any cultural continuity.

The ravages of conquest and barbarism made the prospects for cultural life extremely bleak, and within the narrowing world of culture the place allotted to classical Latin literature was insecure. Education and the care of books were rapidly passing into the hands of the Church, and the Christians of this period were predominantly hostile to pagan literature. Decimated by the continued destruction of war, faced by hostility or neglect at the hands of the new intellectuals, the Latin classics seemed to have a slim chance of survival.

But the fundamental condition for their survival obtained: there were still books. We do not know how much survived of the twenty-eight public libraries of which Rome could boast in the fourth century; but there were remnants at least of the great private libraries of the age of the Symmachi, there were important collections in such ecclesiastical centres as Rome and Ravenna and

Monastic and other centres of Western Europe

Verona, and books were beginning to find a refuge in the monasteries. The luxury copies of Vergil show that the book trade had flourished down to the end of the fifth century and the beautiful monastic productions which survive from sixth-century Italy demonstrate that nothing had been lost in the art of producing books when it passed into the hands of the Church. Many of the handsome capital and uncial manuscripts of the fourth and fifth centuries have survived, though in most cases only in fragments; their contents include remnants of Plautus and Terence, Ovid, Vergil, Lucan, a varied selection of Cicero's works, Sallust, Livy, the Elder Pliny, the tragedies and prose works of Seneca, Fronto, and Gellius. From this and other evidence it is clear that it was still possible in the year 500, at least in Italy, to obtain copies of most of the Latin authors. Some, like Catullus and Propertius, were probably scarce, and much of early Latin literature had been lost for ever, but even in the sixth century a Spanish bishop, Martin of Braga, was able to plagiarize a work of Seneca now lost and which could barely have survived him.

The bulk of Latin literature was still extant; moreover, the machinery for its transmission to later ages was already being set up in the shape of the monastic library and scriptorium. It was the monastic centres which were destined, often in spite of themselves, to play the major part in both preserving and transmitting what remained of pagan antiquity; a more slender, but at times vital, line of descent can be traced through the schools and libraries which became associated with the great cathedrals.

An early and conspicuous example of the monastic tradition was the monastery of Vivarium which Cassiodorus founded some time after 540 on his estates at Squillace in the extreme south of Italy. It owed much of its conception and character to the urgencies of the times, when the devastation of war and conquest was threatening to destroy cultural centres and even the books on which learning and literacy depended. Cassiodorus endowed his foundation with a good working library and put a strong emphasis on education and the copying of manuscripts. His educational program is set out in the two books of his *Institutiones divinarum et saecularium litterarum*, composed c. 562. Although endowed with no exceptional intellectual gifts, Cassiodorus appears in retrospect as a man of vision who foresaw the role which monasteries were to play in succeeding centuries, who grasped the crucial fact that with the disintegration of political life these retreats provided the main hope for intellectual continuity. But he also had a practical bent and an eye for detail in keeping with a long and successful career in the Ostrogothic civil service. He realized the need for Latin translations of the Greek authorities on exegesis, philosophy, and science, and he was influential in both augmenting and disseminating the increasing body of Greek learning available in Latin dress. He had a particular appreciation for the convenience of the omnibus volume and had related texts bound together whenever possible; one of his composite volumes contained Cicero's *De inventione*, Quintilian, and the *Ars rhetorica* of Fortunatianus, a book for which Lupus of Ferrières understandably searched far and wide in the ninth century. He insisted on the importance of the meticulous copying of books, paid great attention to orthography and presentation, and with moving eloquence conferred a new dignity upon the scribe: 'felix intentio, laudanda sedulitas, manu hominibus praedicare, digitis linguas aperire, salutem mortalibus tacitum dare, et contra diaboli subreptiones illicitas calamo atramentoque pugnare' (*Inst.* 1.30.1).

Cassiodorus' services to the classical tradition could easily be exaggerated; indeed, one of his main preoccupations had been to erode the secular monopoly of higher education. The pagan authors found a place in both his library and his educational program, but they were reduced to the rank of teaching books and manuals. The only classical works which to our certain knowledge he put on his shelves were Cicero's *De inventione*, Seneca's *De forma mundi* (now lost), Columella, Quintilian, Apuleius' *De interpretatione*, some Aristotle, and a number of technical works; of the poets, whom he quotes and on whom he had been brought up, apparently nothing. The library of his contemporary Symmachus, for example, who had a much more positive attitude to pagan culture, would probably have had a very different flavour. Nor does Vivarium appear to have played any direct part in the transmission of classical texts. His monastery seems to have died with him, and the theory once held, that its books passed in time to the great monastery of Bobbio, founded in northern Italy in

614, and so provided a direct link between antiquity and the Middle Ages, now lies in ruins: such of its books as can be traced appear to have found their way in the main to Rome, possibly to the Lateran Library, and from there to have been dispersed by the generosity of successive popes. A few manuscripts have been identified which were either written at Vivarium or had ancestors which originated in Cassiodorus' library, among them the famous codex Amiatinus of the Vulgate (see p. 228), but these do not include any classical texts. Cassiodorus is important for many reasons and not least because he provides us with our only example of a sixth-century library; but there must have been other—and from the classical point of view better—collections of which we know nothing.

More limited in aim, but immeasurably greater in effect, was the founding of Monte Cassino c. 529 by Benedict of Nursia, who, by the promulgation of his Rule, laid the foundation on which monastic life in the West was based for centuries to come. Apart from setting aside a period each day for reading—a spiritual rather than intellectual operation—the Benedictine Rule had nothing to say about intellectual pursuits, and the copying of books had no explicit part in the monastic ideal; but, in saying nothing, it left the way open for liberal influences when the time was ripe, and reading could in any case not be carried on without books.

While Italy had enjoyed its late Renaissance in the first half of the sixth century, the blossoming of Visigothic culture in Spain did not come until the late sixth and early seventh centuries. This revival largely owes its place in the history of classical culture to the achievement of its greatest writer, Isidore of Seville (c. 570–636). Owing to the phenomenally rapid spread of his works throughout Europe, an amazing accomplishment for the pre-Carolingian period, Isidore was quickly established as one of the most influential agents in the transmission and elucidation of ancient learning. His *Etymologies* was at the same time the last product of the Roman encyclopedic tradition and the starting-point for most medieval compilations; its most frequently copied section, the first three books covering the subjects of the *trivium* and *quadrivium*, must have contributed enormously to the consolidation of the medieval educational system. This systematically arranged encyclopedia, packed with information and misinformation on every topic from angels to the parts of the saddle, descends so often into false etymologizing and the uncritical parade of absurd bric-à-brac that it cannot be read without a smile. But Isidore wins one's respect, and even affection, by his obvious appreciation of knowledge for its own sake. Hostility to pagan literature is explicit in some of his public pronouncements, and he was more at home in the neutral pages of the scholiast and compiler than the classical authors themselves, whom with a few exceptions he quotes at second-hand; but his curiosity knew no barriers and he took for granted the independent value of profane culture. When he culls from the fathers of the Church the scraps of classical poetry and pagan learning which they contain and re-allocates them to their proper place in the traditional system of knowledge, this bishop is paradoxically recreating in a resecularized form the basic structure of ancient learning.

However, the process which has preserved Latin literature for us could not begin until there was a more sympathetic and more positive attitude to classical authors than generally obtained on the continent in the Dark Ages. Christians still lived in the shadow of pagan literature; its achievement dwarfed their own, and its threat to morals and doctrine was a real one. This was to change when Latin culture was transplanted to a distant soil, where those eager to learn the language of the Church could turn to antiquity without any sense of inferiority or fear, since rivalry was out of the question and men at large were protected from the dangers of ancient paganism by simple ignorance of the Latin language. But this spirit did not percolate on any scale to the continent of Europe until the Carolingian Revival in the late eighth century, and in the meantime much of classical literature perished.

Although few ages are so dark that they are not penetrated by a few shafts of light, the period from roughly 550 to 750 was one of almost unrelieved gloom for the Latin classics on the continent; they virtually ceased being copied. Among the mass of patristic, biblical, and liturgical manuscripts which survive from this period there are precious few classical texts: from the sixth century we have scraps of two Juvenal manuscripts, remnants of one of the Elder and one of the Younger Pliny, but at least two of these belong to the early part of the century; from the seventh century we have a fragment of Lucan; from the early eighth century nothing.

The fate which often overtook the handsome books of antiquity is dismally illustrated by the surviving palimpsests—manuscripts in which the original texts have been washed off to make way for works which at the time were in greater demand. Many texts which had escaped destruction in the crumbling empire of the West perished within the walls of the monastery; some of them may have been too tattered when they arrived to be of practical use, and there was no respect for rags, however venerable. The peak period for this operation was the seventh and early eighth century, and although palimpsests survive from many centres, the bulk of them have come from the Irish foundations of Luxeuil and Bobbio. Texts perished, not because pagan authors were under attack, but because no one was interested in reading them, and parchment was too precious to carry an obsolete text; Christian works, heretical or superfluous, also went to the wall, while the ancient grammarians, of particular interest to the Irish, often have the upper hand. But the toll of classical authors was very heavy: amongst those palimpsested we find Plautus and Terence, Cicero and Livy, the Elder and Younger Pliny, Sallust and Seneca, Vergil and Ovid, Lucan, Juvenal and Persius, Gellius and Fronto. Fronto survives in three palimpsests, fated always to be the underdog. Among the texts which have survived solely in this mutilated form are some of outstanding interest, such as the *De republica* of Cicero (Vat. lat. 5757, Plate X) written in uncials of the fourth or fifth century and covered at Bobbio in the seventh with Augustine on the Psalms, a fifth-century copy of the *De amicitia* and *De vita patris* of Seneca (Vat. Pal. lat. 24) which succumbed in the late sixth or early seventh century to the Old Testament, and a fifth-century codex of Sallust's *Histories* (Orléans 192 + Vat. Reg. lat. 1283B + Berlin lat. qu. 364) which, in France and probably at Fleury, was supplanted at the turn of the seventh century by Jerome. Other important palimpsests are the Ambrosian Plautus (Ambros. S.P. 9/13-20, *olim* G. 82 sup.) and the Verona Livy (Verona XL (38)), both of the fifth century.

II. IRELAND AND ENGLAND

A new intellectual movement which was to put a higher value on classical texts than the price of their parchment had already begun in a remote outpost of Christianity. This was Ireland, possessed of a Latin culture as early as the late fifth century and destined to play a vital part in the civilization of Europe. The amount of actual classical literature known in Ireland in pre-Carolingian times is much debated and appears to have been small indeed; the close acquaintance with Latin poetry revealed by their major literary figure, Columban (c. 543–615), relates to the continental phase of his life and may belong more to the context of late antique culture than that of the monasteries of Ireland. The important feature of their culture was therefore not its classical content but the intensive and uninhibited way in which they read what books they possessed, their enthusiasm and aptitude for learning, however peculiar and bogus that learning sometimes was, and the industry which produced in the course of the seventh and eight centuries a remarkable amount of grammatical and exegetical work. The Irish also had remarkable artistic talents: from the half-uncial manuscripts which they had acquired from Gaul in the fifth and sixth centuries they developed a beautiful half-uncial of their own, seen in its finest form in the Book of Kells, and a more practical and equally individual minuscule script. Their importance for the transmission of classical texts begins when they leave Ireland, impelled by a missionary zeal of far-reaching consequence. The establishment of Iona as the centre of Celtic Christianity outside Ireland by Columba c. 563 marked the effective beginning of the conversion of Scotland and led on in time to the foundation of such important monasteries as Lindisfarne in Northumbria and Malmesbury in the south-west. Even more spectacular was the continental mission of Columban, who blazed a trail across Europe marked out by such important monastic foundations as those of Luxeuil in Burgundy (590), from which Corbie was founded a century later, Bobbio in northern Italy (614), and Saint Gall, which developed from a hermitage which his pupil Gallus established in Switzerland c. 613. The *Scotti peregrini* became a colourful feature of the continental scene in the eighth and ninth centuries and had a large contribution to make, as such men as Virgil of Salzburg, Dungal, Sedulius Scottus, John Scottus Eriugena serve to demonstrate. However much these scholars became part of the Carolingian revival, their learning tended to retain its strong Irish accent.

While the Latin culture of Ireland was percolating through northern England, a more direct link with Rome and its past was re-established in the south when, in 597, Gregory the Great sent Augustine to England with a mission to convert the Anglo-Saxons to Christianity. Canterbury became the centre of Roman Christianity and Augustine its first archbishop. More significant, because more effective, was the second mission of 668, headed by Theodore of Tarsus and Hadrian of Niridanum, which succeeded in establishing the Roman Church throughout the country. Theodore was a Greek, Hadrian an African by birth; both were men of wide learning. An important feature of the renewed contact with Rome was the inflow of books. To Augustine Gregory had sent the necessary vestments and vessels for carrying on divine service *nec non et codices plurimos* (Bede, *Hist. eccl.* 1.29). These would be bibles, service-books, and the like, but most of them were doubtless written in uncials, and it was these books which led to to the development in England of a fine uncial script which enjoyed a couple of centuries of glory before giving way in the eight century to the minuscule introduced into Northumbria by the Irish. Theodore and Hadrian came with an educational and literary program; they must have brought a large number of books, Latin and Greek, probably pagan and Christian, but we have no details. The Anglo-Latin culture which grew out of the converging influences of Ireland and Rome created a need for books of all kinds; some came from France and Spain, but the main source was Italy, Rome, and the South. Wilfrid (c. 634–709), bishop of York and abbot of Ripon, made several journeys to Rome and will not have come back empty-handed, and the same applies to Aldhelm; but the great traveller of the age was Benedict Biscop, the founder of the twin monasteries of Wearmouth and Jarrow (674 and 682), who made no less than six trips to Italy. The fifth is the most famed: *innumerabilem librorum omnis generis copiam adportavit* (Bede, *Hist. abbatum* 6). A distinguished place in English history is owed to Benedict Biscop and his protégé abbot Ceolfrid, who made it possible for a local boy who had apparently never set foot outside Northumbria, Bede, to acquire a breadth of scholarship unrivalled in the Europe of his day and to leap the seemingly unbridgeable gulf which separated his world from that of the later Roman empire. We know of further importations of books in the eighth century, and the result can be seen in the rich libraries which grew up at Canterbury and York.

We know something of the width of reading of the English scholars of the seventh and eighth centuries from the writings of Aldhelm (c. 639–709) and Bede (673–735), the one a product of Wessex and Kent, the other of Northumbria. Their range of reference was doubtless exceptional, but it is evidence of the books available to scholars in England. The impressive roll of classical authors named or quoted shows a healthy respect for the classical tradition rather than first-hand knowledge, for much of it is derived from Macrobius and Isidore and the grammarians. Further reductions of the list may be necessary, but Aldhelm appears to have known Vergil and Lucan, Persius and Juvenal, the Elder Pliny, some Cicero, possibly Ovid, while Bede had first-hand knowledge of a large number of grammarians, Vergil, some books of the Elder Pliny, Macrobius and Eutropius, more dubiously Ovid and Lucan. This is impressive and is corroborated by evidence of a slightly later date which we owe to the fortunate chance that Alcuin (c. 735–804), in a poem in praise of York, gives us a glimpse of the contents of that great library. When it comes to cataloguing, a poem is a far cry from a card-index: some authors and titles are excluded by metrical exigencies, so that the list is vague and incomplete. However, among a rich collection of theological names, we have a number of *auctores*: Vergil, Statius, Lucan, Cicero, Pliny, and Pompeius. Cicero, given the epithet *rhetor*, will mean the *De inventione*, and Pompeius will be Justinus' epitome of Pompeius Trogus. Such hints as we have reveal in England a broader and more systematic knowledge of both Christian and pagan literature than could be paralleled elsewhere at this period.

III. THE ANGLO-SAXON MISSIONARIES

The rich and vigorous culture which blossomed in Anglo-Saxon England soon spread to the continent. The Irish had passed on their missionary impulse, and the most famous of the successors of Columban were Willibrord (658–739), a native of Northumbria, and Boniface (c. 675–754), a product of Wessex. Willibrord set out on his mission to the Frisian people in 690 and so inaugurated a period of Anglo-Saxon influence on the continent which was to last into the ninth century; his consecration as archbishop of the Frisians by the Pope and at the suggestion of Pippin II marked the first step in cooperation between the Carolingian house and the Papacy. Boniface eventually settled on central Germany as his sphere of activity; but his missionary venture, forwarded by the active help of successive Carolingian patrons, particularly Charles Martel, by papal encouragement, and not least by his own tremendous capacity for ecclesiastical organization, so snowballed that it led to the reform of the whole Frankish Church and the establishment of Germany as a province of the Church of Rome. Among his theological opponents was a colourful Irishman, Virgil of Salzburg, who administered the see from 746–84, a man of wide learning with a talent for satire; he claims our interest because his cosmological take-off, the so-called *Cosmographia* of Aethicus Ister, reveals him as the first person north of the Alps to know the geographical work of Pomponius Mela and establishes a link in a chain of transmission which leads from ancient Ravenna to the Renaissance (see pp. 94, 115). One of his countrymen, if not Virgil himself, may well be responsible for the pro-Irish gloss which crept into Mela's text: the unflattering description of the ancient Irish as *omnium virtutum ignari magis quam aliae gentes* (3.6.53) received the comment *aliquatenus tamen gnari*.

One result of this alliance of missionary enthusiasm and temporal interest was the rise of important episcopal centres, like Mainz and Würzburg, and a new wave of monastic foundations, both needing libraries and scriptoria. Among the monasteries were Fulda, founded in 744 by Boniface's pupil Sturmi, and the closely allied Hersfeld, established c. 770 by his helper, the Anglo-Saxon Lullus. But two other important monasteries, Reichenau on Lake Constance (724) and its daughter-house of Murbach (727), were founded by Pirmin, a man of obscure origin, thought to have fled from Visigothic Spain with the coming of the Arabs in 711.

With them the Anglo-Saxons brought a script, books, a liberal intellectual outlook, and the recognition that a well-stocked and well-balanced library was the basis of ecclesiastical education. Books must have been imported on some scale, and not only from England; the letters of Boniface and Lullus are full of requests for books. The Anglo-Saxon script became established in centres under insular influence and was often practised alongside continental hands in the same scriptorium. Pockets of insular writing flourished until the middle of the ninth century, and some of its features, particularly abbreviation signs, were incorporated into the tradition of continental script.

IV. INSULAR INFLUENCE ON CLASSICAL TEXTS

The impact of Anglo-Latin culture on the intellectual rebirth of the continent, which finally culminated in the person of Alcuin, together with the practical provision of books, scriptoria, and scribes, must have had an immeasurable effect on the revival—and hence the survival—of Latin literature. But it is not easy to demonstrate this in detail, as the evidence is fragmentary and disparate. A couple of classical manuscripts have survived which were actually written in the eighth century in Northumbria; these show that part of the textual tradition of these authors actually passed at one stage through northern England. One of these two manuscripts contains the first six books of Pliny's *Natural History* (Voss. lat. F. 4, Plate XII), the other is just a single leaf of Justinus (Weinheim, MS. Fischer). Both manuscripts were written in Northumbria and both the works which they contain were, as we have seen, in the library at York. The Justinus manuscript actually made the journey which one suspects in the case of some other classical texts: it crossed the Channel and found its way to the Carolingian court, where it fathered the transalpine—and best—family of Justinus manuscripts. A recently published fragment containing excerpts of Servius' commentary on the *Aeneid* appears to have been written in south-west England in the latter part of the eighth century (Spangenburg, Pfarrbibliothek S.N.); it is later associated with Fulda and it has been conjectured that it may have been taken to Germany by Boniface or one of his circle.

For some other authors we have manuscripts which were written in insular script on the continent (paradoxically known as 'continental insular'), and the text of these authors clearly owes much to the missionary activity of the English and the Irish. Texts which survive in manuscripts known to have been written or housed in insular monastic and episcopal centres on the continent are equally beneficiaries of the movement, though their script may show no trace of it. The same applies to those texts which show 'insular symptoms', i.e. errors which are best explained as originating in the faulty transcription of letters or abbreviations peculiar to English or Irish hands. These indicate that the text went through an insular tradition at an earlier stage in its history than that represented by the extant manuscripts. But such hypotheses have to be treated with caution: symptoms, especially when few in number, can be wrongly diagnosed, and insular ancestry, like the Scottish grandmother, is more often claimed than substantiated. The authors which go back with at least a high degree of probability to an insular parent include Ammianus Marcellinus, the *Tusculan disputations* of Cicero, the epic poetry of Statius and Valerius Flaccus, the *De architectura* of Vitruvius, and claims can be made for others. The great centres of insular activity were Hersfeld and Fulda, which played a dominant part in the preservation of some texts. But their contribution belongs more to the story of the Carolingian revival, and will be more appropriately described in that context.

V. THE CAROLINGIAN REVIVAL

The classical revival of the late eighth and early ninth centuries, without doubt the most momentous and critical stage in the transmission of the legacy of Rome, was played out against the background of a reconstituted empire which stretched from the Elbe to the Ebro, from Calais to Rome, welded together for a time into a political and spiritual whole by the commanding personality of an emperor who added to his military and material resources the blessing of Rome. Although the political achievement of Charlemagne (768–814) crumbled in the hands of his successors, the cultural movement which it fostered retained its impetus in the ninth century and survived into the tenth.

The secular and ecclesiastical administration of a vast empire called for a large number of trained priests and functionaries. As the only common denominator in a heterogeneous realm and as the repository of both the classical and the Christian heritage of an earlier age, the Church was the obvious means of implementing the educational program necessary to produce a trained executive. But under the Merovingians the Church had fallen on evil days; some of the priests were so ignorant of Latin that Boniface heard one carrying out a baptism of dubious efficacy *in nomine patria et filia et spiritus sancti (Epist.* 68), and knowledge of antiquity had worn so thin that the author of one sermon was under the unfortunate impression that Venus was a man. Reform had begun under Pippin the Short; but now the need was greater, and Charlemagne felt a strong personal responsibility to raise the intellectual and cultural level of the clergy, and through them of his subjects:

igitur quia curae nobis est ut nostrarum ecclesiarum ad meliora proficiat status, oblitteratam paene maiorum nostrorum desidia reparare vigilanti studio litterarum satagimus officinam, et ad pernoscenda studia liberalium artium nostro etiam quos possumus invitamus exemplo (*Epist. gen., MGH, Legum sectio II, Capit. Regum Francorum I* (1883), p. 80).

When it came to creating an educated class out of next to nothing, the Anglo-Saxons were past masters, and it was a shrewd move on the part of Charles to turn to York, at this time the educational centre of England and indeed of Europe, and in 782 to invite Alcuin, the head of its school, to take charge of his palace school and be his adviser on educational matters.

Alcuin was above all an efficient teacher. There was nothing ambitious about the educational system which he transplanted to the continent and there refined: elementary and utilitarian, it aimed at literacy rather than literature, and the classical content, cut and dried, was entirely subsidiary to the Christian purpose. The Carolingian educational program waned before it could become widely established, but the setting up by imperial edict of schools attached to both the monasteries and the cathedrals guaranteed that a basic standard of literacy would be maintained at least here and there in the Europe of the future, to blossom into something greater when circumstances were favourable. But Carolingian culture was not chained to the schoolroom. Alcuin could rise to greater heights when he wished, and the court became the point of fruitful interaction between poets and scholars attracted to it from the whole of Europe, including men of imagination and elegance and learning, such as Peter of Pisa and Paul the Deacon from Italy, the Irish scholar Dungal, the poet Theodulfus from Spain. From this circle there emanated a higher and more secular cultural stream; men were found who rose above the rather constipated limits of much Carolingian thought and literature and approached the ancient classics with genuine intellectual curiosity and honest aesthetic appreciation. An important result of a rapidly developing and highly organized educational program, spreading from the court to the monasteries and cathedrals, was the need for books; these were produced on an unprecedented scale, in a flurry of activity which salvaged for us the greater part of Latin literature.

VI. THE DEVELOPMENT OF CAROLINE MINUSCULE

In keeping with the thoroughness and uniformity of the new order was the universal adoption of a new script, the Caroline minuscule (Plate XIII), which, though it developed too early for Charlemagne or Alcuin to have had a hand in it, doubtless owed its acceptance and refinement to their encouragement. The late seventh and eight centuries had been a period of universal experimentation in the art of writing, inspired by the need for a more economical and up-to-date script. While the Irish and the English had been developing a minuscule script out of half-uncial, other minuscule hands had come into being on the continent. These had a more humble origin, developing not from the uncial book-hands, though in places these influenced their evolution, but from the old Roman cursive which had remained as the script of business and officialdom. Out of this unpromising script was forged a calligraphic book-hand which evolved along its own lines in different regions and produced the 'national hands' of Spain, southern Italy, and Gaul—Visigothic, Beneventan, and Merovingian.

The Visigothic script, which flourished in Spain from the early eighth to the twelfth century, concerns us least, for there are very few extant classical manuscripts written in this hand and very little evidence that it was instrumental in the transmission of classical texts. Beneventan, so called because it was conterminous with the old duchy of Benevento—its designation as Lombardic is now obsolete—has a marked similarity to Visigothic and became the normal script of Italy south of Rome and parts of the Dalmatian coast (Plate XIV). This fine hand, built up entirely from cursive elements, came into being in the eighth century, reached its peak in the eleventh, and lingered on into the fifteenth, though in the thirteenth it gave way to Caroline minuscule as the vehicle for literary texts. The great centre was Monte Cassino (see p. 96), but a modified script emerged under Byzantine influence along the Adriatic coast and particularly at Bari, and a number of classical texts, including works of Terence, Cicero, Sallust, Vergil, and Ovid, are written in this local Apulian variety.

The early minuscule scripts of Merovingian Gaul are important, not as vehicles for the transmission of classical texts—in which they played little part—but as forerunners of the Carolingian hands. From these scripts, more fluid than those of Italy and Spain, the calligraphic urge of the craftsman evolved, after trial and error, a minuscule which was destined to become the normal script of Western Europe. The first calligraphic minuscule of France was produced at Luxeuil and bears the name of that great Irish foundation; it reached its peak about 700. In the eighth century the palm passed to Corbie, where in the second half of the century no less than three scripts can be distinguished, all in use at the same time —known technically as the en script, the ab script, and the Maurdramn type. In the biblical books produced at Corbie under abbot Maurdramn (772-80) we see emerging from these pre-Caroline scripts the first example of a developed Caroline minuscule. The cursive elements are eliminated, the letters are rounded, separate, and regular, and the result is an unsurpassed grace and lucidity, which must have had a tremendous effect on the survival of classical literature by casting it in a form which all could read with both ease and pleasure. It became universal throughout the Carolingian empire in the course of a few decades, crossed to England in the tenth century, and by the end of the twelfth had swept its rivals from the field.

VII. CAROLINGIAN LIBRARIES AND THE LATIN CLASSICS

Recent research has enabled us to see to the heart of the Carolingian classical revival by demonstrating that a list of authors preserved in a manuscript at Berlin (Diez B. 66), and remarkable for the richness and rarity of its content, can be nothing less than a partial catalogue of books in the court library of Charlemagne about the year 790. The list includes Lucan, Statius' *Thebaid*, Terence, Juvenal, Tibullus, Horace's *Ars poetica*, Claudian, Martial, some of Cicero's speeches (the *Verrines*, *Catilinarians*, *Pro rege Deiotaro*), and a collection of orations excerpted from the *Bella* and *Historiae* of Sallust. Other classical works quoted in the court poetry of the time suggest the presence in the library of such additional rarities as Grattius' *Cynegetica* and Statius' *Silvae*. It is reasonable to assume from passages in Alcuin's correspondence that it also possessed a copy of the Elder Pliny. Some of the books in this impressive list will have been ancient codices written in capitals and uncials.

It is clear from the evidence that abbots and bishops who had the right connections could enrich their libraries with copies taken from the books in the palace library; and after Charlemagne's death, although the details of the way in which his library was dispersed are unknown, many of the books found their way to monastic libraries. There is a remarkable correlation between the items in the palace list and the works known to have been copied at Corbie about the middle of the century: the unique Corbie manuscript which contains the well-known collection of speeches and letters taken from Sallust (Vat. lat. 3864) is the most striking example. Another tell-tale item is the group of three Ciceronian speeches which reappear in the important codex Holkhamicus, now in the British Museum (Add. 47678): this was written at Tours in the early years of the ninth century—Alcuin was abbot of Saint Martin's at Tours from 796–804—and it is easy to guess where its parent came from. Again, one of the most famous manuscripts of Livy is the codex Puteanus of the third decade (Paris lat. 5730, Plate XI), written in the fifth century in Italy and the source of all the later manuscripts: this was copied at Tours about the year 800 (its copy is Vat. Reg. lat. 762, Plate XIII) and again at Corbie about the middle of the ninth century (Laur. 63.20), a pattern which strongly suggests that the home of the Puteanus was to be found in the palace. Other classical manuscripts copied in France at the turn of the century may well owe their contents to the same fruitful source, and the science of palaeography, progressing in this field at a breathless pace, will in time doubtless throw much more light on the movement of books.

Gathering impetus with each decade, the copying of books went on apace through the length and breadth of Charlemagne's empire. Such ancient classical manuscripts as could be found, with their imposing majuscule scripts, were transformed, often at speed, into minuscule copies, and these in time begot further copies, branching out into those complex patterns to which the theory of stemmatics has reduced this fascinating process. Some idea of the scale, perhaps exceptional, on which classical books were copied can be had from those Latin manuscripts which were written at Corbie during a short period after the middle of the century. The exemplars from which they were copied came in part from the palace, and the credit for the burst of activity which produced them probably belongs to the Corbie librarian, Hadoard: they include a large collection of Cicero's philosophical works, the first and third decades of Livy, Sallust, Columella, the Elder Seneca, the Younger Pliny, Caesar's *Gallic War*, the *Ad Herennium*, Macrobius' commentary on the *Somnium Scipionis*, Statius' *Thebaid*, Martial, Ovid's *Heroides* and *Amores*, Terence, Vitruvius, and Vegetius. It is clear from extant catalogues of Carolingian libraries and from other evidence that comparable collections existed, or were being built up, at such centres as Tours, Fleury, Ferrières, Auxerre, Lorsch, Reichenau, and Saint Gall. The multiplication of popular texts meant that the contents of these libraries were inevitably somewhat repetitive: rather than examine them in detail, it will be more interesting to single out the more remarkable items and then attempt a survey of what the Carolingian revival had succeeded in rescuing from the wreck of antiquity.

Though a recent foundation (764), the monastery of Lorsch, in Hesse, enjoyed the special patronage of Charlemagne and rapidly built up one of the richest Carolingian libraries. The famous codex Pithoeanus of Juvenal and Persius (Montpellier 125) was written at Lorsch, and it possessed copies of Cicero's *Letters*, which were a

D

rarity at the time. Among the manuscripts which came into its possession were some very remarkable books. These include the fifth-century codex which is our only source for the fifth decade of Livy (Vienna lat. 15) and which had earlier been circulating in the Low Countries; the main manuscript of Seneca's *De beneficiis* and *De clementia* (Vat. Pal. lat. 1547), written in northern Italy about the year 800 and one of the earliest classical manuscripts of the Carolingian period; the codex Palatinus of Vergil (Vat. Pal. lat. 1631), written in rustic capitals of the late fifth or early sixth century; a famous palimpsest from Italy (Vat. Pal. lat. 24), which had been made up from scraps of some of the oldest surviving books of antiquity, including codices of Seneca, Lucan, Fronto, and Gellius.

The importance of the insular foundations of Fulda and Hersfeld has already been mentioned. From these come the two manuscripts of Ammianus Marcellinus from which the rest derive, and we owe the survival of the *Opera minora* of Tacitus and the *De grammaticis* of Suetonius to a manuscript written at either Hersfeld or Fulda and preserved at the former. Besides contributing important manuscripts to the textual tradition of some authors, such as the Younger Pliny and Aulus Gellius, Fulda played a dominant role in the history of other texts: there is good reason to believe that it housed the archetypes of the *Tusculans* and Vitruvius; of the two Carolingian manuscripts of Columella, one was written at Corbie, the other at Fulda; the prime source for the *Historia Augusta* (Vat. Pal. lat. 899) must have been associated with Fulda, for one of its copies is written in the characteristic script; books 1–6 of the *Annals* of Tacitus have come down to us in a manuscript written at Fulda and preserved at Corvey, a daughter-house of Corbie; finally, to end on a lighter note, while one of the early manuscripts of the cookery book of Apicius is a show-piece of the script of Tours, the other (written in a mixture of Anglo-Saxon minuscule and continental script) points almost certainly to Fulda.

Other monasteries and their treasures must be mentioned more briefly. The group of Caesar manuscripts which contain only the *Gallic War* seem to go back to Fleury, which is almost certainly the source of the text of Petronius. Bobbio possessed both a Lucretius and a Valerius Flaccus, two rare poets. Two of the great Vergil codices, the Augusteus and the Romanus (Vat. lat. 3256 and 3867), have the *ex-libris* of the abbey of Saint Denis at Paris and may have been preserved there from this early period. Reichenau possessed a number of scarce items, Ovid's *Metamorphoses* and *Ars amatoria*, Silius Italicus, and the *Natural Questions* of Seneca.

If one were to take stock at the end of the ninth century of the classical books available, it would be clear that some authors were so well entrenched in the literary and educational tradition and so thick on the shelves of the libraries that their survival was no longer in question: to this group we can assign Vergil and Horace (the *Satires* and *Epistles* rather than the lyrics, which were less popular in the Middle Ages), Lucan, Juvenal and Persius, Terence, the epics of Statius, some of the rhetorical and philosophical works of Cicero (the *Letters* and *Speeches* were still rare or unknown), the *Catilina* and *Jugurtha* of Sallust, the Elder Pliny, Justinus, and Vitruvius. The Elder Seneca and Valerius Maximus were available, as were Aulus Gellius and the *Letters* of Seneca, but Gellius and Seneca both circulated in two separate parts, of which one was much less common than the other, and at this period complete copies were rare or non-existent. Quintilian was less common than one would expect (his place had been usurped by the *Ad Herennium* and the *De inventione*), and he too was incomplete; most of the manuscripts were *mutili*, though a complete text was put together in Germany in the tenth century. Martial and Suetonius were not common, though Einhard's *Life of Charlemagne*, thanks to a happy connection with Fulda, is a brilliant adaptation of Suetonius' literary method and a milestone in the development of secular biography. Plautus, Lucretius, Livy, and the Younger Pliny were even scarcer, and the great age of Ovid was still to come. Some authors existed in so few copies—sometimes only one—that their future was still precarious: Cicero's *Letters*, Tacitus, Columella, Petronius, Apicius, Valerius Flaccus, and Ammianus were all copied at this time, but not on a scale which would ensure their survival through wars and acts of God and the less dramatic but ever-present evils of mice and mould; it was going to need another *renovatio* to make their position secure. The few or unique copies of Tibullus and Catullus, Seneca's *Tragedies* and Statius' *Silvae*, were virtually in hibernation, while Propertius, Seneca's *Dialogues*, Apuleius' *Golden Ass*, much of Tacitus, Manilius, Nepos, and Velleius Paterculus were still quite unknown.

One cannot consider these facts without marvelling at the slenderness of the thread on which the fate of the Latin classics hung. In the case of many texts a single copy survived into the Carolingian period, and often a battered one at that. When the great period of the revival was over, some of the great works of Latin literature were still but a single manuscript on a single shelf. The slightest accident could still have robbed us of some of our most precious texts, of Catullus and Propertius, Petronius or Tacitus. There are some extraordinary examples of survival: the fifth-century manuscript of Livy's fifth decade which found a home at Lorsch (Vienna lat. 15) survived until the sixteenth century without ever being copied. A mere mishap, and five more books of Livy would have disappeared without trace.

VIII. CAROLINGIAN SCHOLARSHIP

One of the more obvious aspects of the Carolingian age is the staggering amount of parchment it consumed: there was a tremendous spate of publication, ranging from creative poetry, through history, biography, hagiography, theology, philosophy, and biblical exegesis, to the handbooks on rhetoric, dialectic, metrics, and grammar. All of this has its relevance, for anything that involved a more sophisticated study and exploitation of the Latin language and literature furthered the classical tradition. But if, for our present purpose, we confine our attention to the study of classical literature and put some weight on the word scholarship, there are only a few men who need engage our attention.

One of the earliest glimpses of scholarly activity expended on a classical text in the Carolingian period is provided by the most celebrated manuscript of Lucretius, the codex Oblongus (Voss. lat. F. 30), written in north-eastern France during the first few years of the ninth century. This has been corrected and at times supplemented in an insular hand by the intriguing 'corrector Saxonicus', whose characteristic script has allowed the palaeographer to clothe him with flesh and blood: no Saxon at all, he has proved to be no less a person than the Irish scholar Dungal, the astronomical authority of his day, whom we see taking a not unexpected interest in our oldest extant text of Lucretius. A much larger place in the history of scholarship has been won by another Irishman, Sedulius Scottus, who was active at Liège in the middle of the century. Versatile and gifted, theologian and versifier as well as the author of grammatical commentaries on Priscian and others, Sedulius interests us most as the compiler of a *Collectaneum*, a collection of excerpts from various authors. This is largely a moral rag-bag of the type one meets frequently in the Middle Ages, but he shows some interest in the style of the authors excerpted and is truly remarkable for the range of his reading: he excerpts a large number of Ciceronian works (including the *Philippics, Pro Fonteio, Pro Flacco, In Pisonem*), Valerius Maximus, Macrobius, the military manuals of Frontinus and Vegetius, and the *Historia Augusta*. For Cicero's *Speeches* he seems to have used one of the important extant manuscripts (Vat. Arch. S. Petri H. 25), copied in Italy and probably from an uncial original. A similar collection has been left to us by Hadoard, the *custos librorum* at Corbie (see p. 87), written almost certainly in his own hand (Vat. Reg. lat. 1762 of the mid-ninth century). Hadoard shows much less respect for his authors: his moral maxims are torn from their context, denuded of the names and historical references which tie them to place and period, and Christianized where necessary. But his range is again noteworthy, particularly of Ciceronian works—*Academica priora, De natura deorum, De divinatione, De fato, Paradoxa, De legibus, Timaeus, Tusculanae disputationes, De officiis, De amicitia, De senectute De oratore*. He is of less textual importance than one might imagine, for some of the manuscripts he used are still extant. A more fascinating document, since it reflects the whole career and personal interests of the compiler, is the scrap-book (Saint Gall 878) of Walafrid Strabo (808–49), poet, tutor to the future Charles the Bald, and abbot of Reichenau. The extracts themselves fail to reveal his literary interests: the only pagan works of the classical period which he chose to excerpt were Columella and the *Letters* of Seneca, the first a not surprising choice for the author of a charming poem on his monastery garden. But the scrap-book has helped to demonstrate a more active intervention in the transmission of classical authors than is normal with an excerptor by revealing that the handsome hand which has supplemented and in places written or rewritten our oldest manuscript of Horace (Vat. Reg. lat. 1703 = R) belongs to Walafrid himself.

But the scholar who towers over his contemporaries is Lupus of Ferrières (c. 805–62). Author of the famous dictum *propter se ipsam appetenda sapientia* (Epist. 1), he alone of the men of his age gives a foretaste of the Renaissance. He was educated at Ferrières and completed his studies at Fulda under the greatest teacher of the post-Alcuinian period, Hrabanus Maurus (780–856); he returned to Ferrières in 836 and was abbot from 842 until his death. His letters are of great interest; despite his involvement in the affairs of the world, his correspondence is dominated by his scholarly interests. Anxious to increase the resources of the library at Ferrières, which had been modest enough in his student days, he writes far and wide in his search for books, to Einhard (who had now left the court and retired to Seligenstadt), to Tours, to York, to the Pope himself. However, he was not the only manuscript-hunter in the ninth century: his distinction rests on the fact that he is avid to obtain manuscripts of works which he already possesses, so that by collation he can correct and supplement his own text. He succeeded in filling up some of the gaps in the incomplete Valerius Maximus which had survived from antiquity by drawing on the rare epitome made by Julius Paris in the fourth century. The following extract from a letter written in 847 to a monk at Prüm will illustrate his practice (Epist. 69):

Tullianas epistolas quas misisti cum nostris conferri faciam, ut ex utrisque, si possit fieri, veritas exculpatur. Tu autem huic nostro cursori Tullium in Arato [the *Aratea*] trade, ut ex eo quem me impetraturum credo, quae deesse illi Egil noster aperuit, suppleantur.

Glad to give as well as to receive, Lupus willingly replies to queries on points of grammar, prosody, or exegesis, and gives us a vivid glimpse of the intellectual life of a circle of Carolingian scholars. He wrote little, and the main monument of his humanism, apart from his letters, are the manuscripts of classical authors—more than a dozen in number—which reveal his handiwork. The most important of these in one respect is a manuscript of Cicero's *De oratore* in the British Museum (Harley 2736), written by Lupus himself; those which he has annotated include texts of Cicero, among them the oldest manuscript of the Leiden corpus of the philosophical works (Vienna lat. 189), Livy (VI–X), Valerius Maximus, Aulus Gellius, Macrobius (on the *Somnium Scipionis*), and Donatus (on *Aeneid* I–VI). We know that Einhard sent a Gellius to Fulda at Lupus' request and that Hrabanus was busy having it copied in 836 (Epist. 5). A manuscript of Gellius written at Fulda recently came to light (Leeuwarden, Prov. Bibl. van Friesland 55), but the hope that it might prove to have been the manuscript used by Lupus to correct his own copy of Gellius (Vat. Reg. lat. 597) has been disappointed. His practice of leaving spaces where lacunae are established or suspected, marking corruptions, and recording variants, reveals a sound scholarly approach to classical texts which outweighs the modest quality of his own critical contribution. In the field of biblical studies Lupus' practice of collating manuscripts had been strikingly anticipated by Theodulfus, bishop of Orléans and abbot of Fleury. Before his death in 821 he had made an edition of the Vulgate in which he foreshadowed modern editorial methods by using *sigla* in the margin to distinguish the sources of his variants, such as $\bar{a}$ for the Alcuinian reading, $\bar{s}$ for the Spanish recension.

Lupus was important as a teacher, and among his pupils was Heiric of Auxerre (c. 841–76), himself the teacher of such important figures in the next generation as Hucbald of Reims and Remigius of Auxerre. When one reflects that Lupus was taught by Hrabanus and Hrabanus in turn by Alcuin, one can clearly see one of the threads in the continuity of Carolingian education. Heiric occupies an important place in the history of classical texts. He published collections of excerpts from Valerius Maximus and Suetonius which he had taken down at Lupus' dictation. Lupus' manuscript of Valerius has come down to us (Berne 366). There were texts of Suetonius in the early ninth century at both Tours (Paris lat. 6115) and Fulda, and it was from Fulda that Lupus had tried, and probably succeeded, in obtaining his copy. Heiric is also the first person known to have used the excerpts of Petronius which were circulating in a manuscript now at Berne (357, written c. 870), and he is responsible for a collection of rare texts which have survived in a manuscript written at Auxerre in the years

860-2 and annotated by Heiric himself (Vat. lat. 4929). This odd
little collection of texts is extremely interesting because we know
something of both its earlier and its later history. Among its varied
contents are two texts, Julius Paris' epitome of Valerius Maximus
and the geography of Pomponius Mela, which both have a subscription recording that they were edited at Ravenna in the sixth
century by Rusticius Helpidius Domnulus, a Christian poet who
flourished in the second quarter of the century. Ravenna was the
chief residence of many of the emperors in the fifth and sixth centuries and a thriving centre of intellectual life in late antiquity; after
it was recovered from Byzantine dominion in the mid-eighth century
it may have been, with Rome, one of the main sources of books for
the early Carolingians. At all events, Mela had reached northern
Europe by the second half of the eighth century since his work was
known to Virgil of Salzburg (see p. 80), and both these texts
eventually reached the circle of Lupus and Heiric. The continental
Irish may have taken a hand in their transmission: in addition to
being known to one famous Irishman, Virgil of Salzburg, Mela's
text absorbed a pro-Irish gloss somewhere on its travels. It was
Heiric who in turn passed on Helpidius' little encyclopedia to
posterity: via a twelfth-century copy the contents of the Vaticanus
reached Petrarch, who then ensured their wide distribution in the
Renaissance.

IX. THE CAROLINGIAN TWILIGHT

The intellectual life of the Carolingian revival had been closely
connected with the cohesion and security of Charlemagne's political achievement. During the course of the ninth and tenth century
his empire suffered repeated attacks on all sides from the Vikings,
Saracens, and Hungarians; whole regions were devastated and
monasteries sacked, while internal disagreement led to its being
split up in 843 into the separate political units which already fore-
shadow the fragmented face of modern Europe. However, the
educational machine which Charlemagne and Alcuin had set in
motion, working through the monastic and cathedral schools, had
sufficient momentum to keep going until a new age could take over
the classical tradition and exploit it more fully.

The tenth century was very much a period of transition from the

Carolingian age to the economic and intellectual expansion of the eleventh and twelfth centuries. There was a general sagging in the cultural level and a falling off in the production of classical manuscripts, but the Latin authors went on being studied and copied. Indeed, among the scholars of the age there were two whose breadth of learning could not have been paralleled in the previous century: these were Ratherius (c. 887–974), bishop of Liège and thrice bishop of Verona, and Gerbert of Reims (c. 950–1003).

Ratherius was one of the most turbulent figures in a turbulent century. Indeed, he doubtless owes much of the breadth of his classical knowledge to his varied changes of location, and these in turn to an impetuous temper and a vitriolic tongue, more heavily indebted to the Latin satirists than was comfortable for his fellow clergy, which forced him to scuttle in almost picaresque fashion to and fro across Europe. He claims our special attention for his knowledge of two rare texts, Plautus and Catullus. It is probable that he met the plays of Plautus in France, which was the original home of the Palatine family of manuscripts, and the same may be true of Catullus. For although the great discovery of Catullus' poems took place in Verona, the first sign that they had survived was the inclusion of poem 62 in the *florilegium Thuaneum* (Paris lat. 8071), written in France in the late ninth century. A monument to Ratherius' devotion to the classics still remains in the shape of the most important single manuscript of Livy's first decade (Laur. 63.19 = M), which was copied at Verona on his instructions. Some of the more explosive marginalia readily betray their author. A twin manuscript, possibly copied at the same time and presented to Otto I, found its way to the cathedral of Worms.

The Carolingian traditions were best maintained in Germany, especially under the Ottonian dynasty (936–1002), and as tutor to Otto III Gerbert was at the centre of this intellectual revival. A great teacher, a pioneer in mathematics, and an active collector of manuscripts, Gerbert was an outstanding figure; he was at different times abbot of Bobbio, archbishop of Reims and Ravenna, and finally Pope Silvester II. The emergence of the Holy Roman Empire meant fruitful contact between Germany and Italy, and the German schools of the late tenth and eleventh centuries made a significant contribution to the cause of classical learning. Another famous manuscript of Livy, this time a fifth-century uncial manuscript of the fourth decade, was found at Piacenza and taken to Germany by Otto III. It was given to Bamberg cathedral library by Henry II and now survives as a few scraps of binding; but at least two copies were taken from it, the one our main source for the text (Bamberg Class. 35, written in the eleventh century), the other the parent of two celebrated lost manuscripts, the first at one time at Speyer, the second at Chartres, whence it fathered the whole Renaissance tradition (see p. 115). Further evidence of the scholarly achievement of the German schools of this period is provided by an important omnibus volume of Cicero's works. This manuscript, which is now in the British Museum (Harley 2682), was written in Germany in the eleventh century and formerly belonged to Cologne cathedral. It contains a number of the speeches, letters, and philosophical works, and is a valuable textual witness for some of them.

While the cathedrals continued to increase in importance as intellectual centres, the monasteries had been through a period of decline, but this was arrested by the Cluniac reforms on the continent and the efforts of Dunstan and Ethelwold in England. In the tenth century England begins to import books from the continent and with them the continental script. The most important manuscript of Cicero's *Aratea* (Harley 647), written in France in the Carolingian period, had arrived in England by the end of the century and soon produced a couple of offspring on English soil. Manuscripts of Juvenal and Persius survive from tenth-century England, including an attractive one in insular minuscule (Cambridge, Trinity College O.4.10), which must be among the last of the classical manuscripts written in this script; and a book containing part of Ovid's *Ars amatoria* and written in Wales in the ninth century (Bodleian Library, Auct. F. 4.32) actually belonged to Dunstan.

X. THE RESURGENCE OF MONTE CASSINO

The most dramatic single event in the history of Latin scholarship in the eleventh century was the phenomenal revival of Monte Cassino; the mother monastery of the Benedictine order had her most brilliant hour at a time when Benedictinism was rapidly declining as the cultural force of Europe. The great efflorescence of artistic and intellectual activity which reached its peak under abbot Desiderius (1058–87) was accompanied by a renewed interest in the classics, and in the late eleventh and early twelfth century there was written at Monte Cassino and allied centres a wonderful series of important Beneventan manuscripts of classical and other authors. At one swoop a number of texts were recovered which might otherwise have been lost for ever; to this one monastery in this one period we owe the preservation of the later *Annals* and *Histories* of Tacitus (Plate XIV), the *Golden Ass* of Apuleius, the *Dialogues* of Seneca, Varro's *De lingua latina*, Frontinus' *De aquis*, and thirty-odd lines of Juvenal's sixth satire which are not to be found in any other manuscript. Monte Cassino had strong connections in the eleventh century with Germany, and the Tacitus in particular points back to Hersfeld and Fulda.

XI. THE TWELFTH-CENTURY RENAISSANCE

As we have already noted incidentally, education was gradually passing from the monks and the monasteries to the secular clergy in the cathedral and urban schools. The monasteries remained important for their libraries and scriptoria and indeed as cultural centres, but more creative intellectual life passed to the cathedral schools, which rapidly increased from the middle of the eleventh century and in a few cases later developed into the first universities. By then the intellectual map of Europe had changed dramatically. The great centre for the revival of Roman law was Bologna; the first medical school came into being at Salerno; the Norman kingdom of southern Italy and Sicily fostered the translation of Greek technical works into Latin, and with the reconquest of Spain from the Muslims Toledo emerged as the chief centre for the translating activity which brought Arabic science and scholarship within the reach of the West. To the north the main scene of intellectual activity had shifted to Norman France and Norman England, with Bec and Canterbury to the fore, though it took the English schools a long time to catch up with those of France. The literary side of the classical revival was mainly carried on in the schools of Orléans and Chartres, while philosophy and dialectic chose Paris for their home and made it the intellectual capital of Europe. The literary

output of ancient Rome continued to be the basic stuff of education and remained the chief source of literary inspiration, but now
it had a new role—to cater for the specialized needs of a complex
society with a professional interest in law and medicine, rhetoric
and logic. The exciting books for this age were Euclid and Ptolemy,
the Digest, and such works of the Aristotelian and medical corpus
as were rapidly becoming available. At the same time the study of
ancient literature was both broadened and intensified. Increased
wealth and elegance, together with the secularizing trends in art
and literature, enabled people to take a more robust interest in a
literature which had not been designed for the cloister. An age
which had a rapidly developing literature of its own, both Latin and
vernacular, was able to explore with understanding the techniques
of ancient epic and history. Love poetry and the moral writings of
the satirist were in the greatest demand: ancient literature catered
for both the senses and the conscience. In the process it became
transformed: Vergil was allegorized, Ovid moralized, the satirists
encrusted with glosses and comment rarely in keeping with the
original intention. The results were various. In his *De amicitia*
Aelred of Rievaulx was able to rethink the problem of human relationships in Christian terms and rework Cicero's dialogue in a way
which does no real violence to the model nor detracts from the
charm and originality of his own treatment. Seneca, subtly blended
with material from Christian writers, could inspire some noble
passages, as in William of Saint Thierry, though he loses his identity in the process; in Gautier of Saint Victor, suitably twisted, he
could be made to denounce the study of pagan authors. Borrowings
from Ovid sparkle through some of the most erotic scenes in the
elegiac comedy of the period, but he is commonly exploited as a
manual on morals and much else, his tone and intention so grotesquely distorted that the *Remedia amoris* could become a school text
and even the poet's nose, reputedly large for obvious reasons, be
transformed into an organ supremely capable of discriminating
between virtue and vice.

    Vergil, Horace, Ovid, Lucan, Juvenal, Persius, Cicero, Seneca,
Sallust were the staple literary diet of the twelfth century; Statius
(excluding the *Silvae*) and Terence were popular, Quintilian was
known but not much used, Martial increased in favour, while some

Plautus (the first eight plays) and Livy began to circulate. No age would have taken greater delight in the poetry of Catullus, Tibullus, and Propertius, but the rare or unique copies of these authors which were in existence lay unused, as did those of Tacitus, and Lucretius is a striking example of how a text can circulate in the ninth century and then virtually disappear from sight for the rest of the Middle Ages. The classical emphasis of the revival can be gauged from the fact that in the extant palimpsests the ancient authors begin to appear more frequently in the upper texts: the tables have turned, but attacks on the educational use of the classics continued.

Some notion of the acquaintance with Latin literature enjoyed by the foremost intellects of the period can be derived from the works of two Englishmen, William of Malmesbury (died c. 1143) and John of Salisbury (c. 1110–80), the first the greatest historian of the period, the second the finest representative of the literary revival of the twelfth century. As librarian of Malmesbury, William had at his disposal an excellent library, which he did much himself to improve, and an easy access to the world of books; in addition to the usual run of school texts, he had read parts of Caesar and Livy, Suetonius, Plautus (apparently the *Pseudolus*, one of the rare plays), Petronius, and the *Apocolocyntosis* of Seneca; he was also the first person in the Middle Ages to quote from the whole corpus of Seneca's *Letters*. A real researcher, with strong historical and antiquarian interests, William has earned an honoured place in the history of classical scholarship. His particular concern was to seek out related texts and put them together, and some of his collections, often autograph, still survive. One of his historical collections, containing Vegetius, Frontinus, and Eutropius (Oxford, Lincoln College, lat. 100), is a good example. His massive attempt at an omnibus Cicero still exists in a later copy (Cambridge, University Library, Dd. 13.2); it contains an explicit defence of his classical interests and what is perhaps the first attempt at an edition of the fragments of the *Hortensius* and *De republica*, carefully culled from the works of Augustine. John of Salisbury, educated at Chartres and Paris and unrivalled in the Middle Ages as a stylist, not only absorbed a great deal of patristic, medieval, and classical literature, but was also able to bring it to bear on the practical problems of his day. His favourite reading was Cicero, Seneca, and the *exempla* of Valerius Maximus, but his strong classical interest led him to authors not commonly found, to the *Strategemata* of Frontinus and the *Historia Augusta*, while he was remarkable in knowing the whole extant text of Petronius. He used Heiric's excerpts for Suetonius and may at times be dependent on other *florilegia*. His caustic attacks on the encroachment of dialectic show that the purely literary revival is on the wane.

William of Malmesbury and John of Salisbury were of course exceptional, and among their contemporaries were many who were content to give their writings a spurious air of learning by pillaging the encyclopedists, the grammarians, and the *florilegia*: second-hand learning had come to stay. Robert of Cricklade dedicated to Henry II a nine-book *defloratio* of the Elder Pliny, William of Malmesbury compiled a *Polyhistor*, Étienne of Rouen prepared an abridgement of Quintilian. Some of the miscellaneous *florilegia*, when they were put together by someone who had access to a wide selection of books, are of considerable textual importance in that they tap a tradition at an earlier stage than that represented by the extant manuscripts and draw on a different source. The *florilegium Gallicum*, put together in northern France in the twelfth century, is a good example; it contains extracts from a large number of authors and has some contribution to make to the text of Tibullus, Petronius, Valerius Flaccus, and others. An early thirteenth-century *florilegium* of mainly classical authors (Paris lat. 15155, with portions elsewhere) contains the only pre-fourteenth century extracts from Propertius and also excerpts from the *Laus Pisonis*. Wibald, abbot of Corvey from 1146 to 1158, like William of Malmesbury before him, had the ambitious notion of putting the whole of Cicero into one volume, and he almost succeeded, for there can be little doubt that the most comprehensive manuscript of Cicero's works, written at Corvey in the twelfth century (Berlin lat. fol. 252), is the very volume. Containing oratorical and philosophical works, an imposing range of speeches, and part of the *Epistulae ad familiares*, it is an important textual source and an impressive witness to the humanism of the twelfth century.

If one were to ask how the Renaissance of the late eleventh and twelfth century affected the textual transmission of our classical texts, the answer seems to be that it consolidated the gains of the Carolingian revival. Authors central to medieval education or agreeable to the taste of the time simply poured from the scriptoria; in the case of popular writers like Ovid and Seneca, we have four or five times as many manuscripts from the twelfth century as from all previous centuries put together. Many of these manuscripts are textually worthless, containing nothing of value which is not found in a purer form in earlier witnesses, but often the twelfth-century broadening of the tradition has resulted in gains to the text. The best manuscript of Cicero's *Ad familiares* belongs to the ninth century (Laur. 49.9); but the errors and gaps in its text have to be remedied by calling in the other branch of the tradition, Carolingian in origin but largely represented by manuscripts of the twelfth century. Other texts survive entirely in manuscripts of this period: such texts of Seneca's *Natural Questions* as existed in the Carolingian era have perished and it is the descendants of this tradition, copied in the twelfth and thirteenth centuries, which have preserved the text for us.

XII. THE SCHOLASTIC AGE

In the late twelfth and throughout the thirteenth century the schools and universities were more concerned with assimilating and organizing the material and ideas brought to the surface by the recent intellectual ferment than with making fresh discoveries. The skills employed in the systematization of acquired knowledge and the unification of dogma were those of dialectic and logic, and these subtle sciences dominated not only philosophy, theology, and the fields of specialized knowledge, but grammar and literary exegesis as well. When the classical heritage was absorbed into the systems of contemporary thought, with its strong tendency to allegorize and elaborate, it was bound to become distorted. It also suffered in other ways. With so much else to occupy the mind, the wide reading of ancient authors gave way to the more practical manuals, the *auctores* to the *artes*, and the new grammars and rhetorics which came into use were often scholastic in character. The classics still remained a valuable quarry for moral anecdote and could provide a curious age with information of all sorts; but form and style were no longer part of the attraction, and matter could be more easily assimilated when reduced to excerpts and *exempla*. At the same time the writers of the twelfth and thirteenth centuries took their place alongside the ancient authors; although they did not displace them, the monopoly of the past had been broken.

For these reasons the century which witnessed the final triumph of the Middle Ages in many fields is not a particularly enticing one for the classical scholar. Manuscripts pour on to the market, but the text of those authors who have been copied for generations is getting more and more corrupt; the proportion of grain to chaff is getting smaller, and the manuscripts themselves, with their heavy Gothic appearance, are less alluring than those of previous centuries. Despite all this, the classics survived the tide of scholasticism and made significant advances where least expected. The heroes of the period were the builders of the mighty philosophical and theological systems, but amongst those intent on the organization of knowledge were some who gave an important place to pagan literature. Vincent of Beauvais, who died about 1264, is the most monumental encyclopedist of the Middle Ages; his *Speculum maius* was an attempt to put the whole sum of knowledge into one corpus. Like so many others, he was anti-pagan in principle, but he saw the value of profane texts and defends his use of them with a good conscience. He draws heavily on classical authors; Ovid and Seneca far outdistance the others, Vergil is eclipsed. A large part of his classical quotations are taken from secondary sources, and the appearance of rare authors like Tibullus is explained by his dependence on earlier compilations, in particular the *florilegium Gallicum*.

About 1250 and within a few years of the publication of the *Speculum maius* Richard of Fournival, a native of Amiens and later chancellor of its cathedral, was compiling his *Biblionomia*. In it he lays out the literature and wisdom of the world for the guidance of his fellow citizens in the form of an elaborate garden in which the various branches of knowledge each have their plot. This charming analogy quickly crystallizes into a picture of a library in which the books are laid out on desks according to their subject. This systematic bibliography is not, as has sometimes been thought, the imaginary projection of a bibliophile, but the actual catalogue of Fournival's own carefully collected library. It must have contained about 300 volumes and in size and range could challenge the monastic and cathedral libraries of his day. It contained some rare classical texts and among the most noteworthy are three items in the *opera poetarum*: Tibullus, Propertius, and Seneca's *Tragedies*. His copy of Tibullus may have descended ultimately from the manuscript at one time in the palace library of Charlemagne, for one of the earliest of the *florilegia* in which Tibullus occasionally surfaces also contains a collection of the poetry of the Carolingian court circle. His manuscript passed in 1272, with the bulk of his collection, to the library of the Sorbonne, but it is now lost; had it survived, it would have been our oldest manuscript of Tibullus, if not the source of much of the Renaissance tradition. But Fournival's manuscripts of Propertius and the *Tragedies* do survive and have now been identified. Seneca's *Tragedies* had shown signs of life; some excerpts had appeared in the *florilegium Thuaneum* (Paris lat. 8071), written in France in the ninth century, and our oldest complete manuscript, the codex Etruscus (Laur. 37.13 = E), goes back to the eleventh, but the plays had remained almost unknown. It is not until the thirteenth century that manuscripts of the other and main stream of the tradition (known as A) begin to appear; this re-emerged in northern France, though the oldest of its representatives (Cambridge, Corpus Christi College 406) appears to have been written in England. The manuscript known to editors as P (Paris lat. 8260) was written for Richard of Fournival. Propertius is a new name to the Middle Ages; one of the greatest of the Roman poets, he had to wait until the scholastic age to see the light again, and for his text we are heavily indebted, as with so many discoveries to come, to a new phenomenon, the wealthy private book collector. The book which Fournival had made for him is our manuscript A (Voss. lat. Q. 38), written by the same scribe as copied his Seneca; it is one of the two most important witnesses to the text and the parent of the humanist tradition.

The *Tragedies* were not the only text of Seneca to achieve circulation in northern Europe at this time. The *Dialogues* reached the schools of Paris in the first half of the thirteenth century, having worked their way north from Monte Cassino. They were known to John of Garland as early as 1220 and fifty years later, somewhat tardily but with tremendous excitement, their 'discovery' was announced by Roger Bacon. Though this text too begins to circulate again in northern France, among the first to make use of it were Roger Bacon and John of Wales, both Franciscans and both as much at home in Oxford as in Paris. They serve to draw attention to the less spectacular but not inconsiderable contribution to the promotion of classical studies already being made by the English friars. Some of the English Franciscans actually compiled in the thirteenth century a *Registrum librorum Angliae*, a union catalogue of books available in English libraries, a remarkable bibliographical project in which some classical authors were included. John of Wales's treatises, such as the *Communiloquium* and *Compendiloquium*, were full of references to the ancients and opened a wide and flattering window on classical antiquity; they were intended not only as aids for the teacher and preacher, but also as manuals for polite conversation. Somewhat later Nicholas Trevet, a Dominican but again mainly associated with Oxford and Paris, achieved such a wide reputation for erudition and the exegesis of antique texts that he received commissions from Italy to write commentaries on Livy and Seneca's *Tragedies* (see p. 114). These prepared the way for the classicizing group of friars who have been shown to have been active in England in the early fourteenth century. This loosely knit group, of which the most important are perhaps Thomas Waleys and Robert Holcot, did much to popularize a knowledge of the ancient world by introducing classical allusions to illustrate their biblical commentaries and sermons and helping to create an audience with a taste for ancient history and myth. With his classical scholarship, seen at its best in his commentary on the first ten books of the *De civitate dei*, completed in 1332, his admiration for the ancients, and his knowledge of rare texts, Thomas Waleys comes very close to being a humanist and doubtless owes much of his special quality to periods spent at Bologna and Avignon. He claims to have seen a copy of Apuleius' *Metamorphoses* and can quote from Livy's rare fourth decade, thanks to a book lent to him by the bishop of Modena. The fondness for classical learning common to the group might have developed into humanism had circumstances been different; as it was, their lack of stylistic sophistication, their medieval ways of thinking, their profession, and their lack of contact with a leisured highbrow milieu prevented this from happening; the movement took a different direction and faded out.

Thus more and more was added to the vast body of classical books and learning which had been accumulating over the centuries. Classical studies survived and advanced and were successfully adapted to new tastes and conditions, but in a context in which they were never really emancipated, could never really catch fire. It was left to the humanists of the Renaissance, who drew on this great medieval heritage with curiously little sense of debt, to exploit what had been achieved in a new and vital way.

XIII. GREEK IN THE WEST IN THE MIDDLE AGES

Under the Roman empire Italy had been to all intents and purposes a bilingual country, but with the decline of the empire Greek fell out of use except in the south of Italy and Sicily, where many towns were by origin Greek colonies. Cassiodorus' monastery Vivarium near Squillace is known to have had a collection of Greek books, but there is no sign that they contributed in any tangible way to the preservation of Greek. And in all the other parts of Western Europe, where the language had never been so firmly established, if indeed it was spoken at all, a knowledge of Greek became an attainment of exceptional rarity throughout the Middle Ages. Even diplomatic correspondence was sometimes delayed for lack of suitably qualified translators and interpreters.

For a brief period in the ninth century some interest in Greek can be traced. A few bilingual biblical manuscripts survive, proved by their handwriting to be products of the Latin world; they are thought to come from the scriptorium at Saint Gall. In 827 the Byzantine emperor sent a copy of Pseudo-Dionysius the Areopagite to the French king (still preserved as Paris gr. 437), which served as the basis for a translation of this highly popular forgery into Latin. A few years later the Irishman John Scottus Eriugena used the manuscript for his own translation of these works, and he also made some translations from Gregory of Nyssa, Gregory of Nazianzus, and Maximus the Confessor. But though some of his versions were widely read he did not create a tradition of Greek learning, and no other Greek texts were accessible for the time being except Boethius' versions of some of Aristotle's writings on logic and a version of Plato's *Timaeus* made in the fourth century by Chalcidius.

In the twelfth century the range of translations was increased substantially. Some of the credit belongs to two figures who are still very obscure, Burgundio of Pisa (1110–93), who had spent the years 1135–8 in Constantinople as an interpreter, and James of Venice, a canon lawyer whose version of Aristotle's *Analytica posteriora* was known to John of Salisbury in 1159. Slightly better known are the inelegant and literal versions of Plato, Euclid, and Ptolemy made in Sicily c. 1160 under the aegis of Henricus Aristippus, archdeacon of Catania (d. 1162), who is said to have acquired some manuscripts sent as a gift by the Byzantine emperor to the Norman king of Sicily. Aristippus himself translated Plato's *Phaedo* and *Meno*, some works of Aristotle, and perhaps Hero's *Pneumatica*, which discusses steam-engines, 'penny-in-the-slot' machines, and other gadgets which have a surprisingly modern ring about them. He is praised also for his assistance in making the versions of Euclid, Proclus, and Ptolemy. Another important figure in this circle was the admiral Eugenius, who translated Ptolemy's *Optics* from the Arabic into Latin (the Greek is now lost). The main interests of these men were clearly scientific.

Yet the influence of these translators was perhaps slightly less than would have been expected, for Gerard of Cremona seems to have translated Ptolemy's *Almagest* from the Arabic in Toledo c. 1175, apparently in ignorance of the existing version. For the diffusion of Aristotelianism the work of Arabic scholars in Spain who did not know the original Greek text was also important. Arabic versions and commentaries by Avicenna and other scholars, especially Averroes (d. 1198), were turned into Latin in Toledo in the middle and late twelfth century. A large proportion of the Aristotelian corpus became known and circulated rapidly to other part of Europe.

In the thirteenth century a few eminent men show more than a passing acquaintance with Greek. Robert Grosseteste (c. 1168–1253), though he learnt it late in life and always needed help from native speakers, studied Aristotle and translated the *Ethics*; he also translated Pseudo-Dionysius the Areopagite (his copy of the Greek text is in the Bodleian Library, Canonici gr. 97). His pupil Roger

Bacon (c. 1214–94) wrote a Greek grammar (Oxford, Corpus Christi College 148), but despite his insistence that texts should be studied in the original rather than the often unintelligible translations he had few if any followers. A Flemish contemporary, William of Moerbeke, translated parts of Archimedes and Aristotle, the latter perhaps at the request of Thomas Aquinas. He lived for a time in Greece and can be traced at Nicaea in 1260; later he became the Latin archbishop of Corinth. Another figure of importance was a Greek from Reggio called Nicholas (fl. c. 1308–45), who settled at the court of the Angevin kings at Naples and made versions of many works ascribed to Galen. Some of these survive in his Latin text only.

4. THE RENAISSANCE

I. HUMANISM

It will be convenient for the purpose of this brief survey to regard the Renaissance as the period extending from about 1300 to the middle of the sixteenth century. A cultural movement which is recognizable as humanism, the stimulating force of the Renaissance, was at work in certain parts of Italy by the end of the thirteenth century; by the middle of the sixteenth it had spread to most of Western Europe and had transformed, among so many other things, the transmission and study of classical antiquity. The scholar of the late Renaissance had at his disposal almost as much of the literature of Greece and Rome as we possess ourselves; most of it he could read, at ease and at no great cost, in print; and the translation of Greek into Latin, and of both into the vernacular languages, had made a large part of ancient literature available to the public at large. On the scholarly side, the foundations of historical and textual criticism had been securely laid.

Although humanism eventually acted upon all areas of intellectual and artistic life, it was primarily a literary activity and was closely connected with the study and imitation of classical literature. The origin of the nineteenth-century term 'humanism' has been traced to the word *umanista*, coined in the student slang of the Italian universities of the late fifteenth century, on the analogy of such words as *legista* and *iurista*, to denote the professional teacher of the humanities, the *studia humanitatis*, which by this time had crystallized as the study of grammar, rhetoric, history, poetry, and moral philosophy, a canon as important for what it excluded as for what it contained. The philosophical overtones which humanism later developed are only in part the result of its originally classical emphasis, the teaching, study, and promotion of classical literature.

Many humanists, particularly in the fifteenth century, were professional teachers of the humanities; in this capacity they stepped into the place of the medieval *dictatores*, the men who had taught the art of composing letters, speeches, and other documents essential to diplomacy and public life. But the *dictamen* was an essentially medieval phenomenon, elaborate, stereotyped, smelling of the handbook and fair copy. The cultivation of style depended very little on the use of classical models, poetry was neglected, and classical studies generally in Italy seem to have been in some respects considerably less 'humane' than elsewhere. It is therefore not easy to see why humanism should have emerged from precisely this stable. There appears to be no simple answer, but it has been pointed out that most of the early humanists were notaries or lawyers or in some way associated with the legal profession. The law schools of Italy held a dominant position and the revival of Roman Law at Bologna had reforged a link with antiquity. The *dictatores* had been particularly active in the twelfth and thirteenth centuries, and the strongly grammatical and rhetorical emphasis of the education which lawyers would have received as a preliminary to their legal training, however much it may have lost its classical flavour, would impart a good command of Latin and a strong sense of style. Other important factors were the secular nature of Italian education, the existence of a sophisticated urban culture and of a professional class who had the training and the means and the leisure to pursue their classical interests and yet were sufficiently involved in civic life to make practical use, when the opportunity offered, of the new rhetoric. Some allowance must be made too for the personality of some of the individuals concerned, a Lovato or a Petrarch, who were gifted with the ability to communicate to others their enthusiasm and sense of excitement, and to the simple fact that there were libraries within reach which could provide the right sort of text to give humanism a new direction and emphasize the break with the past. Nor, as humanism broadened and extended its influence to other fields, was the practical aim of the *dictator* superseded, but the way to speaking and writing well was seen to lie in the use of classical models; the Latin classics were revived, not only as an academic study, but as the stuff of which eloquence was made, and it was this command of the Latin tongue which enabled the Renaissance man to impress his peers, denounce his enemies, thunder in defence of creed or city. In turn this led to a more sympathetic and comprehensive study of all aspects of ancient life and to that feeling of identification, however illusory, with the men and ideals of the ancient world which is the mark of neoclassicism.

This attempt to get closer to the classical spirit and to relive and rethink the past in terms of the present completely transcends the medieval approach to ancient letters. At last Latin literature was emancipated from the role for which it had been so badly cast, that of playing second-fiddle to religion; humanism was fundamentally secular, and the thin but unbroken tradition of lay education in Italy had doubtless contributed to this. The humanists were men of the world, sometimes teachers of grammar or literature, more commonly notaries, papal secretaries, chancellors of cities. They were usually book collectors, often on a large scale, and the growth of private libraries and a commercial book trade helped to break the long ecclesiastical monopoly of learning. At the same time the movement quickly gained a foothold within the Church and soon humanists were to be found in the highest positions of its hierarchy.

II. THE FIRST HUMANISTS

The beginnings of humanism are clearly detectable in a small literary coterie which grew up in Padua in the second half of the thirteenth century. The leader of these prehumanists was a Paduan judge, Lovato Lovati (1241–1309), who had a keen interest in classical poetry, a remarkable flair for unearthing texts unknown for centuries, and the ability to communicate his enthusiasm to a circle of friends. His surviving works are some collections of poems, in particular his *Metrical Epistles*. It is evident from these that Lovato was at best a mediocre poet, despite a freshness in his attempt to capture the spirit of his classical models; what is staggering about these poems is the knowledge of Roman poetry which they reveal. Since the clues to his classical models are echoes rather than direct quotations, the evidence is not always as clear-cut as one could wish, but there is enough of it to command respect. An age ahead of his contemporaries, Lovato appears to have been acquainted with Lucretius, Catullus, the *Odes* of Horace, the whole of Tibullus, Propertius, Martial, the *Silvae* of Statius, Valerius Flaccus, and such little-known works as Ovid's *Ibis*. The chronology of humanism has had to be drastically revised: Petrarch was

not the first humanist to know Propertius, or Salutati to possess a
complete Tibullus; Lovato knew Lucretius and Valerius Flaccus
a century and a half before they were discovered by Poggio, and
was making use of Catullus almost fifty years before the traditional
date of his resurrection in Verona. Other members of the same
circle were acquainted with a similar range of Latin poets, unprecedented since antiquity and not equalled again until the fifteenth century.

A dramatic clue to the source of some of Lovato's texts has been
found in a manuscript in the British Museum (Add. 19906), containing *inter alia* Justinus' *Epitome* and Lovato's poems, and written
by Lovato himself about 1290. At the end of the Justinus he copied
the subscription which he found in his exemplar, and this reveals
that the manuscript which he was using had been written in the
monastery of Pomposa, in the Po delta, just before 1100. Among
the classical texts known to have been at Pomposa as early as the
eleventh century was a great rarity, the *Tragedies* of Seneca. The
collateral discovery that Lovato made use of the famous eleventh-
century codex Etruscus of the *Tragedies* (Laur. 37.13) at one swoop
provides a home for the misnamed Etruscus and confirms that
Lovato had succeeded in tapping the resources of one of the great
medieval libraries of northern Italy. It is an easy guess that another
source was the Chapter Library at Verona. However, not all the
questions raised by the richness of his finds have yet been answered;
when these texts were rediscovered later, they came to light in
France and Switzerland and Germany, beyond the ken of this
parochial group. Padua is an isolated and as yet obscure chapter in
the story of the rediscovery of antiquity.

Lovato has also left us a short note on the metre and prosody of
Senecan tragedy, remarkable in that it is derived, not from the
medieval manuals, but from an intelligent study of Seneca's own
practice. It was elaborated by his successors and is an indication of
the intense interest which the prehumanists took in Roman tragedy.
He also tried his hand at archaeology, and identified a skeleton
which some workmen had turned up as the remains of the legendary founder of Padua, the Trojan Antenor, a gorgeous error. From
all this it is clear that something new had begun.

Something of a contrast is provided by another Paduan judge of

the same circle, Geremia da Montagnone (c. 1255–1321), who had
no literary ambitions and trod the well-beaten path of the didactic
florilegist: his *Compendium moralium notabilium*, probably put together in the first decade of the fourteenth century, enjoyed a wide
circulation and was eventually printed in Venice in 1505. Geremia
is more typical of his period; but in some respects his compendium
plants him firmly in the humanist group. His reading is vast, his
excerpts are systematically arranged, with chapter and verse added,
and he seems to be quoting at first hand from the authors themselves; his notions of chronological sequence are not bad for his
time, and he makes a nice distinction (e.g. *poeta* and *versilogus*)
between classical and medieval writers. His quotations from Catullus and Martial, from Horace's *Odes* and Ovid's *Ibis*, together with
his lavish use of Seneca's tragedies, show clearly the influence of
the local humanism.

Lovato's spiritual successor was his friend and fellow townsman
Albertino Mussato (1262–1329). A notary by profession, Mussato
achieved distinction in the worlds of politics, diplomacy, and literature. Strongly influenced by Lovato, he read the same Latin poets
and delved more deeply into Senecan tragedy; he also wrote *Historiae* modelled on Livy, Sallust, and Caesar. His greatest literary
success came in 1315: in order to open the eyes of the Paduans to
the danger of falling into the clutches of the lord of Verona,
Cangrande della Scala, he wrote a Senecan tragedy, the *Ecerinis*,
which dealt in lurid colour with the rise and fall of Padua's own
former tyrant, Ezzelino III. The first tragedy to be written in
classical metres since antiquity was a tremendous literary and
political success; the Paduans crowned its author with laurels and
so revived a Roman custom which caught the imagination of the
Renaissance and was a fitting compliment for the pioneer of
modern classical drama.

Although limited in its influence by the weakness in communi-
cations and the fragmentation of political life in Italy, Paduan
humanism soon percolated to the neighbouring town of Vicenza,
where the notary Benvenuto Campesani (1255–1323) composed in
the early years of the fourteenth century his famous and enigmatic
epigram celebrating the return to Verona of her long-lost poet
Catullus. Verona fostered a more scholarly tradition of humanism.

which was nourished by the Chapter Library. Among its treasures were two important prose texts, the lost Veronensis of Pliny's *Letters* which had been known to Ratherius, and the ninth-century manuscript of the *Historia Augusta*, which had travelled down to Verona in time to have an enormous influence on Renaissance historiography. Both were used by Giovanni de Matociis (fl. 1306–20), custodian of the cathedral, who, in addition to his major work, the *Historia Imperialis*, produced the first critical work on literary history to be written in the Renaissance, his *Brevis adnotatio de duobus Pliniis*. Basing himself on the Verona Pliny and a text of Suetonius, he was able to split the composite Pliny of the Middle Ages into the Elder and the Younger. The Chapter Library also had its own florilegist: in 1329 someone who had access to the books put together a *Flores moralium auctoritatum* (Verona CLXVIII (155)) which, while being partly derived from other florilegia, contained excerpts from rare texts known to have been at Verona, from Catullus, the Younger Pliny, the *Historia Augusta*, Varro's *Res rusticae*, and Cicero's *Letters to Atticus and Quintus*.

III. THE CONSOLIDATION OF HUMANISM: PETRARCH AND HIS GENERATION

Although recent research has shown that the prehumanists had advanced much further along the road to humanism than had been supposed, especially in their acquisition of a new body of Latin poetry, the éclat with which Petrarch (1304–74) makes his dramatic entry has hardly been dimmed. He dwarfs his precursors in every respect: he was an immeasurably greater poet and greater man than any of them; his horizons were wider and his influence, never cramped within the limits of town or province, extended over most of Western Europe; he had the vision and the ability to unite the two existing strands of humanism, the literary and the scholarly, and to combine aims which reached for the moon with the capacity for painstaking research; he went further than anyone else in trying to revive within the framework of a Christian society the ideals of ancient Rome, and his attempts to get close to the great figures of the past, and indeed to rival their achievement, though flirting with the vainglorious, unleashed passions and ambitions which were to reanimate the whole cultural legacy of the ancient world and bring it to bear upon contemporary modes of thought and literature.

It was fortunate for Petrarch, and indeed for the continuity of the classical tradition in the West, that for a critical period in the fourteenth century (1309–77) the papal curia transferred its seat from Rome to Avignon. Avignon was well placed to be a point of cultural contact between the north and the south, and the attraction to the papal court of men of different nationalities and intellectual outlook had important consequences. In particular, educated churchmen and lawyers, whose growing interest in classical texts demanded more knowledge of the ancient world than their schooling had provided, began to draw on the medieval legacy of the north. The monastic and cathedral libraries of France lay within reach, and for help in reading the more difficult classical texts they turned to Oxford, to the polymath Nicholas Trevet, who wrote at the express request of a pope and a cardinal his commentaries on Livy (c. 1318) and the *Tragedies* of Seneca (c. 1315). Thus when Petrarch arrived at Avignon he found an older generation with an active interest in texts which had been little read for centuries. Petrarch owed much to this stimulating society; at the same time he had the imagination and the historical sense to see the inadequacy of looking at antiquity through the eyes of the Middle Ages and broke away to recreate it for himself.

In the British Museum is preserved a manuscript of Livy (Harley 2493, Plate XV) which has been shown to illustrate as well as any single document can the importance of Avignon as a bridge between the Middle Ages and the Renaissance and the part played in this story by Petrarch. This volume, which originally contained books 1–10 and 21–40, was put together by Petrarch when he was still in his early twenties; parts of it he copied in his own hand. The nucleus of the book is a manuscript of Livy's third decade, written about 1200 and ultimately derived, as are all the complete manuscripts which have survived, from the extant Puteanus; to this central portion Petrarch added about the year 1325 a copy of the first decade, then, a few years later, of the fourth. By 1329 he was the proud owner of a Livy which was more complete and had a better text than any other in existence. The various decades of Livy's *History* had followed their separate fates through the Middle Ages and it was a considerable achievement to have put three of them under one cover, expecially as the fourth decade was a great rarity in Petrarch's day; the remaining extant books of Livy (41–5) were not discovered until the sixteenth century. The whole text was supplemented, corrected, annotated—and so in a sense edited—by Petrarch himself; of special value are the variants recorded in his notes to books 26–30, because these were taken from a manuscript independent of the Puteanus. It is evident that for these books, as well as for the fourth decade, he had access to a manuscript of the same tradition as the lost codex of Speyer cathedral used by two scholars, Beatus Rhenanus and Gelenius, for the Froben edition of 1535, from which editors have painfully tried to recover its readings. The story of Petrarch's great find has now been unravelled. In 1328 Landolfo Colonna, a member of the Colonna family whose patronage Petrarch enjoyed and who had for a long time been a canon of Chartres, brought to Avignon a copy of an ancient manuscript of Livy which he had found in Chartres cathedral. The *vetus Carnotensis*, as this manuscript has been christened, was a close relative of the lost Spirensis, and both derive, for the fourth decade, from the fifth-century uncial manuscript which Otto III found at Piacenza and carried off to Germany (see p. 96). Petrarch's great book of Livy later passed into the possession of Lorenzo Valla, whose famous emendations can be found in its margins (see p. 126).

A similar tale has been told of the text of Pomponius Mela. We have already seen (p. 94) how a collection of rare texts, including Mela and Julius Paris, were edited at Ravenna in the sixth century by Rusticius Helpidius and survive in a copy made in the ninth century at Auxerre and annotated by Heiric (Vat. lat. 4929). These texts had a long and important career in the Renaissance, and all the humanist copies derive from the Auxerre archetype via a twelfth-century manuscript, now lost, which Petrarch had acquired at Avignon. We know this because Petrarch's notes were often copied along with the text, and in the earliest of the humanist copies (Ambros. H. 14 inf.) we find, for instance, the revealing remark: *Avinio. Ubi nunc sumus 1335.* The textual history of Propertius too illustrates the same pattern. The earliest manuscript of this author (Gud. lat. 224 = N), which was at one time in the region of Metz, reached Italy in time to influence most of the humanist tradition; but this tradition descends in direct line from the other early Propertius manuscript (Voss. lat. Q. 38 = A), which never left northern Europe. The link between the Vossianus and the humanist manuscripts is a copy of A which had belonged to Petrarch. Via Petrarch's copy we get back to A; and A takes us back, via the Sorbonne library—where it was at the time of Petrarch's trip to Paris in 1333—to the booky garden of Richard of Fournival, and through him to the medieval libraries of northern France. As with Livy, so with Mela and Propertius; amid the gay distractions of papal Avignon the young Petrarch became the converging point of threads of transmission which stretched back through the Middle Ages to antiquity itself, and forward again, with complex ramifications, into the High Renaissance.

This happy conjunction of book collector and scholar meant that in time Petrarch acquired a classical library which for breadth and quality had no equal in his day. We can to a certain extent reconstruct his collection of Cicero texts, an author whom he regarded as his *alter ego* and for whom he scoured the whole of Europe. It is an impressive list: almost all the philosophical works, most of the *rhetorica*, the *Letters to Atticus and Quintus*, and a remarkable range of speeches which he had built up over a lifetime, extending from the *Pro Archia* which he discovered at Liège in 1333 and copied himself, to the *Pro Cluentio* which Boccaccio transcribed for him in 1355 from an eleventh-century manuscript in Monte Cassino (Laur. 51.10). The *Letters to Atticus* were a discovery of supreme importance to him, worthy of an immediate letter to Cicero himself. He found them, as had others before him, in the Chapter Library at Verona, in 1345. It is on these letters, and in practice still more on those of Seneca (whose works he possessed *in toto*) that his own letters, the most charming and valuable of his prose writings, are modelled.

More significant than the mere range of his books was the intensity with which he read and re-read those which he thought important; for it was easy in the Renaissance to degenerate into a mere book collector. The patience with which he corrected and annotated his texts can be seen in the embryonic editions of the Harleian Livy and the Ambrosian Vergil (S.P. 10/27, *olim* A. 79

inf.), his own copy of his favourite poet. By a stroke of good fortune, in addition to reconstructing much of Petrarch's library and seeing him hard at work on his books, we have an intimate record of his literary tastes, for on the flyleaf of a manuscript in Paris (lat. 2201) we have what a brilliant piece of decipherment has proved to be Petrarch's own list of his favourite books. The list is instructive, both for the works which it contains and their order of priority, and for those it does not contain; but it must be remembered that the list belongs to the earlier period of his life and that some of the books which he prized were among his later discoveries. Cicero not unexpectedly heads the list, his 'moral' works taking precedence. Next comes Seneca: the *Letters* have pride of place; the *Tragedies* come later, and in a second and more select list on the same page they are explicitly excluded from the inner circle. The next main section is devoted to history, headed by Valerius Maximus and Livy; there is a special category of *exempla*, in which Macrobius and Gellius find their home. Poetry follows, with Vergil, Lucan, Statius, Horace, Ovid, and Juvenal; Horace is qualified *praesertim in odis*, a complete reversal of medieval taste. At the end come the technical works, grammar, dialectic, and astrology. Augustine is favoured with a list to himself, and with Boethius' *De consolatione* he makes up the sum of the Christian content. The only Greek work is Aristotle's *Ethics* (in Latin, of course), and this disappears from the select list. Of the law, in which Petrarch received his formal education at Bologna, nothing; the writers of the Middle Ages are likewise rejected, made redundant by direct contact with antiquity.

One of the first to fall under the influence of Petrarch's humanism was his younger contemporary Boccaccio (1313–75). Under the patronage of its ruler, Robert of Anjou (1309–43), Naples had emerged as an important intellectual centre quite early in the century and it was here that Boccaccio spent his youth. His early works, written in Italian, belong to the medieval tradition of rhetoric and romance; it was largely his admiration for Petrarch, whom in 1350 he got to know personally, which made him turn from the vernacular to Latin, from literature to scholarship. As a scholar he fell far behind Petrarch; he lacked the patience even to be good at copying manuscripts. He was in the main a gatherer of facts about ancient life and literature, and his encyclopedic treatises on ancient biography, geography, and mythology, enjoyed a considerable vogue in the Renaissance and did much to promote the understanding of classical literature. He had a passionate interest in poetry, and this led him along the lesser-known paths of Latin literature to poetry unknown to Petrarch, to Ovid's *Ibis*, and the *Appendix Vergiliana*; our oldest manuscript of the *Priapea* (Laur. 33.31) is in his hand.

Among the prose works which he possessed was a group which clearly indicate that a new stream of the medieval tradition had broken through to the surface: his acquaintance with the *Annals* and *Histories* of Tacitus, Apuleius' *Golden Ass*, and Varro's *De lingua latina*, can only mean that someone had unlocked the riches of Monte Cassino. It has now been shown that much of the credit for these discoveries lies with a humanist known to both Boccaccio and Petrarch, Zanobi da Strada. As secretary to the bishop in whose jurisdiction Monte Cassino lay, he had access to the monastery and lived there from 1355 to 1357; marginalia in all three of the early manuscripts of Apuleius (including the mysterious *spurcum additamentum* at *Met.* 10.21.1) are in his hand and bear witness to his keen interest in the contents of the library. The texts which Monte Cassino alone had preserved through the Middle Ages were soon in the hands of the Florentine humanists, and the key person in this operation was obviously their man in Monte Cassino, Zanobi da Strada. But Boccaccio played his part in this: we know that in 1355 he returned to Florence from a brief visit to Naples with a Beneventan manuscript (Laur. 51.10) containing *inter alia* two unknown works, Varro's *De lingua latina* and Cicero's *Pro Cluentio*, and that he copied out these texts for Petrarch. His library could boast copies of both Tacitus and Apuleius (his autograph Apuleius is still extant—Laur. 54.32); the Monte Cassino Tacitus eventually turned up in Florence, and Boccaccio has been suspected of playing a sinister part in its removal.

Although he was not in the front rank as a scholar, Boccaccio did put his genius and enthusiasm behind the humanist movement and helped to mark out the lines along which it was to develop. He naturalized humanism in Florence and made the first attempt, even if for the time being an abortive one, to establish Greeks studies in the city which was to become the centre of the teaching of Greek in the West.

IV. COLUCCIO SALUTATI (1331–1406)

The combination of creative genius and humanist inquiry gives Petrarch and Boccaccio an aura which would elude a man who followed mere scholarly pursuits. Coluccio Salutati had little literary talent and his scholarship was not of a very high order; but he was a powerful and critical link in the development of humanism, second in importance only to Petrarch. He had corresponded with Petrarch in his later years, knew Boccaccio well, and was strongly influenced by both. Inspired by the previous generation, he passed on the torch to the next great wave of humanists, many of whom he could claim as his disciples, among them Poggio Braccciolini and Leonardo Bruni. From the death of Petrarch in 1374 until his own death in 1406 Coluccio presided over the humanist movement.

Although a disconcerting taste for allegorical exegesis makes it clear that Coluccio had one foot still in the Middle Ages, he possessed in full measure the characteristic qualities of the humanist. As chancellor of Florence for over thirty years, he was able to consummate the powerful alliance which had grown up between humanism and politics, to use his Latin and his learning to lash his antagonists, whether enemies of Florence or detractors of classical literature. He read the ancient authors passionately and at first hand and achieved that easy intimacy with them which we have seen in Petrarch. To the humanist spirit he added the elements of classical scholarship: he was an active collator of manuscripts, showed remarkable grasp of the ways in which texts are corrupted, made some creditable contributions to textual criticism (his emendation of Scipio Nasica to Scipio Asina in Valerius Maximus (6.9.1) is well known), and has been recognized as a pioneer in this field. Above all, it was he who invited Chrysoloras to Florence (see p. 131) and so made possible, in 1397, the real beginning of Greek studies in Western Europe.

Not the least thing about Coluccio was his library; more than a hundred of his books have been identified. One of them is a classical text copied throughout in his own hand, the *Tragedies* of Seneca

E

(Brit. Mus. Add. 11987), to which he had added Mussato's *Ecerinis*. Although his books have less intrinsic interest than those of Petrarch, this fine collection was an important cultural instrument both during his lifetime and after it was dispersed. Among his more remarkable volumes were the oldest complete manuscript of Tibullus (Ambros. R. 26 sup. = A), one of the three primary witnesses to the text of Catullus (Ottob. lat. 1829 = R), and—his greatest find—a copy of Cicero's *Ad familiares*. Cicero's *Letters* had a special significance for the early humanists; they felt that they now knew Cicero intimately, that they could travel back in time to the classical period and relive moments with the person who was for them the greatest of the Romans. The *Ad familiares* were found in the cathedral library at Vercelli by Pasquino Cappelli, chancellor of Milan, who had instituted a search at Coluccio's instigation. Coluccio was really looking for a manuscript of the *Letters to Atticus*, which Petrarch had known, and he was beside himself with joy to receive (in 1392) the unexpected bonus of a completely unknown collection. In the following year he obtained a copy of the *Letters to Atticus*, and so became the first person for centuries to possess both collections; his copies still survive (Laur. 49.7 and 49.18; the second is the important manuscript M of the *Ad Atticum*). The Vercelli codex was eventually taken to Florence and there it remains (Laur. 49.9), the only surviving Carolingian manuscript of Cicero's *Letters*. It is interesting to observe that the rounded picture of Cicero which emerged from his letters provoked very different reactions from Petrarch and Coluccio. While Petrarch was upset to discover that Cicero had left philosophy for a life of action and intrigue, it was his blending of intellectual pursuits with a political career that roused the admiration of Coluccio and the later Renaissance.

V. THE GREAT AGE OF DISCOVERY: POGGIO BRACCIOLINI (1380–1459)

The gradual rediscovery of ancient literature runs like a powerful current through the Renaissance from the days of Paduan pre-humanism into the second half of the fifteenth century and beyond. Lovato, Petrarch, Zanobi, and Coluccio had been pre-eminent among those who had added to the list of classical works made accessible to the writers and thinkers of their time; but for sheer ability in turning up lost texts they were all outdone by Poggio Bracciolini, an arresting person, who found time as papal secretary to indulge in a variety of literary pursuits, ranging from history and moral essays to polemic and pornography of such accomplished scurrility that it becomes clear that the more robust writings of antiquity had not been rediscovered for nothing.

The great opportunity for another break-through in the discovery of classical texts came when the Council of Constance (1414–17) was summoned to heal the Great Schism and settle other ecclesiastical problems. The whole papal court moved to Constance, and the humanists who were assisting at the conference soon perceived, as men do, that there were interesting activities not included in the agenda; they devoted their spare time to the search for classical texts. Poggio made a number of expeditions, the first in 1415 to the monastery of Cluny in Burgundy, where he found an ancient manuscript of Cicero's speeches, containing the *Pro Cluentio, Pro Roscio Amerino, Pro Murena, Pro Milone*, and *Pro Caelio*. The *Pro Roscio* and *Pro Murena* were previously unknown. This manuscript, which was at least as early as the eighth century, is known as the *vetus Cluniacensis*, and its partial reconstruction from copies and extracts in 1905 is perhaps the greatest achievement of the English Ciceronian scholar A. C. Clark. The text of the lost Cluniacensis is most accurately mirrored in a manuscript which was in part copied from it before it was carried off to Italy by Poggio (Paris lat. 14749). This manuscript has now yielded up its secret and revealed the hand of the French humanist Nicholas of Clémanges.

His next foray was in the summer of 1416, this time to Saint Gall in company with three humanist friends, Bartolomeo da Montepulciano, Cencio Rustici, and Zomino da Pistoia. The result was three major discoveries: a complete Quintilian (previous humanists had had to make do with *mutili*), Asconius' *Commentary* on five of Cicero's speeches, and a manuscript containing four books (i-iv.377) of the *Argonautica* of Valerius Flaccus. Poggio's manuscript of Quintilian is of little value, but for Asconius we depend on three copies which resulted from this trip, one made by Poggio, one (and the best) by Zomino, and one derived from Bartolomeo's autograph. The lost Sangallensis of the *Argonautica* has to be reconstructed from a similar trio, one certainly in Poggio's hand (Madrid, Bibl. Nac. 8514, *olim* X. 81, which also contains his Asconius); but for Valerius we have a complete and more important ninth-century manuscript from Fulda (Vat. lat. 3277), which was itself eventually taken to Italy.

Early in 1417, armed with official sanction, Poggio and Bartolomeo made a highly organized expedition to Saint Gall and other monasteries of the area: their finds included Lucretius, Silius Italicus, and Manilius. The manuscripts which they found have perished, but their legacy remains. The copy of Manilius which Poggio had made is an important witness to the text (Madrid, Bibl. Nac. 3678, *olim* M. 31); his Lucretius fathered the whole race of *Itali*, and all our manuscripts of Silius go back to the copies made as a result of this expedition. At the same time Poggio acquired from Fulda their famous manuscript of Ammianus (Vat. lat. 1873), which he took off to Italy; he also set eyes on their Apicius, and this too was eventually taken to Rome, by Enoch of Ascoli in 1455. Now or at some later date he also obtained a manuscript of Columella (an author already known in Italy), and his manuscript was probably the insular codex at Fulda, which reached Italy in the fifteenth century.

In the summer of 1417 Poggio went on more extended travels in France and Germany. He made two important discoveries. The first was eight unknown speeches of Cicero: the *Pro Caecina*, *Pro Roscio comoedo*, *De lege agraria* i–iii, *Pro Rabirio perduellionis reo*, *In Pisonem*, *Pro Rabirio Postumo*. He found the *Pro Caecina* at Langres, the others probably in Cologne cathedral. His autograph copy of these speeches has now been discovered (Vat. lat. 11458) and so done away with a tedious process of reconstruction. The second find was one of the rarest of texts, the *Silvae* of Statius; our manuscripts of these poems all descend from the copy which was made for him (Madrid, Bibl. Nac. 3678, *olim* M. 31).

When the Council was over, Poggio spent some years in England, where his only find was what he described as a *particula Petronii*, i.e. the *excerpta vulgaria*; it is from this manuscript that all the fifteenth-century copies descend. On his way home in 1423 he found at Cologne a second manuscript of Petronius containing the

Cena Trimalchionis, and from the copy which was made for him descends our unique source for the complete *Cena* (Paris lat. 7989). It disappeared from view while on loan to Niccolò Niccoli, fortunately to reappear at Trau in Dalmatia about 1650.

Poggio's achievements in the field of discovery were prodigious; his personal intervention in the history of many important texts was decisive and influential. But recent studies have added another feather to his cap: he appears to have been the inventor of the humanistic script (Plate XVI). As time went by, and particularly from the beginning of the thirteenth century, Caroline minuscule had become more angular and thick and considerably less attractive, developing into what is known as the Gothic hand. The humanistic script was a deliberate return to an earlier form of Caroline minuscule; the earliest book written in this hand by Poggio can be dated to 1402–3. The influence of Coluccio may have been at work, and it was another of his protégés, Niccolò Niccoli, who seems to have developed the cursive form of the new script. With the advent of printing the formal hand developed into the roman fount, the cursive into italic.

The bulk of Latin literature known to us had now been recovered. The more important of the remaining discoveries may be mentioned more briefly. In 1421, in the cathedral of Lodi, to the south-east of Milan, Gerardo Landriani found a collection of *rhetorica*, including the *De oratore* and *Orator* (previously only known through *mutili*) and an unknown work, the *Brutus*. In 1429 Nicolaus of Cues brought to Rome an eleventh-century German manuscript of Plautus (Vat. lat. 3870), which contained, among others, the twelve plays which were still unknown. The unique manuscript of Tacitus' *Opera minora* (Iesi lat. 8) had been known to Poggio as early as 1425, but attempts to entice it from Hersfeld had failed: in 1455 it was finally brought to Rome, probably by Enoch of Ascoli. The remaining unknown part of Tacitus, *Annals* 1–6, was filched from Corvey and arrived in Rome in 1508. Other fifteenth-century discoveries included Cornelius Nepos, Celsus, Frontinus' *De aquis*, and the *Panegyrici Latini*.

With the finding of a large number of grammatical works at Bobbio in 1493 ended what Sabbadini called the heroic age of discovery. But important texts continued to see the light. In 1501–4

Sannazaro found in France the archetype of the pseudo-Ovidian *Halieutica* and the *Cynegetica* of Grattius (Vienna lat. 277) and its no less interesting and important copy (for the Vienna manuscript is now incomplete) containing the *florilegium Thuaneum*. But most of the discoveries of the early sixteenth century were associated with the scholarly activity now centred at Basle, the home at this time of Erasmus and Beatus Rhenanus and such printers as Froben and Cratander. Beatus Rhenanus discovered Velleius Paterculus at Murbach in 1515 and produced the *editio princeps* in 1520. By using an important new manuscript Cratander was able to print in 1528 an edition of Cicero which contained five letters to Brutus never seen before and for which his book remains the unique source. In 1527 Grynaeus found the surviving books of Livy's fifth decade at Lorsch. Such finds were rarely to be the lot of later scholars, but the excitement of discovery continued, buoyed up by two new sources, palimpsests and papyri.

It should be remembered in this context that the humanists also had a capacity for losing manuscripts. Once they had carefully copied a text, they were liable to have little interest in the manuscript which had preserved it. The Cluny and Lodi manuscripts of Cicero, the Veronenses of Catullus and Pliny have perished; only a few leaves survive of the Hersfeld Tacitus; the *Cena Trimalchionis* was nearly lost again for ever. Other manuscripts unnamed and unsung survived into the Renaissance (their existence can be inferred from their humanist progeny), but not beyond it. In the sixteenth century the situation was worse; many fine codices went along the one-way road to the printing press. Among them were the Murbach codex of the *Historia Augusta* lent to Erasmus, the fifth-century manuscript of Pliny's *Letters* (the unique source for book X, now reduced to a fragment) which Aldus managed to borrow from the abbey of Saint Victor at Paris, the manuscripts of Livy from Worms and Speyer which were used by Beatus Rhenanus and Gelenius. The Murbach codex of Velleius Paterculus which they used for their edition survived but later disappeared, being last heard of in the sale-room in 1786.

VI. LATIN SCHOLARSHIP IN THE FIFTEENTH CENTURY: VALLA AND POLITIAN

The quickened interest in all aspects of ancient life and literature, fostered by the continual excitement of new discoveries, led to a vigorous growth in all the main disciplines and techniques which are necessary to a full understanding of classical antiquity. While archaeology, numismatics, epigraphy, and the study of Roman institutions were launched along sound lines by such men as Flavio Biondo (1392–1463), historical and textual criticism, which are fundamental to the study of classical texts, were developed with singular brilliance by two humanists who may be regarded as representing what was best in the scholarship of the fifteenth century, Lorenzo Valla (1407–57) and Angelo Poliziano (1454–94). As attention will be focused on these two figures, it should be emphasized that they are in a class apart. The average scholar of the time did not reach these heights, though there is evidence that a great deal of sound and scrupulous work was done on Latin texts during this period. A valuable body of corrections and conjectures was rapidly amassed, often depreciated because anonymous. But there were also the dabblers, men whose confidence in emending and elucidating classical texts had outstripped their scholarly equipment and whose facile jottings, even when they were not intended to infect the traditional text, might easily do so. There was a temptation to embellish, to produce the readable and elegant text which the customer expected. Hence the caution with which editors use the manuscripts of this period.

It was now possible to study the works of Latin literature with greater ease and in greater depth. A contributory factor of supreme importance was the increasing number of splendid libraries, founded or enriched by generous and influential patrons, among them the Visconti in Pavia, Duke Federigo of Urbino, Alfonso V in Naples, the Medici in Florence, Pope Nicholas V in Rome. In the train of the library-builders came the highly organized entrepreneur like the bookseller Vespasiano da Bisticci (1421–98), who was prepared to lay on forty-five scribes when a library was on order; and, as the manuscript gave way to the printed book, classical texts and the scholarly work that began to gather around them could be disseminated without restriction or limit.

The critical standards of this surging humanism were carefully probed by Lorenzo Valla. Trained in Latin and Greek by the best teachers of his day, among them Aurispa and Leonardo Bruni, and gifted with exceptional ability, Valla was clearly destined to make his mark. But his vain and aggressive nature, which prompted him to tilt at every sacred cow and was to involve him in a series of venomous polemics, particularly with Panormita and Poggio, might have seriously hampered his career, had it not been for the protection and patronage, first of Alfonso V, then of Nicholas V. Nicholas opened the doors of the Curia to this *enfant terrible*, and under his successor he became papal secretary. From 1450 he held a chair of rhetoric at Rome.

An early victim of his critical powers was the Donation of Constantine, a notorious document, fabricated as early as the eighth or ninth century, which strengthened papal claims to temporal power by recording the legendary gift of Rome and the provinces of Italy by Constantine to the Pope: in 1440 Valla proved, on historical and linguistic grounds, that the Donation was a forgery. It is not surprising that he likewise attacked the authenticity of the spurious correspondence between Seneca and Saint Paul, which had had an undeserved run since the days of Jerome. His most famous work is his *Elegantiae*, dealing with points of Latin style, usage, and grammar. Composed while he was at Naples, it was first printed in 1471; by 1536 it had appeared in no less than 59 editions, a standard authority on the Latin language for both the fifteenth and sixteenth centuries. Its critical and independent scholarship marks the highest point which the study of Latin had so far attained. It was followed, in 1446–7, by his *Emendationes sex librorum Titi Livi* (books 21–26). Written with a scathing brilliance recurrent in later works of this sort, this philological masterpiece was designed to discredit two other scholars at the court of Alfonso, Panormita and Facio, and made it painfully plain that only the best could play at the fashionable game of emending Livy. One of the weapons in his arsenal was the great Livy volume which had been put together by Petrarch, and his autograph notes can still be seen in its margins (Plate XV). He dared to emend the Vulgate itself, and his notes and corrections (1449), based on a study of the Greek original and early patristic texts, were fully appreciated by Erasmus, who had them printed in 1505. He also found time to be a prolific translator from the Greek.

Politian was born at Montepulciano and educated at Florence. He showed a precocious talent and was taken at an early age into the household of Lorenzo de' Medici, who made him tutor to his children and remained his lifelong friend and patron; by the age of thirty he was a professor of such repute that he attracted scholars from all over Europe to his lectures on Greek and Latin literature. As well as being an influential teacher, he was the finest poet of his time, both in Italian and in Latin; and as a scholar he at times transcends his age and moves out of reach of any of his contemporaries.

Politian won his prominent position in the history of the classical tradition both by his exact scholarship and by the way in which he opened the eyes of his contemporaries to the full perspective of ancient literature. Valla had recommended the study of Quintilian, but his insistence on a classical norm in the writing of Latin had tended to foster the predominant cult of Ciceronian Latin. Politian firmly rejected Ciceronianism and chose to create an eclectic style of his own which exploited the whole range of Latin: *'non exprimis'* inquit aliquis *'Ciceronem'*. *Quid tum? Non enim sum Cicero, me tamen (ut opinor) exprimo (Epist.* 8.16). In the same way he was the first to give serious attention to the prose and poetry of the Silver Age.

Politian's great work of scholarship was his *Miscellanea*, a collection of a hundred chapters of varying length on different points of scholarship which well displays the many sides of his learning. The first part (*Centuria prima*) was published in Florence in 1489; an autograph draft of a second series of chapters recently came to light and has only just been printed. The work is similar in style to the *Attic Nights* of Aulus Gellius; again the influence of late authors is evident. A few examples of the topics discussed will show the character of the book: the origin of the names of the days of the week, the original meaning of the word 'panic', the significance of a coin struck by Brutus showing his portrait with a cap and two daggers are typical problems. To settle the question of how to spell the name Vergil Politian invokes the evidence of some

inscriptions and the spelling of very old manuscripts. He uses the
text of Callimachus to emend a corrupt passage in Catullus (66.48).
In an important chapter for the development of textual criticism
(*Misc.* xviii) he points out that the manuscript of the *Epistulae ad
familiares* which was made for Coluccio in 1392 (Laur. 49.7 = P)
is a copy of the Vercelli manuscript (Laur. 49.9 = M), and demonstrates that P itself, in which a number of leaves have been displaced
through an error in binding, must be the parent of a whole family
of later manuscripts in which the sequence of a group of letters has
similarly been disturbed. This methodical application of the principle of *eliminatio codicum descriptorum* (see p. 188) is not found
again until the nineteenth century. In the *Letters to Atticus* (15.4.4)
he emends the vulgate reading *cera* to *cerula* on the strength of the
reading *ceruia* in M, the best of the Italian manuscripts (Laur.
49.18). The principle that conjectural emendation must start from
the earliest recoverable stage of the tradition, employed more than
once by Politian, was not fully exploited until the age of Lachmann.

Although his conviction that later manuscripts are derivative
was too sweeping, Politian's constant recourse to the oldest
manuscripts available and his distrust of humanist copies was
bound to produce solid results. In this he was helped enormously
by the improved library facilities of his day and the advent of the
printed book; between 1465 and 1475 the bulk of the Latin classics
were put into print. He made full use of libraries, both public and
private, in Florence and elsewhere, particularly that of the Medici;
no less than thirty-five Medicean manuscripts were out on loan to
him at the time of his death. Among the many great classical manuscripts which he is known to have examined or collated were such
important witnesses as the Bembinus of Terence (Vat. lat. 3226 of
the fourth to fifth century), the Romanus of Vergil (Vat. lat. 3867
of the fifth to sixth century), the Etruscus of Seneca's *Tragedies*,
the Neapolitanus of Propertius, and (though this is less certain) the
Vaticanus of Valerius Flaccus. Some manuscripts which he used
have been lost and his careful collations, usually entered (by him
or for him) into his copy of an early printed edition, have the
status of important witnesses to the text. Examples are the Parma
edition of Ovid in the Bodleian Library, with his autograph readings from the lost Marcianus of the *Tristia*, his copy of the first

edition of the *Silvae* with his collations of a manuscript which is thought by some to have been the one which Poggio found in 1417, and his *editio princeps* of the *Scriptores rei rusticae*; this contains collations of an early manuscript of Columella (doubtless Ambros. L. 85 sup. from Fulda), and, more important, of the lost archetype of the agricultural works of Cato and Varro.

His keen interest in the more technical writings of antiquity is further illustrated by a massive edition of the Elder Pliny (Rome, 1473) now at Oxford; this contains a transcript of Politian's notes and collations, the latter taken from five different manuscripts (carefully distinguished with the sigla *a b c d e*) and the important critical work of a contemporary scholar, the *Castigationes Plinianae* of Ermolao Barbaro. For Apicius he was able to collate the two ninth-century manuscripts on which the text is based (E and V), from Fulda and Tours respectively. The Fulda manuscript is now in New York, while a fragment of Politian's own manuscript of Apicius, complete with his collations of E and V, eventually came to light in Russia (Leningrad 627/1, *olim* V. 644), a remarkable and colourful history for a cookery book. He studied and copied important medical texts, including the manuscript of Celsus discovered by Giovanni Lamola in Milan in 1427 (Laur. 73.1); and the copy which he caused to be made of an old manuscript of the *Ars veterinaria* of Pelagonius is now the unique source for the text (Riccardianus 1179). Its *subscriptio*, which is typical, demonstrates the sound and scholarly way in which Politian dealt with manuscript evidence:

Hunc librum de codice sanequam vetusto Angelus Politianus, Medicae domus alumnus et Laurenti cliens, curavit exscribendum; dein ipse cum exemplari contulit et certa fide emendavit, ita tamen ut ab illo mutaret nihil, set et quae depravata inveniret relinqueret intacta, neque suum ausus est unquam iudicium interponere. Quod si priores institutum servassent, minus multo mendosos codices haberemus. Qui legis boni consule et vale. Florentiae, anno MCCCCLXXXV, Decembri mense.

VII. GREEK STUDIES: DIPLOMATS, REFUGEES AND
BOOK COLLECTORS

The introduction of Greek studies to the city states of central and northern Italy might have been expected to come about at an early date and without difficulty through contact with the Greek-speaking communities of the extreme south and Sicily. But the south was quite isolated from the rest of the peninsula and had not shared the growth in wealth and other progress of the bigger northern cities, a state of affairs which was not altered until well into the present century. Occasionally men of ability from these regions travelled to the north on diplomatic missions, and in the fourteenth century two of them received an enthusiastic welcome from the leading scholars and writers of the day. It is well known how Petrarch took lessons from the monk Barlaam, whom he met at the papal court at Avignon. But though the monk was admitted by his most bitter theological opponents to be a master of theology and logic, his ability as a teacher left something to be desired, and Petrarch never succeeded in learning enough Greek to read the copy of Homer that a Byzantine ambassador gave him (Ambros. I. 98 inf.). Another opportunity to learn Greek arose in 1360, when Barlaam's pupil Leonzio Pilato was intercepted by Boccaccio at Florence on his way north to Avignon; he was induced to stay and lecture on Greek, in return for an annual stipend from the Florentine government, but being a man of restless and impatient character he did not stay many years. The first translations that he was persuaded to make were some Homer together with about four hundred lines of Euripides' *Hecuba* for Boccaccio and some of Plutarch's *Lives* for Coluccio Salutati. The style of these versions was very rough, and Coluccio set to work to improve the latinity of the Homer translation, which was done in word-for-word style. The opening lines of the *Iliad* ran as follows in Leonzio's version:

> iram cane dea Pelidae Achillis
> pestiferam quae innumerabiles dolores Achivis posuit,
> multas autem robustas animas ad infernum antemisit . . .

More fruitful than the contacts with the south of Italy were those with Constantinople itself. The declining fortunes of the

Greek empire made it necessary to send frequent diplomatic missions abroad to beg help against the Turkish invader; monarchs as far distant as the king of England received these appeals. We have already seen how a knowledge of Latin literature was made available to the Byzantines through Maximus Planudes, who had served on an embassy sent to Venice. It was almost exactly a century later that another Byzantine diplomat, Manuel Chrysoloras, became the first man to give regular lectures on Greek in Italy. He began in Florence in 1397, which is therefore a date of fundamental importance in the cultural history of Europe, and continued his courses for a number of years, combining this activity with diplomatic business. He had several notable pupils including Guarino and Leonardo Bruni. One important result of his teaching was that Latin translations of Greek texts were prepared, and he insisted that the old word-for-word style of translation should be abandoned, and that attention should be given to ensuring some literary merit in the version. An indication of his influence as an instructor is that his textbook of Greek grammar entitled *Erotemata* gained a considerable circulation, and eventually became the first Greek grammar to be printed (in 1471); it was later used by such famous men as Erasmus and Reuchlin.

During the fifteenth century the opportunities for an Italian to learn Greek improved. A number of Byzantines came to live in Italy, and after the defeat of their country in 1453 there was a stream of refugees, who generally reached Italy by way of Crete and Venice, and who were all anxious to earn a living by teaching their native language or copying texts. Fortunately for them the revival in knowledge of classical Latin caused a widespread desire to read the Greek authors so frequently quoted or mentioned in it. But it is difficult to estimate how many Italians in fact learnt Greek to a standard which permitted them to read a text with ease. Enthusiasm for the new language might soon be lost through the lack of a gifted teacher or the irritating drawbacks of unsystematic grammatical textbooks; even Erasmus complained of the effort required to master the language. Some Italians, including Politian, are known to have taught themselves by taking a Latin translation, for example the traditional version of the Bible or Theodore Gaza's rendering of Aristotle, and using it as a key to elucidate the Greek text. In the absence of a teacher or a satisfactory grammar this was an exceptionally difficult undertaking. Many would-be scholars must have been obliged to content themselves with reading Latin translations: a great number of these were produced, especially under the patronage of Pope Nicholas V (1447–55), who commissioned versions of Thucydides, Herodotus, Xenophon, Plato, Aristotle, Theophrastus, Ptolemy, and Strabo. A small minority of students had the energy or the means to seek instruction in Constantinople itself; two of the more famous fifteenth-century figures who did this were Filelfo (1398–1481) and Guarino (1374–1460).

Another reason for travel to the East was the chance of bringing back manuscripts which might well include new texts. Some collectors had remarkable success, and Giovanni Aurispa came back to Italy in 1423 with 238 Greek books (Plate IV); an equally large modern collection of Greek printed texts would be considered substantial, but one must not exaggerate the merits of the Aurispa library, since it doubtless contained a large number of duplicated titles. Probably Filelfo's collection of forty Greek books was more typical of the private libraries formed at the time. Rulers of Italian states collected also. From Florence Lorenzo de' Medici dispatched Janus Lascaris, one of the scholar refugees, on a journey to various Byzantine provinces in 1492 in search of manuscripts. The papal collections also grew rapidly. Venice acquired the basis of its large collection rather differently in 1468 through the gift of Cardinal Bessarion; he had collected for some time with the object of forming a complete library of Greek literature, giving his agents instructions to search in many territories of the former empire, and it is known that a part of his collection, including the newly discovered text of Quintus of Smyrna and perhaps the famous codex Venetus of Aristophanes (Marc. gr. 474), was acquired from the monastery of Saint Nicholas at Otranto.

VIII. GREEK SCHOLARSHIP IN THE FIFTEENTH CENTURY: BESSARION AND POLITIAN

A comprehensive account of Greek studies in the fifteenth century would need to deal with a large number of the more eminent humanists, but for this short introduction it must suffice to select

two of the most notable scholars as typical of the aims and achievements of the period. One of these two represents the learning of the
Greeks, the other shows what the Italians were able to learn from
their masters.

The earlier of the two figures is cardinal Bessarion (c. 1400–
1472). He was born in Trebizond and educated in Constantinople
at the school run by George Chrysococces, where he first met the
Italian Filelfo with whom he was to correspond frequently in later
life. He became a monk in 1423, and spent the years 1431–6 at
Mistra in the Peloponnese in the circle of the freethinker George
Gemistus Plethon, from whom he probably acquired his admiration for Plato. Through Plethon he was introduced to the emperor
and came to be employed on government business; the emperor
made him abbot of a monastery in the capital in 1436 and in the
following year promoted him to the see of Nicaea. In 1438 he came
to Italy as a member of the delegation sent to the Council of Florence and Ferrara to negotiate a union between the Greek and
Roman churches. More than one attempt had been made to restore
church unity, and now the need to end the schism was made acute
by the rapid disintegration of the Byzantine empire, which governed
no more than a tiny proportion of its former territories; hopes of
Western military aid might be realized after a reunion of the
church. The proceedings of the council were protracted, but in the
end an agreement was reached between the two parties, very largely
owing to the forceful arguments of Bessarion, who had to overcome
determined opposition from members of his own delegation. The
union was abortive, since the mass of the population in the Greek
empire, encouraged by many of the clergy, refused to accept the
act of union as a just compromise; the minority who accepted the
union became a separate sect, known as the Greek Uniate Church,
which thus owes its existence to Bessarion. Despite the failure of
the council to have any lasting political effect Bessarion's services
to the Church did not pass unnoticed by the pope; he became a
cardinal and resided permanently in Italy, taking a considerable
part in church affairs, and on more than one occasion he was nearly
elected pope.

The cardinal's house in Rome was a centre of literary activity,
where Greeks and Italians mixed freely; of the former the two

most famous were Theodore Gaza and George Trapezuntios, who translated various works into Latin, while among the Italians were Poggio and Valla. Bessarion's wide knowledge and expert command of Latin caused him to be dubbed by Valla '*Latinorum Graecissimus, Graecorum Latinissimus*'. His library was exceptionally large; the Greek books alone amounted to some five hundred volumes towards the end of his life and included many important copies of classical texts, for his tastes were not confined to theology and philosophy. He took great care over them, as may be seen from the possession-notes, shelf-marks, and other notes he inserted on the flyleaves. He had not always been a keen collector, since he had relied on the book trade in Constantinople as an adequate source of supply; but one of his letters states that the fall of the Greek empire in 1453 made him form the plan of building as complete a collection as possible of Greek books, in the intention of placing it eventually at the disposal of those Greeks who survived the fall of the empire and reached Italy. This statement of his plans shows one of his main reasons for presenting his collection during his own lifetime (1468) to the city of Venice to form the basis of a public library, for it was in Venice that a high proportion of Greek refugees tended to congregate.

Bessarion's own literary work included a Latin translation of Aristotle's *Metaphysics*, and a long book against the critics of Plato. A good many pamphlets and letters also survive. Two of the former are of interest for our present purpose. The first arose out of the negotiations for church unity. The crucial point in the argument between the Greeks and the Latins concerned the procession of the Holy Spirit: is it of the same or merely similar nature to God the Father? Bessarion's great success was that he found a passage in Saint Basil's tract *Against Eunomius* which clearly enunciated the view of the Latin Church, and should therefore have formed the basis of a reconciliation, since the authority of Saint Basil in the Greek Church was beyond criticism. Bessarion's opponents at the council, members of the Greek delegation who wanted a successful conclusion to the discussions only if everything went their own way, claimed that the passage was not a genuine statement by Saint Basil, that an earlier Greek church reformer or the Italians had forged it, and that they had manuscripts which omitted the words in question. Though sure of his ground Bessarion was temporarily at a loss to prove his point and had to rely on other less decisive evidence to convince the opposition. But when he returned briefly to Constantinople he determined to settle the matter to his satisfaction and began to examine all the copies of the text that he could lay his hands on. At the time of the council only one of the six copies of the work that could be found appeared to favour Bessarion's opponents, and that gave every sign of having been tampered with, for the vital passage had been deleted and other words substituted for it. Research in the monastic libraries of the capital soon yielded two old copies of the text, one on paper dated to the middle of the twelfth century, and the other on parchment of still greater age; the text of both these copies supported Bessarion, while only very recent copies of the text, which appeared to have been written at the time of the council or just after, supported the other view. Bessarion used the age of the two old copies as his decisive argument; they were both older than the date of certain earlier Greek churchmen who had favoured union with the West, and so could not have been forged by them; and as to the notion that they had been forged by the Italians, the high quality of the Greek was sufficient reply to the suggestion.

After this example of scholarly method used to refute the unscrupulous manipulation of texts we come to Bessarion's other short work which shows his scholarship to advantage, and here too the context is theological. After a reading from Saint John's Gospel as part of the liturgy conducted in his house in Rome, lively conversation began as to the correct text of John 21 : 22. The reading had been performed from the Latin Vulgate, which erroneously gave the word *sic* instead of *si* (the Greek has ἐάν). Bessarion pointed out in discussion that this was a simple case of a copyist's error, involving only one letter. His audience was not completely persuaded, and so he wrote a pamphlet to prove his point. Here several important principles are enunciated, and the whole matter is discussed with a common sense that seems natural to us but was not welcome to the narrow-minded conservatism of men who regarded every word of Saint Jerome's translation as sacred. Bessarion states that the Greek text is the original and must have precedence over the Latin translation, and is able to claim Augustine's authority for this proposition. He also shows that early quotations of the Greek text in Origen, Cyril, and Chrysostom all have the same wording. Then he shows that the whole context of the passage is not suited to the reading of the Vulgate. The work is of great importance and anticipates the attitude of Erasmus in regarding the Greek text of the New Testament as the only proper basis for interpretation. It may owe something to Valla, who frequently met Bessarion and had previously written but not published a tract entitled *Adnotationes in Novum Testamentum*, in which he called into question the Vulgate's accuracy.

To the Greek bishop who settled in Italy and whose scholarly activity was devoted mainly to theology and philosophy Politian (1454–94) offers a striking contrast. He is famous as a poet in his vernacular language and in Latin, but was equally distinguished as a scholar. Though primarily interested in ancient literature he had a proper understanding of the subsidiary branches of knowledge, such as epigraphy and numismatics, and the contribution that they can make to a general understanding of the ancient world. The combination of poet and scholar in Politian has an interesting analogy in the Hellenistic world; the same description suits Callimachus and Eratosthenes, and it is perhaps not entirely a coincidence that Politian was the first scholar to give serious attention to Hellenistic poetry.

His ability as a Latinist and his appreciation of the importance of old manuscripts have been described above. It may merely be worth remarking in passing that he changed the direction of Greek and Latin studies in rather the same way, by encouraging an interest in post-classical authors; just as in Latin he had pointed out the merits of Quintilian, Suetonius, and the Silver Latin poets, so in Greek he lectured on Callimachus and Theocritus. As a Greek scholar he was the first Italian of whom it was generally agreed that he equalled native Greeks in knowledge of the language. Such a claim appears in his own works. In a latter to Matthias Corvinus, king of Hungary (*Epist.* 9.1), where he offers his literary services, either as a translator of classical texts or official panegyrist of the king's successes, he states that he knows as much Greek as the Greeks themselves, and is the first Italian to do so for a thousand years. The same boast is implied in the opening of his inaugural lecture on Homer. Whatever vanity there may be in this claim, it can easily be justified. Politian is the first Italian of the Renaissance who did work of permanent value on a Greek text, so that his name can still be found in the apparatus criticus of a modern edition. (Valla's contributions to the text of Thucydides are more probably due to the merits of the manuscripts he used than to his own ingenuity.) One other notable testimony to Politian's linguistic power is that from the age of seventeen he composed epigrams in Greek. About fifty of these survive in various metres, and though they are faulty in a number of matters of scansion and prosody they display considerable knowledge of the language, especially in the use of a wide vocabulary.

His works include several translations from the Greek. There is a fluent version of the late historian Herodian and some short essays by Epictetus and Plutarch. But most important prose authors had already been translated, and so Politian could turn his energy in other directions. The work which best displays the many sides of his learning is the *Miscellanea*. Most of the chapters deal with matters of Latin scholarship, but numerous Greek authors are quoted as evidence to justify or reinforce an argument. One example already mentioned is his use of the text of Callimachus to emend a corrupt passage is Catullus (66.48). Perhaps the most significant chapter is the one which gives a text of Callimachus' fifth hymn, *The bath of Pallas*, accompanied by a translation into elegant elegiacs. Here he prints the Greek text without accents in order to avoid anachronism, a point of scholarly precision in which he has not been followed by later generations, and makes a very good job of preparing the first edition of the hymn.

IX. THE FIRST PRINTED GREEK TEXTS: ALDUS MANUTIUS AND MARCUS MUSURUS

While the new art of printing soon led to a spate of editions of Latin classics from the seventies of the fifteenth century onwards, for Greek texts the situation was quite different. Part of the reason for this may have been the difficulty of designing a suitable fount of type, in which the number of sorts would not be unreasonably increased by the various combinations of letters with accents and breathings. Certainly some of the early printers, in a mistaken desire to reproduce in print the appearance of contemporary Greek script, devised founts of type that were expensive to operate with and unsatisfactory in appearance. Even the famous Aldine founts, which served for a very long time as the models for later typographers, are open to both these criticisms. But not all early printers failed in this way; the type-face designed by the famous Frenchman Nicholas Jenson, who worked in Venice, was an excellent piece of work, and still better in some ways was that used for printing passages of Greek in Politian's *Miscellanea*: here the accents and breathings were omitted and ligatures avoided, so that the text bore no close resemblance to written script but was far more easily legible. It is surprising that one of these simpler founts was not immediately accepted as the standard.

More serious than the typographical difficulty was the lack of demand for Greek texts in sufficient numbers to make an edition pay. Knowledge of Greek was quite restricted, and Latin translations could be printed instead in editions large enough to be profitable. A striking example of this is that Plato was not printed in Greek until 1513, but Marsilio Ficino's translation appeared in 1485 in an edition of 1,025 copies. Not only was this an uncommonly large edition, for the average number of copies of all publications at this date is thought to have been 250 or a little more, but it was sold out within six years, and another printing took place. But in contrast to this the Greek text of the *editio princeps* of Isocrates, which appeared in Milan in 1493, sold so slowly that in 1535 the remaining copies were reissued with a new title-page. Before the Aldine press was set up the total number of volumes printed in Greek was scarcely more than a dozen. Several of these were grammars by Chrysoloras and Constantine Lascaris, and the only major classical texts apart from Isocrates were Homer, Theocritus, and the Greek Anthology.

Aldus Manutius (1449–1515) had the idea of setting up a publishing house primarily for the printing of Greek texts. The notion came to him while he was living in Carpi, a town near Modena, acting as tutor to the sons of the ruler. Florence might seem to be the obvious place for the location of this enterprise, in view of its intellectual pre-eminence, but the death of Lorenzo de' Medici had removed the most influential patron of learning and letters. On the other hand Venice possessed a larger library of Greek books than had been assembled by the Medici family; this resulted from the gift of Bessarion. Probably more important to Aldus was the great reputation of Venice as a centre of the printing trade; more than half the books printed in Italy before 1500 were published there. Skilled and experienced workmen would be available for the new firm.

From 1494 to 1515 the Aldine press issued a great series of editions of classical texts: with the death of Aldus in the latter year the firm declined. The printing of Latin texts had advanced to the point that Aldus' books include only one first edition of a Latin text, and an unimportant one at that. But in Greek he was responsible for the first printing of nearly all the major authors, and during his twenty years in business he had almost a monopoly of preparing Greek texts. In Venice and its territories he had privileges from the government which amounted to a patent for the exclusive right to use type-faces designed or commissioned by himself.

His great project could not have been realized without the help of numerous scholarly friends, both Greek and Italian. The man who undertook much the most significant single share of the scholarly work was the Cretan Marcus Musurus (1470–1517). Aldus himself must probably be counted a considerable scholar in his own right. But it is not always easy to tell how much of the work was done by him or Musurus or some other members of the circle. The title-pages of Aldine books and the dedicatory letters written by Aldus often do not name the editor of the text. In such cases the most likely solution to the problem is that the work was shared by several of the publisher's friends. By 1502 at the latest the title-pages refer to the Academy or Neakademia, a club formed by Aldus for the promotion of Greek studies. It had a set of rules drawn up in Greek, one of which was that at meetings Greek should be the only language permitted. About thirty or forty members can be identified. Permanent residence in Venice was not necessary for membership, since Musurus, who taught at Padua and at Carpi for a time, appears to have been a member. Visiting foreign scholars were welcomed; the most famous example was Erasmus.

The quantity of first editions brought out by the press during its most active periods testifies to the enthusiasm of the collaborators and the efficient organization of the printing. The first Greek book to appear was a short text, Musaeus, doubtless chosen as an easy experiment before proceeding to more difficult ventures. After this came a text of Theocritus and Hesiod more complete than the one already in print. Then the press settled to the enormous task of editing Aristotle and Theophrastus, the result being a series of five folio volumes brought out between 1495 and 1498. The only interval in the activity of the firm was caused by the war of the League of Cambrai against Venice, and no Greek books could be produced during the years 1505–7 and 1510–12. The most remarkable years for the publication of major classical texts were 1502–4, which saw the first editions of Sophocles, Euripides, Herodotus, Thucydides, and Demosthenes. But Aldus did not confine himself to major authors: he published Herodian's *History*, Pollux, Stephanus of Byzantium, and Philostratus' *Life of Apollonius*, to mention only a selection. In the preface to the last of these he stated bluntly, with a candour not normal among publishers, what a worthless text he believed this to be (*nihil unquam memini me legere deterius*). Nearly all the Aldine books were classical texts; Christian writers only occasionally appeared. At one time Aldus seems to have projected an Old Testament in Hebrew, Greek, and Latin, together with a New Testament in Greek and Latin, but nothing came of this during his own lifetime.

The task of an editor at this date was full of difficulties. Manuscripts had to be obtained to serve as copy for the typesetters, and if, as often happened, the text was corrupt, the editor might attempt either to emend it or to find better manuscripts. The prefaces give some indications of these hardships. Aldus tells us that in the whole of Italy he had been able to find only one copy of Theophrastus. At the end of his introduction to Thucydides he says that he would willingly have added Xenophon and Gemistus Plethon to the same volume, but had to postpone it for lack of manuscripts. Musurus in his preface to the epistolographi says that some passages in Alciphron were so corrupt that he could not put them right, and asks readers to excuse the unintelligible state of the text as printed. Musurus' procedure can be observed a little more closely in some of his other books. The first large volume for which he was undoubtedly responsible is the Aristophanes of 1498 (Plate VIII),

and it can be established that he worked from at least four manuscripts in preparing it. One of these survives in Modena (Estensis
α. U. 5.10). A text of the comedies had to be constructed from these
four books and submitted to the typesetter. An equally substantial
task was the redaction of the scholia, which were printed in the
margins in just the same position as they had in a medieval manuscript. The scholia in the manuscripts at Musurus' disposal were of
different types, and he had an enormous task in selecting and combining the notes into a form that could be printed. To this clerical
labour was added the need to restore the correct text, which he did
in a number of passages. Similar clerical labour awaited him a
number of years later, when he came to edit the lexicon of Hesychius, a Greek dictionary compiled in the sixth century. This survives in only one manuscript (now Marc. gr. 622). Rather than
write out the whole text afresh to provide the printer's copy
Musurus himself wrote in the manuscript all the necessary corrections and instructions to the printer. As the script contained
numerous abbreviations Musurus wrote out in full, either above
the line or in the margin, each abbreviated word. He also corrected
a large number of mistakes, and the most recent editor has remarked
that every page has some emendation which shows Musurus' skill
and linguistic knowledge. One rather amusing instance of his
skill, which shows him going to greater lengths than modern
critics would think necessary, arises in another text, the third
pastoral poem of Moschus. Here there is a gap in the text between
lines 92 and 93, which Musurus filled by six hexameter lines
of his own. Though these lines consist largely of echoes from the
similar poems of Theocritus, and were probably not intended to
do more than indicate the general sense required by the context,
they have sometimes been regarded as genuine lines of the
poem, supposedly recovered by Musurus from a unique manuscript that is now lost.

Musurus' contribution to classical scholarship is not easy to
estimate exactly, because in most cases the copy of an author which
he submitted to the printer is lost, and the best potential source of
evidence is thereby denied to us. But if he was personally responsible for all the good readings which appear for the first time in
editions that he saw through the press, there can be no doubt that

he was the most talented classical scholar ever produced by his nation.

X. ERASMUS (c. 1469–1536)

We must now turn to consider the level of scholarship that could be achieved by a native of northern Europe. The figure who commands attention is Erasmus. Though originally a monk at Steyn near Gouda, he contrived to obtain permanent leave from his monastery, and it was in Paris that he began to take up Greek. He found the language difficult, and did not benefit much from the tuition of a Greek refugee called George Hermonymus. In 1506 he went to Italy with the intention of improving his knowledge of the language, and in due course made contact with Aldus. Erasmus was by this time tolerably well known in literary circles through the publication of the first edition of the *Adagia*, a collection of proverbs with accompanying comments, and the *Enchiridion militis Christiani*, in which the blunt expression of his view of piety had caused some offence to ecclesiastical authorities. Erasmus had added fuel to the flames in 1505 by supervising the printing of another book that was not welcome to the clerical establishment, Lorenzo Valla's *Adnotationes in Novum Testamentum*, which treated the text of the Bible not as if it were sacred but like any other literary monument. It was therefore natural that Erasmus should soon be in touch with Aldus, and in due course he visited Venice, staying as a guest in the printer's house for several months. In one of his later *Colloquia*, called *Opulentia sordida*, he gives a vivid description of the miserable food and house-keeping, but there is reason to think that this is much exaggerated by Erasmus for the purpose of replying to a scurrilous polemic by Alberto Pio of Carpi. In Venice he naturally had the chance to acquire all the Greek he needed, and read the many texts that Aldus' private library could offer. One immediate result of his stay was the publication of a greatly enlarged version of the *Adagia*, incorporating material from the Greek sources that he had just begun to know well.

Much later in his career he wrote a pamphlet on the correct pronunciation of Greek, which led to the widespread adoption of what is called the Erasmian pronunciation. As a rule the Greek exiles taught classical Greek in the pronunciation of the modern language, which certainly is quite different from that used in the ancient world. Evidence to prove this had already been noted by the Spanish scholar Antonio Nebrija (1444–1522) and some members of the Aldine circle. The epithet Erasmian therefore fails to give credit for the discovery where it is due; but it is only fair to add that Erasmus himself did not claim to be the inventor of the new system, which he may be presumed to have met for the first time while staying with Aldus.

Fruitful and important though Erasmus' association with Aldus had been, he is better remembered for his long collaboration with one of the great printing houses of the north, that of Froben at Basle. Erasmus found the milieu congenial, took an active share in the editorial side of the business, and formed with Froben a friendship of considerable importance for the promotion of Christian humanism. One of the earliest and most spectacular fruits of this alliance was the first publication of the Greek text of the New Testament in 1516. By coincidence the Greek text was being set up in type at the same time in Spain at Alcalá (this edition also included the Old Testament with the Greek and Hebrew texts); but difficulties of various kinds prevented publication until 1520. It is worth noting that while Cardinal Ximénez, the chief editor of the Complutensian Polyglot, as it is sometimes known, recommended study of the Bible in the original languages, his views were perhaps not shared by all his collaborators; in one of the prefatory letters there is at least a hint that the Latin text is more to be trusted than the others. Erasmus, however, was quite clear in his own mind of the importance of establishing the original text of the New Testament. A good deal is known about his editorial procedure. He began working seriously at his projected edition during his stay in England in 1512–13, and had four manuscripts of the Greek text for consultation; one of these has been identified as the Leicester codex, a fifteenth-century copy. During the printing at Basle in 1515–16 he had five manuscripts by him, and one which has marks indicating that it was used as copy for the printer is still preserved (Basle A.N.IV.1). This is a twelfth-century manuscript of no particular value. It seems that Erasmus was aware of the likely value of really old manuscripts, but his palaeographical knowledge was inadequate for his need. In this respect he was clearly inferior to Politian and almost certainly to Bessarion; in general he relied on rather late books of no great merit, despite the evident possibility of discovering better and older texts by inquiry from his many correspondents. Though he rightly regarded codex B (Vat. gr. 1209) as of amazing age, and for a reprint of his edition obtained some collations of it through a friend, it does not seem that he ever used it systematically for the whole text. On the other hand he had a grossly exaggerated regard for a manuscript of the Apocalypse, which he thought might even date back to the apostolic age; modern scholarship has identified it as a twelfth-century codex (Schloss Harburg, I 1, 4⁰, 1).

Among many points arising out of the edition two may be mentioned here. In the book of Revelation his only manuscript lacked the last few verses and was unintelligible at other points; being determined to print a Greek text, Erasmus consulted the Vulgate in these passages and made his own Greek version of it. In so doing he exceeded the duty of an editor as it is now understood, and made some mistakes in his Greek. In the first epistle of John (5: 7) Erasmus had followed the Greek in omitting the so-called *comma Johanneum*, a statement of the doctrine of the Trinity which was found in Vulgate. This caused some controversy, during which Erasmus unwisely offered to insert the words into any reprint of his edition if they could be found in a Greek manuscript. Not surprisingly a manuscript was written for the purpose without delay (Trinity College Dublin 30), and the promise had to be made good. But Erasmus took the chance of indicating his suspicions about the authenticity of the book. The episode shows how a lack of a set of logical principles for the evaluation of manuscripts handicapped scholars in their dealings with opponents who were willing to descend to forgery. Bessarion had had a similar experience at the Council of Florence, but it was easier for him to refute his opponents in controversy, since his aim was to prove a certain passage genuine by showing that it occurred in manuscripts earlier than the date of potential forgers; whereas Erasmus had no equally neat argument at his disposal, and could only appeal to the good authority of very old manuscripts.

Despite its shortcomings in these matters Erasmus' edition of the Greek New Testament represents a very great step forward in scholarship. Against stubborn opposition it established the principles that texts are to be studied in the original language rather than translations, and that texts of scripture are to be discussed and interpreted according to the same rules of logic and common sense as any others. The work of Valla and Bessarion had come to fruition.

Erasmus had been attracted to Basle in the first place because it had already become a centre for the publishing of patristic texts. His New Testament was immediately followed by his first edition of Jerome, and that by a long series of editions of the Fathers which he produced either alone or in collaboration with others, often returning again and again to revise the same author. These include Cyprian, Hilary, Ambrose, and Augustine, and are an impressive monument to his energy and learning, both on account of the massive labour involved and because the patristic writers had received comparatively little critical attention from early editors. While engaged on these mammoth operations, Erasmus still found time to work on classical texts, an essential part of his humanist program. His services to classical Greek are comparatively small, though he produced a number of translations and edited Aristotle and Demosthenes; the only author of whom he produced the *editio princeps* was Ptolemy (1533). His contribution to Latin literature is much greater; the authors he edited include Terence, Livy, Suetonius, the Elder Pliny, and Seneca. The last, which he edited twice (1515, 1529), has been recognized as representative of both his strength and his failings. The first edition was marred by characteristic haste. It went through the press in the absence of its editor, who in any case had enough on his plate with Jerome and the New Testament both in their last stages; the distinction between editor, copy-editor, and proof corrector being more than somewhat blurred, too much was left to others, whom Erasmus afterwards blamed for incompetence and worse. The text benefited from a refreshingly critical approach, but Erasmus knew how much better it should have been and returned to retrieve what he regarded as a disgrace in 1529. The second edition, prefaced by an admirably balanced and sensible essay on Seneca, produced two successful emendations for every one in the first edition and provides convincing proof of the judgement and scholarship of its editor. But again the printing was carried out in something of a fluster, with manuscripts continuing to arrive when parts of the book were already in print. He made judicious use of such manuscripts as he could muster, but they seem to have been an indifferent lot, with one signal exception. He had access to readings from the Lorsch manuscript of the *De beneficiis* and *De clementia* (cf. p. 88), the one manuscript in a large tradition of any real value. But he was inhibited by the critical methods of his day: instead of basing his text of these works upon this prime witness, he drew on it spasmodically to emend what he had before him, and a great opportunity was lost.

5. SOME ASPECTS OF SCHOLARSHIP SINCE THE RENAISSANCE

I. THE COUNTER-REFORMATION; THE HIGH RENAISSANCE IN ITALY

The progress of scholarship in the sixteenth century was hampered by continuing religious controversy. Although Bessarion had been stimulated by such controversy to write two short books of great importance for the development of critical method, it is not easy to discover equally fruitful controversies among the contemporaries of Erasmus or in the next generation. Erasmus himself, though he had exploited the work of Valla and Bessarion for his edition of the New Testament and was aware of Politian's eminence as a scholar, did not possess the palaeographical skill that might have led to further advances; and as he settled at Basle, while most of the best working libraries with manuscript collections were still at that date to be found south of the Alps, he could scarcely hope to add greatly to his experience in dealing with manuscripts. Religious disputes took up much of his time and energy in later years, and in 1524 we find him complaining (*Epist.* 1531) that the struggle between Luther and his opponents had become such a preoccupation in literary circles that the book trade was affected, and in the German-speaking parts of Europe it was hardly possible to sell books on any other topic. Elsewhere, and especially in Italy, the energies of literary men were consumed by another controversy in which Erasmus was once again a leading figure: the question was whether Cicero should be regarded as the one and only suitable model for Latin prose, and though the discussion had been going on intermittently since the days of Poggio and Valla, Erasmus succeeded in giving new life to the argument by publishing at Basle in 1528 a dialogue entitled *Ciceronianus*, in which he held up to ridicule many of the absurdities committed by unduly enthusiastic admirers of Cicero. The debate did not end with Erasmus, whose moderate view failed to win general acceptance. In the middle of the century the extreme pro-Ciceronians seem to have been in the majority, but later there was a change of taste, which affected reading habits and prose style. Literary men became more interested in the works of Seneca and Tacitus than Cicero and allowed this interest to affect their manner of writing both in Latin and the vernaculars; one of the most important representatives of the new movement was the classical scholar Justus Lipsius.

The prospects for classical and biblical scholarship were not improved by the Counter-Reformation. The abolition of intellectual freedom implicit in the decisions of the Council of Trent (1545–63) could lead to nothing but stagnation. The authority of the Vulgate as the text of the Bible was reaffirmed. Erasmus' books were put on the index of prohibited literature, and although the Church did not make a systematic attempt to have them destroyed, the intellectual atmosphere of Catholic countries was not conducive to scholarship. The dispute between Catholics and Protestants was still being carried on bitterly at the beginning of the next century, and one indication of its power to deflect able minds from what might have been more profitable concerns is that Casaubon devoted two years or more to a refutation of the ecclesiastical history compiled by Cardinal Baronius.

However, the dark side of the picture must not be exaggerated. Although most Latin texts had by now appeared in printed editions, there were still some Greek authors of importance that had not been made generally available in the original language by the time of Erasmus' death, and these gradually appeared in the course of the century. In 1544 Josephus and Archimedes came out in Basle, while in Paris the king's printer Robert Estienne (1503–59) was very active during the same decade. His house produced the first editions of the church history of Eusebius and the Roman histories by Dionysius of Halicarnassus and Dio Cassius. He had already made a name by publishing his Latin dictionary in 1531, and he increased his reputation, and equally his unpopularity with the theological faculty at the Sorbonne, by a series of editions of the Bible. Between 1532 and 1540 he is known to have made some search for good manuscripts of the Vulgate, and in the preface to the 1551 edition, which is otherwise famous for the division of the text into verses universally adopted since that date, he makes an interesting comment on the value of the Vulgate. He asserts, not without justice, that it can be taken to represent the Greek text at a very early stage of its history. Despite an apparatus criticus reporting the variants of fifteen manuscripts his edition is critically disappointing in other respects.

The value of a relatively early translation had been correctly assessed in 1549 by the best Italian scholar of the day, Pier Vettori (1499–1585). In his edition of Aristotle's *Rhetoric* he used the medieval Latin version by William of Moerbeke, citing about 300 of its readings. In his preface he shows that its literal and inelegant form can be exploited to reveal precisely the Greek text of the exemplar used by the translator, and its use is chiefly that by being older than the Greek copies it has not suffered as much of the corruption that results inevitably from copying by hand. Vettori notes the frequent agreement of Moerbeke's version with the oldest and best Greek manuscript (Paris gr. 1741), whose readings he was able to use. Though he shows no knowledge of stemmatic theory as such and apparently did not realize that the Paris codex is even older than Moerbeke's version (though not therefore older than his exemplar), his procedure in dealing with this indirect or secondary tradition is of a scholarly competence that deserves mention in even the briefest survey.

Vettori was in touch with the Estienne family, and after Robert had been obliged to leave Paris and set up his printing house in Geneva, Vettori published with his son Henri (d. 1598) an edition of Aeschylus which was the first to include the full text of the *Agamemnon* (previously lines 323–1050 had been omitted). The younger Estienne was a figure at least as important as his father, but as far as classical scholarship is concerned his main achievement was the completion in 1572 of a work begun by his father, the *Thesaurus linguae graecae*. He was not responsible for the first Greek editions of the few remaining authors not yet printed, the most notable of these being Plotinus (1580), Photius' *Bibliotheca* (1601), and the mathematician Diophantus (1621).

Vettori's most able and active contemporary in Italy was Francesco Robortello of Udine (1516–67). He is generally best known for the *editio princeps* of Longinus *On the sublime* (1552) and an important edition of Aristotles' *Poetics* (1548), but he deserves notice here for another reason. In 1557 he wrote a short dissertation *De arte critica sive ratione corrigendi antiquorum libros disputatio,* which is apparently the first attempt to write a brief manual of textual criticism. Robortello claims to be the first to have devised a theory of emendation. After a short and rather slight section on the value of old manuscripts, in which he shows an awareness of the value of Latin texts written in 'Longobardic' script, by which he probably means pre-Caroline minuscule rather than Beneventan, he turns to the principles governing the art of conjecture. The critic is to test his ideas in the light of palaeography, style, and a general understanding of the subject-matter. Then follows a series of eight headings under which emendations can be classified, mostly illustrated with a few examples. The classification is not as clear as might be wished, but it deals with such essential notions as the intrusive gloss that has displaced the original reading and the possibility of error arising from incorrect division of words. The illustrations are mostly taken from Latin authors, but there are a few from Plutarch and Aristotle's *Rhetoric*, where he may have learnt from Vettori. There is no trace of stemmatic theory anywhere in the argument, and the palaeographical knowledge shown is rather disappointing in view of the many good manuscript collections accessible to him. Nevertheless it is very much to his credit that he attempted a systematic account of the way that the critic should go about his task of restoring classical texts to their original state.

The study of the broader aspects of classical antiquity in Italy during this period is well represented by Fulvio Orsini (1529–1600). Cold-shouldered as an illegitimate adjunct to the great family whose name he bore, Orsini owed the bent of his interests and his preferment in the first place to Gentile Delfini, a learned canon of the church of Saint John Lateran, where Orsini began as a chorister, and later to the patronage of the Farnese family, three of whose cardinals he served as librarian. A scholar and collector in the central Renaissance tradition, he had a number of important and original publications to his credit, such as his *Virgilius illustratus* (1567), which filled in the Greek literary background to Vergil, works on iconography (*Imagines et Elogia*, 1570) and numismatics (*Familiae Romanae*, 1577), and the *editio princeps* of the greater part of the fragmentary books of Polybius (1582). It was the breadth of his enthusiasms, ranging over the whole antiquarian world of art, sculpture, inscriptions, coins, and gems, which marked out his contribution to classical studies. He was well placed to make fruitful contacts with scholars of other countries, so that he knew Lipsius, helped Gruter, entertained Daniel and de Thou. His great archaeological collection ended up at Naples, but his books and manuscripts became one of the most important of the early acquisitions of the Vatican. These included a valuable collection of autograph manuscripts of the great humanists, from Petrarch to his own day, but also a number of books of great antiquity, the Augusteus of Virgil (Vat. lat. 3256), a present, not entirely unsolicited, from Claude Dupuy, and others obtained after protracted haggling from the legacy of Pietro Bembo, an important Pindar (Vat. gr. 1312), the Vaticanus of Virgil (Vat. lat. 3225), and the great Terence in rustic capitals which we still call the Bembinus (Vat. lat. 3226). But his activity at the centre of the antiquarian movement of his time was of no less significance than his achievements in the literary field.

Work on patristic authors also made some limited progress in the latter part of the sixteenth century. In 1550 appeared the first edition of Clement of Alexandria, edited by Vettori and printed in Florence but with a dedication to cardinal Cervini, the future Pope Marcellus II. The cardinal was interested in setting up a press at Rome, in order to produce theological texts in editions that would rival and if possible replace those of Erasmus, whose commentaries on the Scriptures and the Fathers were regarded as dangerous if not downright heretical. The creation of the Index in 1558 gave an impetus for several decades to the production of editions in full conformity with orthodoxy, but the results were variable both in quality and in quantity. The fight against heresy could not be entirely beneficial to scholarship, which received a setback in 1587 when Pope Sixtus V, at the foundation of the Typographia Vaticana, decreed that problems of textual criticism too difficult for the editorial staff to solve by their own efforts must be referred to himself. On the other hand it is known that the staff were capable of careful and intelligent work when left to their own devices, as can be deduced from surviving papers relating to a new edition of Saint Augustine.

The most notable literary event of Sixtus V's pontificate was the

F

publication of the Latin Vulgate in 1590, accompanied by the threat of excommunication to anyone who should subsequently dare to change its readings or print the variants from the manuscripts. Notwithstanding the threat his successor Clement VIII in 1592 recalled the unsold copies and issued another edition differing in many passages, which became and remained the official text of the Roman Catholic Church until it began to be replaced by the Benedictine edition published in Rome from 1926 onwards.

The best achievements in patristic studies at this period fall a little later and come from an utterly different milieu. In Oxford, Thomas James (1573–1629), the first librarian of the Bodleian, who took a delight in showing the inadequacy of editions prepared by Catholic scholars on the continent, organized in 1610–12 a team of helpers to collate manuscripts of Gregory, Cyprian, and Ambrose. They found an extremely large number of erroneous or dubious readings in the printed texts and James compared his task to that of cleansing the Augean stables. He and his team are known to have worked on more than fifty manuscripts and he planned without success a series of patristic texts based on the best manuscripts. In this he foreshadowed the work of the Benedictines of Saint Maur, who were able to use some of his material. Still more significant is the edition of Saint John Chrysostom by Sir Henry Savile (1549–1622), Warden of Merton College Oxford and Provost of Eton, published at Eton in 1612 in eight folio volumes. To a considerable extent this edition of one of the most popular and influential of all the Fathers, both Greek and Latin, has not been superseded. Savile's papers for the edition amount to nearly 16,000 pages, and were by no means the only product of a busy life of scholarship in many fields. An indication of his industry is perhaps given by his wife's remark to him: 'Sir Henry, I would I were a book too, and then you would a little more respect me.'

II. THE BEGINNINGS OF HUMANISM AND SCHOLARSHIP IN FRANCE

The speed and vitality with which humanism had taken root and flourished in Italy was unparalleled elsewhere. In France classicism remained more traditionalist and made no such dramatic leap despite its being open to Italian influence, particularly through

Avignon, from the early fourteenth century onwards. But the strength and vitality of French medieval culture meant that French humanism could absorb what it needed from Italy without being too dependent on it and could strike out along its own path within the broad lines of its own tradition. The sensitivity of French scholars on this issue and the frequent signs of a reaction against Italian scholarship reflect both their debt to Italian humanism and the pride they took in the originality of their own achievement.

Pierre Bersuire (d. 1362) had been one of the first to benefit from the cultural interaction fostered at Avignon and from personal contact with Petrarch himself, who gave him his friendship and help with his classical studies. His translation of Livy into French was an important step in reinforcing the historian's new-found popularity and his *Ovidius moralisatus* shows some Petrarchan influence, but his medieval ways of thinking were too strong for even a Petrarch to change and he fell far short of being a humanist. But a powerful group who thoroughly deserved the name had emerged in France towards the end of the century, among them Jean de Montreuil (1334–1418) and his intimate friend Nicholas of Clémanges (c. 1360–1437). Though they owed their wide familiarity with classical authors, particularly Cicero, to contact with Italian humanists and imported texts, their humanism was firmly rooted in the north and they were well able to discover new texts on their own account. Cluny in particular had proved a rich source. Not even a Poggio can turn up a new text every time without being told where to look, and the presence of Jean de Montreuil at the Council of Constance may have had important side-effects. It can hardly have been a coincidence that Poggio found the *Pro Caecina* at Langres, where Nicholas of Clémanges, the great connoisseur of Cicero's speeches, had been canon and treasurer to the cathedral chapter. And although Poggio claims credit for the discovery of the vetus Cluniacensis of the speeches and indeed had it sent to Italy, it must be remembered that the best and most conscientious copy of the lost manuscript is the one made before it went to Italy, by Nicholas of Clémanges. Much of the achievement of this group remains to be told.

The apparently intermittent progress of French humanism was

strengthened by two events which took place in the second half of the fifteenth century, the appearance of the first teachers of Greek and the setting up of the first printing press in France. Earlier attempts to organize Greek studies at Paris had proved abortive and Gregorio Tifernate, who arrived in 1456, stayed only a few years. George Hermonymus of Sparta, who came to France in 1476, is best known for his failure to give much help as a teacher to either Budé or Erasmus. But with the arrival of Janus Lascaris in 1495 and Girolamo Aleandro in 1508, Greek studies began to flourish and became an important element in French humanism. The first printers were German, the first book was a collection of the model letters of the Italian humanist Gasparino Barzizza, but the promoter of the first press to operate in France was Guillaume Fichet, master in theology and librarian of the Sorbonne, who in 1470 obtained authorization to set up a printing press in the College itself. It made a decisively humanistic début; it used the Roman letter exclusively and its first publications were either straight Latin texts, Sallust, Cicero, Juvenal, Terence, and the like, or works bearing on the cultivation of Latin style, such as Valla's *Elegantiae* and Fichet's own *Rhetorica*. The first Greek book to be printed in France appeared in 1507.

The first great classical scholar of France is Guillaume Budé (1468–1540). Born into a wealthy family and not disinclined in his earlier years to the traditional pursuits of the upper class, Budé did not get down to serious study until he was well into his twenties and appears to have been largely self-taught. Years of hard work finally bore fruit. In 1505 he produced his translation of three of Plutarch's treatises into Latin and in 1508 a work of prime importance which established him as one of the founders of legal science. This was his commentary on part of the *Digest*, his *Annotationes in XXIV libros Pandectarum*, an attempt to cut through the medieval accretion of commentary and gloss and reconstitute the text and spirit of Roman law. Neither diplomatic and administrative duties nor a large family nor his fearful headaches stood in the way of Budé's dogged scholarship. In 1515 came his *De asse*, a study of ancient coinage and measures as much a pain to read as a milestone in the establishment of classical studies as a serious discipline. Thanks to a thorough knowledge of the ancient sources, and a practical bent which allowed him to use a balance and consult the local baker, he outstripped previous essays in the field and produced one of the scholarly masterpieces of the century. His *Commentarii linguae graecae* was more lexicographical in character and much of it was afterwards incorporated in the *Thesaurus* of Henri Estienne. His later works, such as his *De philologia* and *De transitu Hellenismi ad Christianismum*, were attempts to define the place of classical, and particularly Greek, studies in contemporary Christian society and justify the position, still somewhat uncomfortable, of the Christian humanist. A monument to one of his many services to scholarship still stands, the Collège de France; it was largely due to the firm pressure applied by Budé that Francis I was finally persuaded in 1530 to institute its precursor, the Collège des Lecteurs Royaux, which gave the study of the ancient languages a certain independence and emancipated them from the prejudices and traditionalist curricula of the university. By giving concrete expression to his view that there is more to humanism than elegance of form Budé initiated a strong trend in the French scholarship of the period, which accorded high respect to solid learning and a thorough understanding of all aspects of ancient life. Though interested primarily in illuminating the content of ancient texts, Budé knew that this depended on a close criticism of the sources themselves and his numismatic researches, for instance, have left an abiding mark on the text of the relevant parts of the Elder Pliny.

While Budé had been reluctantly drawn into the Ciceronian controversy, the Elder Scaliger (Julius Caesar, 1484–1558) had chosen, rather late in life, to make a quick reputation by writing two poisonous orations against the *Ciceronianus* of Erasmus. Though of Italian origin (whether high or low became a matter of lively international dispute), he had left Italy in 1525 to become physician to the bishop of Agen, settled there, and acquired a French wife and fifteen children, one of whom became even more famous than he. His work extends from commentaries on botanical and zoological works of Aristotle and Theophrastus, inspired by his professional interest in medicine, to philology and literary criticism. His *De causis linguae latinae* (1540) is remarkable for its time in aiming at a scientific analysis of the principles of the Latin language, but

the work which earned him the fame for which he thirsted was his
Poetice, published posthumously in 1561. In this he tries in a
lucid and coherent manner to produce a theory of poetry relevant
to Latin literature viewed as a continuum extending from the
classical poets down to his contemporaries Erasmus and Dolet;
nor is it less interesting as an essay in practical criticism.

Budé and Scaliger had not been primarily interested in textual
criticism. But they were followed by a series of scholars who
conspicuously advanced both the standard and the technique of
editing classical texts. The first of these was Adrianus Turnebus
(1512–65), who held chairs at Toulouse and Paris and was Royal
Reader in Greek from 1547 until his death. As director of the
Royal Press (1552–6), he published a series of Greek texts,
including Aeschylus, Philo, and Sophocles. He also worked on
Latin authors and produced an important edition of Cicero's *De
legibus*. His most substantial work is his *Adversaria*, in thirty
books, a miscellany of passages from ancient authors emended and
explained, criticized by Joseph Scaliger as an *abortivus foetus*, not
so much for its content, in which he found much to admire, but
because it continued the Italian fashion of *Adversaria* promoted by
Politian and Vettori. Turnebus is admired for his acumen, judgement, and conjectural gifts. Happy is the man who can leave such
an abiding impression on the text of Aeschylus. His edition of
Sophocles (1553) is also the *editio princeps* of the scholia of Triclinius. His text shows too much Triclinian influence; still, he posed
the problem of the Triclinian recension, gave the text of Sophocles
a new look, and added to the corpus of scholia available in his day.
Though his editorial method was the standard *emendatio ope
codicum* of his time, he saw the need to use older and better
manuscripts than had generally been used for the early printed
editions and knew a *codex vestustus* when he saw one. To him we
owe our knowledge of an important manuscript of Plautus, the
Fragmenta Senonensia, better known as the codex Turnebi. This
was a fragmentary manuscript from the monastery of Sainte
Colombe at Sens, which Turnebus had in his possession for a
time and which may have perished when the monastery was burnt
by the Calvinists in 1567. Apart from the readings quoted in his
Adversaria, a transcript of part of Turnebus's collation made by

the jurist François Duaren in the margins of a contemporary edition of Plautus came to light in 1897. Turnebus's manuscript or his collation of it was known to Lambinus and Scaliger and the book in which his collation is preserved is itself a commentary on the period, having passed from Duaren to the poets Tabourot and Belleau, to Scaliger and Daniel Heinsius.

Turnebus's counterpart in Latin scholarship was Denys Lambin, or Lambinus (1520–72). Before being appointed Royal Reader in 1561, Lambinus had been able to spend considerable periods in Italy, had met such scholars as Faernus and Muretus, and taken the opportunity to collate manuscripts in Italian libraries. This bore fruit when he came to publish his great series of Latin texts, of which the most celebrated are Horace (1561), Lucretius (1563), and the whole of Cicero (1565–6); not the least remarkable feature of these editions is the shortness of the interval between them. Lambinus had an unrivalled knowledge of the literature of the Golden Age, an acute intellect, and a fine feeling for language exemplified in the exquisite elegance of his own Latin style. He had a particular predilection for Lucretius and his masterly edition held the field until Lachmann. One of the five manuscripts he used was the ninth-century codex Quadratus (Leiden, Voss. lat. Q. 94 = Q), one of the two manuscripts on which the text is still based; it was then at the monastery of Saint Bertin, near Saint Omer, and he had access to a collation made for Turnebus. For Cicero's letters he used a manuscript of outstanding merit which belonged to the Lyons printer Jean de Tournes and was last heard of in 1580; for its readings we are dependent on three French scholars of this period, Lambinus, Turnebus, and Bosius.

The manuscript collectors of this age, often scholars and editors themselves, made a signal contribution to classical studies. Conspicuous among them is Pierre Daniel (c. 1530–1603), a jurist of Orléans, whose great coup was to succeed in buying manuscripts from Fleury after its sack by the Huguenots in 1562. His collection, now mainly at the Vatican or Berne, contained such important relics of the scholarly heritage of that region as Lupus's copy of Valerius Maximus (Berne 366). He also published *editiones principes* of the *Querolus* (1564) and the longer version of Servius (1600), still sometimes referred to as Servius Danielis. Another was

Pierre Pithou (1539–96), who published the first editions of the *Pervigilium Veneris* (1577) and the *Fables* of Phaedrus (1596), both based on ninth-century manuscripts which remain prime witnesses to the text. His use of good manuscripts enabled him to publish important editions of Petronius, and he was the first to use the Lorsch manuscript for the text of Juvenal and Persius (1585), the famous codex Pithoeanus, now to be found, with many other manuscripts of his, at Montpellier. Equally important was Jacques Bongars (c. 1554–1612), whose enormous library, partly derived from the collections of Daniel and Cujas and now at Berne, included such choice items as the famous Irish manuscript of Horace (Berne 363) and our best manuscript of Petronius (Berne 357). Indeed, the complicated history of the text of Petronius in the latter half of the sixteenth century epitomizes the activity of a group of French scholars of this period, Pierre Daniel, the Pithou brothers, Bongars, Scaliger, and the great professor of jurisprudence who had taught them all and may have inspired this particular interest, Jacques Cujas. Its complexity is also an indication of the difficulty of piecing together the elaborate web formed by the interrelationship of men and manuscripts in this period, even in the case of central texts, and of how much remains to be discovered about the ramifications of this type of scholarship.

At the end of the century the classical scholarship of Europe was dominated by two great Huguenots, Joseph Justus Scaliger (1540–1609) and Isaac Casaubon (1559–1614). Scaliger was as fortunate as Casaubon was ill-starred. Launched into Latin by his father, Scaliger enjoyed for thirty years the patronage of a French nobleman and when offered the chair at Leiden vacated by Lipsius his eminence as a scholar was such that he was allowed to accept the chair but decline the customary duties attached to it. His scholarship owes its strength to a massive learning in a number of fields and the capacity to treat an author or a subject as an organic whole. It is best seen in his great edition of Manilius (first edition, 1579), a worthy precursor to those of Bentley and Housman, and his *Thesaurus Temporum* (1606), a reconstruction of the chronological systems of the ancient world and a fundamental contribution to the study of history. His special interest in archaic Latin finds expression in his pioneering edition of Festus. His attempts at textual emendation were sometimes violent and spring paradoxically from a more scientific approach to the editing of texts. When editing Catullus, he sought to prove from the nature of corruptions in the manuscripts (the confusion of *a* and *u*) that they all descended from a common parent in pre-Caroline minuscule. Though he happened to be wrong, he did arrive at the notion of a medieval archetype. This concept, reinforced by his critical attitude to even good manuscripts, encouraged his taking considerable liberties with the transmitted text.

Scaliger was far from untouched by the religious troubles of his day, but the way they bedevilled the scholarship of the sixteenth century is more starkly illustrated in the case of his friend and younger contemporary Casaubon. Born in Geneva of refugee Protestant parents, obliged to learn his Greek hiding in a cave in the French mountains, unable to avoid being drawn into the wrangle because of his distinction as a scholar and forced to spend much of his time and talents on arid polemic, this great French scholar finally found rest as a naturalized Englishman in Westminster Abbey. With him the French scholarship of the period ended, as it had begun, on a chalcenteric note. He was a man of vast industry and erudition, but had the rarer gift of being able to use his learning as a commentator to illumine rather than impress. He appears to have chosen to work on those texts which offered the most scope to his wide knowledge, such as Diogenes Laertius, Strabo, and Athenaeus. His choice of difficult and often diffuse texts, with which most students of the classics have but a passing acquaintance, means that his services are not always recognized. For Casaubon is still with us. His *Animadversiones* on Athenaeus formed the core of Schweighäuser's commentary of 1801, Strabo is still usually cited by reference to Casaubon's pages, his notes on Persius loom large in Conington's commentary. Son-in-law to Henri Estienne and for a time sub-librarian to de Thou at the royal library, Casaubon was most at home in the world of books and manuscripts, able to find material for his own needs and to supply scholars all over Europe. His use of manuscript material has not been properly appraised, but he seems to have made no dramatic advances, except that his second edition of Theophrastus' *Characters* (1599) added five more characters (24–8) to those then known.

III. THE NETHERLANDS IN THE SIXTEENTH AND
SEVENTEENTH CENTURIES

Although Erasmus could speak with disgust of the ignorance which obtained in the Netherlands in his youth, it is likely that there was a more widespread general level of literacy than elsewhere. A large measure of the credit for this must go to the Brothers of the Common Life, the members of a community founded at Deventer in the later fourteenth century who devoted a large part of their energy to educational projects and the copying of books. Among the many schools which owed their existence or excellence to them were those attended by Erasmus at Deventer and Hertogenbosch. The general level of literacy and the growth of prosperous mercantile towns helped to create conditions in which learning could flourish despite a late start.

It was the universities and the printing houses, often working closely together, which were largely responsible for the powerful classical tradition of the Netherlands. The university of Louvain was founded in 1425 and the establishment of the Collegium Trilingue for the study of Latin, Greek, and Hebrew in the same town about 1517 further strengthened its claim to be for a time one of the greatest intellectual centres of northern Europe. A similarly dominating position in the northern Netherlands was achieved by the university of Leiden, founded in 1575 to commemorate the heroic resistance of its inhabitants to siege by the forces of Spain. Just as the Protestant north and the Catholic south had their respective centres of higher learning, so they had equally famous traditions of printing. Although the early history of Dutch printing is obscure, it is interesting to observe that such a standard schoolbook as Donatus' *Ars minor* was printed in Holland about 1470, while in the south at Louvain John of Westphalia issued a number of standard classical authors as early as 1475. His successor in the business, Thierry Martens, was himself a scholar and a friend of Erasmus. From 1512 onwards he began to produce classical books to meet the needs of the university and printed the first Greek texts to be published in this part of Europe. In the great age of printing in the Netherlands, in the later sixteenth and seventeenth centuries, it was Plantin who held sway in the south and Elzevir in the north. Christopher Plantin settled in Antwerp in 1550; on his death in 1589 the business passed to his son-in-law Jan Moerentorf (Moretus) and continued on the same premises and in the same family for three centuries, when it was transformed into the Musée Plantin-Moretus. Though his most famous production was the eight-volume Polyglot Bible (1568–73), his vast and varied output contained an enormous number of classical editions, some of them magnificently produced. He was closely associated with such scholars as Canter and Lipsius, and published a number of *editiones principes* of Greek authors, including Nonnus (1569) and Stobaeus (1575). Louis Elzevir had established himself at Leiden, initially as a bookseller, in 1580. His first book, a text of Eutropius (1592), heralded a strong preoccupation with classical books which fortunately coincided with the great period of Dutch scholarship and so ensured a series of good scholarly texts. Particularly influential was the charming little duodecimo series of classical authors, inaugurated by his sons in 1629. At a guilder a volume they appealed to the student and carried both the name of Elzevir and a sound tradition of classical scholarship all over Europe, much as the great series of Greek and Latin texts begun in 1824 was to make the name of B. G. Teubner a household word and provide a sound basis for modern scholarship.

Although the greatest classical scholar to emerge in the Netherlands in the sixteenth century is undoubtedly Justus Lipsius, there were others whose special interests claim our attention. One of these is Wilhelm Canter (1542–75), whose speciality was Greek textual criticism. He is mainly known for his editions of the three tragedians, but he also edited the *editio princeps* of the *Eclogae* of Stobaeus for the Plantin Press. He makes a special claim for his treatment of the lyrics, and his edition of Euripides, printed by Plantin in 1571, is the first to pay particular attention to responsion and its role in emendation. He also wrote a short manual on textual criticism, *Syntagma de ratione emendandi scriptores Graecos*, appended to his Latin translation of the speeches of Aelius Aristides (1566). This is a systematic classification of the different types of error in Greek texts, brought under such headings as the confusion of certain letters, wrong word-division, omissions, additions and

transpositions, errors arising from assimilation or the misunderstanding of abbreviations, and illustrated with examples taken
almost exclusively from Aristides. He provides a brief but business-
like guide to the errors of scribes and, though little that he says
would come as news to the great critics of his day, it is a gain to
have certain valid principles of emendation explicitly set out, even
if the details need refinement. Franz Modius (1556–97) is less
noteworthy for his scholarship, though he edited a number of
Latin texts, than for his insistence that conjecture alone is useless
and even dangerous, that there must be a proper balance between
manuscript authority and emendation, that recension is an essential
preliminary to editing. In this conviction, and also obliged by the
political unrest of the Netherlands to be on the move, he systematically explored the manuscript collections of a wide area, extending
from northern France through the Low Countries to Fulda and
Bamberg. His activity is remarkable for its scale and his reports of
manuscript readings, found in his *Novantiquae lectiones* (1584),
acquire great value when the manuscripts themselves have been
destroyed, as in the case of the Cologne manuscript of Silius
Italicus. The only other first-hand report of the Cologne Silius is
provided by his friend and later enemy, Ludovicus Carrio (1547–
95), who was similarly active on a smaller scale. Jacob Cruquius
worked almost exclusively on Horace and owes his fame to his
invention of the ghostly 'commentator Cruquianus', now exorcized,
and to his timely examination of four Horace manuscripts at the
monastery of Saint Pierre au Mont-Blandin, near Ghent, just
before its destruction in 1566. One of these was the very important,
if controversial, Blandinius vetustissimus, which assures the Bruges
professor a fractional share of that immortality which Horace so
confidently forecast for himself.

It was a singular piece of good fortune for the new university of
Leiden that it should have attracted so soon after its inauguration
one of the most brilliant Latinists of the century. Justus Lipsius
(1547–1606) was a Catholic by upbringing and associated in his
early years with the university of Louvain, but his conversion to
the Protestant faith had opened the way for his being invited to the
chair of history at Leiden, which he held from 1579 to 1591, just
as his reconversion led to his return to Louvain in 1592, where he

was Professor of History at the university and of Latin at the Collegium Trilingue. His achievement was based on a thorough knowledge of the history and antiquities of Rome, reflected in his monographs and discussions on various topics from ancient warfare to dinner parties, and a close reading of the texts, which combined to produce a commentator and critic of the first order. Though he worked with good effect on Plautus and Propertius and Seneca's *Tragedies*, his main contribution was to the prose writers of the imperial period and he is best remembered for his editions of Tacitus (1574, frequently revised) and Seneca (1605). His interest in this period led him to modify his own prose style, initially Ciceronian in character, and to develop a pointed style which had considerable influence on both Latin and vernacular prose writing. His Tacitus is his greatest achievement and a random glance at the apparatus criticus of any modern edition, where his name appears with devastating regularity, will show how he was able to transform the text, despite a basically cautious approach to emendation. As a young man he had spent two years in Italy doing the fashionable things, studying the antiquities, exploring the libraries, and meeting Muretus, but he was luckier with his monuments than his manuscripts. He failed to examine the two Medicean manuscripts of Tacitus and had to rely on copies until his last edition, which appeared posthumously in 1607, where he was able to make use of the collations published in 1600 by an important and rather neglected scholar, Curzio Pichena, gratified to discover how often his conjectures were confirmed. His Seneca is a magnificent folio volume, published, as were so many of his works, by Plantin. He relied on poor manuscript material and his Seneca generally lacked the brilliance of his Tacitus, but it remains a fitting culmination to the labours of a man who had made such a thorough study of Stoicism in preparation for the work that he had been able to revive it as a living force in the troubled days of the Netherlands. His *Manuductio ad Stoicam philosophiam* and *Physiologia Stoicorum* (1604) give the first full account of Stoicism, while his own *De constantia* (1584), which owes much to Seneca in both thought and style, went through thirty-two editions and was translated into several languages.

In the seventeenth century the Netherlands were unaffected by the general decline in the level of classical scholarship which can be discerned in other countries. It maintained its flourishing tradition well into the eighteenth century, when the influence of Bentley, working through Hemsterhuys, contributed to a brilliant revival of Greek studies which more than compensated for the dogged industry of the Elder Burman and the incompetence of Havercamp. Leiden attracted powerful scholars from abroad and Dutch scholarship was enhanced by their influence. Joseph Scaliger had succeeded in 1593 to the chair at Leiden vacated by Lipsius, and occupied it until his death. The same chair, vacant from 1609 to 1631, was then again filled from abroad, to the chagrin of Vossius, by the appointment of the erudite but somewhat dilettante Salmasius (Claude de Saumaise, 1588–1653). He is known for his polemic with Milton, owned the famous codex Salmasianus of the Latin Anthology (Paris lat. 10318), and played a part, much smaller than has at times been supposed, in making known the contents of the famous manuscript of the Greek Anthology at Heidelberg (Heidelberg gr. 23 + Paris suppl. gr. 384); but he had done his best work before moving to Leiden.

G. J. Vossius (1577–1649) helped to give Dutch scholarship a broader basis by treating a wide range of subjects in a systematic and encyclopedic way. He was Professor of Rhetoric at Leiden for ten years until 1632, when he accepted the Chair of History at the newly founded Athenaeum at Amsterdam. He also became a non-resident prebendary of Canterbury. He wrote a comprehensive treatise on rhetoric and later a more influential *Poetic institutions* (1647), two notable contributions to Latin grammar and usage, his *Aristarchus* and *De vitiis sermonis et glossematis latinobarbaris*, while his *De historicis graecis* and *De historicis latinis* (1624, 1627), dictionaries of historians from antiquity to the sixteenth century, took him into the neglected field of literary history. His *De theologia gentili*, still almost medieval in its misconceptions, can claim to be one of the earliest books on classical mythology. His interest in the theory of poetry was shared by his contemporary Daniel Heinsius (1580–1655), the devoted protégé of Scaliger, who in 1611 published an edition of Aristotle's *Poetics* and a short treatise *De tragoediae constitutione*. The latter is a succinct and authoritative restatement of the Aristotelian view of tragedy, filled out with references to Horace's *Ars poetica* and illustrations from Greek tragedy and Seneca, and it had considerable influence on neoclassical drama and the French theatre in particular. He was an elegant versifier and a stimulating teacher, but he had a very mixed success as a textual critic and his greatest gift to this branch of classics was his son.

The editing of Latin authors continued to be the central activity of Dutch scholarship and it was carried on with distinction in the latter half of the seventeenth century by two great friends, J. F. Gronovius (1611–71) and Nicolaus Heinsius (1620–81), who dominated respectively the fields of prose and poetry. Gronovius had travelled in England, France, and Italy before settling at Leiden and had taken the opportunity to examine Latin manuscripts. It was in Florence in 1640 that he came across the codex Etruscus of Seneca's *Tragedies*, neglected since the Renaissance: he immediately recognized its worth and in his edition of 1661 firmly established its authority. He did other useful work on Latin poetry, but is best known for his numerous editions of the prose writers of the imperial period, including Livy, the Elder Pliny, both Senecas, Tacitus, and Gellius, an enormous output distinguished, as was his miscellaneous *Observationes*, by wide knowledge, good judgement, and balanced scholarship. Heinsius was more gifted. He held no academic post and could give to study only such time as remained from an active career in diplomacy and public life. His diplomatic missions had given him the chance to investigate many of the manuscript collections of Europe and his great store of accurate collations stood him in good stead. But his strength lay in his fine feeling for the elegance of Latin poetry, partly derived from his own skill in writing verse, a precise understanding of the niceties of diction and convention which made him a sensitive and almost uncanny critic. His main editions were of Ovid, Vergil, Valerius Flaccus, and the later poets Claudian and Prudentius, but he left notes on others which were published after his death and he did some work on Silver Latin prose. He lives on, and not merely as a model critic: work on the identification of the many manuscripts which he collated, particularly of Ovid, is still in progress, and those editors who follow in his footsteps admit with awe that what Heinsius thought still matters.

Isaac Vossius (1618–89) is best remembered as a bibliophile, or indeed as the free-thinking Anglican convert who dared to read Ovid during divine service in Saint George's Chapel. He had come to England in 1670, was given a doctorate at Oxford and a prebend at Windsor, and became a well-known if somewhat odd figure in the London society of Charles II. His versatile forays into the by-ways of erudition have left no permanent mark, but he had a decisive hand in shaping some of our greatest manuscript collections. Like Salmasius and Heinsius and Descartes, he had been invited to Stockholm by that extraordinary monarch, queen Christina of Sweden, and enjoyed her patronage from 1649 to 1652. Apart from tutoring her in Greek, he aided her in her ambition to build up a library comparable with that of the other courts of Europe. Among the manuscripts which he acquired for her were those of his father, Gerard Vossius, and the French jurist Paul Petau, who had himself bought part of Pierre Daniel's collection. The majority of the queen's manuscripts are now in the Vatican and constitute the Reginenses. But Vossius was not slow to exploit his expertise on his own behalf and he left behind a magnificent library. The Vossiani were offered to the Bodleian Library and Bentley was energetic in trying to promote their purchase, but they went instead to Leiden, and with them the two great manuscripts of Lucretius which, had they not been removed at a critical moment from Bentley's reach, might have changed the course of textual studies.

IV. RICHARD BENTLEY (1662–1742): CLASSICAL AND THEOLOGICAL STUDIES

The next figure of commanding importance in the history of textual criticism is Richard Bentley, who was Master of Trinity College Cambridge from 1699 onwards. Much of his time in that position was taken up by the academic intrigues that were endemic in Oxford and Cambridge colleges in the seventeenth and eighteenth centuries, but his amazing self-control enabled him to avoid being entirely distracted from scholarship, and the list of his works would be more than creditable to many men who enjoyed an undisturbed career. He began to make a name for himself in 1691 by the publication of the *Epistula ad Joannem Millium*. This was a series of observations on the text of John Malalas, an obscure and mediocre Byzantine chronicler of the sixth century, then being printed for the first time. Bentley's extraordinary learning allowed him to emend the text in many places and in passing he offered explanations and emendations of other and better-known authors. It was probably these, in conjunction with the attractive vivacity of his Latin style, which made the work well known in a short time, and his fame spread to a wider public than professional scholars, for in 1697 we find him a member of a small circle that included Newton, Wren, Locke, and John Evelyn.

A few years later Bentley distinguished himself again with his work on the epistles of Phalaris. Once again it was an obscure text of no literary merit that called forth his best efforts, but, as will be seen below, he cannot be accused of confining himself to a pedantic delight in the study of trivial authors. The letters, which purport to be by the early tyrant of Acragas, are in fact a composition of the Second Sophistic age, and there is no explicit testimony to their existence earlier than the anthology of John Stobaeus in the fifth century A.D. Bentley was by no means the first person to cast doubts on their authenticity; Politian had done so already. But there were still some scholars who believed them genuine, and when a new edition appeared the argument began again. It formed a small part of the controversy between the Ancients and the Moderns, and there were some who maintained that irrespective of their dubious authenticity the letters of Phalaris were one of the best literary products of antiquity. Bentley's *Dissertation*, although its conclusions did not win universal acceptance for a long time, was a masterly proof that the letters were a miserable and worthless forgery, marred by every kind of anachronism and composed in a dialect unknown to the supposed author, and the display of learning employed in order to demonstrate the conclusion made it clear that Bentley had no serious rival as a critic or commentator anywhere in Europe.

As a textual critic Bentley is perhaps best known for the work he did on Latin authors at a later stage in his career. His zest for emendation, which is relatively easy in authors whose texts are badly preserved and who have never received the attentions of a good critic, led him astray in dealing with such authors as Horace, and he earned notoriety by the amusing change he proposed to make in the fable of the fox caught in the granary (*Epistles* 1.7.29). Insisting that a fox will not eat grain Bentley proposed to read 'field-mouse' (*nitedula* instead of *vulpecula*), quite oblivious of the consideration that the author of the fable chose the animal as the representative of cunning greed at the expense of the facts of natural history. This insistence on logic, without consideration of poetic and other forms of literary licence, mars Bentley's contributions to the emendation of leading authors that he edited, namely Horace in 1711 and Terence in 1726, and the same is even more true of his attempt to restore the works of Milton to what he supposed to be their original state before a putative interpolator imposed on the blind poet with a series of alterations of the text. On the other hand, where hard facts were at a premium, as in the astronomical poem by Manilius, Bentley's gifts were given a great opportunity, and the opinion of experts is that he made contributions of the utmost brilliance to the interpretation of the hardest passages of this very hard poem, the edition of which appeared in 1739 although the work for it had been done long before.

Bentley made many emendations in the text of other authors, of which a high proportion have been accepted or seriously considered by subsequent editors. But two of his most valuable activities were projects that never came to fruition, editions of Homer and the New Testament. As far as Homer is concerned, his most notable discovery was that the metre of many lines could be explained by postulating the existence of the letter digamma, a notion which contributed as much as any other single discovery to the understanding of this text.

Though Bentley is commonly thought of as a classical scholar pure and simple because of his striking achievements in that field, he was also of sufficient competence in theology to be appointed Regius Professor of Divinity in 1717. Three years later he published a tiny pamphlet called *Proposals for an edition of the New Testament*, in which he announced explicitly that the text would be based on the oldest manuscripts of the Greek text and of the Vulgate. Bentley knew that in English libraries he could lay hands on more than one manuscript a thousand years old, and he arranged for some collations of equally old manuscripts in foreign libraries to be made. With the aid of this information he reckoned to be able to restore the text as it was in the best copies circulating at the time of the Council of Nicaea (A.D. 325). It is interesting to note that he did not hope to establish the authors' text exactly as it stood in the autographs, and in passing it should be said that one of his most distinguished followers, Lachmann, writing in 1830, announced his intention of restoring the text as it was c. A.D. 380. Bentley had already begun collations, and although the work never made much progress he was able to state in the *Proposals* with characteristic confidence 'I find that by taking 2,000 errors out of the Pope's Vulgate, and as many out of the Protestant Pope Stephens', I can set out an edition of each in columns, without using any book under 900 years old, that shall so exactly agree, word for word, and, what at first amazed me, order for order, that no two tallies, nor two indentures, can agree better' (the reference to order is an allusion to the many manuscript variants involving the order of words). He continued, however, with the much less characteristic promise 'I alter not a letter of my own head without the authority of these old witnesses', which is far from the principle he adopted in the textual criticism of secular authors.

Since his edition was never completed, the so-called *textus receptus*, in other words the text in the form which Erasmus and Estienne had given it, continued to be printed. Only very rarely did a bold critic show independence of mind and risk the annoyance of churchmen at large by printing other readings or his own conjectures, and it was not until 1881 that the principles of recension and textual criticism were rigorously applied to the new Testament in the edition of B. F. Westcott and F. J. A. Hort.

While Bentley would therefore appear to be a century and a half ahead of his time, it is only fair to record that his *Proposals* scarcely mark any advance on the work of the cantankerous French priest Richard Simon (1638–1712). For our purpose Simon's chief work is his *Histoire critique du texte du Nouveau Testament*, published in Rotterdam in 1689 (censorship and *odium theologicum* prevented publication in his own country) and translated into English in the same year. This seems to be the first attempt to write a monograph on the transmission of an ancient text, and despite its unattractive appearance and concern with polemic it contains important exemplifications of critical principles in the chapters on the manuscripts, and it is impossible to believe that Bentley did not know and approve of them. After observing that there is nothing in the Greek tradition like the Masoretic system for ensuring textual stability he states as his policy the investigation of the Greek manuscripts, the various versions and the scholia. There follows a survey of the history of the New Testament text from the time of Valla onwards, with comments on the printed editions, chiefly concerned with their success or otherwise in providing a satisfactory apparatus of variant readings. He knows that the great age of a manuscript does not automatically guarantee the truth of its readings, and he follows previous critics in the view that the Greek text should be tested by comparison with early patristic citations, since these are earlier than the schism of the Greek and Roman churches, as a result of which, according to some critics, the Greek text had been deliberately falsified. His use of the versions is admirably shown by his discussion of John 7: 39, where he exploits the Vulgate and Syriac versions in order to arrive at a view of the passage. It leads him to the surprisingly modern and sophisticated view that obscure or ambiguous texts were explained by scholia, and when these scholia were short they easily came to be incorporated into the text. As to the use of early Greek manuscripts, much of his time is spent on readings of the codex Bezae (Cambridge, University Library, Nn. II. 41, commonly known by the symbol D), which has a text very different from most other witnesses and presents some of the most awkward problems of criticism. But he was also aware of the importance of the Vatican codex B (Vat. gr. 1209) and the Alexandrinus (British Museum, MS. Royal I D VIII).

V. THE ORIGINS OF PALAEOGRAPHY

The first steps towards establishing the study of manuscripts on a firm basis were not taken until the end of the seventeenth century. Bessarion and Politian may be credited with some palaeographical knowledge, and the former at least found it useful in refuting his opponents at the Council of Florence. While the technique of editing and the art of textual criticism made steady progress in the

late Renaissance and the following century, little or no interest
was taken in the date and origin of the manuscripts being used for
editions of classical and Christian texts. Once again it was religious
controversy that led to progress. A quarrel broke out between the
Jesuits and the Benedictines; a Jesuit called Daniel van Papenbroeck (1628–1714, otherwise known as Papebroch) proved in
1675 that a charter supposedly issued by the Merovingian king
Dagobert in 646 and guaranteeing certain privileges to the Benedictines was a forgery. The French Benedictine order, which had
recently been revived under the title of the Congregation of Saint
Maur and was devoting itself to various scholarly enterprises,
treated van Papenbroek's work as a challenge. One of its most
able members, Dom Jean Mabillon (1632–1707), spent several
years in studying charters and manuscripts, drawing up in a systematic way for the first time a series of criteria for testing the
authenticity of medieval documents. The result was *De re diplo-
matica* (1681), to which we owe the word diplomatic, normally
used as the technical term for the study of legal and official
documents. Mabillon's work dealt also to a lesser extent with
manuscripts, but was restricted to Latin. It was immediately
recognized as a masterpiece, even by van Papenbroeck, who had a
cordial exchange of letters with Mabillon, acknowledging that his
attempt to prove the spuriousness of all Merovingian charters
was an excess of scepticism. On the other hand his thesis about the
charter of 646 was upheld.

Among the projects of the Congregation of Saint Maur were
new editions of the Greek and Latin Fathers. A large group of
monks was at work at the Parisian house of Saint-Germain-des-
Prés. A knowledge of medieval charters had only limited application, but Mabillon's remarks on manuscripts stimulated one of his
junior colleagues to look more closely at the writing of Greek
manuscripts. Dom Bernard de Montfaucon (1655–1741) had been
ordained in 1676 after illness had enforced his retirement from the
army. Since 1687 he had been working on the edition of the Greek
Fathers, and particularly on Athanasius. In the year after the death
of Mabillon he produced *Palaeographia graeca*, and in this case too
the title of his book invented a word that has been standard ever
since. In its own field it was in some ways a greater achievement

than Mabillon's book, since it remained the best book on the subject for about two centuries and it made the first attempt to understand the history of individual letter forms, which is fundamental to palaeography. The scope of the book is rather different, since very few medieval Greek charters or other documents were available to Montfaucon (they are still mostly to be found in the archives of the monasteries of Mount Athos, which Montfaucon never visited), and in any case the authenticity of these documents raised no issues for Montfaucon and his contemporaries. So he was able to devote himself to studying the manuscripts, and his examination of examples that can be dated with little or no doubt from the subscriptions of the scribes themselves was of permanent value. His other contribution to palaeography was *Bibliotheca Coisliniana* (1715), the first systematic description of a complete collection of manuscripts, in this case the fine collection of about 400 items that had been inherited by Coislin, the prince-bishop of Metz, from Séguier, Chancellor of France under Louis XIV. Although Thomas James, in his *Ecloga Oxonio-Cantabrigiensis* of 1600, had given a very useful list of the manuscripts in the libraries of the two English universities, he did not attempt to describe the manuscripts in any detail, and can scarcely be said to have anticipated Montfaucon. It may be worth adding in passing that Montfaucon was by no means a narrow specialist, concerned with nothing but manuscripts. His other works include a dictionary of classical antiquities in ten folio volumes, to which a further five were subsequently added as a supplement. It appeared in 1719 under the title of *Antiquité expliquée*; 1,800 were sold within ten months, and a second edition of 2,200 copies was called for.

Despite the enormous bulk of their writings, Mabillon and Montfaucon found time to travel, especially in Italy, to visit other manuscript collections that could offer material for their works. In Verona, where the wealth of the Chapter Library had been known to humanists of the Renaissance, the visitor of the late seventeenth century was told that the books could no longer be found. This tantalizing state of affairs roused the curiosity of a local aristocrat and antiquarian, the marquis Scipione Maffei (1675–1755). Besides making a name for himself by writing the tragedy *Merope*, which was a landmark in the revival of the Italian theatre, he found himself involved in historical controversy in 1712, when he wrote a pamphlet against the duke Francesco Farnese. Farnese had been duped into purchasing the grand-mastership of an order of Saint John supposedly set up by the emperor Constantine. The pope and the Austrian emperor swallowed the bait as well, and Farnese was assigned for the use of his order the beautiful church of Santa Maria della Steccata in Parma. Maffei demonstrated that the order must be bogus, since all such orders were of medieval date, a fact which did not save his book from being placed on the index of prohibited literature.

Maffei let it be known to the canon librarian of the cathedral in Verona that he was very anxious to discover the fate of the manu-scripts it had once possessed. One morning in 1712 the librarian found them; they had been piled on the top of a cupboard in order to avoid damage from flooding, and then had been entirely forgot-ten. The news was taken at once to Maffei's house, and he rushed over to the cathedral in his night clothes and slippers. When he set eyes on the books, a wonderful collection mostly of very early date, he thought that he must be dreaming, but the dream proved to be a reality and it was not long before he was studying the manuscripts in his own home. The result of this study was a very important theoretical improvement in the understanding of Latin book hands. Mabillon had divided them into five independent categories, Gothic, Langobardic, Saxon, Merovingian, and Roman. But he had said nothing about any possible relation between them. Maffei hit on the fact that the explanation of the diversity of Latin scripts in the early Middle Ages must be that in late antiquity there were certain basic types, majuscule, minuscule, and cursive, and when the Roman Empire broke apart variations of these scripts arose independently. It was this flash of insight which made palaeography a subject with a clear theoretical basis. The only major advance subsequently is the one associated with the name of Ludwig Traube (1861–1907), whose great contribution was to show that manuscripts, apart from being the primary sources for the texts of classical and medieval literature, can be treated as documents illustrating the history of medieval culture. A manu-script which may be proved utterly useless as a copy of an author's text may none the less be of the greatest value in another way, since if it can be assigned with certainty to its place of origin, or better still, if the scribe of it can be identified with certainty, it will tell us something about the intellectual history of the Middle Ages.

VI. DISCOVERIES OF TEXTS SINCE THE RENAISSANCE

(a) *Palimpsests*

The recovery of an unknown ancient text produces a special sense of excitement and one which the learned world was rarely in a position to experience in the centuries following the Renaissance. But a new series of discoveries, less glamorous but by no means unrewarding, began with the realization that some classical texts still lay hidden in the lower script of palimpsests. Although such palimpsests had long existed in some of the best-known European libraries, in Paris and Rome, Milan and Verona, they were not really exploited until the nineteenth century, when the great discoveries of Mai and Niebuhr conferred an aura of romance on the humble rescript and allowed it to make a spectacular entry into the story of classical scholarship.

The first palimpsest text to be brought to the notice of the public was an early and important manuscript of the Greek Bible, the fifth-century codex Ephraemi (Paris gr. 9, lower script), dicovered by Jean Boivin, the sub-librarian of the Royal Library in Paris, in 1692. The first new classical text to emerge from a palimpsest was again Greek and likewise discovered at Paris, by J. J. Wettstein in 1715–16, though he failed to attribute it correctly: the sixth-century codex Claromontanus of the Pauline Epistles (Paris gr. 107) had at some stage been patched up by the insertion of two leaves from a fifth-century manuscript of Euripides' *Phaethon*, which was then in part reused. This manuscript, supplemented in 1907 by a papyrus of the third century B.C. (P. Berol. 9771), gives us all we have of Euripides' play. Other scholars of the eighteenth century succeeded in anticipating some of the later discoveries, but their ignorance of the chemical means later used to restore faded writing or their reluctance to employ such aids meant that they failed to realize the full significance of their finds. Scipione Maffei had discovered some of the Verona rescripts, including both the palimpsested part and the one unpalimpsested leaf of Gaius' *Institutes* (Verona XV (13)), but it was not until 1816 that the text was correctly attributed. In the middle of the century Dom Tassin, one of the Maurist authors of the *Nouveau traité de diplomatique*, a revised and improved version of Mabillon's work, suggested that one of the primary scripts of a manuscript rewritten at Corbie (Paris lat. 12161) contained a fragment of the then completely unknown writer Fronto. His anticipation of Mai's discovery is hardly more remarkable than the fact that the sixth-century fragment which he had detected was not properly appreciated until 1956, almost exactly two centuries later, when it was identified by Bernard Bischoff as a fragment of one of Fronto's epistles (*Ad Verum* 2.1). In 1772 P. J. Bruns discovered the substructure of Vat. Pal. lat. 24, a rich patchwork of ancient codices, and from it he edited a fragment of Livy Book 91. In the following year G. Migliore extracted from the lower scripts of the same manuscript two fragmentary texts which he took to be Cicero but which were in fact the remains of the *De amicitia* and *De vita patris* of Seneca, later re-edited by Niebuhr and Studemund.

So considerable steps had been taken, faltering though they were at times, to salvage palimpsested texts before the dramatic second decade of the nineteenth century. Then, owing to a combination of circumstances, there was a great leap forward. The main contributory factors were the untiring and almost ruthless energy of Angelo Mai (1782–1854) and his good fortune in being appointed successively librarian of the Ambrosian and of the Vatican, the two libraries which housed the particularly rich collection of palimpsests from Bobbio. He was also the first to make successful use of reagents, which facilitated the detection of palimpsested texts, made the writing more legible, and aided identification; a great measure of his success must be attributed to this. In the space of a few years, beginning in 1814, he published a whole series of new texts, including fragments of some of Cicero's speeches and the *scholia Bobiensia* (Ambros. S.P. 11.66, *olim* R. 57 sup.), the letters of Fronto (S.P. 9/1, 6, 11, *olim* E. 147 sup.), and, from the great Ambrosian palimpsest of Plautus (S.P. 9/13–20, *olim* G. 82 sup.), what remains of the hitherto unknown *Vidularia*. In 1819 he moved from Milan to the Vatican and towards the end of that year crowned his achievements by finding the text for which men like Roger Bacon and Petrarch had passionately searched and which even the most optimistic scholars had given up as lost for ever, the *De republica* of Cicero (Plate X). He published the *editio princeps* in 1822.

Others were quick to enter the palimpsest field, many of them more careful and better scholars than Mai, who had been hasty and uncritical and not over-scrupulous; but he had creamed the collection. One of them was the great German historian Barthold Georg Niebuhr (1776–1831), who arrived in Rome as the Prussian ambassador in 1816, having made on his way to the capital the only find to rival the more spectacular discoveries of Mai. At Verona he succeeded in reading with the use of a reagent the lower script of the Gaius palimpsest, in parts *ter scriptus*, and so made possible the eventual publication in 1820 of the first edition of the complete *Institutes*. Though his greater acumen made relations with Mai somewhat strained, he did contribute to Mai's edition of the *De republica*.

No account of the decipherment and publication of palimpsests, however brief, could omit the name of Wilhelm Studemund (1843–89), who devoted years of an active scholarly life and finally his sight to the patient and meticulous transcription of palimpsest texts. The best known are his transcripts of Gaius (1874) and the Ambrosian Plautus (1889); the latter bears the touching inscription, taken from Catullus 14, *ni te plus oculis meis amarem*. The work of such later scholars was hampered by the earlier employment of reagents, which stained and sometimes corroded the parchment, often with disastrous results. The first reagent to be known was gallic acid and this was the one used by Mai, sometimes with a heavy hand; later scholars used potassium bisulphate or the recipe of a Turin chemist Giobert, which consisted of successive applications of hydrochloric acid and potassium cyanide. They were all harmful in some degree (but infinitely more slowly than might have been expected of such deadly compounds) and had the result that manuscripts so treated are rarely susceptible to the safer and more advanced techniques possible today, especially that of ultra-violet photography, which were perfected in particular by Alban Dold at the Palimpsest Institute of the Abbey of Beuron, in south-west Germany. Consequently the editions and transcripts of the nineteenth century retain their value.

Early in the present century J. L. Heiberg found in Constantinople a palimpsest copy of Archimedes which yielded two works of note (Metochion of the Holy Sepulchre, MS. 355). One, *On floating bodies*, was known already in the Latin translation by William of Moerbeke, but the other, *Method*, was entirely new and of great significance for the history of mathematics, since it showed that Archimedes devised a procedure similar to the integral calculus. Two other fairly recently discovered palimpsests may be worth notice. One is in Jerusalem (Patriarchate MS. 36), and contains part of several Euripidean plays, written probably in the middle of the eleventh century. It is the earliest surviving book with a substantial portion of Euripides' works, but despite its date it does not improve the text much. The other is in Leiden (B.P.G. 60 A), and yields parts of some Sophoclean plays. It is the twin brother of the famous Laurentian codex, written at much the same date.

(b) *Papyri*

Until the end of the last century our knowledge of ancient texts depended almost entirely on copies made during the Middle Ages, whereas manuscripts dating back to the later centuries of the ancient world formed only a tiny proportion of the total number known. From the Renaissance onwards such discoveries as were made of new texts, or more commonly, better manuscripts of texts already known, usually consisted in the unearthing of neglected medieval manuscripts. The only significant exception was the recovery of the charred remains of papyrus rolls from the excavations of Herculaneum; these contained the abstruse writings of the Epicurean philosopher Philodemus. But a remarkable change was brought about when the archaeologists working in Egypt brought to light quantities of ancient books, often generically known as papyri even though a substantial minority of them are in fact written on parchment. The biggest finds were made at Oxyrhynchus in the Fayum by B. P. Grenfell and A. S. Hunt. For the first time scholars could consult a mass of ancient books, which are on average about a thousand years older than the textual witnesses that they had had to rely on before. Discoveries and their publication have continued ever since. Even though the papyri of literary content are outnumbered by documents of various kinds in the ratio of perhaps ten to one, there are many early manuscripts of known texts and a significant number which add to the stock of extant Greek literature. Not all these texts are complete or of the highest quality as literature, but among them are such important books as Aristotle's *Athenian constitution* (P. Lit. Lond. 108), the *Odes* of Bacchylides (P. Lit. Lond. 46), and substantial fragments of Sophocles' satyr-play the *Ichneutae* (P. Oxy. 1174), Euripides' *Hypsipyle* (P. Oxy. 852), Menander's *Dyscolus* virtually complete (P. Bodmer 4), *Epitrepontes* and *Samia* (P. Cairo inv. 43227), and *Sicyonius* (P. Sorbonne 72, 2272, 2273). The authors best represented, however, are those of the schoolroom, and against the handful of really interesting papyri must be set the hundreds of Homer that have survived. Other fascinating discoveries include many important biblical papyri, the most notable being the scrap measuring two and a half by three and a half inches from the Gospel of Saint John that can be dated to the early second century (P. Rylands 457), and the unsavoury documents of ancient racial prejudice known as the *Acts of the pagan martyrs*.

Nearly all the papyri come from Egypt, though there are a few from Dura-Europos on the Euphrates and Nessana in the Negev desert. The vast majority of the Egyptian papyri have been found in a district some way from the capital. The number and variety of the literary finds are rather surprising, since one might not expect to find such evidence of wide reading in a country district. The survival of the papyri was made possible because in the villages refuse, including waste paper, was thrown on to huge rubbish dumps, which rose high enough to make their contents immune from any effects of moisture from the annual inundation or irrigation; with the dryness of the climate the papyri often avoided further damage. A few of them come not directly from the rubbish dumps, but from tombs, like Timotheus' *Persae* (P. Berol. 9875), or from cartonnage, the casing in which mummies were enclosed. This substance was made from layers of papyrus stuck together rather like papier mâché, and unwanted papyri were evidently bought up in quantity to make it. Many of these were damaged books no longer of any use to their owners, and we owe our knowledge of Menander's *Sicyonius* and a hundred lines of Euripides' *Antiope* (P. Lit. Lond. 70) to this fortunate habit of the Egyptian undertakers.

(c) *Other manuscript discoveries*

Since the end of the Renaissance there has been no great stream of discoveries of unknown texts except among the papyri. But for a long time research in manuscript collections was far from systematic, with the result that from time to time it was possible for a fortunate scholar to uncover an ancient text of more than trivial importance, and it is worth recording here the most notable examples.

In 1743 Prosper Petronius, working in the Vatican library, lit upon a unique codex of Theophrastus' *Characters*, which is still the only known witness to the text of nos. 29 and 30 (Vat. gr. 110), and thereby completed the text of this attractive and influential little book. Later in the century a much greater discovery was made in Venice. In 1788 Villoison published the marginal scholia to the *Iliad* found in the codex now known as Venetus A (Marc. gr. 454). They contained a vast fund of new information about the Alexandrian critics of Homer, and this information stimulated F. A. Wolf to write *Prolegomena ad Homerum*, one of the most important books in the whole history of classical scholarship (1795). While Robert Wood, in his *Essay on the original genius of Homer*, had already seen in 1767 that the usual picture of a literate Homer writing down his poems could not be a complete explanation of the present form of the Homeric poems, it was left to Wolf to demonstrate, with the help of the newly found scholia, that the textual problems in Homer were not of the same type as in other authors, and that an explanation for this state of affairs could be provided on the assumption that the text of Homer was not written down until the time of Solon or Pisistratus. Wolf's book marked the beginning of serious discussion of what is traditionally called the Homeric Question.

From the history of Greek scholarship in the nineteenth century it is worth mentioning the discovery of the verse fables by Babrius, found by M. Mynas in a manuscript on Mount Athos that is now in the British Museum (Add. 22087). Sometimes, however, hopes of discovery were deceived. In 1823 the famous Italian poet Giacomo Leopardi, who was also the best Italian classical scholar of his day, found in the Vatican what seemed to be a new piece of classical Attic prose. But the absence of a title in the manuscript and the lack of adequate works of reference conspired to delude his hopes; the text turned out to be a relatively common work of patristic literature written in the best imitation Attic, i.e. Atticist Greek; it was the address of Saint Basil to his nephews on the merits of reading classical literature.

In Latin there is less to record, since most of the great finds of modern times have been made in palimpsests as described above. A significant exception is Petronius' *Cena Trimalchionis*, which, although known for a fleeting moment in the Renaissance, was first printed at Padua in 1664. In 1899 an Oxford undergraduate examining an eleventh-century copy of Juvenal in Beneventan script (Canonici class. lat. 41) found that in satire VI it contained thirty-four additional verses, and though the text is extremely corrupt the balance of opinion now favours the view that they are genuine. And it may be just worth mentioning that an unknown letter of Saint Cyprian came to light not long ago in Holkham lat. 121, and though the letter itself is of no consequence its source at one remove may be a manuscript from Monte Cassino, a possibility which once again shows how important that one religious community was for the transmission of texts. Another recent find is the collection of Latin poems known as the Epigrammata Bobiensia, because the manuscript is a Renaissance apograph of a Bobbio codex (Vat. lat. 2836). Some of the authors represented are Augustan or of the first century, while nos. 2–9 are by Naucellius, a prominent literary figure of the end of the fourth century.

(d) *Epigraphic texts*

While books in their various forms have provided the main vehicle for the transmission of the vast legacy which the Greeks and Romans committed to writing, the large and increasing collections of inscriptions are themselves monuments to the enormous number of texts which have reached us inscribed on bronze, stone, and the like. The valuable contribution which epigraphy and numismatics can make to the illumination of ancient life was appreciated as early as the Renaissance and is in general beyond the scope of this book, but some of the texts which have been preserved by these means should be mentioned, for they are in some cases extensive, of major importance, or useful in that they augment or complement or correct the purely literary tradition.

An obvious example is the *Res gestae Divi Augusti*, a document of crucial importance for the study of Augustus and the early principate. This is the record of his achievements which Augustus left behind him with the express wish that it be engraved on bronze and placed in front of his Mausoleum. Both the original manuscript, which he deposited with the Vestal Virgins, and the original inscription have perished without trace, but copies were set up in the provinces, sometimes with a Greek paraphrase for the benefit of the local population, and the bulk of the text can be recovered from three fragments discovered in Galatia, the largest one, which has been known since 1555, on the walls of a mosque in Ankara. Though it is a rather special and grandiose example, the *Res gestae* belong to the wider tradition of the *laudatio*, or obituary notice, and for obvious reasons this genre is particularly well represented by epigraphic texts, ranging from grandiloquent orations to humble and touching records of personal affection. A famous one is the so-called *Laudatio Turiae* (*ILS* 8393), the funeral oration of a Roman matron of the late first century B.C., a substantial piece of writing. But even stones, as the ancients never tire of telling us, have their own mortality, and much of this stout matron's virtuous career would have been lost to fame had not the pen finally come to the aid of the chisel; for of the six fragments which have turned up in various parts of Rome since the seventeenth century, three have disappeared and now survive only in manuscript copies, which we mainly owe to the Jesuit scholar Jacques Sirmond and J. M. Suárez, the librarian of Cardinal Barberini (Paris lat. 9696, Vat. lat. 9140).

The bronze tablet at Lyons (*ILS* 212) which preserves the speech which the emperor Claudius made to the Senate in A.D. 48 advocating the admission of Gallic nobles is of literary as well as historical interest. For this text, discovered in 1524 and first printed by Lipsius, gives us the unique opportunity of being able to compare Claudius' actual speech, rambling and pedantic, with the taut literary adaptation which Tacitus provides (*Ann.* 11.24). The monument of Antiochus I of Commagene, which was discovered towards the end of the last century on the lofty slopes of an extinct volcano at Nemrud Dagh in eastern Turkey, has won itself an important place in literary history. Its florid text, as elevated in style as in its place of rest, has filled a crucial gap in our knowledge by providing the only example of the ornate 'Asianic' style of oratory which featured so largely in the rhetorical polemic of Cicero's day.

We owe a remarkable philosophical text to the philanthropic urge of Diogenes of Oenoanda, who was so impressed with the efficacy of the Epicurean philosophy that about the year A.D. 200 he had his exposition of the doctrines of Epicurus set up in the market-place of Oenoanda, in Lycia, for the benefit of his fellow citizens. Fragments of this unique text, forty metres long, which number almost a hundred and are still being discovered, lie scattered among the ruins of Oenoanda and provide editors with a jig-saw puzzle of truly monumental proportions. A remarkable feature of the inscription is the way in which its disposition in columns and concern for the convenience of the reader reproduce on an enlarged scale the conventions of the contemporary book. The earliest known example of a Christian hymn in the metrical form characteristic of Byzantium comes from an equally unexpected source: it is an inscription from a catacomb at Kertsch in the Crimea which can be dated to the year 491. It is part of the service for baptism.

More informal contributions to our store of ancient literature have been made by those who write on walls. These include a not inconsiderable body of original poetry, but often graffiti are only quotations from works which have already reached us via more orthodox channels. These are occasionally of interest to textual critics as evidence of indirect tradition. In this way a potsherd of the second century B.C. (Berlin ostrakon 4758) can find its way into the apparatus criticus of Euripides (*Hipp.* 616ff.) and the frequency with which *arma virumque cano* is scrawled on the walls of Pompeii helps to prove that this, and not *ille ego qui quondam*, is the true beginning of the *Aeneid*. A notable example is a distich of Propertius (3.16.13f.) found on a basilica at Pompeii. While the manuscript tradition is united in reading

> Quisquis amator erit, *Scythicis* licet *ambulat* oris,
> nemo *deo* ut *noceat* barbarus esse volet

the inscription (*CIL* iv. 1950) offers

> Quisquis amator erit, *Scythiae* licet *ambulet* oris,
> nemo *adeo* ut *feriat* barbarus esse volet

and is right in at least two of the four places in which it differs from the direct tradition.

VII. EPILOGUE

It is now time to draw together the threads of this rather selective account of the progress of scholarship between the end of the Renaissance and the beginning of what may be properly regarded as modern scholarship in the nineteenth century. Our purpose throughout this book has been to show how the existence of literary texts has been dependent both on material factors, such as the form of the book and the supply of writing materials, and on intellectual movements and changes in educational practice, and how the survival and quality of literary studies have been assisted by the gradual evolution of methods of scholarship. Once printing was established as the means of disseminating texts (and there was some resistance on the part of men such as Federigo duke of Urbino who declared that no printed book should ever form part of his library), one part of our story is at an end, since the survival of texts was assured. But it seemed worth while to pursue the history of scholarly method further, at least as far as the study of texts is concerned, and to highlight some of the developments which permitted a better and fuller use of the legacy of the past. The generally poor quality of the early printed editions shows how much remained still to be done for the theory of textual criticism, how the process of sifting manuscript resources had only just begun, how editing was hampered by a failure to appreciate the complexity of the study of classical civilization as a whole (*Altertumswissenschaft*). There were still obstacles to intellectual freedom, and much had still to be

G

done to establish classical studies as an independent discipline; as late as 1777 F. A. Wolf had to put up a fight to be matriculated at Göttingen, not in the Faculty of Theology, but as a *studiosus philologiae*. To this end we have given a simple account of some of the critical phases in the history of scholarship and their leading figures; although the emphasis is on the editing of texts, we have given some idea of the achievements of these pioneers outside the literary field proper in order to suggest some of the ways in which textual studies have interacted with other parts of the discipline to the benefit of all.

In the present century the study of manuscripts has made a dramatic advance through the provision of moderately priced photography, so that scholars can now obey literally the advice of the Vice-Chancellor of Cambridge University who said, 'Let Mr. Porson collect his manuscripts at home.' With the modern conveniences of microfilm and quick and comfortable travel, it is easy to forget the difficulties which our predecessors faced. The systematic description of manuscripts has also become a branch of scholarship, and the official catalogues of the leading libraries are a source of primary material for the modern scholar that his predecessors generally lacked. Another very important contribution to scholarship has been the decreasing mobility of the manuscript collections. Most manuscripts of Latin and Greek texts are now owned by institutions that may be confidently expected to retain them in perpetuity. But at least up to the end of the last century manuscripts were almost as likely to travel as they had been in the unsettled days of the Middle Ages and Renaissance. In our account we have occasionally alluded to these movements, and some others are explained in the notes to the index of manuscripts. They form a minor but not entirely insignificant facet of the history of culture and scholarship. The accumulation of the primary source material needed to provide the best attainable texts of the ancient authors is now well advanced and parallel to this process is the accumulation and evaluation of the objects, whether inscriptions, documentary papyri, or works of art, unearthed by the archaeologists and serving to throw light on the history, art, and material culture of the ancient world. The interaction between these various fields, the promotion of which was one of the great contributions of German scholarship in the nineteenth century, is the basis of the modern concept of the study of antiquity as a whole and promises a rich and continuing supply of themes as long as classical studies retain their place as an intellectual discipline.

6. TEXTUAL CRITICISM

I. INTRODUCTORY

The foregoing chapters have attempted to give some idea of the ways in which the Greek and Latin classics were handed down through the Middle Ages to the modern world, and to outline some of the more important historical and cultural phenomena which affected the transmission of these texts. The business of textual criticism is in a sense to reverse this process, to follow back the threads of transmission and try to restore the texts as closely as possible to the form which they originally had.

Since no autograph manuscripts of the classical authors survive, we are dependent for our knowledge of what they wrote on manuscripts (and sometimes printed editions) which lie at an unknown number of removes from the originals. These manuscripts vary in their trustworthiness as witnesses to the original texts; all of them have suffered to some degree in the process of transmission, whether from physical damage, from the fallibility of scribes, or from the effects of deliberate interpolation. Any attempt to restore the original text will obviously involve the use of a difficult and complex process, and this process falls into two stages.

The first stage is recension (*recensio*). The object of recension is to reconstruct from the evidence of the surviving manuscripts the earliest recoverable form of the text which lies behind them. Unless the manuscript tradition depends on a single witness, it is necessary (1) to establish the relationships of the surviving manuscripts to each other, (2) to eliminate from consideration those which are derived exclusively from other existing manuscripts and therefore have no independent value (*eliminatio codicum descriptorum*), and (3) to use the established relationship of those which remain (ideally expressed in the form of a *stemma codicum* or family tree) to reconstruct the lost manuscript or manuscripts from which the surviving witnesses descend. When the most primitive state of the text which is recoverable from the manuscripts has been reconstructed, the second main stage of the critical process begins. The transmitted text must be examined and the critic must decide whether it is authentic or not (*examinatio*); if not, his duty is to emend it (*emendatio*), if this can be done with a reasonable degree of certainty, or to isolate the corruption. The task is often complicated by the presence of two or more variant readings, each with a claim to be the transmitted text. The whole of this second stage is sometimes still given its traditional, though misleading, name—*emendatio*.

II. THE DEVELOPMENT OF THE THEORY OF TEXTUAL CRITICISM

The invention of the printed book, and in particular the appearance of the first printed editions of Cicero in 1465, meant that for the first time the future of classical texts was secure. But it had one unfortunate side-effect: the early printers, by the act of putting a text into print, tended to give that form of the text an authority and a permanence which in fact it rarely deserved. The *editio princeps* of a classical author was usually little more than a transcript of whatever humanist manuscript the printer chose to use as his copy, a replica in print of the current manuscript article. The repetition of this text, with only minor changes, from one edition to another soon led to the establishment of a vulgate text; and while there was nothing to prevent one from improving the vulgate by piecemeal emendation, the forces of inertia and conservatism made it difficult to discard it in favour of a radically new text.

Emendation continued to do its work, as it had done in every age; and although the critic's basic equipment—common sense and judgement and taste—were natural rather than acquired gifts, the development of some of the more useful principles of emendation and the rapid progress of classical scholarship in general enabled him to make a sharper attack on textual corruption. But emendation cannot be used to the greatest effect until recension has done its work, and scholars right up to the nineteenth century were in most cases obliged to exercise their critical gifts, which were often of the highest order, not upon the transmitted text as it is properly understood, but upon an entrenched vulgate. This they tried to emend, not only by conjecture, but also by the use of such manuscripts as they could find. There were some very remarkable discoveries, but more often the new manuscripts were no better than those on which the vulgate had originally been based. For in the days when libraries were largely uncatalogued, travel difficult, photography unknown, and palaeography in its infancy, this was a hit or miss process. Worse still, when good manuscripts were found, their usefulness was limited because their aid was sought only when the vulgate was manifestly unsatisfactory.

The first step towards more scientific textual criticism was the rejection of the vulgate text as the basis for discussion and with it the illogical conservatism which regarded the use of manuscripts as a departure from the tradition rather than a return to it. In this, as in other departments of criticism, the first impulse came from New Testament studies, where the problem was more obvious: the wealth of manuscript evidence left little scope for conjectural emendation and the task of choosing the truth from the variant readings was hampered by the almost divine sanction which was attributed to the *textus receptus*. In 1721 Richard Bentley, known to classical students more for the untrammelled boldness of his conjectures, projected an edition of the New Testament based exclusively on the ancient manuscripts and the Latin Vulgate. The conservative attitude of theologians prevented the project from being realized until Lachmann's edition of 1831, but the attack on the *textus receptus* was renewed a few years later by J. J. Wettstein, and in the course of a few decades the same radical approach had percolated to the field of classical philology, where Johann August Ernesti and Friedrich August Wolf restated in the firmest terms the need to make the manuscripts the basis of any critical text.

The relentless accumulation of manuscript evidence through the seventeenth and eighteenth centuries accentuated the need to work out a valid method of sorting the grain from the chaff. Many scholars contributed to the elaboration of the stemmatic theory of recension; this had been formulated in all its essentials by the middle of the nineteenth century and, although his own contribution is much slighter than had been supposed, it is still associated with the name of Karl Lachmann. For all its limitations, it revolutionized the editing of classical texts. There were glimmerings of the genealogical method as early as the humanist age. Politian, as we have seen, saw that manuscripts which derived from an older surviving exemplar were of no value, and effectively applied the principle of *eliminatio* to some of the manuscripts of Cicero's

Letters. In 1508 Erasmus postulated a single archetype from which all the surviving manuscripts of a text descended; and although his notion of an archetype was less precisely defined than ours, he was able to explain how easy it is for all the manuscripts to be wrong. The notion of the medieval archetype seems to have been first entertained by Scaliger, who in 1582 tried to prove from the nature of the corruptions in the manuscripts of Catullus that they were derived from a common parent written in pre-caroline minuscule.

Scaliger was far ahead of his time. No great advance was made towards a theory of recension until the eighteenth century and then the impetus came, once again, from New Testament scholarship. In the thirties J. A. Bengel perceived that the manuscripts of the New Testament could be classified on a genealogical basis. More than that, he spoke of the day when they would be reduced to what he called a *tabula genealogica*, and saw clearly the potentialities of his *tabula* as an instrument for the critical evaluation of variants. His genealogical approach was adopted with varying success by classical scholars of the late eighteenth and early nineteenth centuries, and brought to fruition in a brilliant burst of scholarship in the 1830's. In 1830 Lachmann, preparing the way for his edition of the New Testament, gave a more detailed formulation of the rules which Bengel had expounded for the choice of variants; in 1831 Carl Zumpt, in his edition of the *Verrines*, drew what appears to have been the first *stemma codicum* which the world had seen, and gave it the name which has won general acceptance; the great editions published by Ritschl and Madvig over the next few years refined and established the method. The most famous of all stemmata, that of Lucretius, was constructed by Jacob Bernays in 1847, and it remained for Lachmann, in his edition of 1850, to apply his rules for the mechanical application of the stemma and to give a classic demonstration of the validity of the hypothetical archetype by reconstructing its physical form and telling his astounded contemporaries how many pages it had, and how many lines to the page.

III. THE STEMMATIC THEORY OF RECENSION

The classic statement of the theory of stemmatics is that of Paul Maas. In practice the stemmatic theory has serious limitations, as Maas was well aware, since its successful operation depends on the tradition being 'closed'; these limitations are discussed below. The essentials of the theory are as follows:

(*a*) *The construction of a stemma.* Of fundamental importance in stemmatics are the errors which scribes make in copying manuscripts; for these errors provide the most valid means of working

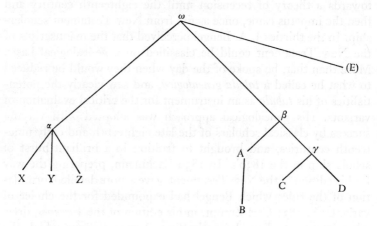

out the relationships of the manuscripts. Special attention is paid to errors of omission and transposition. For stemmatic purposes these errors can be divided into (*a*) those which show that two manuscripts are more closely related to each other than to a third manuscript (conjunctive errors), and (*b*) those which show that one manuscript is independent of another because the second contains an error or errors from which the first is free (separative errors). Care is taken to see that these errors are 'significant', i.e. not such mistakes as two scribes are likely to make independently, or such as a scribe could easily remove by conjecture. On this basis the interrelationships of the various manuscripts and manuscript groups are worked out step by step until, ideally, a stemma of the whole manuscript tradition has been reconstructed.

(b) *The application of the stemma.* The mechanical application of the stemma to reconstruct the reading of the archetype is best illustrated by a hypothetical stemma, as shown above. ω represents the archetype; the intermediate lost manuscripts from which the survivors descend are indicated, as is customary, by Greek letters. The extant manuscripts are eight in number (ABCDEXYZ); for the sake of the illustration, it is assumed that E is a fragment available only for a small part of the text.

1. If B is derived exclusively from A, it will differ from A only in being more corrupt. The first stage, therefore, is to eliminate B.
2. The text of γ can be inferred from the agreement of CD or from the agreement of one of them with an outside witness (A or α).
3. The text of β can be inferred from the agreement of ACD or of AC against D or of AD against C or from the agreement of either A or γ with α.
4. The text of α can be inferred from the agreement of XYZ or of any two of them against the third or from the agreement of one of them (provided the other two disagree with each other) with β.
5. When the texts of the two hyparchetypes (α and β) have been reconstructed, the readings peculiar to the individual witnesses ACDXYZ can be eliminated from consideration (*eliminatio lectionum singularium*).
6. If α and β agree, they may be assumed to give the text of the archetype (ω). If they disagree, either of the two readings may be the text of the archetype. It is the task of *examinatio* to decide which of these two variants is authentic.
7. If at some point in the text we have the evidence of a third independent branch of the tradition (E), then the principle of two against one will operate and the text of the archetype will only be in doubt if all three disagree or if two of them are likely to have fallen into the same error independently.

The application of these principles is sometimes a simple matter. The relationship of the manuscripts may be made clear by one or more glaring faults. Particularly striking examples are afforded when a book has suffered physical damage which is reflected in the copies made from it, whether directly or at more than one remove.

The first scholar to use this form of argument was Politian, in his discussion of Cicero's letters, but the utility of the method remained unappreciated by other scholars for a very long time. In the tradition of Lucretius important inferences were made by Lachmann from physical damage that must have taken place in a lost book. It is evident that at one time there was a copy with twenty-six lines to the page. Some leaves of this fell out and were incorrectly replaced, thus causing serious dislocation of the text in some surviving copies. A more far-reaching conclusion can be drawn from the manuscripts of Arrian's work on Alexander's expedition to India. There are about forty of these, and all have a substantial gap in the text at one point. As a rule this lacuna occurs in the middle of a page and the scribes have copied the text without noticing its existence. But in one manuscript (Vienna, hist. gr. 4) it occurs between the end of one verso page and the beginning of the next recto page, and further investigation shows that there is one leaf missing at this point. All other manuscripts evidently descend from this book after it had suffered mutilation In this case, therefore, the archetype is preserved. Another preserved archetype is the Oxford Epictetus (Auct. T. 4.13, Plate V); here a smudge of dirt has obscured a few words of text, which are missing from all other copies.

But such methods of inference cannot be applied in the majority of traditions. In general it may be possible to establish a few facts about the relation of the later manuscripts of an author from minor textual omissions, but for the main outline of the stemma it will be necessary to classify and arrange the manuscripts by reference to a series of significant errors.

IV. LIMITATIONS OF THE STEMMATIC METHOD

The apparent simplicity and finality of the stemmatic method as outlined above is deceptive. Though it often answers the editor's problem of selecting the right manuscript or manuscripts for his text, there are circumstances in which its utility is restricted. The theory assumes that readings and errors are transmitted 'vertically' from one manuscript to another, that is to say directly from one book to the copies that are made from it. But it has become increasingly evident as scholars have pursued more detailed inquiries that the tradition of many texts, including some of the highest interest and importance, cannot be elucidated by the application of the stemmatic theory. In these cases the manuscripts cannot be assigned to classes or families characterized by groups of errors because there has been contamination or 'horizontal' transmission. Readers in ancient and medieval times did not necessarily copy a text from a single exemplar; as their texts were often corrupt, they compared different copies, entering in their own manuscripts good readings or interesting variants as they found them. In some traditions—an example is Xenophon's *Cyropaedia*—the process was undertaken so often that the tradition has been hopelessly contaminated by the date of the earliest extant manuscripts. Scholarly activity naturally led to this result, and in many manuscripts the process can be observed, since variant readings are quoted in the margins or between the lines. It follows that the texts most commonly read, including those prescribed for the school syllabus, are most likely to show serious contamination. But the tradition of more recondite authors is not exempt from this feature, as the example of Diogenes Laertius shows.

A further difficulty in the theory lies in its assumption that all surviving manuscripts can be traced back to a single archetype, datable to the late ancient world or early middle ages. In practice thorough examination of manuscript variants has often suggested that this is not so, but that the tradition is 'open'. It may be possible to account for almost all the variants on the assumption of a stemma leading back to an archetype, but some readings refuse to fit the pattern, and if they are apparently ancient readings (a question of judgement arises here), another source has to be postulated for them. This source may be one or more manuscripts representing a different branch of tradition, which ceased to be copied as a whole but was consulted by scholars for some readings; these readings became variants within the main tradition, whether incorporated into its 'archetype' or at a later stage (see pp. 53–54). The plays of Aeschylus and Euripides which came to be prescribed for school reading probably went through this process.

Occasionally the facts are even more puzzling. In 1899 an Oxford manuscript of Juvenal (Canonici class. lat. 41) was found to contain thirty-four lines in satire VI that appear nowhere else, except that two of them are quoted by a scholiast. The passage has been regarded as spurious, but it is probable that interpolators would have lacked the powers or the motive to insert it; on the other hand if it is genuine, how are we to explain its survival in an otherwise mediocre copy and in only one of some five hundred manuscripts? A similar puzzle arises in the letters of Saint Cyprian. Recent work revealed the existence in a single copy (Holkham lat. 121) of a letter hitherto unknown and yet beyond all reasonable doubt genuine. Here too the tradition is copious and contaminated. No satisfactory explanation has yet been devised, but one feature is common to both cases: the Juvenal manuscript was written at Monte Cassino, while the Cyprian manuscript is very closely related textually to another book from the same monastery, which possessed so many unique texts.

One final complicating factor is the possibility that the ancient author himself made corrections or alterations to his original text after publication. Sometimes these would be extensive enough to justify us in speaking of a second edition. Under the conditions of the ancient publishing trade a second edition was much less likely to supplant its predecessor than in the modern world. Cicero's attempts to revise or eliminate errors in his works did not affect all the copies from which our archetypes descended (see p. 23). The two versions circulated side by side throughout antiquity with horizontal transmission taking place. Where a stemma cannot now be worked out this may be the reason. One or two examples can also be given in which authors' revisions are visible but have not affected the stemma so seriously. At Martial 10.48.23 it looks as if the name of a charioteer stood in the first edition of the book, but for the second edition, prepared after his death, the no longer topical name was replaced by a word indicating the team to which he belonged. A possible explanation of the incoherence of a scene in Aristophanes' *Frogs* (1437–53) is that some of the lines come from a revised version of the play. Similarly Galen (15.624) attributes the confused state of one of Hippocrates' works to marginal additions and revisions by the author.

V. AGE AND MERIT IN INDIVIDUAL MANUSCRIPTS

The notion of a best manuscript is sometimes found in discussions of textual problems, and there was a time when an appeal to the authority of the *codex optimus* was the normal or the most common way of discriminating between variant readings. But this procedure has rightly been criticized, since it was frequently used without regard to stemmatic method, and in any case it involves an error of logic. One cannot hope to identify the best manuscript of an author until one has considered the readings of all the significant manuscripts at all the points where they diverge; significant manuscripts are those extant or reconstructed books which the stemmatic method, in so far as it is applicable, proves to be of use for constituting the text.

When this has been done it is possible to draw up lists of passages in which the various manuscripts individually offer the reading which is best for literary, linguistic, historical or other reasons, and the manuscript which has the largest tally of such readings to its credit has a right to be termed the best manuscript. The utility of the term is often limited, particularly if there are one or more other manuscripts which have an almost equal number of good readings. In textual traditions where the term may reasonably be employed its use is confined to passages where there is a variety of readings among the manuscripts and there are no grounds for preferring one of these readings to another. Since the best manuscript is that which gives the greatest number of correct readings in passages where there are rational grounds for decision, it is more likely than the others to give the correct reading in passages where no such grounds exist. It is this argument from probability which justifies the appeal to the best manuscript in the circumstances indicated.

Here it is necessary to mention a variation of the faulty argument referred to above. This consists of an appeal to the authority of the oldest manuscript, usually implying that the antiquity of a manuscript guarantees its merit; conversely manuscripts of the Renaissance are dismissed as unimportant merely because of their date. There is of course no doubt that in general a certain relation exists between the age of a manuscript and the quality of the text that it offers, since it is a reasonable supposition that a late manuscript is separated from the original text by a larger number of intervening transcripts, each of which is to be presumed more corrupt than its predecessors. In many textual traditions investigation will show that the oldest manuscript is the best. But there are some exceptions which serve to show that the generalization must not be carelessly applied. A general argument may be drawn from the evidence of the papyri; though these are many centuries earlier than the medieval manuscripts, they do not as a whole offer markedly superior texts, and one of the most famous and important, containing Menander's *Dyscolus* (P. Bodmer 4), is astonishingly corrupt. Medieval manuscripts yield a number of instructive examples. Several manuscripts of Greek authors which date from the Palaeologan Renaissance (see p. 68) are of much the same value to editors as the more famous manuscripts of the same texts that are as much as three centuries earlier (e.g. Vienna supp. gr. 39 of Plato, Paris gr. 1734 of Thucydides, Laur. 32.16 and Wolfenbüttel Aug. 2996 of Apollonius Rhodius). A more extreme example is the sixteenth-century Vienna manuscript of the minor works of Xenophon (phil. gr. 37), which is clearly at least equal in importance to the other witnesses, being the unique source of many correct readings. The same phenomenon can be observed among Latin texts. Here one outstanding example is the Renaissance copy of Lucretius *l* 31 (Laur. 35.31), the unique source of many correct readings, all apparently the work of a clever humanist. A slightly different case is the notorious Leiden Tacitus (B.P.L. 16 B) which offers a few good and many specious readings. As a result of the discovery of these late manuscripts that are of interest to the editor and textual critic a principle has been established, which is usually expressed by the formula *recentiores, non deteriores*. Printed editions too can have a similar importance; indeed some of the letters of Cicero and Pliny are preserved only in print.

These late manuscripts pose a problem for the editor; what is the source of their good readings? In some cases it is clear beyond any reasonable doubt that they represent a branch of tradition that cannot otherwise be traced; the good readings are such that they could not possibly have been invented by a scholar of the Middle Ages or Renaissance. The copy of Xenophon mentioned above is a case in point: it supplies words missing from the text, in some places where the gap had not even been demonstrated beforehand. But often it is not so easy to come to a conclusion; Renaissance scholars were capable of acute conjectures, at least in Latin texts, and it is often impossible to say with any certainty whether or not a particular conjecture would have been within their powers. The same considerations apply to Byzantine scholars, but recent investigations have tended to suggest that their ability in conjectural restoration of a text was rather more limited than has sometimes been assumed in the past.

VI. INDIRECT TRADITION

Apart from ancient and medieval books (and occasionally translations into other languages) the editor and critic sometimes has another source of help in the secondary or indirect tradition. This is the term applied to quotations of one author by another, who may on occasion preserve the correct reading when all the ordinary manuscripts of the author quoted are in error. There are one or two famous examples of this phenomenon. In Vergil's fourth *Eclogue* (62–3) the manuscripts give

> cui non risere parentes,
> nec deus hunc mensa, dea nec dignata cubili est.

But Quintilian (9.3.8; though his MSS. too are corrupt) evidently read *qui* at the beginning of the relative clause, which led to the necessary conjecture:

> qui non risere parenti.

And it is not only ancient authors whose quotations hint at the right text. Some good manuscripts that are now lost survived until late in the Middle Ages and were consulted by scholars of that period. A striking case has already been mentioned in another connection: Eustathius quotes Sophocles *Antigone* 1165–8 complete, whereas all manuscripts of Sophocles omit 1167 (see p. 61). It is interesting to note that this same quotation of the passage occurs in the late ancient author Athenaeus (c. A.D. 200) (280c, 547c); Athenaeus was known to Eustathius and could have been his source for the quotation, but the manner in which he introduces the lines rather suggests the opposite. Another medieval source of correct quotations is the *Suda* lexicon (see p. 58).

It should not be supposed, however, that secondary tradition is an unfailing source of correct readings. Ancient and medieval writers were even less inclined than their modern counterparts to follow the advice of Dr. Routh and verify their references. Quotations were usually made from memory and there were good reasons for this practice. Ancient books of the roll type did not facilitate quick reference, and when the codex form was adopted readers still could not count regularly on such aids as page numbering, chapter division, and line numbering, which are part of every modern text. These considerations must be borne in mind in cases where the manuscripts of an author offer one reading, and there is an acceptable but not absolutely certain alternative in the secondary tradition. Either reading may be what the author wrote. But in the majority of cases editors will probably be right to follow the primary tradition; the divergent reading of a quotation is likely to be right only if the purpose of the quotation was to emphasize or illustrate the divergent words or phrases, whereas if the divergence is incidental to the quotation it is probably due merely to lapse of memory.

The difficulty of enunciating firm principles may be shown by a few examples:

(*a*) Aristophanes, *Acharnians* 23: the MSS. have οὐδ᾽ οἱ πρυτάνεις ἥκουcιν, ἀλλ᾽ ἀωρίαν|ἥκοντεc κτλ. The *Suda* lexicon quotes the line with the reading ἀωρίᾳ, in the article which is devoted to this word. In principle there is some reason to hope that this might be an accurate quotation, but the dative is less idiomatic than the accusative in this type of adverb and for that reason is rejected by the editors.

(*b*) In the same play at 391–2 the MSS. offer:

εἶτ᾽ ἐξάνοιγε μηχανὰc τὰc Cιcύφου,
ὡc cκῆψιν ἀγὼν οὗτοc οὐκ εἰcδέξεται.

These lines are quoted in the *Suda* article on Sisyphus, but with two differences: in the first line εἶτα is replaced by ἀλλά, and in the second εἰcδέξεται by προcδέξεται. Since the quotation is not intended to illustrate either of these words, there is not much reason to trust its accuracy. Yet on other grounds ἀλλά may well be right, and προϲδέξεται is as likely to be right as the rather puzzling εἰϲδέξεται.

(c) Lucretius 3.72 is given in the MSS. as:

crudeles gaudent in tristi funere fratres.

Macrobius quotes the line in a passage where he is comparing Lucretius and Vergil (6.2.15), and gives the variant *fratris*. This is clearly superior, but the quotation was not made to illustrate any single word in the line.

(d) In the same book at 676 the MSS. have:

non, ut opinor, id a leto iam longius errat.

The grammarian Charisius (p. 265, Barwick[2]) quotes the line with the variant *longiter*, and says that it was his purpose to exemplify the form by this quotation. For this reason editors usually, though not invariably, adopt the reading.

VII. SOME OTHER BASIC PRINCIPLES

The critic may find himself in a position where he has to choose between two readings that are equally acceptable in respect of the sense and the linguistic usage of his author, but feels that it is unsafe or impossible to argue from the merits of the manuscripts. In such situations there are two maxims that are frequently invoked, *utrum in alterum abiturum erat* and *difficilior lectio potior*. The first of these is a general principle, and the basis of it can be easily explained. Given the tendency of scribes to corrupt texts it is reasonable to suppose that careless copying or a desire to simplify a difficult passage encouraged certain types of alteration. The maxim *difficilior lectio potior* is strictly speaking no more than an application of this general principle. It embodies the notion that if one of the available readings is more difficult to understand, it is more likely to be the correct reading. The justification of this view is that scribes tended, sometimes consciously, sometimes inadvertently, to remove from the text the rare or archaic linguistic forms that were no longer readily understood, or to simplify a complex process of thought that they could not master. Alternative terms to describe these activities are interpolation and trivialization. Many references to the maxim *difficilior lectio* will be found in commentaries, and there is no doubt of its value. But it has probably been overworked, for there is a temptation to use it as a defence of anomalous syntax or usage; in such cases the more difficult reading may be more difficult because it is wrong.

VIII. CORRUPTIONS

In order to extract the truth from the manuscript evidence the scholar needs to have some acquaintance with the various types of corruption that occur. The primary cause of these was the inability of scribes to make an accurate copy of the text that lay before them. The majority of errors were involuntary, but at the end of this section we refer to an important category of which this is not true. Although it seems surprising at first sight that the concentration of the scribes should have failed so often, anyone may soon verify for himself by experiment how difficult it is to make an entirely accurate copy of even a short text. If due allowance is made for the length of time during which copying by hand was the only means of transmission, it is perhaps remarkable that more ancient texts were not reduced to an unintelligible condition. Many different pitfalls lay in the path of the scribe if he once allowed his attention to wander. Some of the possibilities are indicated in the list below. They are to be regarded as a small selection divided into rough and ready categories. It must be emphasized that scribal errors have never been made the subject of a statistical study, and so it is not possible to establish with any degree of precision the relative frequency of the various types. Another important warning is that the assignment of an error to a class is not always as easy as it might appear. Cases arise in which it is possible to attribute a mistake to one of several causes or to a combination of them. A third consideration to be borne in mind is that not all causes of error were active at all times. A case in point is that the use of some abbreviations which were liable to cause difficulty to scribes can be set within chronological or geographical limits.

A. Mistakes induced by any feature of ancient or medieval handwriting may be taken as a first class of error. It might be supposed that this class is much more numerous than any other, but the careful study of an apparatus criticus casts doubt on this view. Typical causes of error within this class are (i) the lack of division between words in many manuscripts, (ii) a close similarity of certain letters in a script which results in their being confused, (iii) the misreading of an abbreviation; apart from ordinary signs representing syllables or common short words there was a special method of abbreviation for certain key terms of Christian theology; these are known as *nomina sacra*, and are frequent in both Greek and Latin texts. In both languages abbreviations are so numerous and complex that the study of them forms a subject in itself (Plate V). (iv) Since numerals were represented by letters in both languages they were often incorrectly transmitted, a fact which is a serious hindrance to students of economic and military history. Perhaps one may add here (v) the confusion of two words of similar shape or spelling even when there is no immediate cause of confusion in the forms of the individual letters.

(i) 1. Petronius, *Cena* 43.
   Quid habet quod queratur? *abbas secrevit*.
   ab asse crevit   Scheffer. (Cf. also G (i).)

   2. Aeschylus, *Eumenides* 224.
   δίκας δ' ἐπ' ἄλλας τῶνδ' ἐποπτεύσει θεά.
   δὲ Παλλὰς Sophianus.

(ii) The following letters are commonly confused in Latin scripts:
   In capitals: ILT EF PT PF PC BR HN OQ COG and such combinations as M NI.
   In uncials: ILT FPR CEOGU and such combinations as U CI. Characteristic of uncial, as opposed to capital, is the confusion of EU (now rounded in form) with the group COG.
   In minuscule: *au oe cld nu sf ct* and various letters or combinations of letters made of one or more downstrokes (minims), e.g. the letters in *minimum*. The confusion of *pr rn ns* is characteristic of insular script; in Visigothic the peculiar *t*, and in Beneventan both the *t* and the *a* cause difficulty (see Plate XIV).

1. Seneca, *Epist.* 81.25.

Manifestum etiam *contuenti* discrimen est.

coniventi codd. recc.

2. Lucretius ii.497.

quare non est ut credere possis
esse infinitis distantia *femina* formis.

semina Oᶜ

Groups of letters liable to be confused with each other in Greek script are:

In uncials: *ΑΔΛ ΕΘΟC ΙCΚ ΓΤ*.

In minuscule: *βκμ μν α ευ*.

1. Aristotle, *Poetics* 1462 b 3.

λέγω δ' οἷον εἴ τις τὸν Οἰδίπουν θείη τὸν Cοφοκλέουc ἐν
ἔπεcιν ὅcοιc ἢ ἰδίαc.

ἢ ἰδίαc MSS.: *ἤ 'Ιλιάc* a humanist corrector (confusion of Δ and
Λ).

2. Julian, *Epist.* 23.

δόc μοί τι κατὰ τοὺc μελικτὰc εἰπεῖν ῥήτοραc.

μελικτὰc Aldine edition: μελητὰc VL: μελίτουc N: βελτίcτουc
Jackson. β and μ are very similar in minuscule; here the corruption is aided by the uncial confusion of IC and K.

(iii) 1. Curtius Rufus, vi.11.30.

Intellego non prodesse mihi quod praesentis sceleris *expressum*.

expers sum   codd. recc.

The symbols for *per pro prae* (usually p ꝑ p̄) are one example of the many *notae* which are open to misinterpretation.

2. Seneca, *epist.* 76.7.

Quare *autem* unum sit bonum quod honestum dicam.

autem] ħ V: hoc M: om. P: in b. The manuscript V has preserved the insular abbreviation for *autem* which has been the undoing of MPb.

3. Scholium on Aristophanes, *Knights* 505.

τοῦτο πρῶτον τὸ δρᾶμα δι' αὐτοῦ καθῆκε, τὰ δ' ἄλλα δι'
ἑτέρων ἀπων.

ἀπων V: προσώπων ΕΓΘΜ. In V's exemplar there were two
compendia, α (= προ) and ∼ (= ω).

4. Aeschylus, *Eumenides* 567–8.

†ἤ τ᾽ οὖν διάτοροc† Τυρσηνικὴ
cάλπιγξ βροτείου πνεύματος πληρουμένη.

οὖν seems to conceal the *nomen sacrum* οὐρανόν (ο̄υνο̄ν), which
has been further corrupted.

(iv) 1. Cicero, *Att.* i.13.6.

Messalla consul Autronianam domum emit HS CXXXIIII.

Other MSS. offer CXXXVII or CXXXIII or XXXIII. HS
13,400,000 is an astronomical price for a house. A plausible emen-
dation is |X̄X̄X̄I̅I̅I̅| = 3,300,000 (Constans), but certainty is in the
circumstances unattainable.

2. Thucydides, iii.50.1.

τοὺς δ᾽ ἄλλους ἄνδρας οὓς ὁ Πάχης ἀπέπεμψεν ὡς αἰτιωτάτους
ὄντας τῆς ἀποστάσεως Κλέωνος γνώμῃ διέφθειραν οἱ Ἀθηναῖοι
(ἦσαν δὲ ὀλίγῳ πλείους χιλίων), καὶ Μυτιληναίων τείχη
καθεῖλον καὶ ναῦς παρέλαβον.

χιλίων MSS.; but this number seems too large for the ringleaders
of a revolt in Mytilene, and τριάκοντα has been suggested instead.
χιλίων would be written ͵A (in uncials), τριάκοντα Λ' (cf. A (ii)
above).

(v) 1. Seneca, *Epist.* 102.22.

Tempus hic ubi inveni relinquam, ipse me diis reddam.

corpus   Pincianus.

2. Pindar, *Pythians* 4.90.

καὶ μὰν Τιτυὸν βέλος Ἀρτέμιδος θήρευσε κραιπνόν.

κραιπνόν correctly most MSS.: τερπνόν C.

B. Other corruptions arose out of changes in spelling and pronunciation. For instance in late Latin the sounds *ae* and *e* became
identical, while *b* came to be sounded as a fricative and was confused with *v*. In Greek several vowels and dipthongs were reduced to the single sound of iota, as in the modern language.
Error resulting from this change is known as iotacism. Beta became
fricative as in modern Greek, and so did upsilon in diphthongs.

The distinction between omicron and omega was lost. The diphthong alpha-iota became identical with epsilon. Orthographical errors are of extreme frequency, but the majority of them are of no consequence for the establishment of the text and are not recorded in the apparatus.

1. Quintilian 6.3.93 (quoting Domitius Afer).

   Pane et aqua *bibo*.

   vivo   Haupt. (Most MSS. inevitably have *panem et aquam bibo*.)

2. Diogenes Laertius, *Vitae philosophorum* ix.10.

   (ἔφη) ἡμέραν τε καὶ νύκτα γίνεσθαι καὶ μῆνας καὶ ὥρας αἰτίους καὶ
   ἐνιαυτοὺς ὑετούς τε καὶ πνεύματα καὶ τὰ τούτοις ὅμοια κατὰ τὰς
   διαφόρους ἀναθυμιάσεις.

   αἰτίους BP: ἐτείους F.

C. Omissions constitute a third large class of error. Here again subdivision is possible. Sometimes we find (i) omission of not more than a few letters; if this occurs in a passage where the scribe has written a sequence of letters only once when they should be repeated, the term haplography is used. This mistake arises if the scribe is moving ahead too quickly with his task, and an extended form of the same mistake is sometimes referred to as (ii) *saut du même au même*. Here the scribe, finding the same word twice within a short space, copies the text as far as its first occurrence; then looking back at the exemplar to see what he must copy next he inadvertently fixes his eye on the second occurrence of the word and proceeds from that point. As a result the intervening words are omitted from his copy. Mistakes are also caused if two words in close proximity have the same beginning or ending; the technical terms for these are homoearcton and homoeoteleuton. The same fault of eyesight was responsible for similar errors which it is convenient to list as a slightly different category, (iii) the omission of a whole line of text. This error is often found in the manuscripts of the poets, and its informative value to scholars trying to establish a stemma is obvious. Examples can be found in prose texts also. It should be added, however, that a large number of omissions occur for no apparent reason except the carelessness of the scribe; this is particularly common with small words.

(i) 1. Lucretius, iii.135.

> Quidquid ⟨id⟩ est, habeant; tu cetera percipe dicta.

> id suppl. *l* 31.

   2. Aristophanes, *Acharnians* 221–2.

> μὴ γὰρ ἐγχάνοι ποτὲ
> μηδέ περ γέροντας ὄντας ἐκφυγὼν Ἀχαρνέας.

> ὄντας is omitted by most MSS., but is clearly necessary.

(ii) 1. Cicero, *Att.* vii.9.4.

> Praeteriit tempus non legis *sed libidinis tuae, fac tamen legis*;
> ut succedatur decernitur; impedis et ais 'habe meam rationem'.

> sed . . . legis C: om. Ω.

   2. Aristophanes, *Acharnians* 692–5.

> ταῦτα πῶς εἰκότα, γέροντ' ἀπο (λέ-
> σαι πολιὸν ἄνδρα περὶ κλεψύδραν,
> πολλὰ δὴ ξυμπονήσαντα καὶ θερμὸν ἀπο-)
> μορξάμενον ἀνδρικὸν ἱδρῶτα δὴ καὶ πολύν.

> The MS. A omitted the section enclosed in parentheses.

(iii) 1. Seneca, *de ira* 3.7.1.

> tenerique iam visa cum ipso cadunt ita fit ut frequenter inrita
> sit eius voluntas

> These words form one line of the Ambrosianus: they are
> omitted by a number of the later manuscripts, which in this
> way reveal their derivation from A.

   2. The omission of Sophocles *Antigone* 1167 in all the manuscripts
has been mentioned already in connection with Eustathius and the
importance of the secondary tradition. A stemma of the Sophocles
manuscripts is facilitated by the omission of *Oedipus Tyrannus* 800
from the famous Medicean MS. (Laur. 32.9) and its twin brother,
the Leiden palimpsest (Leiden, B.P.G. 60 A).

D. A fourth group may be termed errors of addition. The sim-
plest of these are no more than the repetition of a few letters or
syllables, which is referred to as (i) dittography. More substantial
is the addition to the text of explanatory or illustrative material.
The most frequent type in this category is (ii) the addition of a
gloss. Most Greek manuscripts have a number of brief interlinear

notes explaining rare or difficult words. These glosses were easily added to the text in the course of transcription. In poetry a simple addition of this kind may be immediately obvious because of the violence it does to the metre; but sometimes the word used as a gloss had the same metrical value as the word in the text and replaced it without impairing the metre, and examples of this process are not easy to detect. The detection of (iii) glosses in a prose text is often of the greatest difficulty. Many passages contain explanatory phrases which are not strictly required for the sense but offer no offence to grammar or syntax. These phrases present problems which may remain insoluble. Two texts which scholars have recently discussed in detail in the light of these questions are Petronius' *Satyricon* and Cicero's *Tusculan Disputations*. (iv) A rare but interesting corruption is the addition to a text of a parallel passage originally written in the margin of a book by a learned reader. This may happen in verse or prose. Cases are known from Greek tragedy, and Galen (17(1).634) noticed that it had happened in one of the Hippocratic treatises.

(i) 1. Seneca, *Epist.* 78.14.

Quod acerbum fuit ferre, *retulisse* iucundum est.

tulisse   Bartsch.

2. Song quoted by Athenaeus 694d.

γελάςειας, ὦ Πᾶν, ἐπ᾿ ἐμαῖς
εὐφροςύναις ταῖςδ᾿ ἀοιδαῖς, ἀοιδέ, κεχαρημένος.

εὐφροςύναις A: εὔφροςι Wilamowitz
ἀοιδαῖς ἀοιδέ A: ἀοιδαῖς Hermann

(ii) 1. Aeschylus, *Agamemnon* 549.

καὶ πῶς; ἀπόντων τυράννων ἔτρεις τινάς;

So F: Triclinius restored the metre by substituting κοιράνων for τυράννων.

2. Plautus, *Truculentus* 278.

Cumque ea noctem in stramentis pernoctare perpetim [totam].

The Ambrosian palimpsest gives both the gloss (*totam*) and the word which has been glossed (*perpetim*); the Palatine family give the correct text.

(iii) 1. Seneca, *Epist.* 42.4.

Eadem velle [subaudi si] cognosces: da posse quantum volunt.

The words *subaudi si* ('understand *si*'), corrupted to *subaudis* and worse in the MSS., were put in the margin to help the reader with the paratactic conditional sentence and then incorporated into the text.

2. Diogenes Laertius, *Vitae philosophorum* v.76.

λέγεται δ' ἀποβαλόντα αὐτὸν τὰς ὄψεις ἐν ᾿Αλεξανδρείᾳ κομίcαcθαι αὖθιc παρὰ τοῦ Cαράπιδοc.

ἀποβαλόντα BP: τυφλωθέντα F, which is a gloss.

(iv) 1. In the margin of the Medicean Aeschylus at *Persae* 253 the line Sophocles *Antigone* 277 has been written. In copies of M this line has been incorporated into the Aeschylean text.

2. Vergil, *Aen.* ii.76.

ille haec deposita tandem formidine fatur.

Sinon is about to explain himself. This line is omitted in P and added at the foot of the page in M by a later hand. It is a doublet of iii.612, where it is in place, and has been added here because of the similarity between this passage and that in book iii.

E. Errors of transposition are another well-known class. (i) Transposition of letters is common. (ii) In poetry verses are often copied in the wrong order. (iii) In all kinds of text word order is subject to fluctuation. The number of variants of this kind is large enough to suggest that inferences about the word order of Latin and Greek prose should be made with great care.

In Greek texts of both verse and prose there were special causes leading to corruption of word order during the middle ages. (iv) One of these affected the text of tragedy. A common metre in Byzantium was a twelve-syllable line rather like the classical iambic line but subject to different rules, the most important being that the penultimate syllable must carry an accent (at this date a stress accent). As a result some scribes altered, probably unconsciously, lines of tragedy in order to make them conform to this rule. The process is known as *vitium Byzantinum*. (v) In Byzantine prose there was a rule affecting the order of words; in general it was necessary that the last two stressed syllables of a sentence should be separated by two or four unstressed syllables (in special cases by none or six). The effect of this is sometimes visible in manuscripts of classical prose writers.

(i) 1. Lucretius, iii.170.

> Si minus offendit vitam vis horrida *leti*
> ossibus ac nervis disclusis intus adacta . . .
> teli Marullus.

2. Aeschylus, *Agamemnon* 1205.

> βαρύνεται γὰρ πᾶς τις εὖ πράσσων πλέον.

So Triclinius' autograph; but F has the correct reading ἀβρύνεται.

(ii) This extremely frequent error may be found exemplified in the text of any author.

(iii) 1. Seneca, *Epist.* 117.24.

> Deos vitam et salutem roga.

So Bθ. Other manuscripts read *vitam roga et salutem* or *salutem et vitam roga*. Manuscript authority and rhythm (double cretic) decide.

2. Pindar, *Nemeans* 7.37.

> ἵκοντο δ' εἰς Ἐφύραν πλαγχθέντες.

So the MSS.; Boeckh restored metrical responsion by reading πλαγχθέντες δ' εἰς Ἐφύραν ἵκοντο.

(iv) Aeschylus, *Agamemnon* 1106.

> ἐκεῖνα δ' ἔγνων. πᾶσα γὰρ πόλις βοᾷ.

So M, correctly, but F and Triclinius have βοᾷ πόλις.

(v) Plutarch, *de curiositate* 13 (522).

> ὁμοίως οὐδ' Ἀλέξανδρος εἰς ὄψιν ἦλθε τῆς Δαρείου γυναικὸς ἐκπρεπεστάτης εἶναι λεγομένης.

So most MSS.: the Λ-family alter to give a Byzantine clausula: τῇ Δαρείου γυναικὶ εὐπρεπεστάτῃ λεγομένῃ τυγχάνειν.

F. In a sixth group one may include errors induced by the context. (i) The inflection of a word may be wrongly assimilated to that of an adjacent word. (ii) The scribes allowed themselves to be influenced by words or phrases that they had recently copied or were just about to copy.

(i) 1. Catullus, xxxiv. 17.

  tu cursu dea *menstrua*/metiens iter annum
  rustica agricolae bonis/tecta frugibus exples.

  menstruo   B. Guarinus.

  2. Euripides, *Helen* 1243.

  κενοῖϲι θάπτειν ἐν πέπλοιϲ ὑφάϲμαϲιν.

  πέπλοιϲ L: πέπλων Scaliger.

(ii) 1. Seneca, *Epist.* 114.9.

  Ubi luxuriam late felicitas fudit, *luxus* primum corporum esse diligentior incipit.

  cultus   Muretus.

  2. Euripides, *Rhesus* 776–7.

  ἤπυϲα δ᾽ αὐτοῖϲ μὴ πελάζεϲθαι ϲτρατῷ,
  κλῶπαϲ δοκήϲαϲ ϲυμμάχων πλάθειν τινάϲ.

  At 776 V has πλάθειν for πελάζεϲθαι by anticipation.

G. Some mistakes betray the influence of Christian thought. As all readers in the Middle Ages were more or less devout Christians it would be very surprising if they had succeeded in copying thousands of manuscripts without committing mistakes of this kind.

1. Petronius, *Cena* 58.

  Sathana tibi irata sit curabo.

Sathana H: Athana   Heinsius. (Cf. also D (i). As the previous sentence ends with *habeas*, this could be a case of dittography.)

2. Aristophanes, *Knights* 1302–4.

  οὐδὲ πυνθάνεϲθε ταῦτ᾽, ὦ παρθένοι, τὰν τῇ πόλει;
  φαϲὶν αἰτεῖϲθαί τιν᾽ ἡμῶν ἑκατὸν εἰϲ Καρχηδόνα,
  ἄνδρα μοχθηρὸν πολίτην, ὀξίνην ῾Υπέρβολον.

  Καρχηδόνα RVΦ: Χαλκηδόνα Γ² and a scholiast.

Carthage is more likely to be right than Chalcedon, a city of little importance in the Athenian empire but well known to every orthodox Greek in the Middle Ages because of the famous church council held there in A.D. 451.

H. There is also a class of mistakes that derives from the deliberate activity of the scribe. As has been seen above, ancient and medieval readers tried to emend passages that they found difficult or corrupt, and their attempts were sometimes misguided or ill-informed. A typical example is that Triclinius mutilated some Euripidean lyrics because he knew that metrical responsion ought to be restored, but was not well enough acquainted with the language of classical poetry to make the correct emendations. Such faulty corrections are often referred to as interpolations, though the term is not quite apt. Deliberate alteration on a larger scale can be seen in attempts to bowdlerize. This process was not as widespread, however, as might be expected. It seems that schoolmasters of late antiquity and the Middle Ages were not as anxious to suppress obscene or otherwise embarrassing passages as more recent editors have been. The excisions found in some modern school editions of Aristophanes do not seem to be anticipated in medieval manuscripts. But there are manuscripts of Herodotus which omit the account of sacred prostitution at 1.199, and there is a family of Martial manuscripts in which some of the blatant obscenities have been replaced by less offensive words. Another type of interpolation, for which scribes were not responsible, is that made by the actors in the texts of Greek tragedy (see pp. 14–15).

1. Juvenal, viii.148.
   Ipse rotam adstringit sufflamine mulio consul.

In some manuscripts this has been, not unnaturally, corrupted to *sufflamine multo*. At this point deliberate interpolation steps in and restores the metre: other manuscripts read *multo sufflamine*.

2. Tacitus, *Annals* 13.39.1.
   Et Corbulo, ne irritum bellum traheretur utque Armenios ad sua defendenda cogeret, exscindere parat castella.

So M. In the Leiden Tacitus interpolation has run riot, producing specious nonsense:

> Et Corbulone irritum bellum trahente ut Armenios ad sua defendenda cogeret exinde repetit castella.

3. Euripides, *Electra* 435-7.

> ἵν' ὁ φιλάδελφος ἔπαλλε δελ-
> φὶς πρώραις κυανεμβόλοι-
> σιν εἱλισσόμενος.

So the first hand in L; Triclinius used his knowledge of strophic responsion and the quotation of this passage at Aristophanes *Frogs* 1314ff. to make one good alteration (φίλαυλος), but then committed a bad error (κυανεμβόλοις εἱειλισσόμενος).

4. Plutarch, *de curiositate* 7 (518).

> φέρε γὰρ Ἡρόφιλον ἢ Ἐρασίστρατον ἢ τὸν Ἀσκληπιὸν αὐτόν, ὅτ'
> ἦν ἄνθρωπος, ἔχοντα τὰ φάρμακα καὶ τὰ ὄργανα, κατ' οἰκίαν παριστ-
> άμενον ἀνακρίνειν, μή τις ἔχει σύριγγα περὶ δακτύλιον ἢ γυνὴ
> κάρκινον ἐν ὑστέρᾳ.

The *Λ*-family here alter δακτύλιον to δάκτυλον and delete ἐν ὑστέρᾳ.

The diversity of the causes of error brings with it a consequence of great importance to the critic. He cannot approach his task in the belief that any one class of error is predominant. In practice many scholars appear to have assumed that errors arising from palaeographical causes are the commonest; certainly this is the conclusion to be drawn from the numerous and often elaborate palaeographical justifications that accompany proposed emendations. The only safe method is to follow the rule explicitly enunciated by Haupt, and reiterated by Housman: 'the prime requisite of a good emendation is that it should start from the thought; it is only afterwards that other considerations, such as those of metre, or possibilities, such as the interchange of letters, are taken into account. . . . If the sense requires it I am prepared to write *Constantinopolitanus* where the MSS. have the monosyllabic interjection *o*.' In order to drive home their lesson Haupt and Housman quoted an extreme example. In fact when a critic has decided on grounds of sense how a corrupt passage might be restored, he considers various possibilities in the light of the types of error listed above, and is influenced by them in his choice between different restorations of the text. When really serious corruption has taken place it may well be necessary to print between obeli (††) the text of the archetype and indicate in the apparatus the best conjectures; in such passages certainty is unattainable even with the critic's sharpest weapons.

IX. CONCLUSION

In this account of the function and methodology of textual criticism we have described some of the principles and criteria which have been most commonly and most usefully employed by those who attempt to reverse the process of transmission and restore the words of the ancients as closely as possible to their original form. In order to reduce to the length of a chapter a subject which normally fills a book and even then is no more than a guide, we have confined our account to basic and well-tried techniques. This will inevitably give the impression that textual criticism is a tidier and more cut-and-dried process than it proves to be in practice. While general principles are undoubtedly of great use, specific problems have an unfortunate habit of being *sui generis*, and similarly it is rare to find two manuscript traditions which respond to exactly the same treatment.

One omission is obvious. While giving space to the limitations of the stemmatic theory, we have not explored the complicated and sometimes controversial methods which have been devised to deal with contaminated traditions. The more open a tradition is, the less fruitful the stemmatic approach is likely to be, and other methods must be tried. These range from empirical, common-sense approaches which accept the necessities of an imperfect world, to elaborate statistical techniques which aim at more objective results. In some cases it is possible to adopt a flexible modification of the genealogical method. The manuscripts are classified as far as is possible into broad groups and the editor chooses his readings eclectically, persuaded more by their intrinsic merit than by considerations of affiliation and authority and taking care to balance these factors to suit the nature of the tradition. But if contamination has gone so far that, in the words of Housman, 'the true line of division is between the variants themselves, not between the manuscripts which offer them,' various approaches may be adopted which all tend to concentrate on the variants themselves rather than on the manuscripts which carry them. These may involve sophisticated mathematical techniques, which are particularly tempting at the present time, now that the development of computers and allied mechanical and electronic devices have made them more feasible. We have given no account of distributional and statistical methods, which would be a study in itself, nor of their automatization, which is at an experimental stage and already generating a body of literature not readily intelligible to most students of the humanities. It is not yet clear whether elaborate mechanized techniques, however valid as a theoretical study, will yield practical results which justify the labour and expense entailed or are markedly superior to those produced by traditional means and 'nature's own computer, located between the ears of the investigator.' In any case their future seems to lie more in the biblical and patristic fields and with vernacular languages than with classical texts, where the material is more easily controlled and not usually unmanageable by traditional methods accompanied by the limited use of scientific aids. Ultimately, the basic essential equipment is taste, judgement, common sense, and the capacity to distinguish what is right from what is wrong in a given context; and these remain the perquisite of human wit. But where the tradition is large and complex, computers can be usefully employed in building up a provisional picture of the interrelationship of texts. Outside the field of recension, machines can be used, if great caution is observed, in stylistic studies, and they have already proved their worth for information retrieval and in the making of concordances; and the fruits of these activities have a real bearing on the editing of texts.

NOTES

I

The growth of the book trade in classical Athens is described by
E. G. Turner, *Athenian books in the fifth and fourth centuries* B.C.,
London 1952. The exact period at which it becomes legitimate to speak
of a trade is uncertain, but it is worth emphasizing that Xenophon,
Anabasis 7.5.14, speaks of books (βίβλοι γεγραμμέναι) as forming part
of the cargo of ships wrecked off Salmydessos on the north coast of
Thrace; the inference seems inescapable that books were an article
exported (from Athens?) to the cities of the Euxine coast as early as
the year 399 B.C. If this is so, our inability to extract more precise
information from the passages of Eupolis and Plato cited in the text
is of little importance.

On the form and appearance of books in Greece from the classical
period until the end of the Roman Empire the reader should consult
E. G. Turner, *Greek papyri*, Oxford 1968, and his companion volume,
Greek manuscripts of the ancient world, Oxford 1971, which offers a well-
chosen album of plates with commentary.

The supply of papyrus was precarious in the classical period, if we
can trust the evidence of the letter from Speusippus to Philip of
Macedon (p. 50 in L. Köhler's ed., *Philologus Supplement-Band* 20,
Leipzig 1928); the text indicates a shortage of papyrus c. 342 B.C.
owing to the Persian occupation of Egypt. But though this letter is
now regarded as genuine by many authorities, its status is not entirely
above suspicion.

The use and gradual refinement of punctuation are still debated;
apart from Turner's book cited above see R. Pfeiffer, *History of classical
scholarship*, Oxford 1968, pp. 178–81; his view is essentially shared by
R. Renehan, *Greek textual criticism, a reader*, Cambridge, Mass., 1969,
pp. 76–7; but see the reservations expressed by N. G. Wilson, *CR*
19 (1969), 371, and note that the passages cited by Renehan do not all
prove as much as he thinks. Perhaps the best view is that of H.-I.
Marrou, *Histoire de l'éducation dans l'antiquité*, Paris 1965⁶, p. 602 n. 30,
that books with full punctuation never passed into general use but were
confined to teachers and pupils (though Marrou appears to be making
this suggestion about books in the Roman period). An interesting

example of a conjecture that finds part of its justification in the absence of punctuation from ancient texts is given by H. Lloyd-Jones, *The justice of Zeus*, Berkeley 1971, p. 193 n. 23.

II

The standard work on Alexandrian scholarship is R. Pfeiffer, *History of classical scholarship: from the beginnings to the end of the Hellenistic age*, Oxford 1968, reviewed by N. G. Wilson, *CR* 19 (1969), 366–72. This is the first volume of a work that will replace Sir J. E. Sandys, *History of classical scholarship*, vols. 1–3, Cambridge 1903–8 (some volumes subsequently revised), reprinted 1958, which is still of considerable use as a reference book. On the Museum and library see P. M. Fraser, *Ptolemaic Alexandria*, Oxford 1972, chapter 6.

The monograph of Lloyd W. Daly, *Contributions to a history of alphabetization in antiquity and the Middle Ages*, Brussels 1967 (= Collection Latomus, vol. 90), is of interest; since it is there shown that Zenodotus and Callimachus used the principle of alphabetical order in some of their writings, one may conjecture that the same principle was employed to some extent in the arrangement of the library in the Museum.

The so-called 'wild' papyri of Homer were re-edited by S. R. West, *The Ptolemaic papyri of Homer*, Cologne 1967.

G. P. Goold, *TAPA* 91 (1960), 272–91, expressed extreme scepticism about the idea that copies of Homer in the old Athenian alphabet found their way into the Alexandrian library; but his conclusion if right does not necessarily apply to all other authors.

The primary sources about the use of the critical signs are corrupt and confused, but the facts were reasonably well sorted out by A. Gudeman in *RE*, s.v. Kritische Zeichen.

The statistics of Aristarchan emendations generally adopted in the text of Homer come from T. W. Allen's edition of the *Iliad*, Oxford 1931, vol. 1, pp. 199–200; on pp. 201–2 similar calculations are given for readings ascribed to Zenodotus and Aristophanes. Subsequent publications will not have altered the figures substantially.

On Aristarchus' principle of interpreting Homer from Homer see N. G. Wilson, *CR* 21 (1971), 172.

The actors' interpolations are discussed by D. L. Page, *Actors' interpolations in Greek tragedy*, Oxford 1934; on the passage mentioned in the text see A. M. Dale, *Wiener Studien*, 69 (1956), 103–4 (= *Collected papers*, Cambridge 1969, pp. 126–7), and M. D. Reeve, *GRBS* 13 (1972), 263–4.

H

III

For the archaeological discoveries at Pergamon see E. Akurgal, *Ancient civilisations and ruins of Turkey*, Istanbul 1970², pp. 79–80.

Didymus' commentary on Demosthenes was edited by H. Diels and W. Schubart, Berlin 1904; for the exact definition of the type of literature to which it belongs see F. Leo's review in *NGG* (1904), 254–61 (= *Kleine Schriften*, vol. 2, pp. 387–94), but note also the reservations of S. West, *CQ* N.S. 20 (1970), 288–96.

IV

The Latin book does not receive very much specific treatment in the standard works on books in the ancient world, since it is similar in all essentials to its Greek counterpart, and the bulk of our evidence comes from Egypt, where there was comparatively little interest in Latin. The degree of punctuation enjoyed by a reader in the classical period is as much in dispute for Latin books as for Greek, owing to the extremely limited palaeographical evidence and the ambiguous nature of statements casually made by our literary authorities. The view that Latin books, down to the end of the first century A.D., were provided with more in the way of punctuation and aids to the reader than was customary in antiquity, was propounded by R. P. Oliver, *TAPA* 82 (1951), 241–2, and has been further developed by E. O. Wingo, *Latin punctuation in the classical age*, The Hague etc., 1972. For a more sceptical view, see G. B. Townend, *CQ* N.S. 19 (1969), 330–3. In general, see R. W. Müller, *Rhetorische und syntaktische Interpunktion*, Diss. Tübingen 1964. The Roman contribution to the development of the codex is discussed in VIII.

Pending the appearance of R. Pfeiffer's second volume in the *History of classical scholarship*, there is no full and comprehensive account of scholarship during the Roman period. The primary material can be found in G. Funaioli, *Grammaticae Romanae fragmenta*, vol. 1, Leipzig 1907, and its continuation, A. Mazzarino, *Grammaticae Romanae fragmenta aetatis Caesareae*, vol. 1, Turin 1955. Brief accounts are given by F. Leo, *Geschichte der römischen Literatur*, vol. 1, Berlin 1913, pp. 355–68; G. Funaioli, *Studi di letteratura antica*, vol. 1, Bologna 1946, pp. 206ff. Much can also be derived from Leo's *Plautinische Forschungen*, Berlin 1912², and G. Pasquali's *Storia della tradizione e critica del testo*, Florence 1952².

The history of the text of Plautus in antiquity throws some much needed light on the beginnings of Roman scholarship, murky though that story sometimes is: cf. W. M. Lindsay, *The ancient editions of Plautus*, Oxford 1904; F. Leo, *Plautinische Forschungen*, pp. 1–62; Pasquali, *Storia della tradizione*, pp. 331–54. The date of the alternative ending of the *Andria* of Terence has been most recently discussed by O. Skutsch, *RhM* 100 (1957), 53–68. There is a good account of the history of the text of the dramatic poets in ancient times, with particular reference to Ennius, in H. D. Jocelyn, *The Tragedies of Ennius*, Cambridge 1967, pp. 47–57.

On the *Anecdoton Parisinum* and the critical activity of Aelius Stilo and his circle see S. F. Bonner, *Hermes*, 88 (1960), 354–60.

Attention focuses on Atticus because of the wealth of information in Cicero's letters, in contrast to our ignorance of the book trade at Rome before his time. His precise role has been discussed by R. Sommer, *Hermes*, 61 (1926), 389–422; see further R. Feger, *RE*, Suppl. 8 (1956), 517–20, K. Büchner in *Geschichte der Textüberlieferung der antiken und mittelalterlichen Literatur*, vol. 1, Zürich 1961, p. 328. The evidence is conveniently presented (and interpreted with predictable bias) by J. Carcopino, *Les Secrets de la correspondence de Cicéron*, vol. 2, Paris 1947, pp. 305–29. The nature of 'publication' in antiquity and the concept of 'edition', so different from ours, have been discussed by H.-I. Marrou, *VCh* 3 (1949), 208–24; H. L. M. Van der Valk, *VCh* 11 (1957), 1–10; B. A. van Groningen, *Mnem.* Ser. 4, 16 (1963), 1–17.

For a general account of the book trade in Rome, see T. Kleberg, *Buchhandel und Verlagswesen in der Antike*, Darmstadt 1967, pp. 22–68.

V

The gnomic quality of *Aen.* 10.284 and the danger of drawing any general conclusion from it have been pointed out to us by Sir Roger Mynors.

The importance of Probus in the history of scholarship is highly controversial. The exaggerated esteem of earlier scholars, such as Leo (*Plautinische Forschungen*, pp. 23ff.), has given way to a much more cautious assessment: cf. Pasquali, *Storia della tradizione*, pp. 339ff.; N. Scivoletto, *GIF* 12 (1959), 97–124; K. Buchner in *Geschichte der Textüberlieferung*, pp. 335–9. See also R. Hanslik in *RE*, 8 A.1 (1955), 195–212, and, for a detailed consideration of the crucial chapter in Suetonius, A. Grisart, *Helikon*, 2 (1962), 379–414. The reputation of Hyginus has similarly declined; for a critical view of his Vergilian textual criticism, see G. P. Goold, *HSCP* 74 (1970), 161–2, and J. E. G. Zetzel, ibid. 77 (1973), 237–8.

VI

A general account of the second-hand book trade in Rome is given by T. Kleberg, 'Antiquarischer Buchhandel im alten Rom', *Annales Acad. Reg. Scient. Ups.* 8 (1964), 21–32. J. E. G. Zetzel, in the article cited above, has cogently demonstrated that many of the imposing volumes reported to exist in the second century and later were forged by alert entrepreneurs to meet the demand of antiquarian enthusiasts, and that Lampadio's Ennius and Tiro's Cicero and some of the more 'authentic' copies of Vergil should be numbered among such fakes. This is an understandable phenomenon, as easily paralleled in antiquity as at other times (cf. p. 7), and a testimony to the strength of the archaic revival, if not to the expertise of the antiquarian scholars. At the same time one should perhaps not be too sceptical about the existence of early texts at this period. Evidence which the Elder Pliny provides for the previous century is less suspect in that it predates the change in literary fashion and therefore the motive for forgery on a large scale: he claims (*NH* 13.83) to have seen documents written by the Gracchi, adding that autographs of Cicero, Augustus, and Vergil were common. He may be referring primarily to letters and similar documents. The theory that the collection of Ciceroniana bought by the bookseller Dorus (Seneca, *Ben.* 7.6.1) was part of Atticus' legacy is pure conjecture, based on a philosophical *exemplum*.

An accurate text of the subscription to the *De lege agraria* was first given in *Codices Vaticani Latini: Codices 11414–11709*, rec. J. Ruysschaert, Vatican 1959, pp. 93–5, and is printed as it stands in Poggio's manuscript except for the expansion of *Dom* to *Domitium* and the emendation *oratio XXIIII* for *oratio eximia*. The last is due to Zetzel, who discusses the textual problem posed by the subscription and its significance in general, op. cit., 226–30.

VII

For the audacious fraudulence of the author of the *Historia Augusta*, see Sir Ronald Syme, *Ammianus and the Historia Augusta*, Oxford 1968, and in particular p. 9.

VIII

The now classic account of the codex is that of C. H. Roberts, *Proc. Brit. Acad.* 40 (1954), 169–204. See further E. G. Turner, *Greek papyri*, pp. 6ff.; T. C. Skeat, 'Early Christian book-production: papyri and manuscripts', *Cambridge history of the Bible*, vol. 2, ed. G. W. H. Lampe,

Cambridge 1969, pp. 54–79. On the dating of the fragment *De bellis Macedonicis*, cf. J. Mallon, *Emerita*, 17 (1949), 1–8.

IX

Aspects of the conflict between paganism and Christianity in the fourth century are discussed in the essays edited by A. Momigliano, *The conflict between paganism and Christianity in the fourth century*, Oxford 1963; of special relevance is the contribution by H. Bloch, pp. 193–218. Alan Cameron has redated the *Saturnalia* of Macrobius and put it into a new perspective, *JRS* 56 (1966), 25–38. For the Christianization of the senatorial class, see P. Brown, *JRS* 51 (1961), 1–11.

For a more general treatment of the confrontation between the two cultures, see M. L. W. Laistner, *Christianity and pagan culture in the later Roman Empire*, Ithaca, N.Y., 1951 (Cornell Paperbacks 1967); *Thought and letters in Western Europe, A.D. 500–900*, London 1957[2], pp. 25–53. A real assessment of the attitudes and practice of the two most influential figures of the fourth century, Jerome and Augustine, has been made possible by the detailed studies of H. Hagendahl, *Latin Fathers and the classics* (Studia Graeca et Latina Gothoburgensia, vol. 6), Göteborg 1958; *Augustine and the Latin classics* (Studia Graeca et Latina Gothoburgensia, vol. 20), Göteborg 1967.

On the question of style and taste, see C. E. Chaffin in *The classical world* (Literature and Western Civilization, ed. D. Daiches and A. Thorlby), London 1972, pp. 461–86.

X

Many editions of the subscriptions have been projected, but we are still dependent on the fundamental work of Otto Jahn, 'Über die Subscriptionen in den Handschriften römischer Classiker', *Berichte über die Verhandlungen der Sächsischen Gesellschaft der Wissenschaften, Phil.-hist. Classe*, 3 (1851), 327–72. Much of the historical detail is filled in by H. Bloch, in Momigliano, *The conflict*.

Whether the Asterius subscription in the Medicean Vergil is an autograph or not has long been in dispute; for a negative view, see e.g. O. Ribbeck, *Prolegomena critica ad P. Vergili Maronis opera maiora*, Leipzig 1866, p. 223. W. Clausen provides a warning against attaching too much importance to the revision of the gentleman amateurs who feature so often in the subscriptions, *Hermes*, 91 (1963), 252f. For the imperial fora as intellectual centres, see H.-I. Marrou, *Mélanges d'archéologie et d'histoire de l'École française de Rome*, 49 (1932), 94–110.

CHAPTER 2

I

In general see Sandys, *History of classical scholarship*. The ancient grammarians' contributions to syntax are noted by J. Wackernagel, *Vorlesungen über Syntax*, Basle 1950². There is no satisfactory modern treatment of Atticism and its effects on scholarship and literature; the basic reference book is still W. Schmid, *Der Attizismus in seinen Hauptvertretern*, Stuttgart 1887–96.

II

On the Christians and education see H.-I. Marrou, *Histoire de l'éducation*, pp. 451–71. The early Christian apologists are well presented by H. Chadwick, *Early Christian thought and the classical tradition*, Oxford 1966. W. Jaeger, *Early Christianity and Greek paideia*, Harvard 1961–Oxford 1969, is a good introduction to another side of the question. A sketch of the influence of the Church on scholarship, mainly in the Byzantine period proper, will be found in N. G. Wilson, *Antike und Abendland*, 16 (1970), 68–77.

Various views have been taken of Saint Basil's intention in his so-called twenty-second homily (it is in fact addressed to his nephews). Marrou, p. 462, emphasizes that it does not consist of a recommendation to study the classical authors; its advice is rather that, given the existing curriculum of pagan texts, there are ways of ensuring that these do the pupil good instead of harm. On the other hand it is probably wrong to see in Basil no more than a grudging recognition; the tone of the treatise is not unfriendly.

On Apollinaris it should be added that he also recast the Gospels and Epistles in the form of Platonic dialogues (Socrates, *Hist. eccl.* 3.16).

The burning of books is discussed by C. A. Forbes, *TAPA* 67 (1936), 114–25. The documents relating to ecclesiastical censorship in the twelfth century are nos. 1003 and 1008 in V. Grumel, *Regestes des actes du patriarcat de Constantinople*, Istanbul 1947.

III

On the closure of the philosophical school at Athens see A. D. E. Cameron, *Proc. Camb. Phil. Soc.* 195 (1969), 7–29, and R. C. McCail, ibid. 196 (1970), 79–82.

On the school at Gaza and the formation of scholia see the tentative hypothesis advanced by N. G. Wilson, *CQ* 17 (1967), 244–56 and 18 (1968), 413.

Wilamowitz's theory of the selection of plays for use in schools was put forward in his *Einleitung in die griechische Tragödie* (vol. 1 of his edition of Euripides' *Herakles*), 1895[2] and subsequently reprinted, pp. 175–80, 196–8. Its main features had been anticipated by T. Barthold in a Bonn dissertation of 1864.

The evidence that Menander was still being read in the school at Gaza may be found in J. Irmscher's essay in *Menanders Dyscolos als Zeugnis seiner Epoche*, ed. F. Zucker, Berlin 1965, p. 209. (The article by A. Dain on the survival of Menander in *Maia*, 15 (1963), 278–309, contains an error and a dubious interpretation on this point.) J.-M. Jacques, *Bull. Assoc. G. Budé* (1959), 200–15, has shown that Menander may have been read in Byzantium as late as c. 600 by the historian and epistolographer Theophylactus Simocatta.

The history of the other schools or universities of late antiquity is much more obscure. Some idea of the law school at Beirut may be had from the attractive picture in M. L. Clarke, *Higher education in antiquity*, London 1971, pp. 116–17 (with further references). For Alexandria the best guide is H. D. Saffrey, *REG* 67 (1954), 396–410.

IV

A recent review of the use of local vernacular languages in the eastern provinces is given by R. MacMullen in *AJP* 87 (1966), 1–16.

Oriental versions of the New Testament are discussed by B. M. Metzger, *The text of the New Testament*, Oxford 1968[2], pp. 67–84, 265–8, and K. Aland (ed.), *Die alten Uebersetzungen des Neuen Testaments, die Kirchenväterzitate und Lektionare*, Berlin 1972.

Syriac translations of Greek texts are listed by A. Baumstark, *Geschichte der syrischen Literatur*, Bonn 1922. On the schools of Nisibis and Edessa one may consult A. Vööbus, *History of the school of Nisibis*, Louvain 1965. For studies of particular authors see e.g. A. Baumstark, *Jahrbücher für classische Philologie*, Supp.-Band 21 (1894), 357–524, *Aristoteles bei den Syrern*, Leipzig 1900, G. Uhlig's edition of Dionysius Thrax, Leipzig 1883, pp. xliv–xlvi, M. Aubineau's edition of Gregory of Nyssa, *De virginitate* (= Sources Chrétiennes, vol. 119), Paris 1966, pp. 223–5, M. D. Macleod–L. R. Wickham, *CQ* 20 (1970), 297–9.

The best introduction to Arabic translations and Hunain ibn Ishaq is by R. Walzer, *HSCP* 63 (1958), 217–31, where further bibliography will be found There is also quite a useful bibliographical survey by F. Gabrieli, *Al-Andalus*, 24 (1959), 297–318. For a recent and instructive illustration of the difficulties to be overcome and the gains to be expected from the use of an Arabic version, see R. Kassel, *Der Text der aristotelischen Rhetorik*, Berlin 1971, pp. 88–92, 125–6, 141–2.

Joseph Needham, *Science and civilization in China*, vol. 1, Cambridge 1954, p. 219, draws attention to a fascinating episode in the life of the great Arab physician and alchemist Rhazes, who dictated some of the works of Galen to a Chinese scholar visiting Baghdad.

For Armenian translations see M. Leroy, *Ann. Inst. de phil. et d'hist. orient.* 3 (1935), 263–94, who gives the reference to Callimachus; there does not seem to be a more recent survey of the field. For some recent work on the Armenian version of Plato see W. S. M. Nicoll, *CQ* 16 (1966), 70–4.

It may be worth adding that occasionally one has to reckon with a translation into another Oriental language (Hebrew or Persian), but these cases are very much rarer, and the number of them discovered so far did not seem to justify a mention of them in the main text.

V

Byzantine scholarship from its beginnings to the middle of the tenth century is dealt with by P. Lemerle, *Le Premier Humanisme byzantin*, Paris 1971. Since this will evidently be the standard work for some time to come, we refer the reader to it without listing earlier contributions to the subject, and we only mention here a few articles in English that have remained unknown to the author and some matters of palaeography that require comment.

(1) p. 119: L. says that minuscule script brought with it accentuation, word-division, and punctuation. However, in the earliest minuscule only the last of these three features is found.

(2) p. 168: L. says that MS. Vat. gr. 1 of Plato's *Laws* was written for Arethas by John the Calligrapher, who was the scribe of his copies of Plato and Aristides. But the scribe is certainly not John the Calligrapher, and M. Ch. Astruc, as quoted by L. in n. 73, is probably right in saying that the marginalia are not in the hand of Arethas. For a further note on this MS. (and a general account of Byzantine libraries) see N. G. Wilson, *GRBS* 8 (1967), 53–80.

(3) On Photius it may be as well to say that the new early dating of the *Bibliotheca*, though ingenious, is not without its difficulties; see N. G. Wilson, *GRBS* 9 (1968), 451–6. On the nature of the circle or club of which Photius was the central figure see the postscript to the same writer's article on books and readers in Byzantium in *Dumbarton Oaks Papers* (forthcoming). As to the absence of poetry from the *Bibliotheca* (except from one codex), it should be noted that in letter 150 Photius shows knowledge of Aristophanes' *Plutus*, which he is likely

to have encountered in the school curriculum; and a close reading of his works might well reveal acquaintance with a number of other poetic texts, most probably known to him for the same reason.

(4) p. 215: there is no strong reason for associating MS. Paris gr. 1807 with Arethas; on palaeographical grounds it is likely, but not certain, that the book was written before Arethas began to form his library.

VI

The identification of scribes, and very rarely scriptoria, through features of handwriting or book production, is one of the chief means by which our knowledge of Byzantine scholarship advances. Autographs of the leading scholars are still being recognized, and our knowledge of scriptoria is making slow progress. For the methods involved see J. Irigoin, *Scriptorium*, 12 (1958), 208–27 and 13 (1959), 177–209. The objection of principle raised by B. Hemmerdinger, *BZ* 56 (1963), 24, remains a serious difficulty, but need not be held to invalidate all the results of this method of inquiry (known in some circles as codicology). A successful application of the method may be seen in Irigoin's identification of a group of manuscripts of the Greek historians all written with thirty-two lines to the page: *Annuaire de l'école pratique des hautes études*, 1968–9, section IV, pp. 137ff.

There is no satisfactory study of Psellus (the article by E. Kriaras in *RE* leaves a good deal to be desired). What is said in our text may need to be substantially revised in due course. Psellus' literary interests can be seen for instance in his short essays comparing the novels of Achilles Tatius and Heliodorus and the verse of Euripides with that of George of Pisidia, a Byzantine versifier of the seventh century; but since neither of these texts is available in an adequate edition judgement must be reserved.

Anna Comnena's circle was unearthed by R. Browning, *Proc. Camb. Phil. Soc.* 188 (1962), 1–12.

For Eustathius see R. Browning on the patriarchal school in *Byzantion*, 32 (1962), 167–202, 33 (1963), 11–40. This is the appropriate place to mention that though the school is well attested as an institution in the twelfth century, the evidence for its existence at other periods is very weak (see H. G. Beck, *Polychronion, Festschrift Dölger*, pp. 69ff.); yet it may be hypercritical to deny its existence at any time other than the twelfth century. Eustathius' commentary on the *Iliad* is now being edited from the surviving autograph manuscript by M. van der Valk (vol. 1, Leiden 1971, with prolegomena of considerable value for assessing Eustathius' sources and methods of scholarship). The superior text of Sophocles' *Antigone* possibly comes from a reading of Athenaeus, who quotes the passage; but this does not diminish Eustathius' merit in recalling as he read that the Sophoclean text, as he knew it, was faulty at that point. His work on Aristophanes was brought to light by W. J. W. Koster–D. Holwerda, *Mnemosyne*, 7 (1954), 136ff., 8 (1954), 196ff.

On Tzetzes see C. Wendel in *RE*. His scholia on Aristophanes have been edited by L. Massa Positano, D. Holwerda, and W. J. W. Koster, Groningen 1960–4. The philological club is mentioned in his notes to *Frogs* 897.

For Michael Choniates see G. Stadtmüller, *Michael Choniates Metropolit von Athen*, Vatican City 1934. The incorrect name Acominatos is ingeniously explained by J.-L. Van Dieten, *Niketas Choniates, Erlaüterungen zu den Reden und Briefen nebst einer Biographie*, Berlin 1971, pp. 4–8. See also O. Lampsidis, *BZ* 64 (1971), 26–7.

Constantine Lascaris' statement about Diodorus Siculus is in Migne, *PG* 161.918: he had seen a complete copy in the emperors' library.

A general account of literature and learning in the kingdom of Nicaea is given by A. A. Vasiliev, *History of the Byzantine Empire*, Madison, Wis., 1952, pp. 548–63. On the contribution of southern Italy to Byzantine culture see J. Irigoin, *JÖBG* 18 (1969), 37–55; pp. 51–3 concern the thirteenth century.

Sketches of Palaeologan scholarship and related matters are given by Sir Steven Runciman, *The last Byzantine Renaissance*, Cambridge 1970, and D. M. Nicol, *Studies in church history*, 5 (1969), 23–57.

For Planudes see the article by C. Wendel in *RE*. Two further facts about his scholarship may be worth adding here to what is said in the text. In preparing his edition of Plutarch from a damaged exemplar he seems to have instructed his scribes to pay attention to the length of each lacuna. Less to his credit is that he bowdlerized the Greek Anthology and his translation of Ovid. The autograph of his text of Aratus has now been discovered in the Advocates Library in Edinburgh (MS. 18.7.15); see I. C. Cunningham, *Scriptorium*, 24 (1970), 367–8 with plate 24. Planudes' alterations to the text are found exactly as expected. The translations of Ovid's amatory works cannot be ascribed to him with the same degree of certainty as the other translations; on this side of his activity see W. O. Schmitt, *JÖBG* 17 (1968), 127–47, and E. J. Kenney, *Hermes* 91 (1963), 213–27.

On Triclinius see A. Turyn, *The Byzantine manuscript tradition of the tragedies of Euripides*, Urbana, Ill., 1957, pp. 23ff., 32ff.; N. G.

Wilson, *CQ* 12 (1962), 32–47; G. Zuntz, *An inquiry into the transmission of the plays of Euripides*, Cambridge 1965, *passim*; A. Wasserstein, *JÖBG* 17 (1968), 153ff.

An observation about the Byzantine school curriculum may be added here. There are sporadic references in authors of widely differing dates to the *quadrivium* (τετρακτύς), but the evidence does not enable us to say whether the concepts of *trivium* and *quadrivium* were as influential in Byzantium as they were in the educational practice of Western Europe. See A. Diller, *Isis*, 36 (1945–6), 132, who points to the existence of these concepts in a work dating from A.D. 1008.

CHAPTER 3

I

Among the most relevant general works on the intellectual and cultural history of the Dark Ages mention should be made of P. Courcelle, *Les Lettres grecques en Occident de Macrobe à Cassiodore*, Paris 1948²; P. Riché, *Éducation et culture dans l'Occident barbare, vie–viiie siècles* (Patristica Sorbonensia, vol. 4), Paris 1962; B. Bischoff, 'Scriptoria e manoscritti mediatori di civiltà dal sesto secolo alla riforma di Carlo Magno', *Settimane di studio del Centro italiano di studi sull' alto medioevo*, 11 (Spoleto 1963), 479–504, reprinted in his *Mittelalterliche Studien*, vol. 2, Stuttgart 1967, pp. 312–27; also the works earlier cited by Laistner and Marrou. The fundamental work is E. A. Lowe, *Codices latini antiquiores*, vols. 1–11 with Supplement (Oxford 1934–71), now complete except for further indexes to be published and containing facsimiles and descriptions of all Latin manuscripts prior to the ninth century (abbreviated *CLA*).

Martin of Braga's *Formula vitae honestae*, dedicated to the Suevic king Mir and written between 570 and 579, is an adaptation of a lost work of Seneca, probably the *De officiis* (cf. E. Bickel, *RhM* 60 (1905), 505–51). Unlike his *De ira*, a carefully constructed mosaic of borrowings from Seneca's treatise of that name, which survives in only one medieval manuscript, the *Formula* was an extremely popular work in the Middle Ages and later. Often entitled *De quattuor virtutibus cardinalibus*, it was commonly attributed, with perspicacity if not a sense of poetic justice, to Seneca. For further information see C. W. Barlow, *Martini episcopi Bracarensis opera omnia*, New Haven, Conn., 1950.

For bibliographical material on Cassiodorus see the important article by A. D. Momigliano, 'Cassiodorus and the Italian culture of his time', *Proc. Brit. Acad.* 41 (1955), 207–45, reprinted (with a more select bibliography) in his *Secondo contributo alla storia degli studi classici* Rome 1960, pp. 219–29, and *Studies in historiography* (London 1966, paperback 1969), pp. 181–210. The theory that the oldest Bobbio manuscripts came from Vivarium was advanced by R. Beer in *Anz. Akad. der Wiss. in Wien, Phil.-Hist. Kl.* 48 (1911), 78–104. For some of the important stages in its demolition see E. A. Lowe, *CQ* 19 (1925), 205 (= *Palaeographical papers 1907–1965*, ed. L. Bieler, vol. 1, Oxford 1972, p. 198), and *CLA* 4 (1947), xx–xxvii; G. Mercati, *Prolegomena* to the facsimile edition of the palimpsest of Cicero's *De republica*, Vatican 1934, pp. 1–174; P. Courcelle, *Les Lettres grecques*, pp. 357–88, who has made the most positive contribution to the problem (but cf. Bischoff, *Karl der Grosse*, p. 44 n. 17). For a survey of the question see the important review of *CLA* 4 by H. Bloch in *Speculum*, 25 (1950), 277–87. *Cassiodori Senatoris institutiones*, ed. R. A. B. Mynors, Oxford 1937, provides a critical text of the *Institutiones* and valuable indexes.

A full-length study of Isidore and his classical sources is provided by J. Fontaine, *Isidore de Seville et la culture classique dans l'Espagne wisigothique*, 2 vols., Paris 1959. It seems dangerous to draw firm conclusions about the classical content of the episcopal library at Seville from Isidore's *Versus in bibliotheca* (ed. C. H. Beeson, *Isidor-Studien* (Quellen und Untersuchungen zur lateinischen Philologie des Mittelalters, 4.2, Munich 1913), pp. 157–66). The remarkable story of the dissemination of his works has been most recently and authoritatively treated by B. Bischoff, 'Die europaische Verbreitung der Werke Isidors von Sevilla', *Isidoriana. Estudios sobre San Isidoro de Sevilla en el XIV centenario de su nacimiento*, León 1961, pp. 317–44, reprinted in *Mittelalterliche Studien*, vol. 1, Stuttgart 1966, pp. 171–94.

A celebrated manuscript long attributed to the sixth century, the Morgan Pliny (Pierpont Morgan Library M.462) has been recently redated to the late fifth century (*CLA* XI.1660).

For the facts and figures about early palimpsests, which can be supplemented from the volumes of *CLA*, see E. A. Lowe, 'Codices rescripti', *Mélanges Eugène Tisserant*, vol. 5, Vatican 1964 (Studi e Testi, 235), 67–112, reprinted in *Palaeographical papers*, vol. 2, pp. 480–519.

II

The extent to which the early Irish knew the classics is as controversial as many Irish problems, and the scope of their classical knowledge has doubtless been exaggerated at times. The controversy tends to turn on the rather subjective question of whether Columban's familiarity with classical poetry, evidenced for instance in his *Carmen ad Fedolium*, was acquired at home or on the continent. The negative view has recently been put by E. Coccia, 'La cultura irlandese precarolina—miraculo o mito?', *Studi medievali*, 3rd ser. 8 (1967), 257–420. For a judicious defence of Irish classical culture see L. Bieler, 'The classics in Celtic Ireland', *Classical influences on European culture A.D. 500-1500*, ed. R. R. Bolgar, Cambridge 1971, pp. 45–9. The works of Columban have been recently edited by G. S. M. Walker, *Sancti Columbani opera* (Script. Lat. Hiberniae, vol. 2), Dublin 1957, who however makes some exaggerated statements about classical culture in Ireland: see the review by M. Esposito, *C&M* 21 (1960), 184–203. There are two valuable articles on the scholarly activity of the Irish by B. Bischoff, 'Il monachesimo irlandese nei suoi rapporti col continente', *Settimane di studio del Centro italiano di studi sull' alto medioevo*, 4 (Spoleto 1957), 121–38, and 'Wendepunkte in der Geschichte der lateinischen Exegese im Frühmittelalter', *Sacris Erudiri, Jaarboek voor Godsdienstwetenschappen*, 6 (1954), 189–279; both are reprinted in *Mittelalterliche Studien*, vol. 1, pp. 195–205, 205–73. For a handsome introduction to early Irish culture, see L. Bieler, *Irland, Wegbereiter des Mittelalters*, Olten etc. 1961 (English edition, *Ireland, Harbinger of the Middle Ages*, Oxford–London 1963).

For a survey of the books known to the English scholars of this period, see J. D. A. Ogilvy, *Books known to the English* (Mediaeval Academy of America Publications, no. 76), Cambridge, Mass., 1967. Bede's classical sources are thoroughly studied by M. L. W. Laistner, 'Bede as a classical and a patristic scholar', *Tr. Royal Hist. Soc.*, 4th ser. 16 (1933), 69–94, and 'The library of the Venerable Bede', in *Bede: his life, times, and writings*, ed. A. H. Thompson, Oxford 1935, pp. 237–66; both are reprinted in his collected essays, *The intellectual heritage of the early Middle Ages*, ed. Chester G. Starr, Ithaca, N.Y., 1957, pp. 93–116, 117–49. On Bede see also R. W. Southern, *Medieval humanism and other studies*, Oxford 1970, pp. 1–8.

Alcuin's lines on the contents of the library at York are to be found in his *Versus de sanctis Euboricensis Ecclesiae*, 1535ff., ed. E. Dümmler, *MGH, Poetae latini aevi Carolini*, vol. 1, Berlin 1880–1, pp. 203–4.

III

W. Levison's *England and the continent in the eighth century*, Oxford 1946, remains the authoritative work on the missionary activity of the Anglo-Saxons: see especially pp. 132–73.

We owe the brilliant identification of Virgil of Salzburg as the author of the *Cosmographia* to H. Löwe, *Ein literarischer Widersacher des Bonifatius, Virgil von Salzburg und die Kosmographie des Aethicus Ister* (*Abhandl. der Akad. der Wissenschaften und der Literatur in Mainz*, 11), 1955. For further details about the tradition of Pomponius Mela see p. 94 and the notes to VIII.

IV

One of the difficulties of assessing the part played by the Irish and the English in the transmission of classical texts is the imprecise nature of the term 'insular tradition'. This may be postulated in a variety of circumstances: when one or more manuscripts of a text were actually written in Britain, or written in insular script on the continent, or associated with some Irish or Anglo-Saxon foundation, or showing traces, more or less conjectural, that a lost exemplar belonged to one of these categories. The route which the flow of cultural life followed from Italy to Britain and then back again to the continent is very much the *romantische Strasse* for the transmission of texts and it can be dramatically documented for some biblical traditions, as in the case of the Fulda and Echternach Gospels and, still more clearly, the codex Amiatinus (Laur. Amiat. 1) where the part played by England in the story is beyond doubt. This great Bible was written at Wearmouth or Jarrow as part of Ceolfrid's project to produce three pandects of the Bible and was almost certainly used by Bede himself, but much of its decoration was modelled on that of the lost *codex grandior* of Cassiodorus, written at Vivarium and brought from Rome to Northumbria by Ceolfrid as one of the fruits of his journey with Benedict Biscop in 678; he was taking the Amiatinus to Rome, as a present for the pope, when he died at Langres in 716 (cf. R. L. S. Bruce-Mitford, *Journal of the British Archaeological Association*, 3rd ser. 32 (1969), 1–25). Unfortunately, it is not easy to substantiate such romantic journeys for classical texts and some of the hastily posited insular traditions once fashionable have evaporated, such as the insular pre-archetype of Lucretius, a text which does not appear to have reached England before the late fifteenth century.

For the manuscripts of Pliny, Justinus, and Servius, see *CLA* X.1578, IX.1370, *Suppl.* 1806.

V

The educational aims of Charlemagne are fully and explicitly set out in the mandate which he sent to Baugulf, abbot of Fulda, between 794 and 800. This document has been edited and fully discussed by L.

Wallach in *Speculum*, 26 (1951), 288–305, reprinted in his *Alcuin and Charlemagne*, Ithaca, N.Y., 1959, rev. ed. 1967, pp. 198–226. Of particular interest is Wallach's demonstration, from the thought and style of the mandate, that Alcuin had taken a hand in its composition. For the educational role of the Palace School, see F. Brunhölzl, 'Der Bildungsauftrag der Hofschule', in *Karl der Grosse, Lebenswerk und Nachleben*, vol. 2, *Das geistige Leben*, ed. B. Bischoff, Düsseldorf 1965, pp. 28–41.

VI

This brief account of the history of the national hands and the development of Caroline minuscule, complex and at points controversial, has been simplified to accord with the scope and nature of this volume. For the Beneventan manuscripts, which are of most interest to classical scholars, see E. A. Lowe, *The Beneventan script*, Oxford 1914, and 'A new list of Beneventan manuscripts', *Collectanea Vaticana in honorem Anselmi M. Card. Albareda*, vol. 2, Vatican 1962 (Studi e Testi, 220), pp. 211–44. The introductory matter from both of these has been reprinted in *Palaeographial papers*, vol. 1, pp. 70–91, and vol. 2, pp. 477–9. S. Prete (*Observations on the history of textual criticism in the medieval and Renaissance periods*, Collegeville, Minn., 1971, p. 16 n. 46) has drawn attention to two Visigothic manuscripts of classical authors. There appear to be at least three: a ninth-century manuscript of Ausonius, actually written by Spanish emigrants at Lyons (Leiden, Voss. lat. F. 111), an eleventh-century Terence (Madrid Vitr. 5.4), and a Lucan of the late eleventh or early twelfth century (Vat. Ottob. lat. 1210 + Vat. Pal. lat. 869). The possibility of lost exemplars in pre-Caroline minuscule may have been underplayed: for another view see S. Timpanaro, *Maia*, 22 (1970), 288.

VII

For the key to the Palace Library see B. Bischoff, 'Die Hofbibliothek Karls des Grossen', in *Karl der Grosse*, pp. 42–62. It is noteworthy that the compiler of the book-list, an Italian, was interested in jotting down the titles of only the classical books in the collection. For Hadoard and the Corbie manuscripts, see B. Bischoff, 'Hadoardus and the manuscripts of classical authors from Corbie', *Didaskaliae. Studies in honor of Anselm M. Albareda*, ed. S. Prete, New York 1961, pp. 41–57, reprinted (in German) in *Mittelalterliche Studien*, vol. 1, pp. 49–63.

The survey of the classical books in Carolingian libraries is mainly derived from such catalogues as survive or deduced from the manuscript traditions of the individual texts concerned. The information from the catalogues, though in places out of date, is conveniently assembled in M. Manitius, *Handschriften antiker Autoren in mittelalterlichen Bibliothekskatalogen* (Zentralblatt für Bibliothekswesen, Beiheft 67), Leipzig 1935. See also B. Bischoff, 'Panorama der Handschriftenüberlieferung aus der Zeit Karls des Grossen', *Karl der Grosse*, vol. 2, pp. 233–54.

VIII

The true identity of the 'Saxon' corrector, which has teased generations, was finally revealed by B. Bischoff in the catalogue to the 1965 Charlemagne Exhibition at Aachen: cf. *Karl der Grosse, Werk und Wirkung*, Aachen 1965 (= *Charlemagne, œuvre, rayonnement et survivances*, Aixla-Chapelle 1965), pp. 202–3. For further information on Dungal, see Bischoff, 'Die Bibliothek im Dienste der Schule', *Settimane di studio del Centro italiano di studi sull' alto medioevo*, 19 (Spoleto 1972), 410–12. For Hadoard, see the notes to VII; also C. H. Beeson, 'The Collectaneum of Hadoard', *CPh* 40 (1945), 201–22. Walafrid Strabo's scrapbook is identified and described by Bischoff in 'Eine Sammelhandschrift Walafrid Strabos (Cod. Sangall. 878)', *Aus der Welt des Buches, Festschrift Georg Leyh* (Zentralblatt für Bibliothekswesen, Beiheft 75), Leipzig 1950, pp. 30–48; this article is reprinted and enlarged in *Mittelalterliche Studien*, vol. 2, pp. 34–51, the addenda including the discovery of Walafrid's role in the Horace tradition. For the Seneca excerpt, see L. D. Reynolds, *The medieval tradition of Seneca's letters*, Oxford 1965, pp. 92–3 and Plate 1; for Columella, Å. Josephson, *Die Columella-Handschriften*, Uppsala 1955, pp. 39–41.

For a general study of Lupus see P. E. von Severus, *Lupus von Ferrières, Gestalt und Werk eines Vermittlers antiken Geistesgutes an das Mittelalter im 9. Jahrhundert*, Münster in Westf. 1940. C. H. Beeson has edited a facsimile of the manuscript of the *De oratore* written by Lupus: *Servatus Lupus as scribe and text critic* (Mediaeval Academy of America Publications, no. 4), Cambridge, Mass., 1930. For an up-to-date list of the other books which he has annotated or corrected see E. Pellegrin, 'Les Manuscrits de Loup de Ferrières', *BEC* 115 (1957), 5–31. His scholarly interests are vividly illustrated by his letters, edited by L. Levillain, 2 vols., Paris 1927–35. See also M. L. W. Laistner, *Thought and letters*, pp. 252ff.

For Theodulfus' Bible see G. Pasquali, *Storia della tradizione*, p. 155 n. 2.

We now have a good edition of Heiric's *florilegium*: R. Quadri, *I 'Collectanea' di Eirico di Auxerre* (Spicilegium Friburgense, 11), Fribourg 1966. The whole story of the transmission of the collection of texts which include Mela and Julius Paris, one of the most fascinating of all since it can be traced almost continuously from antiquity to the Renaissance, has been told by Gius. Billanovich, in 'Dall' antica Ravenna alle biblioteche umanistiche', *Annuario dell' Università Cattolica del S. Cuore-Milano*, 1955-7, pp. 71-107; an earlier version appeared in *Aevum*, 30 (1956), 319-53.

IX

For Ratherius and the text of Livy's first decade, see Gius. Billanovich, 'Dal Livio di Raterio (Laur. 63,19) al Livio del Petrarca (B.M. Harl. 2493)', *IMU* 2 (1959), 103-78. The early history of the Catullus tradition and Ratherius' part in it remains as puzzling as the epigram by Benvenuto Campesani (cf. p. 112) which should have thrown some light on it. For different views see B. L. Ullman, *Studi in onore di Luigi Castiglioni*, vol. 2, Florence 1960, pp. 1031f.; G. Billanovich, op. cit., pp. 164-5.

The fundamental article on the history of Livy's text, and in particular the third and fourth decades, is Gius. Billanovich, 'Petrarch and the textual tradition of Livy', *Journal of the Warburg and Courtauld Institutes*, 14 (1951), 137-208. For the early history of the fourth decade see pp. 183ff.; also A. H. McDonald, in the preface to the Oxford Text of Livy XXXI-XXXV (= vol. 5), pp. x ff.

The manuscript containing Ovid's *Ars amatoria* in early Welsh minuscule is a very remarkable book: R. W. Hunt, *Saint Dunstan's classbook from Glastonbury* (Umbrae Codicum Occidentalium, 4), Amsterdam 1961.

X

For Monte Cassino and its manuscripts see the notes to VI. On the whole, it seems to have kept its manuscripts to itself during the Middle Ages. With the exception of the *Dialogues* of Seneca, what one may call the 'Cassinese texts' did not begin to circulate until the Renaissance. A facsimile of the Tacitus was published by E. Rostagno, *Codices graeci et latini photographice depicti*, vol. 7, pars 2, Leiden 1902. It and the Apuleius have been discussed at length by Lowe: *CQ* 14 (1920), 150-5 (= *Palaeographical papers*, vol. 1, pp. 92-8), and *Casinensia*, Monte Cassino 1929, pp. 257-72 (= *P.P.* 1.289-302). For Seneca and Monte

Cassino, see L. D. Reynolds, *CQ* N.S. 18 (1968), 355–72; for Juvenal, J. G. Griffith, *Hermes*, 91 (1963), 104ff.

XI

For general accounts see C. H. Haskins, *The Renaissance of the twelfth century*, Cambridge, Mass., 1927: G. Paré, A. Brunet, P. Tremblay, *La Renaissance du douzième siècle*, Paris 1933; C. Brooke, *The twelfth century Renaissance*, London 1969. England is put into its context by R. W. Southern, 'The place of England in the twelfth century Renaissance', *Medieval Humanism and Other Studies*, Oxford 1970, pp. 158–180, which is based on an earlier paper printed in *History*, 45 (1960), 201–16. See also R. W. Hunt, 'The deposit of Latin classics in the twelfth-century renaissance', *Classical influences*, pp. 51–5. On John of Salisbury, H. Liebeschütz, *Mediaeval humanism in the life and writings of John of Salisbury*, London 1950; J. M. Martin, 'John of Salisbury and the classics', summarized in *HSCP* 73 (1969), 319–21; on William of Malmesbury, H. Farmer, 'William of Malmesbury's life and works', *Journal of Ecclesiastical History*, 13 (1962), 39–54.

The *florilegium Gallicum* has been discussed in relation to the classical texts it contains by B. L. Ullman in a series of articles in *Classical Philology*, 23–7 (1928–32); for a summary see the last, pp. 1–42. Also A. Gagnér, *Florilegium Gallicum*, Lund 1936. It was used by the author of another important twelfth-century *florilegium*, the *Moralium dogma philosophorum* (ed. J. Holmberg, Uppsala 1929), and in the thirteenth century by Vincent of Beauvais (cf. p. 102).

XII

The *Biblionomia* of Richard de Fournival was edited by L. Delisle, *Le Cabinet des manuscrits de la Bibliothèque nationale*, vol. 2, Paris 1874, pp. 518–35. For recent contributions to the subject of his library and its transmission to the Sorbonne, see: P. Glorieux, 'Études sur la "Biblionomia" de Richard de Fournival', *Recherches de Théologie ancienne et médiévale*, 30 (1963), 205–31; R. H. Rouse, 'The early library of the Sorbonne', *Scriptorium*, 21 (1967), 47–51, and 'The "A" text of Seneca's tragedies in the thirteenth century', *Revue d'Histoire des Textes*, 1 (1971), 93–121. A further and important article by Rouse is forthcoming in vol. 3 of the *Revue d'Histoire des Textes*. Valuable pioneering work was done by B. L. Ullman, who identified Fournival's Propertius with the extant Voss. lat. Q. 38 and established some links between his library and that of Corbie: cf. in particular 'The library of the Sorbonne in the fourteenth century', *The septicentennial celebration of the founding of the Sorbonne College in the University of Paris*, Chapel Hill, N.C., 1953, pp. 33–47, reprinted in *Studies in the Italian Renaissance*, Rome 1955, pp. 41–53. Ullman's identification of the Propertius has been confirmed by Rouse's researches and his discovery that a number of Fournival's books, including the Propertius and the Seneca, were written by the same scribe. Corbie is just twelve miles from Amiens and a likely source for some of his classical manuscripts, but the evidence is circumstantial: Rouse argues for Paris. Another interesting manuscript which belonged to Fournival is the oldest surviving copy of Aristippus' translation of the *Phaedo* (see p. 106); this is Paris lat. 16581, probably the parent of Petrarch's manuscript (cf. *Plato latinus*, vol. 2: *Phaedo*, ed. L. Minio-Paluello, London 1950, pp. xi f.).

The relevant Tibullus *florilegium* is Venice, Marc. Z.L. 497, of the eleventh century: cf. F. Newton, *TAPA* 93 (1962), 259ff. For the most recent comprehensive study of the manuscript tradition of Seneca's *Tragedies*, see R. H. Philp, *CQ* N.S. 18 (1968), 150–79; for the history of the A-text, Rouse, op. cit.

The medieval tradition of the *Dialogues* is discussed by L. D. Reynolds, *CQ* N.S. 18 (1968), 355–72. The early history of this text belongs entirely to Italy and is particularly interesting for that reason. The whole essential process, from the copying of the archetype through contamination and correction to the appearance of a vulgate, took place in Italy, in a period—between the end of the eleventh and the middle of the thirteenth century—in which such a lively interest in the classics has rarely been assumed.

The activities of the English friars have been illuminated and brought into focus by Beryl Smalley, *English friars and antiquity in the early fourteenth century*, Oxford 1960.

XIII

For the ninth-century translators see P. Lemerle, *Le Premier Humanisme byzantin*, pp. 13–16. He underestimates the possibility of some knowledge of Greek at Saint Gall; see L. Bieler's introduction to the facsimile of the Basle Psalter (MS. A.VII.3), published as vol. 5 of Umbrae Codicum Occidentalium, Amsterdam 1960, esp. p. xix.

Burgundio of Pisa is discussed by E. M. Buytaert in the preface to his edition of *St. John Damascene, de fide orthodoxa, versions of Burgundio and Cerbanus*, Saint Bonaventure 1955. James of Venice is dealt with by L. Minio-Paluello, *Traditio*, 8 (1952), 265–304.

Basic information on the twelfth-century translators and much else can be found in C. H. Haskins, *Studies in the history of medieval science*,

Cambridge, Mass., 1927², pp. 141–241. E. Grant, *Speculum*, 46 (1971), 656–79, casts serious doubt on the idea that Hero's *Pneumatica* were known in Latin as early as the twelfth century.

Grosseteste's copy of Pseudo-Dionysius was recognized by R. Barbour, *Bodleian Library Record*, 6 (1958), 401–16.

Moerbeke's activity can be studied in the various volumes of the *Aristoteles Latinus* series and a convenient résumé of the current state of knowledge is given by B. Schneider, *Die mittelalterlichen griechisch-lateinischen Uebersetzungen der Aristotelischen Rhetorik*, Berlin 1971, pp. 5–9. Moerbeke's translations were very popular; there are 98 surviving manuscripts of his *Rhetoric*, and Dante shows that he knew the work in this version.

In general medieval translations were made word for word, and a sign of their unidiomatic character is that from 1266 onwards Moerbeke felt impelled to reproduce the Greek definite article by using the French 'le'; the lack of an article in Latin had made it impossible to deal properly with many abstract expressions.

On matters related to this section two papers by B. Bischoff may be recommended: 'The study of foreign languages in the Middle Ages' (*Speculum*, 36 (1961), 209–24) and 'Das griechische Element in der abendländischen Bildung des Mittelalters' (*Byzantinische Zeitschrift*, 44 (1951), 27–55; both are now reprinted (the first in an enlarged form) in his *Mittelalterliche Studien*, vol. 2, pp. 227–45 and 246–75.

CHAPTER 4

I

The first important discussions of the origin of the term 'humanist' appeared almost simultaneously: P. O. Kristeller, 'Humanism and scholasticism in the Italian Renaissance', *Byzantion*, 17 (1944–5), 346–74, and A. Campana, 'The origin of the word "humanist"', *Journal of the Warburg and Courtauld Institutes*, 9 (1946), 60–73. For recent bibliography and further discussion, see R. Avesani, 'La professione dell' "umanista" nel cinquecento', *IMU* 13 (1970), 205–323.

The wider problem of the origin of Italian humanism and its place in the context of the Renaissance is beyond the competence of this book, but some of the more general studies which have influenced the shape of this chapter may be conveniently mentioned here: P. O. Kristeller, various essays and lectures collected together in *Studies in Renaissance thought and letters*, Rome 1956, and *Renaissance thought*, vols. 1–2, New York 1961–5; Kenneth M. Setton, 'The Byzantine

NOTES 235

background to the Italian Renaissance', *Proc. Amer. Philosoph. Soc.* 100 (1956), 1–76; F. Simone, *Il Rinascimento francese*, Turin 1961 (updated English version by H. Gaston Hall, *The French Renaissance*, London 1969); Beryl Smalley, *English friars*, pp. 280–98; B. L. Ullman, *Studies in the Italian Renaissance*, Rome 1955; R. Weiss, *The dawn of humanism in Italy*, London 1947, *The spread of Italian humanism*, London 1964, and *The Renaissance discovery of classical antiquity*, Oxford 1969.

Though in many respects out of date, the fundamental works on the rediscovery of classical texts remain those of R. Sabbadini: *Le scoperte dei codici latini e greci ne' secoli xiv e xv*, 2 vols., Florence 1905–14, reprinted with author's additions and corrections and an appreciation by E. Garin, Florence 1967; *Storia e critica di testi latini*, Catania 1914, of which a second edition has now been produced (Medioevo e Umanesimo, no. 11, Padua 1971) with new indexes and a full bibliography of Sabbadini's works.

II

The first real indication of the strength of Paduan prehumanism was given by Gius. Billanovich in *I primi umanisti e le tradizioni dei classici latini*, Fribourg 1953. The evidence for the wide knowledge of Latin poetry shown by members of this circle is set out by Guido Billanovich, '*Veterum vestigia vatum*', *IMU* 1 (1958), 155–243. Their poetry is still not properly edited or easily accessible; for a bibliography see Guido Billanovich, ibid., p. 181. Mussato's *Ecerinide* was edited by L. Padrin, Bologna 1900, and texts pertaining to the study of Seneca's *Tragedies* at Padua have been edited, with full discussion of this topic, by A. Kh. Megas, Ὁ προουμανιστικὸς κύκλος τῆς Πάδουας (Lovato Lovati– Albertino Mussato) καὶ οἱ τραγῳδίες τοῦ L. A. Seneca, Thessalonica 1967 (English summary, pp. 229–33). For a good account of Lovato, see R. Weiss, *Italian Studies*, 6 (1951), 3–28. Geremia da Montagnone is dealt with by Weiss, *Il primo secolo dell' umanesimo*, Rome 1949, pp. 15–20, and Ullman, 'Hieremias de Montagnone and his citations from Catullus', *CPh* 5 (1910), 66–82, reprinted in *Studies*, pp. 81–115. For Benvenuto Campesani, see Weiss, *Bollettino del Museo Civico di Padova*, 44 (1955), 129–44.

III

The study of Petrarch's manuscripts and his work on the text of classical authors is proceeding at such a pace and covers so much ground that it was necessary to be very selective in this section and concentrate on the most important examples. For Petrarch's contribution to the tradition of Livy and Mela, see the articles by Giuseppe Billanovich cited on p. 231; for Propertius, B. L. Ullman, 'The manuscripts of Propertius', *CPh* 6 (1911), 282–301, *Studies*, pp. 181–92. Good discussions of Petrarch's list of favourite books are provided by Ullman, 'Petrarch's favourite books', *TAPA* 54 (1923), 21–38 (reprinted in *Studies*, pp. 117–37), and H. Rüdiger, in *Geschichte der Textüberlieferung*, 1. 526–37; it was Ullman who first demonstrated the precise significance of the list. A. Petrucci, *La scrittura di Francesco Petrarca* (Studi e Testi, 248), Vatican 1967, provides a list of Petrarchan manuscripts and a most useful bibliography. The pioneering work of P. de Nolhac, *Pétrarque et l'humanisme*, 2nd ed., vols. 1–2, Paris 1907, should not be forgotten, though inevitably out of date in many respects.

The importance of Avignon emerges from the study of any text which passed through it. The significance of its role in channelling manuscripts to Italy was pointed out by Ullman in 1941 (*Philological Quarterly*, 20 (1941), 213–17 = *Studies*, pp. 29–33) and recent studies of individual texts have dramatically substantiated his theory. For broader discussions of Avignon as a cultural centre, see F. Simone, *Il Rinascimento*, pp. 9–24; W. Braxton Ross, 'Giovanni Colonna, historian at Avignon', *Speculum*, 45 (1970), 533–45.

Billanovich, *I primi umanisti*, pp. 29–33, deals with the rediscovery of the Monte Cassino manuscripts and Zanobi da Strada's part in it.

IV

We are fortunate in having a recent full-length study of Coluccio by B. L. Ullman: *The humanism of Coluccio Salutati* (Medioevo e Umanesimo, no. 4), Padua 1963. His book on *The origin and development of the humanistic script*, Rome 1960, should also be consulted.

V

The fantastic tale of Poggio's discoveries is still best followed in Sabbadini, though the details need to be checked against recent work on the individual texts concerned. See also A. C. Clark, *Inventa Italorum* (Anecdota Oxoniensia, Classical Series, Part 11), Oxford 1909. Poggio's expedition to Cluny in the spring of 1415 remains dubious: cf. T. Foffano, *IMU* 12 (1969), 113–28. The works by Ullman cited in the preceding section contain important material, particularly on Poggio's contribution to the development of the new script, and manuscripts in Poggio's hand continue to turn up. One of the most important recent identifications was that of Poggio's autograph copy (Vat. lat. 11458) of the eight Cicero speeches which he found in 1417, made by A. Campana: cf. *Codices Vaticani Latini*, vol. 8 (1959), pp. 93ff. The detailed work of C. Questa on Poggio's contribution to the textual tradition of the twelve plays of Plautus permits some assessment of his philological ability: *Per la storia del testo di Plauto nell' umanesimo* 1: *La 'recensio' di Poggio Bracciolini*, Rome 1968. The standard biography is that of E. Walser, *Poggius Florentinus: Leben und Werke*, Leipzig 1914; a new one is needed.

The discovery that the best copy of the lost vetus Cluniacensis is the handiwork of Nicholas of Clémanges was made by Gilbert Ouy (cf. *Annuaire de l'école pratique des hautes études* (IVe Section. Sciences hist. et philol.), 1965–6, 259); his work on the manuscripts of Nicholas of Clémanges has still to be published.

The traditional view that the humanists did not possess a complete text of Quintilian until Poggio's discovery of the Saint Gall manuscript (now Zürich, Stadtbibl. 288) in 1416 is not invalidated, as some have thought, by Sabbadini's attempt to prove that Nicholas of Clémanges possessed the whole text (*Le scoperte*, 2. pp. 84–5; *Storia*, pp. 283–4). Nicholas could indeed have found a complete Quintilian north of the Alps, had he looked in the right places, but the evidence adduced by Sabbadini does not prove more than that he had access, as did other early humanists, to a *mutilus* plus the excerpt from book 10 (1.46–107) which circulated separately or in conjunction with the incomplete text: cf. P. S. Boscoff, *Speculum*, 27 (1952), 71ff.; M. Winterbottom, *CQ* N.S. 17 (1967), 339 n. 5. But startling evidence that there was a complete Quintilian in Italy as early as the first half of the fourteenth century is provided by Winterbottom, *Problems in Quintilian, Bulletin of the Institute of Classical Studies*, Supplement 25 (London 1970), pp. 20–1.

The evidence for the survival of the Murbach Velleius into August 1786 was published by A. Allgeier in *Miscellanea Mercati*, 6 (Studi e Testi, 126,) 1946, 457ff.

VI

E. J. Kenney has written a penetrating article on the limitations of humanist philology and the problems of its assessment: 'The character of humanist philology', *Classical influences*, ed. Bolgar, pp. 119–28.

We now have a detailed study of the building up of one of the richest and most influential of the Renaissance libraries: B. L. Ullman and P. A. Stadter, *The public library of Renaissance Florence: Niccolò Niccoli, Cosimo de' Medici and the Library of San Marco* (Medioevo e Umanesimo, no. 10,) Padua 1972.

The *Opera omnia* of Valla have been reprinted with a preface by
E. Garin and other material, 2 vols., Turin 1962. A different recension
of his *Adnotationes in Novum Testamentum* from that printed by
Erasmus has been discovered and edited by A. Perosa, Florence 1970.
Good examples of his work on Latin texts are provided by Livy and
Quintilian. For Livy see Gius. Billanovich, *Journal of the Warburg and
Courtauld Institutes*, 14 (1951), 137ff., *IMU* 1 (1958), 245–64 (with
M. Ferraris) and 265–75; for Quintilian, M. Winterbottom, *CQ* N.S. 17
(1967), 356ff.

A good idea of the range of Politian's activities is given by the
catalogue of an exhibition held at the Biblioteca Laurenziana in 1954
(*Mostra del Poliziano*, a cura di A. Perosa, Florence 1955). See also
Il Poliziano e il suo tempo, *Atti del IV convegno internazionale di studi
sul Rinascimento*, Florence 1957; I. Maier, *Les Manuscrits d'Ange
Politien* (Travaux d'humanisme et Renaissance, no. 70), Geneva 1965.
The Greek epigrams were edited by A. Ardizzoni, Florence 1951; the
Miscellanea will be edited with an important commentary by A. Perosa
in the near future. The recently discovered Centuria has now been
published as *Angelo Poliziano, Miscellaneorum Centuria Secunda*, ed.
critica per cura di V. Branca–M. Pastore Stocchi, vols. 1–4, Florence
1972. On his contribution to the development of the stemmatic method,
see S. Timpanaro, *La genesi del metodo del Lachmann*, Florence 1963,
especially pp. 4–6. Whether Politian used the Vaticanus of Valerius
Flaccus and the lost copy of Statius' *Silvae* is disputed and depends
very much on one's opinion of his accuracy as a collator. For two views
on the former question see W. Wolfgang Ehlers, *Untersuchungen zur
handschriftlichen Überlieferung der Argonautica des C. Valerius Flaccus*
(Zetemata 52), Munich 1970, pp. 102ff., E. Courtney, *CR.* N.S. 22
(1972), 216f.; for the latter, M. Pastore Stocchi, 'Sulle *curae statianae*
del Poliziano', *Atti del Istituto Veneto, Classe di scienze morali*, 125
(1966–7), 39–74.

VII

The primary sources for this section, together with an extensive discussion, will be found in A. Pertusi, *Leonzio Pilato fra Petrarca e
Boccaccio*, Venice–Rome 1964 (pp. 62ff. deal with his copy of Homer).
F. Di Benedetto, 'Leonzio, Omero e le "Pandette" ', *IMU* 12 (1969),
53–112, has shown that Leonzio Pilato owned the Florentine Pandects
and translated into Latin the Greek quotations of the *Digest*. Petrarch's
copy of Plato has been identified as Paris gr. 1807 by A. Diller, *CP*
59 (1964), 270–2.

For Chrysoloras see G. Cammelli, *Manuele Crisolora*, Florence 1941. The way that most humanists had to learn Greek is made clear by R. Sabbadini, *Il metodo degli umanisti*, Florence 1922, pp. 17–27, who cites a letter of Ambrogio Traversari about his own experience and a latter of Aldus to Alberto Pio referring to the use of these methods by Ermolao Barbaro, Pico della Mirandola, and Politian. G. Cammelli, *Demetrio Calcondila*, Florence 1954, p. 7, quotes a letter of Giovanni Antonio Campano in which he complains that he has not yet been able to learn Greek for want of a tutor.

On the discovery of manuscripts in general see R. Sabbadini, *Le scoperte dei codici latini e greci ne' secoli xiv e xv*, reprinted with additions, Florence 1967.

VIII

A short and up-to-date account of Bessarion is given by L. Labowsky in the *Dizionario biografico degli Italiani*. The fundamental work is L. Mohler, *Kardinal Bessarion als Theologe, Humanist und Staatsmann*, Paderborn 1923–42; in the third volume, sub-titled *Aus Bessarions Gelehrtenkreis*, pp. 70–87, will be found the pamphlet expounding his views on the status of the Vulgate translation. His palaeographical researches are outlined in his letter to Alexios Lascaris Philanthropenos. See also J. Gill, *The council of Florence*, Cambridge 1959. To mark the quincentenary of his donation to Venice an exhibition was mounted; the catalogue, which contains also a text of his act of donation, was published as *Cento codici Bessarionei*, a cura di T. G. Leporace e E. Mioni, Venice 1968.

For Valla's *Adnotationes* see the edition by A. Perosa cited above (VI) and in particular p. xxxiv n. 64.

The relevant bibliography on Politian has been given in the notes to section VI.

IX

The authorities on the early printing of Greek are R. Proctor, *The printing of Greek in the 15th century*, Oxford 1900, reprinted 1966, and V. Scholderer, *Greek printing types 1465–1927*, London 1927; see also a paper by the latter on 'Printers and readers in Italy in the fifteenth century', *Proc. Brit. Acad.* 35 (1949), 1–23. The great reduction in book prices brought about by the new invention is made clear by Giovanni Andrea De Bussi, bishop of Aleria, in his preface to the Rome edition of Saint Jerome's letters printed in 1468; he says (fol. 1ᵛ) that books are now available at one fifth of the price that they used to

command. But this boast naturally applied to Latin and vernacular
texts only. Knowledge of Greek remained for some time a rarity; one
may wonder if the frequent tags and quotations of it in the writings of
Erasmus, who could count on a very wide readership, imply that the
situation had changed for the better in the first two or three decades of
the sixteenth century.

On Aldus and Musurus one may consult D. J. Geanakoplos, *Greek
scholars in Venice*, Cambridge, Mass., 1962, reprinted 1973 with the
title *Byzantium and the Renaissance*. It does not, however, discuss the
scholarship of either man in sufficient detail to permit us to form an
estimate of their capacities as textual critics, and here further research
is required. The favourable judgement on Musurus' edition of Hesychius comes from K. Latte's edition, vol. 1, Copenhagen 1953,
p. xxxiii; the addition to the text of Moschus is dealt with by W. Bühler
in his edition (Hermes Einzelschriften 13), Wiesbaden 1960, p. 14;
fresh light was thrown on the Aristophanes scholia by N. G. Wilson,
CQ 12 (1962), 32–47 (Musurus' contribution is less substantial than
was once believed).

For the history of the Marciana library, which was very badly
housed and difficult of access for more than half a century after
Bessarion's donation, see J. Valentinelli, *Bibliotheca manuscripta ad
S. Marci Venetiarum, Codd. Mss. Latini*, vol. 1, Venice 1868, pp. 10–55.

X

Erasmus' classical scholarship has not been the subject of a properly
informed study; one must await the publication of the next volume of
Professor Pfeiffer's *History of classical scholarship*. In the meantime
one may refer to his paper in *Historisches Jahrbuch*, 74 (1955), 175–88
(= *Ausgewählte Schriften*, Munich 1960, pp. 218–21): this deals with
Erasmus' concept of the relation between classical and theological
scholarship. Pfeiffer cites a revealing aphorism: incorrect punctuation,
a tiny detail in itself, is enough to give rise to heresy (*tantula res gignit
haereticum sensum*). P. S. Allen, *Proc. Brit. Acad.* 11 (1924), 349–68,
argues that Erasmus' chief services to learning were in editing patristic
texts, mainly of Latin Fathers (his attempts to assemble material for an
edition of Chrysostom never made enough progress for printing to
begin). See also the essay of M. M. Phillips in *Erasmus*, ed. T. A.
Dorey, London 1970, pp. 1–30.

For the preparation of the Alcalá Bible and Erasmus' New Testament see the summary in B. M. Metzger, *Text of the N.T.*, pp. 96–103.
Erasmus' use of manuscripts for his edition and its subsequent revised

impressions has to be worked out from various sources, including his letters and passing remarks in his commentaries on the New Testament (the idea of a systematic exposition of the manuscripts used for an edition is relatively modern). The facts stated in the text depend on P. S. Allen's introduction to letter 373 in vol. 2 of *Opus epistolarum Desiderii Erasmi Roterodami*, Oxford 1906–54, pp. 164–6. Allen's account seems to be reliable, with the possible exception of his statement about the Leicester codex. With regard to the Vatican codex B (Vat. gr. 1209), Erasmus had learned of its existence in 1521, and when he was reminded of its importance some years later by the Spanish humanist and theologian Sepúlveda he failed to respond as he should have done. In his reply to Sepúlveda he suggested that a Greek manuscript which supported some readings of the Vulgate had probably been tampered with, not realizing that the great age of B made this relatively implausible; and he advanced the exaggerated but not entirely unreasonable proposition that the only way to be sure of recovering the original Greek was to go back to the text as cited by patristic authorities of the third, fourth, and fifth centuries (letter 2905, written in 1534).

A good way of approaching the *Adagia* is to read M. M. Phillips, *The 'Adages' of Erasmus*, Cambridge 1964; on pp. 65–9 there is an account of the polemic arising from Erasmus' stay in Aldus' house. His stay is also described by D. J. Geanakoplos, *Greek Scholars in Venice*; see especially pp. 273–5 for the question of the so-called Erasmian pronunciation of Greek.

For further orientation and bibliography, P. Petitmengin, 'Comment étudier l'activité d'Érasme éditeur de textes antiques', *Colloquia Erasmiana Turonensia*, vol. 1 (Paris 1972), pp. 217–22. See also E. Bloch, 'Erasmus and the Froben Press: the making of an editor', *Library Quarterly*, 35 (1965), 109–120.

On Seneca, L. D. Reynolds, *The Medieval Tradition of Seneca's Letters*, Oxford 1965, pp. 4–6, W. Trillitzsch, *Philologus*, 109 (1965), 270–93, M. M. Phillips, op. cit., 15–17.

CHAPTER 5

I

Erasmus' *Ciceronianus* has been edited with substantial prolegomena by A. Gambaro, Brescia 1965. He discusses the history of the controversy, but it is also worth consulting '*Attic' and baroque prose style: the anti-Ciceronian movement*, essays by Morris W. Croll, edited by Patrick-Evans-Wallace, Princeton, N.J., 1966 (paperback 1969). For the

Estienne family see especially E. Armstrong, *Robert Estienne, royal printer*, Cambridge 1954. Vettori's work on the Latin Aristotle is discussed by B. Schneider, *Die mittelalterlichen griechisch-lateinischen Uebersetzungen der Aristotelischen Rhetorik*, Berlin 1971, pp. 73–6. Robortello's scholarship has been discussed by A. Carlini, 'L'attività filologica di Francesco Robortello', *Atti dell' Accademia di Udine*, 7 (1967), 36ff. On Fulvio Orsini the standard work is still P. de Nolhac, *La Bibliothèque de Fulvio Orsini* (Bibl. de l'École des Hautes Études, 74), Paris 1887. For the Vatican edition of Saint Augustine see P. Petitmengin, 'Le Saint Augustin de la typographie vaticane', *Recherches augustiniennes*, 4 (1966), 199–251. For Thomas James see N. R. Ker, 'Thomas James' collation of Gregory, Cyprian and Ambrose', *Bodleian Library Record*, 4 (1952), 16–32.

II

For the progress of studies on early French humanism one may consult, in addition to F. Simone, *Il Rinascimento francese*, and other works mentioned in the notes to the previous chapter: *Humanism in France at the end of the Middle Ages and in the early Renaissance*, ed. A. H. T. Levi, Manchester 1970; E. Ornato, *Jean Muret et ses amis Nicolas de Clamanges et Jean de Montreuil*, Geneva 1969.

Short accounts of Budé are provided by L. Delaruelle, *Guillaume Budé: les origines, les débuts, les idées maîtresses*, Paris 1907; J. Plattard, *Guillaume Budé et les origines de l'humanisme français*, Paris 1966. See also R. R. Bolgar, 'Humanism as a value system with reference to Budé and Vives', *Humanism in France*, pp. 199–215, and the Catalogue of the Budé Exhibition, *VIIIᵉ Congrès international Guillaume Budé*, Paris 1968.

There are not as many recent studies of individual French scholars of this period as one would wish. An exception is V. Hall, *Life of Julius Caesar Scaliger* (1484–1558) (*Trans. Amer. Philosoph. Soc.*, N.S. 40, Part 2), Philadelphia, Pa., 1950, and Mark Pattison's classic *Isaac Casaubon* (2nd ed., Oxford 1892) retains its value. For a brilliant demonstration that Julius Caesar Scaliger was plain Giulio Bordon, see M. Billanovich, 'Benedetto Bordon e Giulio Cesare Scaligero', *IMU* 11 (1968), 187–256.

For Turnebus's manuscript of Plautus, see W. M. Lindsay, *The codex Turnebi of Plautus*, Oxford 1898. The significance of Joseph Scaliger's work on Catullus has been pointed out by Timpanaro, *La genesi del metodo*, pp. 9–10.

III

The study of the scholarship of the Netherlands is facilitated by some good articles in the *Biographie Nationale*, published by the Académie Royale des Sciences et des Lettres et des Beaux-Arts de Belgique (1866–1944, with later Supplements). Isaac Vossius qualifies for an entry in the *Dictionary of National Biography*. Also useful are L. Müller, *Geschichte der klassischen Philologie in den Niederlanden*, Leipzig 1869; G. Cohen, *Écrivains français en Hollande dans la première moitié du XVIIᵉ siècle*, Paris 1920.

It is not surprising, in view of the amount of time and effort expended on editing texts and producing critical miscellanea, that there should be a market for theoretical studies of textual criticism. Canter, who had been anticipated by Robortello, was succeeded in 1597 by a German scholar, Caspar Schoppe, whose *De arte critica* did for Latin texts what Canter had done for Greek; it also attempts a brief history of textual criticism by reviewing critics ancient and modern. Exactly a century later appeared the first edition of the more ambitious *Ars critica* of Jean Le Clerc.

Modius' search for manuscripts has been fully documented and discussed by P. Lehmann, *Franciscus Modius als Handschriftenforscher* (Quellen und Untersuchungen zur lateinischen Philologie des Mittelalters, 3.1), Munich 1908.

For two recent views on the Blandinius of Horace, see Pasquali, *Storia della tradizione*, pp. 381ff.; E. Fraenkel, *Horace*, Oxford 1957, pp. 97ff.

Lipsius' methods have been studied by J. Ruysschaert, *Juste Lipse et les Annales de Tacite: une méthode de critique textuelle au XVIᵉ siècle*, Louvain 1949. His work on Tacitus is assessed critically by C. O. Brink, 'Justus Lipsius and the text of Tacitus', *JRS* 41 (1951), 32–51; F. R. D. Goodyear, *The Annals of Tacitus*, vol. 1, Cambridge 1972, pp. 8–10.

N. Heinsius collated manuscripts of Ovid on such a scale that their identification and evaluation have been slow, despite the fact that the Heinsius material is available in Oxford and Berlin and that the manuscripts he used are still extant. The latest contributions of importance are H. Boese, 'Zu den Ovidkollationen des N. Heinsius', *Philologus*, 106 (1962), 155–73; F. W. Lenz, 'Die Wiedergewinnung der von Heinsius benutzten Ovidhandschriften II', *Eranos*, 61 (1963), 98–120. An article by M. D. Reeve is forthcoming (*RhM* 1974).

IV

Bentley is treated at considerable length here because of his position in both classical and biblical studies, and it did not seem possible to do justice to him without giving some details of his life and work. Sir R. C. Jebb, *Bentley*, London 1882, is a lively and entertaining account with bibliography. *The Epistola ad Joannem Millium* has been reprinted with an introduction by G. P. Goold, Toronto 1962 (note that the date of Malalas is incorrectly given as the eighth or ninth century).

The history of biblical scholarship is set out by B. Metzger, *The text of the New Testament*, pp. 95ff., but we have given here rather more detail of Bentley's *Proposals* and taken a different view of the importance of Richard Simon; on him one may consult the study of Jean Steinmann, *Richard Simon et les origines de l'exégèse biblique*, Desclée de Brouwer 1960, but there too the important details are not always fully brought out. The facts recounted in the text are drawn from chapters 29–33 of his *Histoire critique*, principally from 29.

V

For a convenient sketch of the history of palaeography one may consult L. Traube, *Geschichte der Paläographie*, printed in vol. 1 of his *Vorlesungen und Abhandlungen*, Munich 1909, pp. 13–80. David Knowles, *Great historical enterprises: problems in monastic history*, London 1963, pp. 33–62, gives an attractive short account of the achievements of the Maurists in scholarship, without giving quite as much detail as one might wish about palaeography. His essay on the Bollandists, ibid., pp. 1–32, should also be consulted for the life and work of van Papenbroeck; he was one of the continuators of Jean Bolland's great project for a comprehensive edition of the lives of the saints, *Acta Sanctorum*; an impressive series of volumes has been, and is still being, produced by a small team of Jesuits in Belgium, who despite some interruptions due to wars and revolutions have maintained an astonishing academic tradition over the centuries. See further P. Peeters, *L'œuvre des Bollandistes*, 2nd ed., Brussels 1961.

Traube and Knowles give all the essential guidance for further reading about the Maurists and Maffei. But on the latter one may also refer to an essay by A. Momigliano, 'Mabillon's Italian disciples', in *Terzo contributo alla storia degli studi classici e del mondo antico*, Rome 1966, pp. 135–52. Maffei's letters, in addition to the works mentioned by Traube, contain some statements about palaeography; see nos. 158 and 160 in the *Epistolario*, ed. C. Garibotto, Milan 1955, pp. 199–201, 203–4.

VI

(a) The first comprehensive account of Latin palimpsests is that of E. Chatelain, 'Les Palimpsestes latins', *Annuaire, École pratique des hautes études, Section des sciences hist. et philol.* 1904 (published 1903), pp. 5–42. This has now been largely superseded by E. A. Lowe, '*Codices rescripti*: a list of Latin palimpsests with stray observations on their origin', *Mélanges Eugène Tisserant*, vol. 5, Vatican 1964 (Studi e Testi 235), 67–112, reprinted in *Palaeographical papers*, 2. 480–519. S. Timpanaro provides an excellent account of both Angelo Mai and the early history of palimpsest discovery in 'Angelo Mai', *Atene e Roma*, N.S. 1 (1956), 3–34. For the new palimpsest fragment of Fronto, still absent from all editions, see B. Bischoff, 'Der Fronto-Palimpsest der Mauriner', *Sitz. Bayer. Akad. der Wiss., Phil.-Hist. Kl.* (1958), p. 2. Further information can be sought in the editions of the texts concerned.

(b) On papyri in general see the works by E. G. Turner, cited above on Chapter 1 (I). It is also worthwhile to read Sir H. I. Bell, *Egypt from Alexander the Great to the Arab conquest*, Oxford 1948, which is still an excellent introduction from a cultural and historical point of view.

The codex containing Menander's *Dyscolus* has given us in addition a substantial proportion of his *Aspis* and *Samia* (edited by C. F. L. Austin, Berlin 1969); the fragments of the latter overlap to some extent with those already known, with the result that in these passages we possess two uncommonly early witnesses to the text of a classical author.

Literary papyri, including the very small number of Latin texts among them, are listed with a bibliography by R. A. Pack, *The Greek and Latin literary texts from Greco-Roman Egypt*, Ann Arbor, Mich., 1965. For statistics showing how the main authors are represented at various dates see W. H. Willis, *GRBS* 9 (1968), 205–41.

(c) A history of the Homeric Question is given by Adam Parry in the introduction to the collected papers of his father Milman Parry, *The making of Homeric verse*, Oxford 1971, pp. xiii–xv.

Leopardi's disappointing experience is recounted by S. Timpanaro in *Differenze*, 9 (*Studi in memoria di Carlo Ascheri*), Urbino 1970, pp. 357–79.

Heiberg's find of Archimedes was announced in *Hermes*, 42 (1907), 235ff. On Juvenal VI and Saint Cyprian see J. G. Griffith, *Hermes*, 91 (1963), 104–14. For the new letter of Saint Cyprian see also M. Bévenot, *The tradition of manuscripts: a study in the transmission of St. Cyprian's treatises*, Oxford 1961. The Epigrammata Bobiensia were edited by

A. Campana and F. Munari, Rome 1955. More recent still is the recovery, from a strip of parchment used for binding, of 39 mutilated
lines of Rutilius Namatianus: see M. Ferrari, 'Spigolature bobbiesi,
I: In margine ai *Codices Latini Antiquiores*, II: Frammenti ignoti di
Rutilio Namaziano', *IMU* 16 (1973), 1–31.

(d) Roberto Weiss, in *The Renaissance discovery of classical antiquity*,
Oxford 1969, traces the beginnings of an interest in the tangible remains of antiquity. For the impact of inscriptions on literary texts,
see the section 'Rapports avec la littérature' of the 'Bulletin epigra-
phique' of J. and L. Robert in the *Revue des études grecques*.

The *Res gestae* of Augustus, sometimes referred to as the *Monumen-
tum Ancyranum*, has been frequently edited and it will suffice to mention the editions of J. Gagé, Paris 1935, and P. A. Brunt–J. M. Moore,
Oxford 1967. The *Laudatio Turiae* has been edited with a translation
and commentary by M. Durry, *Éloge funèbre d'une matrone romaine*,
Paris 1950.

For the monument of Antiochus of Commagene and its importance
for the history of ancient prose style, see K. Humann and O. Puchstein,
Reisen in Kleinasien und Nordsyrien, Berlin 1890, and E. Norden, *Die
antike Kunstprosa*, 2nd ed., Leipzig–Berlin 1909, vol. 1, pp. 140ff.

Diogenes of Oenoanda has been recently re-edited and studied by
C. W. Chilton, *Diogenis Oenoandensis fragmenta*, Leipzig 1967; *Diogenes
of Oenoanda: The Fragments*, Oxford 1971. There is an important
article on the inscription by J. Irigoin, *Studi filologici e storici in onore di
Vittorio De Falco*, Naples 1971, pp. 477–85; and for recent progress in
the finding of new fragments, see M. F. Smith, *AJA* (1970), 51–62
and plates 11–16, ibid. (1971), 357–89 and plates 81–4.

For the early Christian hymn, see P. Maas, *Kleine Schriften*, Munich
1973, p. 315.

Pompeian graffiti have been collected and edited by E. Diehl,
Pompeianische Wandinschriften und Verwandtes, 2nd ed. (Kleine Texte
für Vorlesungen und Übungen 56), Berlin 1930. For the corpus of
epigraphic poetry, see the relevant parts of the *Anthologia latina* edited
by F. Bücheler and E. Lommatzsch, vols. 1–3, Leipzig 1930², 1897,
1926; E. Engström, *Carmina latina epigraphica*, Gothenburg 1911.
The occurrence of *arma virumque* on ancient walls is documented by
R. P. Hoogma, *Der Einfluss Vergils auf die Carmina Latina Epigraphica*,
Amsterdam 1959, pp. 222f. The text of Propertius 3.16.13f. is discussed by M. E. Hubbard in 'Propertiana', *CQ* N.S. 18 (1968), 318f.

CHAPTER 6

Our account of stemmatic theory and the history of its evolution depends on P. Maas, *Textual criticism*, Oxford 1958, and S. Timpanaro, *La genesi del metodo del Lachmann*, Florence 1963, revised and translated into German under the title *Die Entstehung der Lachmannschen Methode*, Hamburg 1971. Timpanaro's second and third appendices are also important explorations of areas of stemmatic theory. Maas' exposition is so brief as to verge on the obscure, and some of the finer points of stemmatic theory require a full statement in order to make latent assumptions explicit. Timpanaro, *Maia*, 23 (1970), 289, pointed to one such assumption in the fourth of the inferences from our hypothetical stemma on p. 191, where we have added a parenthesis to meet the case: the agreement of one of the MSS. XYZ with β indicates the reading of α, *provided that* the readings of the other two of the MSS. XYZ disagree with each other; if they agree, as can happen, the tradition has been affected by contamination or emendation. L. Canfora, *Belfagor*, 23 (1968) 361–4, has directed attention to some other obscurities in Maas's presentation of the theory.

Limitations of the stemmatic method were emphasized by G. Pasquali, *Storia della tradizione e critica del testo*, 2nd ed., Florence 1952, and they have been urged more recently, but perhaps too passionately, by R. D. Dawe, *The collation and investigation of manuscripts of Aeschylus*, Cambridge 1964. We have tried to make it clear in our text that controversy on this subject is largely misplaced. Maas knew as well as anyone else that there is no simple answer to the problems of a contaminated tradition, but some critics have failed to notice his explicit statement on the matter. Others, perhaps unduly impressed by the wealth of examples in Pasquali's rather discursive but deservedly famous book, most of which is devoted to unusual traditions, have assumed that contamination is the rule rather than the exception, and that consequently Maas's theory is of no practical use. We doubt whether Pasquali could have wished to create this impression, and it must be stressed that in many traditions the amount of contamination that has taken place is not sufficient to prevent the useful application of stemmatic theory. It may be worth adding here that an interesting *eliminatio codicum* has recently been performed in the stemma of Aristotle's *Rhetoric*, where the tradition is not entirely free from contamination; see R. Kassel, *Der Text der Aristotelischen Rhetorik*, Berlin 1971, pp. 54–5.

I

G. B. Alberti, *SIFC* 40 (1968), 44–60, has observed that the term 'open tradition' has come to be used in more than one sense. Pasquali's original use meant that judgement rather than the application of automatic rules was needed in order to infer the readings of the archetype, and in this sense the word can obviously be applied to traditions in which there is no single archetype.

The facts about Saint Cyprian and Juvenal VI have been commented on above in Chapter 5, section (VI) c.

The standard work on second editions in antiquity is H. Emonds, *Zweite Auflage im Altertum*, Leipzig 1941. For the question of author variants in the case of Longus, and for a recent bibliography of the whole subject, see M. D. Reeve, 'Author's variants in Longus?', *Proc. Camb. Philol. Soc.*, 195 (1969), 75–85 (with a reply by D. C. C. Young, ibid. 197 (1971), 99–107); for Ovid, add A. S. Hollis, *Ovid, Metamorphoses Book VIII*, Oxford 1970, pp. x–xi, xxvii. A most instructive discussion of the problems raised by indirect tradition is offered by S. Timpanaro, *Maia*, 22 (1970), 351–9.

The principle of *difficilior lectio* seems to have been first expressly formulated as a criterion by Jean Le Clerc (Clericus) in his *Ars Critica*, vol. 2, Amsterdam 1697, p. 389: cf. S. Timpanaro, *La genesi*, p. 21.

Two other critical principles which are useful from time to time may be briefly mentioned here. One is the so-called geographical criterion, which appears in two forms. The first of these involves the notion of survivals on the periphery of a culture, and is an application of a notion that has been fruitful in comparative philology: if there is agreement in striking variants between manuscripts written in two or more peripheral areas of a culture, these readings are probably survivals from a very ancient state of the text. It is not often that we are in a position to know enough about the place of origin of the manuscripts in question, especially if they are Greek, to apply this criterion. The other form of the geographical criterion was worked out by critics of the New Testament, by which one or more manuscripts are assigned to a region, whether peripheral or not, and reference is still frequently made to the Western, Caesarean, and Alexandrian text or family of manuscripts.

Another useful principle in the criticism of prose authors is Wettstein's canon *brevior lectio potior*. This too was devised because of the problems of editing the New Testament, and in particular because of the many additional phrases and sentences found in the Western text, represented notably by the codex Bezae. On both these principles one should consult B. M. Metzger, *The text of the New Testament*.

Valuable advice on dealing with contaminated traditions is given by M. L. West, *Textual criticism and editorial technique* (Stuttgart 1973), pp. 37–46. This book is intended to replace to a great extent both Paul Maas's *Textkritik* and O. Stählin's *Editionstechnik*, 2nd ed., Leipzig 1914.

For other methods of recension, see H. Quentin, *Mémoire sur l'établissement du texte de la Vulgate*, Rome 1922, *Essais de critique textuelle*, Paris 1926; W. W. Greg, *The calculus of variants*, Oxford 1927; A. A. Hill, 'Postulates for distributional study of texts', *Studies in Bibliography, Papers of the Bibliog. Soc. Univ. Virginia* 3 (1950–1), 63–95; V. A. Dearing, *A manual of textual analysis*, Berkeley 1959. The rapidly increasing number of publications on the use of computers in textual and related studies presents a problem in that much of it demands a measure of familiarity with current mathematical theory. But a representative picture of methods and progress in this field may be obtained from Dom J. Froger, *La Critique des textes et son automatisation*, Paris 1968; H. Love, 'The computer and literary editing: achievements and prospects', in *The computer in literary and linguistic research*, ed. R. A. Wisbey, Cambridge 1971, pp. 47–56; B. Fischer, 'The use of computers in New Testament studies, with special reference to textual criticism', *JTS* N.S. 21 (1970), 279–308; W. Ott, 'Computer applications in textual criticism', *The computer in literary studies*, ed. A. J. Aitken, R. W. Bailey, N. Hamilton-Smith, Edinburgh 1973, pp. 199–223. Two practical demonstrations of the application of the methods of numerical taxonomy to the classification of manuscripts, intelligible to both literate and numerate, are given by J. G. Griffith: 'A taxonomic study of the manuscript tradition of Juvenal', *Mus. Helv.* 25 (1968), 101–38; 'Numerical taxonomy and some primary manuscripts of the Gospels', *JTS* 20 (1969), 389–406.

Our account of textual criticism may give the impression that once a text has been printed for the first time its form is static except where an editor deliberately alters it. In fact there is sometimes more error and fluctuation than might be supposed, as has been shown in a particular case by A. Severyns, *Texte et apparat: histoire critique d'une tradition imprimée*, Brussels 1962.

In conclusion we mention a small selection of books and articles on textual criticism which supplement the information given above:

(a) M. Bévenot, *The tradition of manuscripts: a study in the transmission of St. Cyprian's treatises*, Oxford 1961.

   A. C. Clark, *The descent of manuscripts*, Oxford 1918, reprinted 1969.

A. Dain, *Les Manuscrits*, 2nd ed., Paris 1964.

H. Fränkel, *Einleitung zur kritischen Ausgabe der Argonautika des Apollonius*, Göttingen 1964. The theoretical sections were translated into Italian under the title *Testo critico e critica del testo*, Florence 1969.

B. A. van Groningen, *Traité d'histoire et de critique des textes grecs*, Amsterdam 1963.

L. Havet, *Manuel de critique verbale appliquée aux textes latins*, Paris 1911.

A. E. Housman, *Selected prose*, ed. J. Carter, Cambridge 1961. (see also the complete prefaces to the editions of Juvenal, Lucan, and Manilius).

J. Jackson, *Marginalia scaenica*, Oxford 1955.

W. M. Lindsay, *An introduction to Latin textual emendation*, London 1896.

B. H. Streeter, *The Four Gospels*, Oxford 1936⁵.

J. Willis, *Latin textual criticism* (Illinois Studies in Languages and Literature, 61), Urbana 1972.

(b) R. Browning, 'Recentiores non deteriores', *BICS* 7 (1960), 11–21.

W. Bühler, 'Gibt es einen gemeinsamen Archetypus der beiden Überlieferungsstränge von Tertullians Apologeticum?', *Philologus*, 109 (1965), 121–33.

W. Headlam, 'Transposition of words in MSS', *CR* 16 (1902), 243–56.

J. Irigoin, 'Éditions d'auteur et rééditions à la fin de l'antiquité (à propos du "Traité de la virginité" de Grégoire de Nysse), *Rev. phil.* 96 (1970), 101–6.

A. H. McDonald, 'Textual criticism', in *The Oxford Classical Dictionary*, 2nd ed., Oxford 1970.

R. Merkelbach, 'Interpolierte Eigennamen', *Zeitschrift für Papyrologie und Epigraphik*, 1 (1967), 100–2.

R. M. Ogilvie, 'Monastic corruption', *Greece and Rome*, 18 (1971), 32–4.

T. C. Skeat, 'The use of dictation in ancient book production', *Proc. Brit. Acad.* 38 (1952), 179–208.

D. C. C. Young, 'Some types of error in manuscripts of Aeschylus' *Oresteia*', *GRBS* 5 (1964), 85–99.
'Some types of scribal error in manuscripts of Pindar', *GRBS* 6 (1965), 247–73.

INDEX OF MANUSCRIPTS

Note: the number of collections, both public and private, which contain Greek and Latin manuscripts of direct importance for the subjects treated in this book, is very considerable. Guides to printed descriptions or handwritten catalogues are given for Greek by M. Richard, *Répertoire des bibliothèques et des catalogues des manuscrits grecs*, 2nd ed., Paris 1958, with a *Supplément*, Paris 1965, and for Latin by P. O. Kristeller, *Latin manuscript books before 1600*, 3rd ed., New York 1965. The history of manuscripts since their discovery in the Renaissance is in some cases very complicated. The formation of some of the major libraries has been made the subject of specialized monographs which are outside the scope of the present book. It would be useful if students were able to refer to a short account of the movements of manuscripts from the Renaissance to the present day, which would explain the names and present location of the various collections and would incidentally cast an interesting light on a section of European cultural history. At the moment there does not seem to be a study which precisely fills this need, but the chapter on the 'Nomenclature of manuscripts' in F. W. Hall, *A companion to classical texts*, is still valuable; and for a selective treatment of the subject see M. R. James, *The wanderings and homes of manuscripts* (Helps for Students of History no. 17), London 1919, G. Laurion, 'Les Principales Collections de manuscrits grecs', *Phoenix*, 15 (1961), 1–13.

A: MANUSCRIPTS

ATHOS
Almost all the monasteries on Mount Athos have a number of manuscripts; some of the collections are extremely large and have a nucleus of books acquired in the Middle Ages.
Lavra 184: 59
Vatopedi 747: 59

BAMBERG, Staatliche Bibliothek
Class. 35: 96

BASLE, Universitätsbibliothek
A.VII.3: 233
A.N.IV.1: 143

BERLIN, Deutsche Staatsbibliothek
This library is in East Berlin; during the Second World War the books were removed for safety, but some were lost and others are now provisionally held in West Berlin. A good many of the manuscripts come from the library of the nineteenth-century English eccentric Sir Thomas Phillipps.
Diez B.66: 86
lat. fol. 252: 100
lat. qu. 364: 76

Gregory XV in return for financial assistance, and most of the manuscripts are still in the Vatican Library. In 1797 Napoleon removed some of the books to Paris (a fate suffered by many other Italian libraries), and when the books were restored in 1815 the University of Heidelberg, aided by the king of Prussia, persuaded Pope Pius VII to let a few volumes return to their original home.
Pal(atinus) gr. 23: 59, 164

HOLKHAM, Library of the Earl of Leicester
Since 1954 the Greek manuscripts of this collection have been in the Bodleian Library at Oxford.
lat.121: 180, 194

IESI, Library of Count Balleani
lat. 8: 88, 123, 124

ISTANBUL, Metochion of the Holy Sepulchre
355: 177

JERUSALEM, Patriarchate
36:177

LEEUWARDEN, Provincial Library of Friesland
B.A. Fr.55: 93

LEICESTER, City Museum
Greek MS. of the New Testament: 143, 241

LEIDEN, Bibliotheek der Rijksuniversiteit
This contains among other collections those of Heinsius, Lipsius, Scaliger, and Vossius.

B(ibliotheca) P(ublica) G(raeca) 60 A: 177, 205   L(atina) 16 B: 196, 211
Voss(ianus) lat. F. 4: 81, 228, Plate XII   Q. 38: 103, 116, 232
         F. 30: 90, 166, 230   Q. 94: 157, 166
         F. 111: 229

LENINGRAD, National Public (Saltykov-Shchedrin) Library
gr. 219: 52

LENINGRAD, Library of the Academy of Sciences
627/1: 129

LONDON, British Museum
The Burney collection is that of Charles Burney the younger (1757–1817), brother of Fanny Burney. The Harley collection was built up by Robert and Edward Harley, 1st and 2nd earls of Oxford; the second Lady Oxford sold it to the nation in 1753 for £10,000.

Royal 1 D VIII: 170   Burney 86: 14
Add(itional) 11987: 120   Harley 647: 96
         19906: 111   2493: 114, 116, 126, 231, Plate XV
         22087: 180   2682: 96
         34473: 3   2736: 92, 230
         47678: 86

MADRID, Biblioteca Nacional
3678 (*olim* M. 31): 122   Vitr. 5.4 (*olim* Hh.74): 229
8514 (*olim* X. 81): 122

MILAN, Biblioteca Ambrosiana
This library, named after the famous bishop of the city, was founded in 1609 by Cardinal Borromeo, and is not therefore such an early foundation as one might expect in a great Renaissance city.

A. 79 inf. (now S.P. 10/27): 116

E. 147 sup. (now S.P. 9/1,6,11): 175

G. 82 sup. (now S.P. 9/13–20): 19, 22, 76, 175, 176, 206

H. 14 inf.: 115

I. 98 inf.: 130

L. 85 sup.: 88, 122, 129

O. 39 sup. (now S.P. 11.251): 43

R. 26 sup.: 120

R. 57 sup. (now S.P. 11.66): 175

MODENA, Biblioteca Estense
The Este were the ruling family of Ferrara; when the direct line died out in 1597 the illegitimate prince who became the next ruler transferred the capital and with it the library to Modena. The collection has a number of books that belonged to Alberto Pio of Carpi.
gr. 127 (olim α. U. 5.10): 141

MONTPELLIER, Bibliothèque de la Faculté de Médecine
An important group of books including the one listed below came from the collection of the jurist Pierre Pithou (1538–96).
125: 87, 158

NEW YORK, Pierpont Morgan Library
M. 462: 124, 226

ORLÉANS, Bibliothèque municipale
192: 76

OXFORD, Bodleian Library
Since its foundation by Sir Thomas Bodley in 1602 many collections have been added. The Auctarium shelf-marks date from a rearrangement of the library in 1789; the collections named below come from Giacomo Barocci, a Venetian collector, acquired 1629; the Italian Jesuit Matteo Luigi Canonici (1727–1805); E. D. Clarke, professor of mineralogy at Cambridge (1769–1822); J. P. D'Orville, professor at Amsterdam (1696–1751).

Auct(arium) F. 4.32: 96, 231

T. 4.13: 192, Plate V

V. 1.51: Plate IV

Barocci 50: 59

109: Plate VI

Canonici class. lat. 41: 97, 180, 193

gr. 97: 106, 234

E. D. Clarke 39: 57, Plate III

D'Orville 301: 57

Holkham gr. 88: Plate VII

Gr. class. a.1(P): Plate I

OXFORD, Corpus Christi College
148: 107

OXFORD, Lincoln College
lat. 100: 99

PARIS, Bibliothèque Nationale
This exceptionally rich collection comprises the manuscripts of the old Royal Library, which was particularly active in acquiring books in the sixteenth and seventeenth centuries, and numerous other libraries which it incorporated at

various times, among them those of Saint Germain (including the major block of early Corbie manuscripts), Saint Victor, the Sorbonne, and Notre Dame.

RAVENNA, Biblioteca Classense

SAINT GALL, Stiftsbibliothek

SPANGENBURG, Pfarrbibliothek

VATICAN CITY, Biblioteca Apostolica Vaticana
This was already a large collection in the Renaissance and has since been enormously enlarged. The collection of the dukes of Urbino was brought to Rome in 1657 at the order of Pope Alexander VII. In 1769 Clement XIV bought the Ottoboni collection, which by then included that of queen Christina of Sweden (*Reginenses*), collected for her largely by Isaac Vossius and Nicolaus Heinsius. Other famous families whose collections have found their way to the Vatican are the Barberini, Borgia, Chigi, and Colonna.

B: PAPYRI

After publication many papyri have been distributed to libraries or other
institutions which bore part of the cost of the excavations in Egypt. In such
cases they usually receive a shelf-mark in the library in question, in addition
to retaining their serial number in the original publication.

GENERAL INDEX

NOTES TO THE PLATES

I. Oxford, Bodleian Library, MS. gr. class a.1(P). 2nd cent. The papyrus known as the Hawara *Iliad*. The fibrous nature of the material is clearly visible.

II. Venice, Biblioteca Marciana, MS. gr. 454, fol. 41ʳ. 10th cent. This famous book from the collection of cardinal Bessarion is generally known as Venetus A of the *Iliad*.

Plates I and II illustrate the relation between the Alexandrian critical signs and the commentary. They both show the same passage of the *Iliad* (ii. 856ff.); the papyrus has the critical signs in the margin but no scholia, the manuscript has both. It is not surprising to find that the signs are not quite identical. A *diplē* seems to be the correct sign at 856, but the papyrus apparently has the *diplē periestigmenē*; the scholia have simply a geographical note about the Alizones and add that there was another Hodios in the Greek camp, but there is no indication of a difference between Aristarchus and Zenodotus here. At 858 the papyrus has a *diplē*, and the manuscript a note that the name Chromis is else-where given as Chromios. 859–61 are obelized in the papyrus, 860–1 in the manuscript, and the ground given in the latter is that in the battle by the river the death of Chromis is not related, whereas Homer is careful to record the death of any commander of a contingent; this is a good example of an argument that does not satisfy the modern reader. At 863 both books have a *diplē*, and the manuscript gives a geographical note on the use of the name Phrygia.

III. Oxford, Bodleian Library, MS. E. D. Clarke 39, fol. 113ʳ. A.D 895. Plato; the plate shows the opening of the *Sophist*. The text was written for Arethas by the scribe known as John the Calligrapher, who also prepared for Arethas a copy of Aelius Aristides (MSS. Laur. 60.3 and Paris gr. 2951). The marginal scholia are in Arethas' own hand; the first note begins: αὕτη ἡ ἐλαία οὐχ ὥϲ τινεϲ ὑπέλαβον τῆϲ Ἰωνίαϲ ἐϲτιν ἀλλὰ τῆϲ Ἰταλίαϲ, εἴ τι δεῖ Ϲτράβωνι πείθεϲθαι τῷ γεωγράφῳ.

IV. Oxford, Bodleian Library, MS. Auct. V. 1.51, fol. 94ʳ. Late 10th cent. Notes on the *Odyssey*. The plate shows the outline of the story of Book XI (the descent to the underworld), followed by the beginning of the vocabulary list for that book. Such aids were necessary for readers in the Middle Ages and their existence throws light on the school curri-culum. This MS. is from the collection of Giovanni Aurispa and later belonged to the monastery of San Marco in Florence. The opening clause reads: ἀπαγγέλλει πῶς κατὰ τῆς Κίρκης ἐντολὰς λαβὼν εἰς Ἅιδου κατῆλθεν.

V. Oxford, Bodleian Library, MS. Auct. T. 4.13, fol. 132ʳ. 11th cent. The archetype of the works of Epictetus. It is thought that Arethas possessed a manuscript of this text, of which the Oxford MS. is perhaps a direct copy. The script displays a certain number of abbreviations. The opening words read: ἐλεύθερος ἐστιν ὁ ζῶν ὡς βούλεται, ὃν οὔτ' ἀναγκάσαι ἔστιν οὔτε κωλῦσαι οὔτε βιάσασθαι.

VI. Oxford, Bodleian Library, MS. Barocci 109, fol. 167ʳ. 15th cent. This late copy of Aratus' *Phaenomena* is one of the few which have the lines interpolated by Planudes. The plate shows line 480 followed by the interpolation. The name Triclinius in the right-hand margin is thought to indicate his authorship of the scholium at the foot of the page explaining what Planudes had done. It reads as follows: ἰστέον δὲ ὅτι ἡ τοῦ Ἀράτου σφαῖρα οὐκ ἀκριβῶς ἔχει πρὸς τὴν θέσιν τῶν κύκλων ἐκτεθειμένα τὰ ζῴδια. ἡ δὲ τοῦ Πτολεμαίου λίαν ἠκριβωμένως ἐκτίθεται. ταύτῃ γοῦν τῇ τοῦ Πτολεμαίου σφαίρᾳ ἑπόμενος ὁ σοφὸς Πλανούδης κατὰ τὴν ἐκείνης θέσιν ἐκδέδωκε τοὺς παρόντας στίχους, ἐναλ<λ>άξας ὅσα μὴ καλῶς εἴρηκεν ὁ Ἄρατος. διὸ οἱ ἐντυγχάνοντες ταύταις καὶ μάλιστα τοῖς περὶ τούτων λεχθεῖσι παρὰ ἀμφοτέρων ἔχουσιν ἀκριβῆ τὴν περὶ τούτων κατάληψιν, ἀμφοτέρους [ἐπὶ τούτοις] εὑρίσκοντες ἐπὶ τούτοις συμφωνοῦντας.

VII. Oxford, Bodleian Library, MS. Holkham gr. 88, fol. 207ʳ. 15th cent. Aristophanes. This copy shows the text and scholia in the recension prepared about a century earlier by Demetrius Triclinius; it is the only known manuscript source for his scholia to four of the plays. Note in this plate Triclinius' scholium on metre at the foot of the page (beginning ἡ εἴσθεσις τοῦ παρόντος δράματος) and his misleading title to the main body of scholia, 'old scholia by Aristophanes the grammarian'.

VIII. The *editio princeps* of Aristophanes, Venice 1498, at the Aldine press. Text and scholia were prepared by Musurus, who had among his manuscript materials at least two copies of the Triclinian recension. In the style of type-face and arrangement of text and scholia there is a close resemblance to contemporary manuscripts. The marginal scholia, after the lemma ὀρθὴν κελεύεις, begin with the metrical note of Triclinius shown in the previous plate.

IX. Florence, Biblioteca Medicea-Laurenziana, MS. Laur. 39.1, fol. 8ʳ. This is the codex Mediceus of Vergil, written in Italy in the 5th century. It was corrected at Rome by Asterius, consul in 494, and later found its way to Bobbio. The script is rustic capital. The plate shows the end of the *Eclogues* (10.61–77). Abbreviations are few, here restricted to *B·* (*bus*) and *Q·* (*que*). Among the corrections, apparently by Asterius himself, we may note in line 62 the change from *DRUSUM* to *RURSUS* and *NABIS* to *NOBIS*, and in line 70 *HAES* corrected to *HAEC*. In line 63 the reading *RURSUSM* suggests a *duplex lectio* at an earlier stage in the tradition (*RURSUS/M*). In the space left vacant at the end of the *Eclogues* Asterius has added a subscription recording his work on the manuscript, rounded off with a poem in elegiacs. The subscription is written in a small hand and is somewhat defaced; the first part reads (the abbreviations are expanded and enclosed within brackets): *Turcius Rufius Apronianus Asterius v(ir) c(larissimus) et inl(ustris), ex comite domest(icorum) protect(orum), ex com(ite) priv(atarum) largit(ionum), ex praef(ecto) urbi, patricius et consul ordin(arius) legi et distincxi codicem fratris Macharii v(iri) c(larissimi) non mei fiducia set eius cui si et ad omnia sum devotus arbitrio XI Kal. Mai(as) Romae.*

X. Biblioteca Apostolica Vaticana, MS. Vat. lat. 5757, fol. 171ʳ. The famous palimpsest of Cicero's *De republica*. Originally a *de luxe* edition of Cicero, it was reused in the 7th century at Bobbio to copy a text of Augustine on the Psalms. The primary script is a bold uncial of the late 4th or early 5th century, the secondary script is a small uncial of the 7th century. Here we have part of *De republica* 2.33. The lower text reads: *ENIM SERPIT/SED VOLAT IN/OPTIMUM STA/TUM INSTITU/TO TUO SERMO/NE REMP·POS^{S}^{T}/TUM NUMAE/POMPILI NEPOS/EX FILIA REX/A POPULO EST/ANCUS MAR/CIUS CONSTITU/(TUS).*

XI. Paris, Bibliothèque Nationale, MS. lat. 5730, fol. 77ᵛ. This uncial manuscript of Livy's third decade was written in Italy in the first half of the 5th century and is the parent of all the complete extant manuscripts of this decade. A direct copy of it, written at Tours about the year 800, is shown on Plate XIII. For the history of this manuscript in the Carolingian Renaissance see p. 86. The parchment is so fine and thin that in places, as here, the writing shows through from the other side of the leaf. Both this plate and Plate XIII show the beginning of Book XXIII; in line 11 a second hand has 'corrected' *MOPSIORUM* to *COMPSINORUM*, and this further change in an already corrupt passage has established itself in the text of the copy (Plate XIII).

274 NOTES TO THE PLATES

XII. Leiden, Bibliotheek der Rijksuniversiteit, MS. Voss. lat. F. 4, fol. 20ᵛ. This beautiful manuscript of the Elder Pliny, written in Anglo-Saxon majuscule, was produced in Northumbria in the first half of the 8th century. The plate shows the opening of Book IV of the *Naturalis Historia*, beginning: *tertius europe sinus acrocerauniis incipit montibus finitur helisponto amplectitur praeter minores simus* (i.e. *sinus*) *XIX.XXV passuum*. The first three words are repeated in the margin in minuscule.

XIII. Biblioteca Apostolica Vaticana, MS. Vat. Reg. lat. 762, fol. 32ʳ. Caroline minuscule. This manuscript of Livy's third decade was written at Tours about the year 800 and copied directly from the 5th-century uncial manuscript shown on Plate XI. Both plates show approximately the same passage from the beginning of Book XXIII. The survival of both ancient exemplar and minuscule copy enable one to examine the mistakes which arise when a medieval scribe copies an ancient book, and the errors made in this transcription have been collected and studied (F. W. Shipley, *Certain sources of corruption in Latin manuscripts*, New York 1904). The words are divided for the most part, there is little punctuation, and abbreviations are few, e.g. *q*; (*que*), *b*; (*bus*), *p̄* (*prae*). Some cursive elements survive from earlier scripts, the open *a* which appears along with the other forms of the letter and the ligatures of *et*, *rt*, *st*. The open *a* disappeared in time, and the majuscule *N*, here used alongside the minuscule form, later had a more restricted use.

XIV. Florence, Biblioteca Medicea-Laurenziana, MS. Laur. 68.2, fol. 6ᵛ. This is the manuscript which has preserved for us *Annals* XI–XVI and the *Histories* of Tacitus. It was written at Monte Cassino during the latter half of the 11th century and provides an example of Bene-ventan script of the best period. The plate shows the last words of *Annals* XI and the beginning of XII. The end of Book XI is seriously corrupt and reads: *sed ex quis* (glossed with *quibus*) *deterrima orerentur tristitiis multis*.

XV. London, British Museum, MS. Harley 2493, fol. 101ᵛ. The history of this manuscript of Livy, written about the year 1200 and later in the possession of both Petrarch and Valla, is told on pp. 114–15. The plate shows one of the passages of Livy (21.46.3) used by Valla to discredit the scholarship of his rivals Panormita and Facio (see p. 126). The manuscript offers the corrupt *ex quo propinquo*. Valla points out that, while his rivals had failed to see anything wrong with the transmitted text, Petrarch had long since altered *ex quo* to *ex loco*, and Petrarch's correction can still be seen in the text. In the margin Valla has written his own conjecture *exque*, an emendation accepted by modern editors. One may note in passing the increased use of abbreviation at this period.

XVI. Florence, Biblioteca Medicea-Laurenziana, MS. Laur. 48.22, fol. 121^r. This manuscript contains Cicero's *Philippics* and *Catilinarians* and was written by Poggio in 1425. Here we have the end of *In Catilinam IV*.

PLATE I

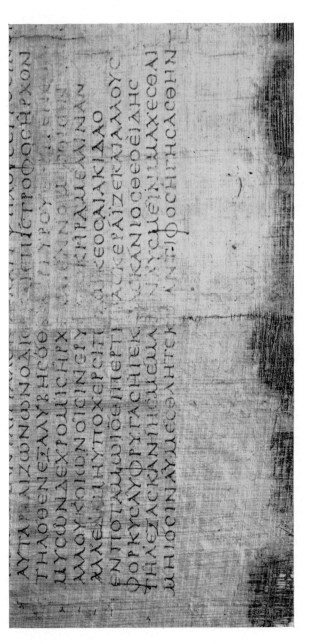

PLATE II

PLATE III

PLATE IV

PLATE V

PLATE VI

PLATE VII

PLATE VIII

PLATE IX

ATQVE EGO SILLIXIALIS HOMINVM MITIS CEI DISCAT
IAMINEQ·AMIAIDAIADESDAVSVAINECCAMINANABIS
IESAELACENTIESAERVASVSMCONCIDITESILVAI
NONILLVMNOSTRIPOSSVNTMVTARELABORIS
NECSITRIGORIB·MEDIISHIBRAVAIQ·BIBAMVS
SITHONIASQ·NIVISHIEMISSVBEAMVSAQVOSAI
NECSICVMMORIENSALTALIBERAREIINVLMO
AETHIOPVMVERSEMVSOVISSVBSIDERECANCRI
OMNIAVINCETAMORETNOSCIDAMVSAMORI
HAESSATERIIDIVAEVESTRVMCECINISSEPOETAM
DVMSEDETETGRACILIFISCELLAMTEXITHIBISCO
PIERIDESVOSHAECFACIETISMAXIMAGALLO
GALLOCVIVSAMOMANTVMMITIICRESCITINHORAS
QVANTVMVERENOVOVIRIDISSESVBICMALNVS
SVRGAMVSSOLETISSEGRAVISCANTANTIPVMBRA
IVNIPERIGRAVISVMBRANOCENTETFRVGIBVSVMB
ITEDOMVMSATVRAEVENITHESPERVSITECAPE[L]

P VIRGILI · MARONIS

BVCOLICON   LIBER   EXPLICIT

INCIPIT   GEORGICON

PLATE X

116

Nemoenim minetur domui ubies
quasialiquiddomuinoceat sice
dicens. Nequenum audiusest
adeseminee... quifaciebantoc
titioned̄ı· quianonproillorum
meritisabrahaeparceretei·s· et
coerceret... suamadur
... inquibuperarum· quan
utbaptizarenturinaquapaenite
... talese... enaniqu
... niuluaborneachannan
penderunt dm̄ ipsorumfilierant
... quisostenditūobi
... paenitentiae·etnedi
... dēlapidibusistis·
lapidestuncudebatincampissal
... quifiudicantisunt
coomietur domui· quasidicat· s
estulli utcoaedificeturēthabeat

PLATE XI

haecHANNIBALPOSTCAN
NENSEMPUGNAMCAPTA
ACDIREPTACONFESTIM
EXAPULIINSAMNIUM
MOUERATACCENUSINHIR
MNOSASIATIOROUICEN
TESSECOMPSXMTRAD TU
RUMCOMPSXNOSE
TREBIUSNOBILISINTER
SUOSSOIRE
MOPSTERU
MILITEPER
MANUCLU
POSTEXPU
SISPUGNX
QUETREBIS
ADUENTU
USCOMCOMPSXN
BEOIEXCESXISSEN SI
NERARILXORIUELR
TAURPSPOENORUOS
OIKINOACCEPIUMOS
EIBISRAEDXORININIO
INUPEDIMENIISRELIO
TISEXERCIIUSPXRIIO
MACONEMUERIONIS

PLATE XII

TERTIVS EVRO PE SINVS

tertius europe
sinus

Oceno cenarumis incipit montib;
pincun. helipponto complectitum.
praeterp. inniones sinus .xix. xxii.
paessuum meo epspo sa. cocpnaemae.are-
toliae phocis locrus araxiae. messenid,
lacomicae. acrtolicis megarus atrice-boecid.
tepum que. abadio macru exaedem phocis
& locrus doius phiaetis thesaeliae. mar-
nesiae. maecedoniae. thnarciae. omnisquaeae
fabulosraes. sicut & litterenarum clacru
tars ex hoc. primum sinu expulsit. quae.
propterp. parulum meo commonrabimum.
Epsnos universum aeppellarae. araeniae.
unus incipit montibus inaea primi chae.
ones aequibus chomiae. dentes prot i arita
tonenses locos haoprnon & pestipenae arui
bus exaelacio. cestrum-per. aebi. quonum.
mons pi ndus caessopaei. chno pes sello.
epilopes molosi aepire. quos clodonaeei.

PLATE XIII

INCIPIT LIBER VICESIMUS TERTIUS·

Haec hannibal post cannensem pugnam castraque capta ac direpta con
festim ex apulia in samnium moverat· accitus in hirpinos a sta
tio pollicentes se compsam traditurum· Compsanus erat ex trebius nobilis inter
suos· sed premebat eum comp sino rufacio familiae pergraeciae romano
rum potentia post fugiam cannensis pugnae uolg graeciaeque crebri sermoni
b; aduenta tibi annibalis cum compsam urbem excessissent fine certamine
tradita urbs poeno praesidiumque acceptatest· ibi praedam omnis atque; impedi
mentas relicas exeratu praedato magone regionis eius urbes atque defic
entias ab romanis accipere aut detractantas cogere ad defec ao nem uba
Ipse peragra tu campanum mare inferum petit oppugna turus neap olim
urbemacram com bebere· Ubi sine neapol racnorum introutitnu
mides praedam insidias explorque que augiuntur· ae sinu tique occulta quae
cumque; aptae poterat disposuit alios prae actaemp praeda peraguit oraen

PLATE XIV

sed egos decerpimur ostendat artistatis multas ::

Cornelii taciti LIBer

vndecim; EXP. Incip xii

EDE MESSALINE.

conuulsa principis domo; optator apud

libertos consultarni qs deligeret

uxore claudio caelibis uita et Inconanciam. & coluga

Imperatoris obnoxio ne minus ambitu fe

minis excerpseran. sua quisq; nobiliaratē.

formae opes conatendersc ac dignae arcnar

matrimonio ostendatisc. Sed maxime certabi

gebatur Inter lolliae paulinae. Cn. lolli cōsularis.

& Iuliae agrippinae germanico genitae. huic

pallas. illi callistus fauentes adeponēt. at

aelia petina ex familia aubetorum narcisso

fouebatur. Ipse huc modo. mox illuc. ut quisqū

q; suadentium audierant in diuersus. discordem

aces Inesilium uocaret. ac primase senatum sta &

PLATE XV

Prodigia.

PLATE XVI

affimo me muro septum esse arbitrabor. Quod si mea spe
uis improbor. fefelleritt atqz supauerit. comendo uobis
paruű meum filium. cui profecto satis erit presidij ñ solű
ad salutem uerz etiam ad dignitate. si cuiusqui hec oia suos so
lius periculo conseruauerit illum filium esse memineritis.
Quapropter de summa salute uestra populiqz. r. de uris com
iugibus achliberis de aris ac focis. de fanis atqz templis de
totius urbis tectis ac sedibus de imperio ac libertate de sa
lute italie de uniuersa . r. p. decernite diligenter ut instt
tuistis ac fortiter. Habetis eum consulem qui & parere ue
stris decretis non dubitet. & ea que statueritis quoad ui
uet defendere & per se ipsum prestare possit.

FINIS. LIBRI. SCRIPSIT. POGGIVS.
.ROMAE.